Critical acclaim for Elise Title and

ROMEO

"**ROMEO** IS PSYCHOLOGICALLY INTRIGUING—A STUDY OF HUMAN CHARACTER, BROKEN SPIRITS, AND THE SHEER WILL TO SURVIVE. YET IT'S STILL A GOOD WHO-DUN-IT. . . . GREAT READING."
—*St. Louis Post-Dispatch*

"FILLED WITH RAW PASSIONS, FROM KINKY SEX TO UNSPEAKABLE VIOLENCE . . . FEW READERS WILL BE ABLE TO PUT IT DOWN."
—*The Brazosport Facts*

"PLENTY OF SUSPECTS . . . PLENTY OF CLUES AND RED HERRINGS. PLENTY OF SURPRISES . . . A PAGE-TURNER."—*Sunday Monitor*

"[**ROMEO**] WILL PROPEL MS. TITLE INTO THE UNIVERSE ILLUMINATED BY THE GENRE'S BRIGHTEST STARS AND MAKE HER A FORCE TO BE RECKONED WITH IN THIS SELECT FIELD."
—*Affaire de Coeur*

"WELL WRITTEN . . . ONE OF THE BETTER ONES."
—*Star Tribune*, Minneapolis

"A NEAT PSYCHOSEXUAL THRILLER WITH PLENTY OF SUSPECTS AND A GRITTY HEROINE . . . SPEEDS TO AN EXCRUCIATINGLY TENSE CLIMAX."
—*Library Journal*

"THIS BOOK WILL KEEP YOU GUESSING UNTIL THE END."—*Boston Weekly*

ROMEO
Elise Title

BANTAM BOOKS
New York Toronto London
Sydney Auckland

This edition contains the complete text
of the original hardcover edition.
NOT ONE WORD HAS BEEN OMITTED.

ROMEO

A Bantam Book

PUBLISHING HISTORY
Bantam hardcover edition published / February 1996
Bantam paperback edition / February 1998

ISBN 0-553-57206-7

Published simultaneously in the United States and Canada

Bantam Books are published by Bantam Books, a division of Bantam
Doubleday Dell Publishing Group, Inc. Its trademark, consisting of the
words "Bantam Books" and the portrayal of a rooster, is Registered in
U.S. Patent and Trademark Office and in other countries. Marca Regis-
trada. Bantam Books, 1540 Broadway, New York, New York 10036.

PRINTED IN THE UNITED STATES OF AMERICA

OPM   10 9 8 7 6 5 4 3

To my husband, Jeff
A man after my own heart!

I would like to thank many people for their help, guidance, and support: the homicide detectives and coroner's office of the SFPD, psychologists Deanna Spielberg and Anna Salter, psychiatric social workers Marilyn and Bill Dawber, physicians Ted Spielberg and Joseph Schwartz, attorneys Joan Rosenberg Ryan, Thomas Ryan, and Howard Zaharoff, my friend Marilyn Breselor, my sister Jane Atkin, and my sister-in-law Jacqueline Title, an indomitable researcher.

Special thanks to my longtime friend and agent, Helen Rees, my foreign rights agent, Linda Michaels, Jeffrey Rees, and to the hardworking folks at Bantam. To Irwyn Applebaum for his warm welcome to the Bantam family. To my editors extraordinaire Nita Taublib and Kate Miciak for their terrific suggestions, guidance, and much appreciated attention to detail.

All my love and gratitude to my Dad, Irving Kaplowitz, and children, David and Rebecca, and most especially, to my husband Jeff Title, who not only provided me with enormous psychological expertise thanks to his background in rehabilitation and prison counseling and clinical psychology, but endless hours of editorial work, encouragement and good laughs when I needed them most.

ROMEO

Lifeless surrender is numbness, a void, a prickly black hole, death. Yet, there is another altogether tantalizing form of surrender. The act of giving in with a vengeance.

M.R. diary

Prologue

The anticipation is palpable. Under her skin. Inside her head. Tingling all over—the pads of her toes, between her thighs, her breasts, her tongue, even her eyelids. Reverberating throughout the bedroom. Permeating her cool mauve and cream cocoon.

She can feel the thrumming giving way to a relentless churning. Setting the inescapable chaos into motion. Would she escape it if she could? No. Without the chaos, she would feel limbless. In limbo.

Guilt is the only problem. Creeping insidiously, gnawing, leaving festering sores. Carefully disguised, naturally. She is a master of deception as well as perception. Clutter set aside. An encapsulated force that's carefully kept within its prescribed confines. Prescribed by her.

Slowly, humming a tune from some long-ago time—a lullaby—she rakes her bloodred nails over her small breasts. Pain is her aphrodisiac because only pain stops the wheels from spinning in her mind. Only pain stops the critique of her damaged psyche. Whose psyche isn't damaged?

Her glossy manicured nails move across the soft flesh. Then over the nipples. Leaving angry red lines against ivory skin. Her nipples are rigid, stinging with anticipation. She twists them lightly between her index fingers and her thumbs. She gasps in a breath, suffering an unexpected stab of pain as the air fills her lungs. At thirty-six, surely not a heart attack. She's in great shape, works out daily, plays squash, tennis, eats a low-fat diet. Had her annual check-up less than a month ago and got a clean bill of health. What then? She knows.

An attack of conscience. Sweeping over her like a tempest. A feeling she hates. *Watch it, Melanie. You want to cruise the edge, not do any real damage. Even you could lose your footing.*

Her right nipple—the one she's pinched so hard—throbs. She focuses her mind on the pain there, letting it take over, letting it cleanse her. Instant repression. Exorcism.

The sweat begins to evaporate on her skin. A late October chill from the open window. The sounds of the street filtering in as the night fog rolls over San Francisco. A quarter moon. The sky eerily luminescent.

A firm rap on the door leading to her upstairs apartment. Freeze frame. Everything jams. Even her breath. Then swiftly she pulls herself together. She stops at the full-length mirror in her bedroom, gives herself a cool, detached study. She's chosen her outfit carefully. Rose silk man-tailored shirt. Soft, flowing black silk slacks. Black sling-backs on her bare feet. Still sophisticated, but with an air of added enticement, heat. She runs a comb through her thick, straight auburn hair that falls in a blunt cut to her shoulders. A quick reappraisal. Yes. She is ready.

An ironic smile twists her lips even as a wave of vertigo makes her sway and grab on to the wall. The dizziness passes quickly. She has willed it away. She can do that. Nothing to worry about. She smiles. The chaos has shifted into something with shape and substance. Something she can manipulate.

She steps into her living room, taking in the space with the restless, critical eye of a woman who is constantly assessing what she has accomplished. Like the rest of her Pacific Heights Victorian townhouse, this room is punctuated with style and elegant understatement. Not a hint of clutter. Stucco walls in the palest peach. Windows shaded with teakwood-slatted blinds. Moroccan rug in muted tones—tan, burnt umber, gray—over a white-washed, planked oak floor. Two matching love seats in a pale caramel silk facing each other. Pine coffee table set with a vase of chrysanthemums, two crystal goblets. Large bay window perfect for plants, but there are none. She doesn't have a green thumb and doesn't want to see a living thing die a slow death at her hands.

Grief or despair over failure? She's not sure. The two often bleed into each other.

The doorbell doesn't ring again, but she knows he will be standing in the hall, patiently waiting. Understanding that she is stretching out the anticipation. As he is, too. She is sure of that. The thought alone arouses her.

She smiles as she opens the door. In her haste to put her disguise back in place, she senses that it's slightly skewed.

He makes no move, studying her unabashedly, his face devoid of emotion. Tabula rasa.

Her gaze falls to the package in his hands. Champagne. Interesting. Provocative. A warped kind of playfulness. She stops. She will not analyze.

Sitting together on her love seat, she watches him observing her as they drink the champagne from her crystal goblets. She can tell by his eyes that he's pleased. She has soft jazz playing—Branford Marsalis. The lights are dim, candles lit, the mood serene and romantic. He toys with a few strands of her hair as he sips his drink.

She is careful to conceal that she is only marking

time. The fear is behind her now that he is here. She trusts him. Sees him as a master conductor of a great symphony. And she his all-encompassing instrument.

He ever so lightly strokes her cheek. She feels the caress like a charge of dynamite.

"You look like a little girl tonight," he says.

She's taken aback. But secretly pleased. "A little girl?"

"You try to conceal it, but you can't."

He puts his arm around her, gently guiding her head to his shoulder. They sit like that in tender silence, the candles flickering, listening to Marsalis wail on his tenor sax.

The prelude.

At the armoire changing the CD. Not sure what to choose. He comes up behind her. She starts to turn toward him, but he rests his hands on her shoulders, holding her in place. When he releases her, she dutifully stays put. His fingers skim seductively down her back, over her buttocks.

She imagines him smiling at his discovery that she isn't wearing a bra or panties beneath her grown-up clothes, but she won't move—even her head—to check out whether she's right. Being obedient is too much of a turn-on.

He tugs her shirt out from the waistband of her trousers, slips his cool hands underneath, palms flat on her spine, fingers spread over her back. She stands very still in anticipation.

"Pick something out. Something with a hot beat," he murmurs in her ear.

She wants to press into him, rub against his groin, see if he's hard, but she appreciates the languid rhythm he's setting. Appreciates his style. It suits her. There is a strong simpatico between them.

She selects a Bob Marley CD. The erotic strains of reggae spill out of the speakers. She sways to the beat.

Closes her eyes. Confident she will not lose her way. He is the perfect guide for her journey.

He does not sway with her, but his hands move slowly round to her rib cage, creep up to her breasts.

His mouth in the crook of her neck. "Undo your pants." His tone a cool yet enticing command.

His abrupt shift in the tempo catches her by surprise. She suspects he delights in this. Her hands give her nervousness and eagerness away, but she manages it, unbuttons the waistband, starts to lower the zipper. He is smiling now. She is certain. Even though she is still facing away from him.

Her slacks puddle at her ankles. He remains behind her, kneading her bare ass as she continues to sway to the music.

"You have a dimple."

She feels a momentary flutter of alarm. An imperfection? "Is that bad or good?" There's a tremor in her voice.

He laughs softly. "Very good."

She feels a glowing pleasure. A victory.

Sitting in her armchair, completely naked now. He's kneeling between her spread-eagled legs. She can't see his face. Buried in her breast. She inhales deeply, arching, reaching for him.

"Not yet," he tells her softly, his tongue beginning its descent. "This time is just for you. But you mustn't move."

His generosity brings her close to tears. It has been ages since any man has put her needs before his.

He leans her back, his hands beneath her ass, lifting her up to him, a precious offering.

His ministrations are expert, brilliant. She is pitched on the edge of pleasure and pain, a sensation that makes her whole body rock and tremble.

He draws his head away, looking up at her, his lips glistening with her juices. "Have you had fantasies about this?" he asks, his smile so boyish, she feels a little tug on her heart. This is a surprise to her. Her heart has always been a thing separate. A well-protected organ. Until now.

"Have you?" he persists.

"Yes." She smiles shyly. Girlishly. The woman is beginning to evaporate.

Sitting together on the edge of her bed. His eyes not on her but on her reflection in the bureau mirror across from them. Watching with that same intent and yet removed expression.

An edge of frustration. Wanting him to get undressed. Become a more active participant. Feeling a little self-conscious.

"Tell me what you like to fantasize." His voice is low, seductively coaxing.

She blushes. "That's very personal." The absurdity of her remark makes her laugh.

"You don't have to hold anything back from me," he says, his voice seductive, mesmerizing. "That's what this is all about."

Her shyness begins to recede, the exciting naughtiness of it too enticing to resist.

She begins tentatively. "I've broken down on a highway. It's night. A trucker stops. He approaches me, but it's so dark I can't see him. Cars are whizzing by us. I can smell the exhaust fumes. Their headlights flash on us, but for some reason only I'm reflected in their lights. He manages to remain in shadow."

"What does he do?"

"He looks under the hood but says my car can't be fixed. Then he slams the hood down. He's standing very close to me." Her breathing has changed. Quicker. Erratic.

"Are you afraid?"

"Yes. There's something brutal about him." Her heart is racing. "But I'm excited, too," she confesses. She doesn't say why, but it's the danger, the exposure, the dread, the illicit desire to succumb against her will.

"What does he do?"

"He strips me. Right there on the side of the road. With all the cars passing. I struggle, but he slaps me a few times and warns me that he'll hurt me worse if I don't behave. When I'm naked, he lifts me up on the hood of the car and pushes me down across it. He spreads my legs wide. He's very rough. Cars are driving by more slowly. I beg him to take me inside my car where no one can see."

"Is that what you really want?"

"No, no, no. I'm getting very hot. I'm wanting him. It's thrilling, being exposed like that, helpless." She feels that way now. Fantasy transformed to reality.

"Go on."

"He's on top of me, taking me right there on the cold hood of the car. Hard, furious thrusts. Hands pinning my wrists. A car's slowing down. Three young men getting out. Oh God, I realize they're all going to take me—"

She's speaking in a rush now, the words spilling over themselves. She can no longer focus on his image in the mirror. She can no longer see either of them. Everything is dissolving.

Curled up on her bed. She smiles demurely—the novice, the initiate—as he stands over her, looking down at her.

"Tell me what to do," she murmurs. "How can I please you? I'll do anything to please you."

He smiles as his eyes travel up and down her body. "You've got little-girl titties."

"I hate them," she confesses, feeling the shame spread over her. More than anything, she doesn't want to displease him.

He strokes her breasts gently. Reassuring her. She smiles tremulously. Until he moves to her nipples, pinching them, his fingers like pincers. She winces, but she can feel an adrenaline rush.

Yes, yes, make me hurt. This is what I deserve.

In the bathtub. Being washed by him. He is being very gentle, especially where she is bruised. She is both aroused and touched by his efforts. His tenderness adds greatly to the excitement, the drama of the evening.

"Are you Daddy's little girl?" he asks, his voice playful, loving, tender. A new game.

The naughty little girl is all innocence now. "Yes, Daddy."

She stands in the tub, the dutiful child, arms at her side while he scrubs and inspects her. Being so closely examined is as much a turn-on for her as the touching.

"You want to be very clean, don't you?"

Yes, it's true. Wash away the sins. Purify my body. Make it all new again.

He is on his knees, scrubbing his way down her belly now.

"Do you like when I wash you here?" He begins rubbing her with his soapy fingers. Roughly. Just the way she likes it.

"Yes."

"And here?" He dips inside her vagina. She's very aroused, but is he? He is still dressed, his body too close to the tub for her to detect an erection through his trousers.

"Yes, yes." She has to hold on to the tile wall for support.

He stops abruptly, brusquely turns her around. She almost slips but catches herself. He doesn't seem to notice. He begins working on her back, her ass.

"Scrub harder," she commands.

That makes him mad. He doesn't like being ordered about by his little girl. He has a scrub brush by her ass, his arm viselike around her waist.

She cries out as he swats her hard with the bristles. Once, twice—

Yes, punish me. Make me be good. I want to be good.

On the rug at the foot of her bed, arms and legs splayed, hands grasping the brass bar of the footboard. She isn't bound, but he's commanded her not to let go. She plays the willing victim—a part that fits her like a second skin.

Meanwhile her whole body is aching, throbbing. Wanting, wanting, wanting. He makes her say it over and over again. "I want you. I want you. I want you."

His smile no longer bears any trace of boyishness. It is wily, amused. The line between fantasy and reality blurring. Deception stripped away. He has invaded those private recesses of her mind and body, claiming them. He slaps her across her breasts. She hardly feels the pain as she arches up to him, white-knuckled as she clutches the bar.

He slaps her again. "Are you a whore?"

"No." The cry is forced out of her mouth with the second blow to her breasts. She winces this time, but she is losing herself in the pain.

"Are you a whore?"

"No, no."

He hits her again. "Liar. Liar."

Even as she panics that he is getting carried away, a guttural desire clots her throat. She stares up at him, her brown eyes huge and liquid with lust. She wants him inside of her.

Should she ask? Demand? Beg? She's a little afraid. He's losing himself, too. His joy in inflicting the pain has heightened. She can see it on his face, in his eyes. If he starts to get too rough, she'll have to call a stop to this. And the hideous, awful truth of it is, she doesn't want to.

■   ■   ■

Over his knees. Facedown on the bed. Hard to breathe. Pain mounting, but the desire escalating. Excruciating.

Something soft and silky flits across her ass. She turns her head, catches a glimpse. A scarf. A white silk scarf.

A sharp intake of breath. Images flash in her head—four young women, their once-lovely faces bruised and battered, their bodies bound, raped, mutilated—

So horrible. So ghoulish. And yet—this fascination. To be utterly at someone's mercy. Forced to give up all control. All responsibility.

She twists her head. He smiles like he knows what's lurking deep inside of her.

"You can trust me, Melanie. And satisfy your curiosity at the same time."

She starts to protest, but the words die in her throat.

He smiles tenderly as he holds the scarf out to her as an offering.

Her eyes meet his for only an instant. Long enough for him to know that the new game is go.

A terrible pulsing in her head. The contorted position of her bound body is becoming intolerable. Her jaw throbs; her teeth feel like they've loosened from his harsh slaps. What's even worse, he keeps tormenting her to the brink of orgasm with his hands, his mouth—but never his penis.

She feels thoroughly debased. And mortified by her own acceptance of this reprehensible treatment, her bizarre reluctance to stop. But she must. Or else she's sure she'll truly lose complete touch with reality, fall into the abyss. And take him with her.

"Please untie me. It hurts."

"I thought you wanted to experience their pain, Melanie."

She feels a clenching in her chest. She was certain he'd cooperate.

"This isn't turning either of us on." She says this lie very soberly.

He smiles. Knows the truth.

Panting and trembling on the Moroccan rug on the living-room floor, still bound, her ankles and wrists quite numb, the strain to her back excruciating. Her skin is red and raw. Welts. Horrible welts surface on her flesh.

"Tell me," he whispers, letting his fingers skim across her bruised cheek. "Do you still want me, Melanie? Tell me the truth."

She can't answer. She doesn't know what's true or real anymore. She's drowning in confusion and chaos.

"More champagne?" he asks almost conversationally.

She shakes her head. Alcohol will sting her bloodied lip. Hysteria quivers across her flesh.

"Let's take a break, huh?" she says, forcing a smile. "Cool it for a little while. We forgot all about dinner. Why don't we eat and then—"

He isn't paying attention. He kneels beside her; he jams the crystal goblet against her lips.

She starts to shake her head again. "Please—"

He grabs her hard by the back of the neck, starts pouring the champagne into her mouth. She gags, coughs, spits it out. She's angry now.

He smiles warmly, lovingly, at her, but there is nothing in his eyes. If the eyes are the mirror to the soul, then tonight his soul has abandoned him. And her.

He rises and goes to the armoire, thumbing through her CDs. Finding the one he wants, he puts it on. He turns back to her, still smiling as the strains of Gershwin's *Rhapsody in Blue* fill the room.

"You've played it before, haven't you, Melanie? Not the same as it is hearing it now. Why did Romeo play it for each of his victims? You wondered, didn't you?"

"Yes, I wondered." Her voice is a bare croak.

He changes the subject. "They shared their darkest

fantasies with him. As willingly as you did. They got off on it. Just like you, Melanie."

What was he saying? He can't know what those women shared with the serial killer before he killed them. He's still playing with her. But enough is enough.

It is only then that she sees he's wearing clear, thin rubber surgical gloves. When did he put them on? She's been so out of it, he could have been wearing them practically the whole time.

"No," she whimpers, clinging to denial like a lifeline.

I know this man. I trust this man. This is a game. Only a game—

He leans close enough so that she can smell the champagne on his breath, smell his excitement.

" 'Romeo, Romeo, wherefore art thou Romeo?' " he whispers as he tenderly cups her chin. "Romeo's right here, Melanie."

The killer punch. The final blow to her self-deceit. She is no longer in control. A low moan of pure anguish escapes her lips. She cannot breathe. Cold, stark terror—a lightning bolt impaling her.

His prick's hard as a rock now. No mystery why. Not for the eminent Dr. Melanie Rosen, leading psychiatric expert in the unholy compulsions of serial killers. How demoralizing to think that in the end it would be her own unholy compulsions that would destroy her.

Her knees digging painfully into the rug. He's sitting on the love seat. His hand circles his penis as he presses her head against his thigh. She is too weak to object. Knows it would do no good anyway.

"I was touched when you dubbed me Romeo on *Cutting Edge*. 'Romeo. A brutal psychopath who woos his victims and steals their hearts.' "

He pauses to laugh. A laugh devoid of humor.

"You look great on TV, Melanie. I never missed a segment."

He gives her a thoughtful glance. "What would you tell all those eager-beaver viewers about me now, I wonder? That would be quite a show, Melanie. A firsthand account. 'My Night With Romeo.' Bet the ratings would skyrocket with that one."

He strokes himself in a trancelike motion. She remains very still. Wants him to keep talking. Give her more to work with.

"I did like your theory about my victims' hearts. Taking them to keep the women alive in my perverted mind. Until they start to rot. Until I'm compelled to exchange a smelly old heart for a nice fresh one." He grins. "That was good, Melanie. Bullshit, but very good bullshit."

"It's really about hurt," she says quietly. "A hurt twisted up with rage and a desperate need to feel powerful —in control." She knows it isn't only him she is analyzing now.

"But then you spewed out all that hackneyed Oedipus complex shit on the show the other night. Cheap shot, Melanie." He smiles sardonically, but as she turns her head to glimpse his face, she sees that he's entering a fugue state.

"Children are vulnerable. A lot of people can hurt them," she says. "And that hurt gets bottled up—"

He's slid down beside her on the carpet. His fingers are poking absently between her thighs now. She tries not to show any physical reaction.

He presses his lips to her damp hair. His fingers find their way into her. To her horror and despair, she realizes she is still wet. He's smiling at her. Not the least surprised.

"You're just like the other cunts."

"No. No, I'm not." She can hear the pleading in her voice. Wrong note to sound, but she can't help it. "You know me. You feel . . . something for me. You don't want to do this . . . to me."

He shoves her away abruptly. He's sweating profusely as he leans back against the leg of the love seat and smiles down at her. For a moment she thinks he must have come. A silent, self-induced orgasm. She thinks she's been granted a reprieve.

But he's still ramrod hard.

He grabs hold of her chin, yanking her head his way. "Say it. *Romeo.* I want to hear it from your lips, whore."

She sees the rage flare up in his eyes. She's not connecting with him. Panic flooding her. Feeling delirious from the pain and the fear. But she can't give up. She can find a way. She always has before. She must now.

"I was having a very good time," she says quietly.

"I know. They all were." He says it so offhandedly, all the hairs on her raw, naked body stand on end. "For a time. Then they wanted to stop. Just like you. Spoilsports. Cockteases. Fucking whores. If you can't pay, don't play."

A feeling of futility sweeps over her, but she rallies herself. Is it her fierce desire to survive or a contest of wills that drives her on? At this point she doesn't even know.

"You're tired," she says softly, yet she is the one who is steeped in physical exhaustion. "Each time, you think about stopping. You want to stop. Afterward you're filled with self-loathing."

And what about me? My self-loathing?

He's amused. "This is a date, Doctor, not a session."

"I care about you. I know how much you're suffering."

He laughs softly. "You think you're so clever, so brilliant, so insightful. You think you know the truth about me. You——don't——know——jackshit——bitch."

He moves closer to her. His prick presses against her thigh. It's hard, cold, damp. He leans back on the sofa, closes his eyes, hums to the music.

"Isn't this romantic?" he croons, his words a demented mockery.

She's nauseated, the champagne soured by terror. "I feel sick. . . ."

He ignores her. Leaves her. Returns humming. Caressing her thigh. Then stroking her hair.

She smells something fetid. Loathsome. His voice echoes in her head. *Until they each, in turn, start to rot, and I exchange a smelly old heart for a nice fresh one . . .*

"Please. I'm really sick—" She has begun to shake convulsively.

"Poor baby," he soothes.

"Oh God—" She throws up all over herself, over the rug. The retching seems to go on forever.

Wracking sobs. He's wiping her with a sponge. Must have gotten it from the kitchen. She's so out of it, she hadn't even noticed he'd left her.

"Say it, Melanie," he prods gently as he wipes the vomit off of her.

Tears flow down her face. "Don't do this. Let me help you. I can help you."

"You are helping me, Melanie."

She feels it happening. A blackness descending. She looks for something of herself to grab on to, but there's nothing. She's evaporating.

He's standing before her. A knife in his gloved hand. The silver blade glints with a reflection of the chrysanthemums in the bronze vase on the coffee table.

He steps closer. Her eyes skid from the knife to his penis. She can't stop staring.

"Do you want it?"

Her heart is racing. Her skin is tingling. To her horror, her revulsion, her whole body is throbbing. She's lost herself. Lost in him.

The room is black. She can't see him. She can only feel him. His penis pulsating against her hip. Honed tip of the knife against her breast.

"Say it. Say, 'I want you, Romeo.' " His arm circles

her waist, sways with her to the strains of *Rhapsody in Blue.*

Even as she faces death, she remains the voyeur. Hasn't she been dancing with Death forever?

"Say it, Melanie. Say it and you'll be saved," he murmurs seductively.

Yes, saved. Not really giving in, but reclaiming all that I've lost.

"I want you, Romeo." She barely breathes the ultimate—the final—confession—as she sinks deeply inward. It's all that exists. This final act of letting go, the extraordinary arousal and paradoxical feeling of power that consume her.

The music reaches a crescendo as the knife descends. Melanie cannot hear the scream. She is drowning in it.

He gazes down at her and smiles reverently. He is coming in a fierce, hot jet even as he enters her, the explosion of his semen and her blood forever merged in his psyche. In a heartbeat. Melanie's last.

.

Romeo's need to kill before he can rape is a key element in his ritual. Because when he reaches orgasm he—like all of us—loses control, exposing his vulnerability. . . . Something he can't allow his victims to witness for fear they'll use it against him. Dead, these women pose no threat.

Dr. Melanie Rosen
Cutting Edge

1

The last time Sarah Rosen spoke with her sister Melanie was very early on the day of Melanie's murder. Normally, Sarah would have been pissed as hell to be jarred awake before her alarm went off, but she was having such a torturous nightmare—a huge, menacing hand with thick, hairy fingers circling her throat, a voice in the dark calling out hoarsely, "Sarah, Sarah"—that the call was actually a relief. Until she heard who was at the other end of the line.

"I should have known it was you," Sarah said groggily, pushing a sagging strand of her short-cropped, spiky auburn hair back from her forehead. She dug around for her glasses on her bedside table amidst the mess of magazines, papers, alarm clock, books, and a half-filled glass of white wine that she inadvertently toppled in the process.

Ignoring the spill, she continued her hunt. The glasses, their gold-rimmed, John Lennonesque frames slightly bent, along with an empty dessert plate from a midnight snack of peanut butter and jelly, somehow turned up underneath her pillow. Retrieving the glasses caused the china plate to hit the wooden floor, shattering.

"What was that?" Melanie asked.

"Nothing. A plate," Sarah said, sticking her glasses on. Whenever Sarah had to deal with difficult people or, to be fair, with people she had difficulty dealing with, she tried to hedge her bets by having things in focus.

"You're such a slob, Sarah," Melanie scolded lightly.

"I function better in chaos." Her bedroom did look like the scene of a break-in, all her bureau drawers hanging open, jerseys, socks, underwear spilling out in tiers as if a slipshod burglar had been on a furious search for hidden valuables. What valuables there were—a tangled mass of costume jewelry, a chipped coffee mug, a lopsided earring tree, and a clumped-up pair of pantyhose—were out for the taking on top of the bureau. Her one chair, an old wooden porch rocker abandoned by the last tenant, was piled with the clothes she'd worn the day before. Adding to the chaos were cartons stacked against the far wall, untouched since she moved into this ground floor, one-bedroom apartment in the Mission District nearly a year ago.

Melanie had been horrified by her sister's move. Drive-by shootings in the Mission were an almost daily event. She'd accused Sarah of being masochistically reckless. Actually, Sarah was as big a coward as they came. It was just that worrying about what was going on outside distracted her from what was going on inside of her, which scared her even more.

"You can't put your life in order, Sarah, until you put some order into your life," Melanie said tartly.

"A homily? All those years of psychoanalytic training, and that's all you can come up with?" Sarah said dryly. "But then, it's early in the morning, Mel. Maybe you're not warmed up yet."

"It's almost seven o'clock. Don't you have to be at work by nine?"

"Yes. Which means I still had a good half hour of sleep to go." She wasn't about to thank her sister for waking her from that nightmare. The first thing Melanie would want to do was analyze it.

"I don't have much time," Melanie said briskly. "My first patient is due in ten minutes."

That suited Sarah just fine since she could only take her big sister in very small doses. "What do you want?"

"You know what I want, Sarah. I want you to go see Dad."

Sarah fell back on her pillow and yanked her plaid comforter up under her chin. A shoe that had gotten tangled in the cover thumped to the floor. "It's too early in the morning—"

"I was going to drag you over there with me this evening, but I've got a date. We'll go tomorrow during lunch instead. I'll stop by your office and pick you up."

"No," Sarah said. "I'll go alone." As upsetting as it was to make the trek to the nursing home to see her father, turning it into a family reunion would be infinitely worse.

"When will you go, Sarah? It's been weeks," Melanie badgered. "The other night, he went on and on about how he never sees you. How you've deserted him."

"Don't guilt-trip me, Mellie." Sarah knew how much her sister hated being called anything but Melanie. Melanie, after the renowned Austrian psychoanalyst, Melanie Klein. Her father's choice. Naturally.

"Give it a rest, Sarah."

"You're the good daughter, I'm the shit. So what else is new?"

"I'm not guilt-tripping you. You're feeling guilty, and you're taking it out on me. And I don't have time for it. When will you go see him?"

"Saturday." Sarah figured she could get her good pal Bernie to go with her. For moral support. She sighed. "There. Are you happy?"

"Happy? No, Sarah, I'm not happy. How can I be happy when my father, who was once one of the most distinguished psychoanalysts in the world, thinks I'm five years old and wants me to sit on his lap so he can rock me to sleep with a lullaby?"

Sarah winced. But when she spoke, her tone was deliberately cool and perfunctory. "The man's got Alzheimer's disease. Aren't you the one who's always on my case about coming to grips with reality? Actually, I think you stole that line from Dad. Not that he has much use for it anymore."

"Don't you have any feelings for your father at all? For chrissake, Sarah, you're not a child anymore. You can't blame everything on me being Daddy's favorite—"

Sarah pushed a book out of the way so she could check her bedside clock. "It's three minutes to seven, Mel. You don't want to keep your patient waiting. Or is there some kind of countertransference going on?"

"I'll call you tomorrow," Melanie said with more resignation than indignation. "After I visit Dad. I'll only have a minute to give you an update because I've got to see Feldman at two."

"Be sure to give him my love," Sarah said dryly.

"Dad or Feldman?"

"You figure it out, sis. You're the shrink."

"Tell me what you see."

Sarah put her glasses on as she stood in front of an easel in a small top-floor studio in SoMa, a derelict area of warehouses southeast of the Tenderloin. The place was thick with the smells of oil paints and turpentine, coupled with the lingering aroma of fried bacon from Hector Sanchez's breakfast.

"Well?" the artist prodded impatiently when Sarah didn't immediately respond.

She cleared her throat. Hector's painting unsettled her and yet held her transfixed. "It reminds me of the sea in a storm. Lots of turbulence. Ferocity. Rage. But it's thrilling, too. There's a lot of power here."

"How does it compare with—" His voice faltered. He dropped his head, like it was too heavy for his neck to support. "You know," he mumbled.

Sarah turned to her client. Hector Sanchez didn't look like an artist. When he'd first walked into her office at the Department of Rehabilitation a couple of months back, she'd taken him for a laborer. Her guess was, a dock worker. He was in his late twenties, broad and muscular with an acne-scarred face, short black hair, dark Latino skin, and a chip on his shoulder the size of a boulder.

"Would you believe me if I told you it's better?" Sarah'd viewed Hector's *pre-accident* works a few weeks ago, before he'd gone ballistic on them with a kitchen knife in a violent fit of rage, frustration, and despair.

"Don't bullshit me."

Sarah shrugged. "See what I mean? Why'd you bother to ask?"

Sanchez tore off his sunglasses and flung them angrily across the studio. "It's all crap. I don't know why the fuck I ever let you talk me into this. It's fucking nuts. You call this rehab? You've got to be one fucked-up broad to have come up with this crazy scheme. I'm going to be a goddamn laughingstock."

Her bangle bracelets jangling, Sarah strode purposely over to where Hector sat perched on a wooden stool, his hands dug deep in the pockets of his paint-stained jeans. She stared him in the face, not shying away from the rivulets of scar tissue circling both eyes that the sunglasses had hidden, his shriveled lids still half-concealing his raisin-dark pupils. Before his motorcycle accident he must have had very sexy bedroom eyes, she imagined with a pang of sadness.

"You're not a laughingstock, Hector. You're an artist."

"I'm fucking blind."

"You're a fucking blind artist. And whatever you couldn't see with your eyes when you were painting this canvas, you saw with everything else inside of you. It came spewing out—violent and vivid, dark and ominous. And whether you like it or not, it's fucking *good*."

Hector Sanchez's hard-lined mouth broke into a sudden grin. "Cursing? That ain't very professional, Ms. Rosen."

Sarah jabbed the artist's shoulder. "Give me a break, pal. I've got a couple of other clients left to check on this morning, and there's a mountain of paperwork waiting for me back at the office."

"Jesus, your life sounds dull, Sarah. Seems to me you could use a little rehab yourself." He reached out for her, fingers closing around her upper arm. "How 'bout we go out for a bite tonight?"

"You know the rules, Hector. I can't date my clients."

"Rules, schmules. You gotta eat. You're skinny as a rail. Your arm feels like a chicken leg."

"I eat like a pig. Just burn it up, is all," she said, a touch defensively.

He stared at her with his sightless eyes. "Tell me what I'm seeing, Sarah."

She gave a little start. "What?"

"You know. Describe yourself, like you did the painting."

"What, you want a blow-by-blow description?"

"Yeah," he said, smirking. "Start at the top and work your way down."

"Come on, Hector. I haven't got the time." She wriggled her arm free of his hold.

"I'll tell you what I know from my little subversive grabs at you here and there," he said with a lascivious grin, "and you fill in the blanks. Like, I know you got this real short hair that feels like a porcupine—probably chop it off yourself. And you dress like a fucking gypsy. Long, gauzy skirts, big, soft, shapeless tops, sandals."

"How do you know about the sandals?"

"They flap when you walk. Where was I? Oh yeah. And you decorate yourself like a goddamn Christmas tree. Lots of gold—"

"Silver," she interrupted. "I'm not a gold person."

"Right, silver fits. And beads wherever you can hang them. Big earrings, necklaces, bracelets. I said skinny, but my bet is you're hiding more of a shape than you wanna let on."

Sarah shifted restlessly. "What the hell do you want, Hector? My bra size?" she chafed.

"Thirty-two B?"

"You sure you're blind?"

"I think you're probably a knockout, but you do your best not to let it show."

She gave a derisive laugh. "Win one, lose one. I've got to go. See you in a couple of weeks. Oh, and Arkin from the Beaumont Gallery will be up to see your masterpiece here, tomorrow afternoon, three o'clock. Don't give him a hard time, okay?"

She removed her glasses, tucking them into the big tapestry tote bag that was slung over her shoulder, and started for the door.

"Hey, Sarah—" he called out to her.

"Yeah?"

"You do like guys, don't you?"

"Not when they're pains in the ass." She opened the door. "See ya, Sanchez."

He laughed. "See ya, Rosen. In my dreams."

It was close to noon on that last Thursday in October. A misty rain started falling over the city as Sarah left the Eddy Street Rehabilitation Training Center and made her way on foot down Van Ness to her office near the Civic Center. It hadn't rained in San Francisco in weeks—flawless day after flawless day had driven the local weathermen nuts because it made their weather reports so boring. A little rain would brighten their spirits even if it didn't hers. Sarah had nothing against perfect weather. Rain, on the other hand, bummed her out.

She flashed on an image of herself as a tall, gawky girl —just turned thirteen—standing at her bedroom window shortly after they'd settled into the rambling Victorian house on Scott Street. Her face pressed to the cool pane of glass, the rain coming down as she stared off at the bay, the Golden Gate Bridge smeared by fog. Her tears falling on the inside pane of glass.

She hated that house in Pacific Heights then. Still hated it. Her father's house. Now her sister's. Fine with her. She didn't want it. Nothing but bad, sad memories in that place. Ironic really, since they'd moved there from Mill Valley to escape other bad, sad memories. Some things there was just no escaping. Unless you put your mind to it. Or more to the point, got your mind off it. Sarah didn't think of herself as having many talents. But she did have one. She had a talent for turning forgetting into an art. Most of the time.

Today, because she felt so down, her talent was flagging. Memories kept flashing like blinking yellow warning lights. Sarah blamed the disquieting visions on the rain. On that dumb nightmare. On the phone call from her sister that morning. Had Melanie actually climbed onto her father's lap at the nursing home? Sarah shut her eyes, feeling an unpleasant heat coursing through her, despite the damp wind whipping around as the misty rain got soupier.

A woman wrestling a Toyota coupe into a tight space at the curb in front of Davies Hall accidentally hit the horn with her elbow. Sarah's eyes popped open.

A gull that strayed a bit far from the bay—maybe lost its way—swooped above her, its wings spread wide, cutting across the fast-darkening sky. She wanted desperately to fly. *Fly, fly away.*

Sarah was thoroughly soaked and chilled by the time she got to the Rehabilitation Department offices, housed in an architecturally void skyscraper on the corner of Van Ness and Hayes.

She'd been working there for the past six years, ever since she'd gotten her master's degree in rehabilitation counseling from San Francisco State. The pay was marginal—far below what her father and her sister felt she, as a Rosen, was capable of earning—but Sarah didn't have their expensive tastes. Nor their bent for overachievement. Anyway, except for the paperwork, she enjoyed being a rehab counselor. It gave her a sense of purpose. She felt needed. And she liked most of her caseload, which currently consisted of forty-six physically disabled clients—or physically *challenged,* as they were supposed to be called if you wanted to be politically correct. Most of Sarah's clients didn't give a damn what they were called. They just wanted to get their lives back in order, find something they could learn to do that would earn them enough to get by on, and be left alone. Sarah felt much the same way herself.

As she stepped into the drab lobby of the office building, her stomach growled. She remembered Hector's remark about her being skinny. She did have a habit of forgetting to eat. Doing an about-face, she turned and headed back out of the building and over to the coffee shop just around the corner to grab a bite of lunch.

Ready-made wrapped sandwiches were lined up at the front of the counter. She bought a turkey deluxe, dropped it in her tote bag to take back to her office. She was tucking the change away when she spotted her colleague and best pal, Bernie Grossman. Bernie had his wheelchair pulled up to one of the gray Formica tables at the rear of the coffee shop, where he was devouring a bowl of chili con carne.

He glanced up at her as she approached. "You're wet," he said.

Bernie, in his early forties, had a face that reminded Sarah of a cherub. "It's raining."

He reached up and patted her damp face with his napkin.

She brushed his hand away as she slid into a chair beside him. "Save it. You need it more than me. Christ, you're a slob, Bernie." Flecks of chili were embedded in his thick salt-and-pepper beard.

He grinned. "I know. It's driving Tony crazy. He's such a priss when it comes to tidiness."

Sarah retrieved her sandwich from her tote bag but paused to peer suspiciously over at her friend before unwrapping it. "Did you say Tony?"

Bernie plucked a scrap of chopped beef off the front of his blue denim shirt, the buttons of which were straining from the paunch around his middle. "I didn't tell you about Tony?"

Sarah unwrapped her sandwich, gave it a closer inspection. Shit. The label said turkey with mayo, but there was mustard slathered all over the rye bread. Screw it, she wasn't all that hungry anyway.

"Bernie, you told me Tony was a tight-assed bastard and he'd be the last guy in the universe you'd ever take up with."

Bernie put his spoon on the table. The spastic tremor in his right hand forced the utensil into a little drumroll before it settled down. "When did I tell you that?"

Sarah mulled it over while she picked off a piece of the crust and popped it into her mouth, trying to ignore the biting taste of the mustard. "Let's see. Today's Thursday. You were out sick yesterday. Tuesday. You told me on Tuesday that the guy was a shit."

"Don't ad lib, Sarah. I specifically said *tight-ass*. Which depending on how one looks at it isn't necessarily a put-down."

Sarah groaned. "Do you mind, Bernie?"

He grinned. "One of these days, Sarah, you're going to admit you love it when I talk dirty."

"Yeah, yeah. Along with admitting I really still believe in the tooth fairy?"

"Gracious, Scarlett, where would we be if we didn't believe in fairies," he teased.

"Yuck, yuck."

"I know. I could be a stand-up comedian instead of a rehab counselor if I could only stand up." He gave the wheels of his chair a friendly little rap.

Sarah flashed a wry smile.

"Okay, maybe it's not funny enough. Anyway, while I was home nursing a lousy stomach virus yesterday, guess who showed up to take care of me?"

"Florence Nightingale himself?"

"Tony happens to be a legitimate registered nurse."

"Who had his license revoked for stealing 'ludes from the hospital cookie jar. Come on, Bern. The last thing in the world you need is a guy who messes with drugs."

No one knew that better than Sarah. Except Bernie himself.

Bernie Grossman had been one of Sarah's first *cases* at the rehab department. A college-educated, homosexual, Jewish drug addict who'd gotten the shit kicked out of him so bad outside a gay bar on Castro Street that he landed in the emergency room of San Francisco General with several broken vertebrae. After six months of physical rehab combined with two months at a drug treatment center, Bernie had entered her office cleaned up, bound to a wheelchair, still Jewish, still gay, and thinking that maybe he should finally, at the age of thirty-five, become the *mensch* his immigrant parents down in Pasadena had raised him to be.

A little more than two years later, thanks in large part to Sarah's constant *kvetching,* he ended up with a master's degree in rehabilitation counseling and, thanks to Sarah's finagling, landed a probationary position as a rehab counselor at the department and was put under her supervision. Six months later, he was still off drugs, passed the civil service test, and landed a permanent staff position. Now he was coming up on his fourth clean and successful year on the job.

"How am I supposed to stay away from druggies, Sarah?" Bernie asked after downing another spoonful of chili. "Practically my entire caseload's made up of ex-druggies. Granted, some are more ex than others."

"I'm not talking about clients," Sarah said pointedly.

"Tony's been clean for seven months, dear heart. You

have my devout word that if he swallows anything other than an aspirin, I'll kick him right out the door." He grinned. "Figuratively speaking, naturally. Point being, my dear Sarah, I will still screw, thank God, but I will not screw up. As my good old dad says, some of us *schmendriks* gotta learn our lessons the hard way."

"Speaking of good old dads—"

Bernie's crooked smile revealed eyeteeth that three years of orthodontia had not been able to set straight. "You hate your dad."

"Did I ever actually say I hated him?"

"In so many words?" His toothy smile broadened. "Yes."

Sarah sighed. "We don't always say exactly what we mean."

"Or not all of what we mean, anyway," Bernie tacked on.

"What is this? Fuck-with-Sarah's-head day?"

"Touchy, touchy," he said but gave her short, damp hair an affectionate ruffle. "Tell Bernie all about it."

"Look, my sister's on my case about my not visiting my dad. He's been asking for me."

Bernie buttered a piece of bread, then dunked it into his chili. "I thought he didn't even recognize you last time you went to see him."

"He didn't. But he fades in and out. Sometimes he's amazingly with-it." She sighed. "I don't know which times are worse." She recalled with a sinking feeling her visit about a month earlier, when he'd remembered her all too well.

She'd spent an agonizing thirty minutes with her father that afternoon, listening in stony silence while he tongue-lashed her for being incompetent, inarticulate, lazy, sneaky, and bizarrely enough, judgmental. Sarah couldn't blame the harangue on his illness. It was the same one she'd heard many times over during the years he was supremely lucid.

When she was younger and her father was in top

form, he'd occasionally break her down. Then he'd zero in for the kill, accusing her of having a Cinderella complex, insisting she deal with her neurotic feelings of inadequacy and paranoia in psychoanalysis. Sarah, always there with a quick retort, would say that if she was Cinderella, where the hell was her fairy godmother and when was Prince Charming going to show up with her glass slipper? It was her considered opinion that most of the men she met who weren't pigs were frogs. And no amount of kissing was going to turn them into princes.

"Do you honestly want to go see him, Sarah?" Bernie gave her one of his inimitable I-can-see-right-through-you looks, which always made Sarah uneasy. Even though she considered Bernie her best friend and had certainly confided in him more than she had anyone else in her life, she was still a very private person. There were a lot of things she never shared with anyone.

"I promised Melanie I'd go on Saturday."

Bernie shook his head as he broke off a piece of the sodden bread and popped it into his mouth. "When are you gonna stop letting those two bully you around, dear heart? You're thirty-two fucking years old, for chrissake."

"I didn't fuck my way through all thirty-two years."

Bernie picked his spoon back up again and waved it at her—a little wildly because of his tremor. "Yeah, and that's precisely your problem. When's the last time you got laid, Sarah?"

"Sex is overrated."

Bernie grinned. "No, it isn't. Come on, let's share war stories. Wanna know the last time I got laid?"

"No. I wanna know if you'll come with me to see my dad on Saturday."

"All right, already. I'll come. Now, can I give you the delicious details of my escapade with Antonio yesterday? Do you know he's the first lover I've had in months that I haven't had to shut my eyes and work up a good, juicy fantasy in order to really enjoy myself? With most of the others, what with all their grunting and groaning, I couldn't concentrate and—*nada.* Tony's a whole different story. He can do things with grape jelly—"

Sarah raised her hand. "Please. Spare me the lurid details. Grape jelly happens to be a staple in my diet. Do me a favor and let me keep it that way."

Close to nine that evening, Sarah stood at her open refrigerator door in her narrow galley kitchen, finally getting around to thinking about her dinner. Not much to choose from. A couple of slices of leftover pizza, a slab of cheese that would require excising its moldy edges, a half-container of take-out pork lo mein. The lo mein was her first choice, until she remembered that it had been in there for well over two weeks.

Her eyes lit on the jar of Welch's grape jelly on the top shelf. One corner of her mouth turned up. Definitely not a night for a peanut butter and jelly sandwich, thanks to Bernie.

Sarah sighed, wondering just what it was Bernie's lover had done with that jelly. Maybe it was the lack of grape jelly in her sex life that made it so dull. Or the lack of lovers. She hadn't had a date in a couple of months. As for sex itself . . .

Sarah wondered for the first time who her sister was seeing tonight. Someone new? Had Melanie mentioned his name on the phone? She didn't think so. Not that Melanie shared much of her private life with her. Then again, she didn't share much of hers with Melanie. True, there wasn't all that much for her to share. Though Melanie would be the last person she'd freely confide in. They never had been very close, despite Melanie having always been there for her in the crunch times. But more as a shrink than a sister.

Not wanting to think about Melanie or her own pathetic social life, Sarah focused back on the problem at hand. What to eat. She settled on a slice of pizza, giving it a one-minute zap in her microwave. Heating it up that way made the crust soggy and chewy, but the pizza hadn't been particularly good to start out with.

After eating her pizza, Sarah debated whether to attack the week's worth of dishes piled up in her sink, call a friend and take in a late movie, or climb into a hot bath and then get an early night's sleep.

Fifteen minutes later she was sliding down into her old-fashioned claw-footed tub of steamy water. Being five foot eight, she couldn't immerse her whole body at the same time, so she opted to let her legs dangle over the rim.

Sarah rarely looked at her body, but as she lay there soaking in the tub, she replayed her conversation with Hector Sanchez earlier that day about her appearance and gave herself a dispassionate survey. She was bony all right, but in a reasonably lanky, athletic way. Odd, since other than walking, which she did a great deal of, she wasn't and never had been particularly interested in sports. Something about her fear of competition had been her father's diagnosis.

Naturally, her big sister Melanie had been a star athlete all through school—captain of the girls' lacrosse team in high school, number three on her college tennis team. Recently, Melanie had taken up squash with a vengeance, her most frequent opponent none other than her ex-husband and fellow psychiatrist, Bill Dennison. Despite having been divorced for nearly two years, Melanie and Bill had remained close professionally, covering each other's patients during vacations or conferences. And they still seemed to enjoy doing battle together. At least on the squash court.

Sarah had watched them play once—she and Melanie were going to have one of their rare dinners out together afterward—and all Sarah could think, witnessing Melanie in action, was that there was something fierce and disquietingly erotic about the way her sister gave herself so completely over to the game. She made mincemeat out of Bill and seemed to love pounding him. Sarah wondered if Melanie responded that way with all her opponents, or if she was still working out unresolved issues with her ex. If so, Sarah knew all too well that her sister wasn't the only one who had unfinished business with Dr. Bill Dennison.

Sarah glanced down at her body and saw, with a start, that her hands were cupping her breasts. She saw, too, that her nipples were taut. For a few moments, she contemplated masturbating. But no sooner had the idea of a little self-gratification come into her head than she lost all desire. She ended up smiling sardonically, remembering Hector's accurate guess about her bra size—32B. Nothing to write home about, but she supposed Hector had also been right when he'd said that she was shapelier than her clothes revealed.

She let her hands slip down the curves of her rounded hips as she lifted first one leg, then the other, straight up in the air like a ballet dancer. Good legs. Her mother's legs.

Her mother once dreamed of being a dancer and then transferred those dreams to her younger daughter. With a rueful snicker, Sarah wiggled her toes. Great legs, but two left feet. After six lessons, the ballet teacher had suggested to her mother that she might want to try her daughter in tap instead. Sarah suffered through three agonizing months of tap before her mother finally accepted she would never make it in the world of dance and let her quit. Strongly against her father's wishes. He felt that his younger child needed to see things through and not give up so easily. It was one of the rare times Sarah ever remembered her mother going against her father. They'd had an actual blowup—the first Sarah had ever witnessed between her parents.

And the last.

Sarah washed quickly, vigorously, then got out of the tub, toweled off, slipped on a man-size white terry robe, and padded into her living room. After a hot bath she usually felt relaxed and sleepy, but tonight she felt edgy, restless. She flopped down on her sofa, rummaging in the cushions until she came up with the remote. She flicked on the TV. The reception was lousy. Dark images, snow across the screen. Picture tube probably going. One of these days she'd get around to buying a new set.

She stayed with CNN for a few minutes, listening more than watching—continued problems with jury selection in the O.J. case, Feinstein was closing the gap on Huffington to hold on to her Senate seat from California, and there was still no settlement in sight for either the baseball or the hockey strike.

She idly surfed the channels, not really paying attention. Until a familiar voice brought her up short.

"Because when he reaches orgasm he—like all of us— loses control, exposing his vulnerability."

Melanie. Sitting with two men in what looked for all the world like a squad room straight out of one of those cop shows.

Sarah fiddled with the controls, trying to brighten the picture. That only produced more snow, making the images even fuzzier. By this point, the camera'd cut from her sister and the two men to a close-up of a dark-skinned woman with short-cropped hair and huge hoop earrings.

"I'm Emma Margolis, and this is *Cutting Edge.* Don't go away. When we come back, we'll return to noted psychiatrist Dr. Melanie Rosen's scintillating discussion with Homicide detectives John Allegro and Michael Wagner about Romeo, the serial killer who 'steals women's hearts.' Taped live this afternoon at the Homicide squad room at the Hall of Justice, right here in San Francisco."

Sarah almost changed the channel. Although she'd heard Melanie had made several appearances on the nightly newsmagazine show *Cutting Edge,* she'd assiduously avoided watching any of them. She found her sister's fascination with this warped killer, Romeo, disturbing. Not only had Melanie been retained by the local tabloid TV show to analyze the madman who was wreaking havoc on the city, she had also become the expert consultant to the special SFPD task force created to apprehend him.

Sarah's curiosity, however, got the better of her. Instead of changing the channel, she pressed the mute button, sitting through a beer commercial and an ad for AT&T. When the show came back on, the interview between Melanie and the two detectives resumed. Their names flashed at the bottom of the screen as the camera moved in for close-ups, first of Melanie, then the younger cop, Detective Wagner, last the older one, Detective Allegro. Hard to see their features clearly because of the lousy reception.

John Allegro was talking when Sarah switched on the sound—

"Our experience has been that most serial killers usually hit on 'bad women'—prostitutes, druggies, the homeless. Or they're the Bundy types who go after schoolgirls— young, defenseless, impressionable. But this guy's MO is different. He's striking out at successful, smart, very attractive career women. His victims have been a lawyer, a professor, a stockbroker, a business executive. And there's not even a common physical type."

"To have power over a prostitute or a schoolgirl may seem too easy and unchallenging to Romeo." Melanie spoke with the assured, clipped voice of authority. "The thrill for him is in dominating the kind of women who appear on the surface to be powerful and seemingly in control."

"And beneath the surface?" Detective Wagner broke in. "I gather you're referring to information we dug up that a couple of the victims, in any event, have dabbled in a little S&M."

Melanie faced him squarely. "I believe some need, some longing, some secret yearning to be sexually dominated drew those victims to this man. They went along . . . up to a point."

Wagner leaned forward. "Why would they do that? Why would any woman want to be a victim?"

"Some women have so little self-worth, they feel they deserve the abuse, Detective Wagner," Melanie told him, using her lecturing voice. Once again the camera framed her face. "Abuse can become an obsession. Like a drug. Romeo could give these women the 'fix' they craved. Fulfill their wildest fantasies, their deepest needs. Without judgment."

"No, he didn't judge them," Allegro snarled. "He just eviscerated them."

There was a brief silence, broken by Detective Wagner. "What else can you tell us about this creep?"

"That's the problem," Melanie responded coolly. "You wouldn't guess Romeo's a creep to look at him; even to spend some time with him. On the surface, he's most likely quite appealing."

"You mean good-looking?" Wagner asked.

Melanie shrugged. "Looks are subjective, Detective. I'd say magnetic, charming. However violent things ultimately got in the end for his victims, Romeo was initially able to win their confidence. From what you've found at the crime scenes, all these encounters apparently started out as dates. Three out of the four victims even had their tables set for romantic dinners for two. Candlelight and champagne."

"So you're saying there's no looking at this guy and knowing he's a psycho case?" Allegro demanded.

"If by psycho case, you mean criminally insane," Melanie said, again the voice of authority, "you're heading up the wrong alley. Romeo is a sexual psychopath. Legally, he'd never be judged insane. Because the true sexual psychopath has no trouble discerning right from wrong. We're talking here about a compulsion—an unrelenting drive. Romeo, like all sexual predators, feels secretly powerless. Only rage and fury help to fend off that feeling. This ritualized killing and mutilation make him feel powerful. And his frantic need to feel powerful extends beyond his victims. I think he gets off on the power he has over authority figures like the police, as well."

"Yeah, right," Allegro said brusquely. "Four women raped, brutalized, and vivisected, and we haven't been able to get so much as a crumb of a lead on him. What do you say, Doc? Is Romeo really all that clever, or has he been just plain lucky so far?"

"Quite a bit of both, it seems to me," Melanie said.

"Too bad his victims weren't a little more of both," Wagner observed sourly.

For the first time, Melanie's voice faltered. "Too bad? Detective, I'd say it's tragic."

Sarah hit the off button on the remote. She found this whole business about Romeo revolting. It made her sick to imagine that such a demented, sadistic creature existed. That there were women out there who seemed so together on the surface, only to be harboring some sick, desperate need for domination and subjugation. That her own sister had made this madman killer her personal cause célèbre.

It's you alone who understands my struggle. If I lose you, I lose me.

M.R. diary

2

At 8:20 on Friday morning, Detective-Sergeant John Allegro and his partner, Detective Michael Wagner, arrived at Dr. Melanie Rosen's home on Scott Street. The area was already secured. The uniform positioned at the front door gave them a nod and stepped aside. In the vestibule, they were greeted by Johnson and Rodriguez, the Homicide detectives who'd been on call when the body was discovered. The paramedics were heading out. Not much question on this one.

"Who's crying?" Allegro asked Rodriguez, hearing sobs coming from upstairs.

Rodriguez, a wiry man in his midthirties, shrugged. "The guy who found her and called it in. He's pretty much a basket case. We've had no luck getting anything out of him except his name. Perry. Robert Perry. And that he was one of her patients. Maybe you two can brace him up while we go canvass the neighborhood. Looks like it happened sometime late last night. We'll see if anybody around here saw someone either coming or going. You never know. Gotta get a break one of these times, right?"

Allegro's nod lacked any sign of optimism. Four dead women. Now five. No witnesses. Endless hours, weeks,

months of tracking down clues, and they were still on this
wild-goose chase. Every possible lead that had come in—
and there hadn't been all that many that had the ring of
legitimacy about them—had been checked out, only to
lead to another dead end. Romeo was running them
around in circles.

After Rodriguez and his partner took off, Allegro and
Wagner, following the sound of sobs, found Robert Perry
up one flight of stairs. Wailing mournfully, Perry lay
curled in a fetal ball on the beige-carpeted foyer floor just
outside the arched entrance to the psychiatrist's living
room.

"Jesus H. Christ," Allegro said hoarsely, bile rising to
his throat, as he spotted Dr. Melanie Rosen's naked,
bound, and grotesquely mutilated body splayed on one of
the living room's caramel silk love seats, her open, sightless eyes aimed out across the room. The stench of blood,
vomit, and rotted flesh filled his nostrils. It was a smell he
was all too familiar with, but it didn't make it any easier.
Especially this time.

Wagner felt his guts twisting inside of him as he
looked into the room, but he didn't say a word. Instead,
he quickly shifted his gaze, focusing in on Robert Perry.
Feeling none too steady on his feet, the detective knelt
down beside the sobbing man. "Let's go downstairs, Mr.
Perry. It'll be easier to talk down there."

Perry made no response to the suggestion. His hands
were clamped between his thighs, his complexion chalky
white, his shaggy sandy-colored hair damp with sweat. He
looked truly awful, but his underlying handsomeness
wasn't completely camouflaged. Wagner was reminded of
a young Robert Redford type, right down to his outdoorsy
clothes. The red plaid flannel shirt, blue jeans, and hiking
boots could have come straight from an L.L. Bean catalog.

While Wagner dealt with Perry, Allegro slipped on a
pair of surgical gloves and walked resolutely toward the
corpse.

He bent over the body, clinically noting the same MO

he'd seen in all four of Romeo's prior victims—the gaping chest cavity, the white silk scarf binding the wrists and ankles behind the back. And then there was the shriveled, decayed heart resting over the left breast. No doubt the autopsy report would come back with the finding that the heart belonged to victim four, Margaret Anne Beiner.

What was it Melanie had said? *The killer always leaves something of himself at the scene, and takes something with him.* True enough. What he'd taken from each scene was his victim's heart. What Melanie had called the killer's totem or souvenir. And what he'd left behind was the old totem. Melanie had her theories as to why he did this, but what it boiled down to, in her expert opinion, was that Romeo was obsessive and very intelligent.

He'd been smart enough so far to avoid leaving any prints at any of the crime scenes. Allegro was certain the killer's other signature items—the bottle of Perrier-Jouët champagne on the coffee table, the CD jewel box of Gershwin's *Rhapsody in Blue* on the floor beside the couch, the disk itself inside the CD player—would all come up clean this time, just like the others. And all the items could have been purchased or swiped in any one of hundreds of shops in San Francisco or the surrounding area. Endless liquor stores, fabric shops, and record stores had already been canvassed by investigators, to no avail.

Romeo may have managed the print problem easily enough. He couldn't, however, wipe away the traces of sperm found inside and around each dead woman's vagina. The DNA testing on the sperm samples taken from the four prior victims were a perfect match. The same man had committed all four brutal murders. Or else it was a pair of identical twins.

The only problem was, the distinctive profile gleaned from the DNA testing didn't lead them to a suspect. No DNA match-up on file at the FBI. No killings with a similar MO reported from any other county or state. Romeo was sticking to San Francisco—at least for the time being.

The DNA findings would nail the perpetrator, but

first they had to nab him. And to nab him they needed some clues as to his identity—a credible eyewitness or at least something left behind that would provide a connection.

Allegro stared down at the rosewood-handled blade on the floor beside the body. The murder weapon—a carving knife. Nothing fancy or unique. Certain to be clean.

"John!" Wagner shouted from the hall. "I'm gonna need some help here."

Allegro nodded, more grateful for the interruption than he'd ever admit. It was impossible to be dispassionate —this wasn't just another victim. He'd worked closely with Melanie Rosen—had strong feelings for her.

He returned to the foyer, silent and grim-faced, and helped his partner half-carry, half-drag the traumatized, sobbing young man downstairs. They were both eager to get Perry away from the horrific sight of his mutilated analyst before their CSU set to work.

The rest of the investigating team arrived less than two minutes after Allegro and Wagner got Perry to the office waiting room: a police photographer with his Nikon and video camera, a criminalist and his assistant, and the medical examiner. All set about their business with quiet efficiency. The procedure was the same as always—go over the victim and her living quarters with a fine-tooth comb, tweezers, and a vacuum, checking for fingerprints, weapons, threads, buttons, any physical evidence that might provide a lead. Couch cushions, sheets, towels would be carefully bagged and tagged and taken to the forensic lab for tests. Along with the murder weapon and the items Romeo'd probably brought along for the *date*. And of course, the discarded heart.

With Dr. Rosen dead, every investigator and cop in that house knew that the shit was really going to fly now. The psychiatrist had become a kind of local star during the building hysteria of the previous months. The mayor, the DA's office, the chief of police—each would be feeling the pressure and passing it right on down the line. The tabloids would have a field day. In the past months, Romeo had become a household word in the city. Now his name would spread clear across the country. And panic, which was already escalating to a fever pitch, was going to reign supreme in San Francisco until Romeo was brought in. There was even word that a TV movie of the week was already in the works. The only holdup was casting Romeo. The producers were stalled until the real one was caught. And now there'd be a casting call for Dr. Melanie Rosen look-alikes.

"I feel sick," Perry mumbled pathetically as he slumped in a chair in the waiting room, limp as a rag doll.

"You gonna puke?" Allegro asked him. "You want to go to the bathroom?"

Perry shook his head. Wagner poured him a paper cup of water from the water cooler. Perry waved it away, and Wagner swallowed the water down himself in one long gulp. Allegro pulled out a stick of gum from the pocket of his wrinkled gray wool jacket, hoping to combat the sour taste in his mouth. Perry started crying again, quietly.

Shafts of sunlight broke through the morning's milky fog, streaming into the room through a big bay window that framed a picture-postcard view down one of the city's steep hills toward Lombard Street and the Marina District. Wagner looked idly about the compact, pristine space, its ecru-painted walls punctuated with tasteful Japanese prints. Four gray-and-white tweed upholstered chairs were squared off around a glass coffee table with a cube-shaped marble base, an eclectic mix of magazines neatly splayed out on the top.

"We need to go over a few things, Mr. Perry." Allegro settled into the chair beside the weeping patient.

Perry shook his head, waving them away with his hand. Allegro looked up at Wagner, who was standing by the window. Wagner shrugged and pulled out a pack of Camels from the inside pocket of his blue blazer, flipping it open and tapping a cigarette out with the expertise of a longtime smoker.

"Thought you quit," Allegro said.

"Yeah, I thought so, too," Wagner said, lighting up. "Mr. Perry says he got here a little before eight." He looked over at Perry. "Isn't that right?"

Perry didn't respond.

"And that the front door downstairs here was unlocked when he showed up," Wagner continued. "Isn't that what you said, Mr. Perry?"

This time Perry managed a faint nod.

"What made you go upstairs?" Allegro asked.

"She . . . didn't . . . come out . . . to get me."

Allegro rubbed the heel of his palm across his stubbled jaw. "So you decided to go up there and get her?"

"She's . . . always . . . on time. First I . . . went across . . . the hall."

From the arched entrance of the waiting room, Allegro could see across the hall to the closed mahogany pocket doors leading to Dr. Rosen's consulting room. "You thought maybe she was running late with another patient?"

Perry shook his head, still sobbing quietly. "No. I'm her . . . first . . . on Fridays."

The detectives shared a look, both picking up something about the way Perry had said "first." Like it was a point of pride. Like it made him feel special.

"So what did you do?" Allegro asked. "Check to see if she was in there?"

Perry nodded. He wiped his wet face with the cuff of his flannel shirt-sleeve, then wedged his hand back between his tightly pressed-together thighs.

"And after you saw she wasn't?" Wagner prodded.

"I got . . . worried. I thought . . . maybe she . . . was sick . . . or fell . . . or something."

"You knock first before you walked into her apartment?" Allegro asked.

Perry gave him a quick red-eyed look. "Of course I knocked." An edge of hostility crept into his voice.

"Ever been up there before?"

A muscle in Perry's jaw started popping. "No." He got the word out without moving his lips.

"You're gonna have to hang around here for a while," Allegro told him. "Maybe you want to call the place you work, let 'em know you're—"

"I don't . . . have a job. I was laid off. I'm a software engineer. A damn good one," Perry said acerbically. Boastfully.

Allegro shot Wagner a look. What happened to the grieving patient?

"How about your family?" Allegro asked.

"My wife walked out on me." Perry sounded more angry than upset. "All her damn friends told her I was a loser."

"How'd you know that? Wife tell you?"

"I don't want to talk about her. She's got nothing to do with—anything. Just drop it. I'm telling you, I can't take much more. Can't I go home now? I've told you everything. You've got no right—"

"You seeing someone else? Got a girlfriend?" Allegro persisted.

Perry's features crumbled, his face once more a landscape of anguish. "There's no one now. No one. Okay? Satisfied?" Sobs wracked him again as he rocked and clutched himself with added fervor.

Wagner, who had smoked his cigarette practically down to the filter, looked around the room for an ashtray. There wasn't any. He remembered Melanie saying once that she didn't allow her patients to smoke in either her waiting or consulting room. He felt a little guilty for breaking the rule, then felt like a jerk. What difference did it make now? He snuffed the cigarette out on the bottom of his loafer and, after a moment's hesitation, stuck what little was left of the butt in his jacket pocket.

Allegro decided to hold off on asking Perry any more

questions for the time being. He nudged Wagner. They went out into the hall.

"Romeo's signature's all over the place. As far as I can tell, there was no forced entry."

"Meaning she let the bastard in," Wagner said gruffly. "Meaning it must have been some kind of a—date." *Like the others* remained unspoken.

They stood there, awkward and ill at ease, neither successful at concealing the depth of his upset.

"Listen," Wagner mumbled, "I'm not saying that she —I don't mean—well, you know. All that stuff about the victims being into S&M, giving off sick vibes—"

"Shit, there are a lot of possibilities here," Allegro snapped. His voice was louder than he intended. "Who's to say it wasn't one of the wackos she treated? Maybe she was on to him and figured she could get him to confess— give himself up."

"And not say a word to either of us?"

"Patient-doctor confidentiality. If she thought it was a patient, she wouldn't be able to give him away. She'd have to get him to do it himself."

Wagner looked doubtful. "Why would she have brought him upstairs if he was a patient?"

"Maybe she didn't *bring* him," Allegro snapped. "Or maybe she thought it would be one way to win his trust. How the fuck do I know how she worked?"

Wagner looked back in on Perry. "You thinking that our engineer in there could be the doer? He could have been here all night. Killed her and then hung around—"

"We'll get a blow-by-blow account of every move he's made for the past twenty-four hours. If there's anything, we'll trace his movements for the other victims. And have a chat with the ex-wife."

"What about Dr. Rosen's case files? Maybe she wrote something about Perry that could give us a lead. Or if not Perry, maybe one of her other psycho cases."

Allegro shook his head. "We can't go into those files. You know that, Mike. Those records are protected, whether she's alive or dead. Overlooking that point, nothing we dug up without a warrant would be admissible evidence. Not to mention we'd be putting our asses on the line if we got caught."

"We could try for a subpoena."

"Yeah, but we'll need something to go on first. For starters, let's get a list of her patients from her appointment book. Even if we can't get into their files, we can check them out ourselves. Starting with Perry."

"I say we go back in there and lean on him," Wagner said with grim determination.

"No. Let's give him a little more time to stew." Allegro rubbed his thumb across the prickly stubble over his upper lip. He hadn't shaved that morning. When the call came in from the department, he was still in bed. Nursing a world-class hangover. Within fifteen minutes of receiving the call, he'd upchucked in his toilet, relieving some of the pain in his head, thrown on the same wrinkled gray suit he'd worn all week, swallowed down some of the prior day's cold stale coffee still sitting on his stove, and headed for the door. He raced to the scene in his beat-up vintage red '78 MG, which he'd bought "for a steal" off a drug dealer he'd sent up the river about seven years back. The car, like its current owner, was in need of a thorough overhaul.

"Anyway," Allegro added, "we don't know it was a patient. She could have met the bastard at a party or at a conference or through a friend. Or maybe those spots she did on that TV show got to him after all. Made him decide to target her. She said he was real intelligent. Maybe he wanted to see just how smart *she* was."

The muscles in Wagner's face tightened. "Not smart enough."

Allegro swallowed a curse.

A uniformed cop came down the stairs. He approached the grim-faced detectives.

"Morgan says there's a carving knife missing from a set in the kitchen. The murder weapon's a match. I wonder what the bastard'd do if he found himself a victim that didn't cook. You think he brings along his own blade just in case?"

"Anything else?" Allegro wasn't up for humor.

The cop eyed him skeptically, then shrugged. "Kelly's ready to take the lady to the morgue. Wants to know if you want a last look."

Truth was, neither one of them had the stomach to view the mutilated remains of Dr. Melanie Rosen again.

Allegro answered for them both. "No. Tell Kelly to go ahead. Have him take the body out the back way. Might as well keep this low-profile for as long as we can," he said tonelessly.

"Yeah, like maybe the next sixty seconds or so," the uniform said dryly.

"A comedian," Allegro groused. He didn't look at his partner as the uniform took off.

"I'm not smiling," Wagner said, lighting up another cigarette.

Allegro stared at the flare of the match. "You think he is?"

Wagner took a deep drag of his cigarette. "Who? That cop?"

"No. Romeo."

Wagner slowly exhaled a long stream of smoke. "We've got to find that fucker, John."

Allegro nodded grimly, the grooves on his weather-beaten face deepening.

One of the uniformed cops from the street popped his head in the door. "There's a lady outside. Won't give her name. Demands to know what's going on. Says she's got a nine o'clock appointment with the doc."

"Shit." Wagner looked over at Allegro. "We should have thought of that. Dr. Rosen probably had patients lined up all day. They'll be arriving every hour."

Allegro nodded. "You go out there and have a talk with this one, Mike. I'll check out the doc's office and see if I can find her appointment book, and we'll have one of the boys call the other patients she had scheduled for to-day."

Glancing into the waiting room, Allegro saw that Perry was still pretty much out of it, holding his head in his hands, whimpering. "Better bring someone in to baby-sit our boy here first."

Wagner nodded but hesitated before taking off. "What about that ex-husband of hers? Dennison? He's a shrink, too. Maybe he should contact her patients instead of one of us. Some of them might take it real hard."

"Give Dennison a call after you talk to the patient outside," Allegro said. "Not that we can count on him right off the bat after he hears the news."

Wagner's eyes narrowed. "Yeah. Unless he's our perp. Like you said, John, it could be someone she knew. Maybe she and her ex—remember that time he came to pick her up at headquarters a few weeks back? The way he looked at her before and after she brushed him off? We both know he still had the hots for her. He's a possibility."

"Everyone's a goddamn possibility," Allegro said sharply. "That's what's driving me so goddamn nuts."

"What about the rest of her family? Shouldn't we let them know before they catch it on the news?"

"Who've we got?" Allegro's mind was drawing a blank, even though he knew the psychiatrist did have some immediate family. Fucking hangover.

"There's her dad," Wagner said, "but I think she said something about him being in a nursing home. I don't know if he's in any condition—"

"Didn't Melanie once mention a sister?" Allegro asked, glad he could remember something.

Wagner gave his partner a questioning look. It was the first time he could recall hearing John refer to the psychiatrist by her first name. In their meetings with her, it was always "Dr. Rosen" or "Doc." Same for him. And the same even when they discussed her between them-selves.

Allegro cleared his throat. He, too, had noticed the slip. How would she have analyzed it?

Wagner, picking up on his partner's discomfort, glanced away from him, pretending to be studying a Japanese drawing of a tiger that hung on the far wall. "She did mention a sister. We can check around for the doc's address book. Gonna need it in any event for the investigation."

"See if anyone upstairs found one. If not, try the phone book."

Wagner nodded and took off. Allegro remained in the foyer, reluctant to go upstairs where his people were invading every nook and cranny of the psychiatrist's apartment. All the details of Dr. Melanie Rosen's life and grisly death would be scrutinized, analyzed, questioned, judged. In life she'd made a profession out of prying—in death the tables were being turned.

Pounding from the waiting room drew Allegro's attention. He found Perry slamming his fist into the palm of his other hand. Perry stopped abruptly when he saw Allegro. "You don't know what it's like . . ." he whimpered.

"Just a few more minutes. I know you want to do everything you can to help us, right?"

Perry moved his head faintly, but Allegro couldn't tell whether it was a nod or a shake.

Helen Washington, a young plainclothes officer, entered the room. Allegro gave her a quick study. She was trim, brunette. She wore a simple gray linen jacket, slightly flared black skirt, and sensible black pumps. She looked professional and very efficient.

"Detective Wagner asked me to come in and—" She left off and glanced over at the slumped Perry.

Allegro approached her. "Keep Mr. Perry here company for a few minutes. If he should feel like talking, make sure you get it on tape," he said softly, handing her his own minirecorder from his jacket pocket. "And just in case he decides to make life easy for us and confess, you be sure you read him every word of his Miranda."

Washington flashed him a sarcastic, white-toothed smile—what was she, some rookie who needed to be told what to do? She slipped the machine inside her own jacket pocket and sat down in the armchair closest to Perry.

Allegro crossed the hall. He reached the entry to the psychiatrist's consulting room just as Frank Kelly from the medical examiner's office, a short, balding man with a pug nose and a mouth set in a permanent smirk, was heading downstairs. Behind him, two blues maneuvered a stretcher carting a dark green plastic body bag.

Allegro felt sick to his stomach again as he observed the maudlin procession. His hands started to shake. He dug them deep into the pockets of his jacket, fists clenched.

He flashed on the way Melanie Rosen's face looked when he'd examined her remains—brown eyes glazed and bulging, horribly swollen, bruised lips slightly parted, bruised cheeks, all the color drained from her face. Then her naked, contorted, bound body—the surgical slice right down her breast plate, the gaping cavity where her heart had been.

He remembered their first meeting—remembered thinking that it had to be difficult for her patients not to be distracted by her beauty. She had been beautiful.

Hard to hold on to that memory as the medical examiner, cops, and the bagged corpse passed by him. Kelly stopped to confirm what Allegro already knew—that it looked like "a Romeo job, all right," commenting that the knots in the silk scarf binding the victim's wrists and ankles were identical to the ones found on the other victims. And again, there were traces of semen that would be shipped off to the lab for DNA testing.

"Coming down for the postmortem on this one, John?" Kelly's face didn't show it, but Allegro could hear an uncharacteristic note of sadness in the medical examiner's voice. This wasn't just another victim for any of them.

"No," Allegro said brusquely. "Get the report to me ASAP."

The medical examiner nodded, but they all knew there wasn't much chance they'd get anything more from this autopsy than they had from the others. They were batting a big fat zero.

Impassively, Allegro watched the somber group head around the stairs and down the foyer to the back door, where a van from the morgue was waiting. Once they were gone, he turned toward the psychiatrist's consulting room and slid apart the heavy mahogany doors.

As he stepped inside the cherrywood-paneled office, his eyes tracked from the forest-green chaise and black leather Eames chair along one side of the room to the pair of black leather club chairs facing a simple Shaker-style desk at the far end. He'd sat on the club chair on the right that first day. Uncharacteristically nervous. And distracted. Not that he'd given himself away.

Breaking off the memory, he turned to shut the heavy pocket doors behind him, catching a glance from Washington in the waiting room across the hall. He gave her an awkward grimace, then pulled the doors closed.

An eerie silence surrounded him, which he was quick to attribute to the excellent soundproofing. Still, it made him think of a mausoleum. All he could hear was his own breathing. And it wasn't sounding all that steady.

He shuddered, wished he could dash out for a quick belt. A few months ago he would have been able to unobtrusively slip out a flask from his inside jacket pocket.

Thing was, he'd stopped carrying that flask back around the same time Wagner had quit smoking. It wasn't only that Wagner had started getting on his case about his drinking. Allegro knew that it was only a matter of time before his chief would be "suggesting" that he have a few sessions with a police psychologist. So he quit drinking while he was on duty. For the most part.

After hours—that was another story. A couple of beers with dinner, a few shots of Jim Beam with beer chasers as the evening wore on. Not every night, but enough of them so that he often didn't remember getting into bed. He'd made a lot of vows over the past few months to cut back, but now—with this latest blow—he knew things weren't likely to get much better anytime soon.

He forced the desire for that drink from his mind, pulled himself together, and wasting no more time in the consulting room, strode purposefully toward the open door that led to the doctor's private office.

He stepped inside the rectangular room that ran across the back of the house—it must have originally been the kitchen but was now the doctor's private office. His mouth was fixed in a resolute line as he headed straight for the L-shaped oak desk in front of a bank of built-in bookcases lined from floor to ceiling with professional texts. He immediately took note of the calendar sheet for the month's appointments next to the Macintosh computer and checked the Friday schedule. Melanie had patients stacked up from eight until noon. Perry was indeed her eight o'clock. Noon to two had been blocked off, then a notation at two of a meeting at "the Institute." Probably the Bay Area Psychoanalytic Institute, where she consulted.

Picking up the calendar sheet for Mike to pass on to Dennison, his gaze fell on the computer.

We can't go into those files. You know that, Mike. Patient-doctor confidentiality. We'd be putting our asses on the line if we got caught.

Lips tightly compressed, Allegro sat down at the desk and hit the button on the keyboard that turned on the computer. There were things that went beyond job security. The screen glowed, flashed the warm-up routine, then presented the hard drive directory. He went directly to FAST FIND and, after a moment's hesitation, began typing in the prescribed space the letters—GRACE ALLEGRO

A moment later, the psychiatrist's case notes appeared on the screen.

Patient: Grace Allegro
Address: 1232 Bush Street, S.F.
Phone #: 555-7336
Marital Status: Separated
DOB: 4/25/53
Diagnosis: Major Depressive Episode, Recurrent

Initial interview 1/15—patient arrived with her estranged husband, John Allegro, age 44, Homicide detective with SFPD. Patient very agitated and withdrawn following what husband describes as an abortive suicide attempt. Husband, who lives on Washington Street, less than five minutes from wife, says he received a "hysterical" call from Grace at 11:40 last night saying that she was about to slit her wrists. When he arrived at her apartment five minutes later, she had a small penknife in hand and had made a few surface cuts on her arms. She relinquished the knife to him almost immediately and agreed to seek treatment if husband would attend at least the first session with her. Her former therapist, Dr. Carl Eberhart, recently retired, referred her to me, and I agreed to see her for an emergency interview on this date. . . .

Allegro scanned down toward the bottom of the full-page screen, where there was a brief notation about Dr. Rosen's initial observations of him.

This is not a comfortable setting for John. He appears ill at ease. Looks like he'd rather be at the corner bar. Catch him giving me furtive glances. Obvious he finds me attractive and that adds to his discomfort.

Allegro smiled ruefully. So much for imagining he'd hid any of his feelings from her that first day. He continued reading to the end of the screen.

> John is clearly concerned about his wife but makes a point of saying there's no chance of a reconciliation between them. They've been separated on and off for close to two years, but because she has been so unstable he's felt guilty about going ahead with divorce proceedings. He reports that wife has been "in a bad way" for the past six years, ever since their only child, a boy age eleven, died. John doesn't want to talk about the boy—

Dr. Rosen had been right on target about his not wanting to talk about Daniel's death. He didn't want to think about it either, which was where the booze came in. Not that there weren't plenty of other reasons why he needed to dull his senses.

The file on Grace wasn't long—it amounted to a little more than five screens of notes. She'd seen Dr. Rosen alone for eight sessions in January and early February.

Allegro didn't read the rest of his wife's file. None of his business. Anyway, he didn't really want to know what had made Grace tick. He'd given up wanting to know that a long time ago. Or maybe he was afraid to find out. Maybe he didn't want to feel any more guilty and miserable than he already felt. About his wife, his kid, his whole fucking screwed-up life.

Grace's last visit to Dr. Rosen had followed on the heels of another botched suicide attempt—this time with her prescribed antidepressants. Dr. Rosen insisted that Grace voluntarily commit herself to a private psychiatric inpatient hospital in Berkeley. After a two-week observation period, the psychiatric team at the hospital recommended a thirty-day commitment. Grace had railed against staying, but then sank into an even deeper clinical depression and admitted that, if she were released, she would try to kill herself.

That was at the end of February. John remembered Dr. Rosen telephoning him at home. She asked him to come in to see her that evening, explaining that she was signing the papers on his wife, and wanting to give him the opportunity to ask any questions he might have.

She'd left it all very open-ended. He recalled thinking, driving over to her office a short while after her call, that he didn't really have any questions. All he felt was relief that Grace would be someone else's responsibility for at least another month, a feeling he wasn't about to share with Dr. Rosen. He didn't want her to think he was a real shit. Even if he thought he really was, he wasn't eager to have her agree with him. So why was he going? Why had he made a big point of driving over there sober? Even changed to a fresh shirt and buffed his shoes. Who the fuck was he kidding?

Allegro stared at the computer screen, but he wasn't seeing the typed report. He was seeing Melanie. The way she looked that day. And remembering the way he'd felt.

She comes to get him from the waiting room. She's wearing another of her spiffy designer-type suits. Slate gray, the wide-lapeled double-breasted jacket tucked at her narrow waist, the straight skirt a good two inches above her knees. She has on high heels and pale gray stockings that look to be slightly iridescent, making those lovely legs of hers shimmer.

Everything about her shimmers that day, and he isn't inside her consulting room one minute before he has a roaring boner. And she damn well knows it, too. He sees the way her eyes skid briefly down to his crotch as he crosses the room and sits down. He has the distinct impression she takes such things as a given. How the hell did her male patients ever concentrate on their problems? Then he recalls that during that first meeting when he'd

*been there with his wife, while he'd found her just
as striking, he hadn't really gotten turned on. He
can't figure out why it's different this time. But
then it comes to him. This second time—in addi-
tion to being alone together—the doc's sending off
a whole different set of signals. Vibes. Oh, they're
real subtle, but his prick got the message posthaste.
Just took a little longer for his brain to catch on.*

A knock on the door brought him up short. "Just a sec,"
he shouted, quickly dragging his wife's computerized file
to the trash icon, emptying the trash, and shutting down
the computer. Then, spotting a leather-bound appointment book poking out from beneath a stack of journals,
he snatched it up and stuck it inside his jacket pocket.

Scowling, he opened the door. Washington, Perry's
baby-sitter, stood there. Her eyes shone with excitement.

Allegro gave her a skeptical look. "Don't tell me he
confessed?"

"No. Not exactly."

"Then what?" he asked impatiently.

"Just that he's babbling all kinds of crazy stuff."

"What's that mean?"

"Well, he's saying that he and Dr. Rosen—" She
paused. "He's alleging that they were—lovers."

Romeo takes a sadistic pleasure in showing his victims—these successful, independent, professional women—how powerless they are on all levels—physical, psychological, sexual. His heightened arousal is in direct proportion to their heightened debasement.

Dr. Melanie Rosen
Cutting Edge

3

Michael Wagner could feel the tremor in his hands even as he white-knuckled the leather steering wheel of his zippy two-year-old silver Firebird. He flipped on the radio. A scratchy recording of Billie Holiday crying out the blues. Perfect. He drove down Mission Street, the singer's haunting notes washing over him. Tears slipped down his cheeks.

Traffic was heavy on Mission, a bustling, gritty commercial strip lined with palm trees and spilling over with pawnshops, Latino bars blasting salsa music through their doors, poolrooms, military surplus stores, and even a few hippie joints, holdovers from the sixties.

He passed a boarded-up tenement right next to a building with a huge colorful mural. Slick-looking punks in black leather, their arms and thighs circled with studded belts, leaned against the mural wall, talking to a couple of peroxide blondes sporting nose rings. Genuine San Francisco. Wagner knew this grimy section of town well. Working Vice, he'd been over this way plenty of times.

When he got to Sixteenth Street, he hooked a right onto Valencia. He pulled up at the curb in front of a three-story stucco building, its flaking yellow paint clashing with its garish bright orange trim. This shabby tenement, wedged between a porno bookstore and a Mexican bodega, was certainly quite a contrast from Melanie's classy Pacific Heights abode.

No one buzzed him in when he pressed the button beside Sarah Rosen's name, so he tried the one under it. Vickie Voltaire. The buzzer went off, and he opened the door, stepping into the first-floor hallway.

A striking woman somewhere in her midthirties stepped out of the door of apartment 1C. She was about five foot ten, flaming red hair piled high on her head with sexy little tendrils falling about her large-boned, exotic face. Her full lips were painted a shocking pink. She was dressed for action in a black leather miniskirt, scooped-neck fuzzy white wool sweater, and gold mules. She smiled seductively as the detective approached, but the smile never got anywhere near her heavily made-up eyes.

"Hiya, sweetie. Can I do ya something?"

The low, breathy voice made Wagner look a little closer at the woman, who now had one hand draped on her jutting hip, the other gracefully placed at her throat. He realized at once that the imposing *she* was actually a *he*.

A shudder went through Wagner. All those years on Vice, and it still amazed him how the best of them could really fool you. He flashed on that stunning little blond-haired number he'd picked up at a SoMa nightspot only a month ago. It wasn't until they were dancing that he'd felt *her* hard-on.

"The name's Vickie Voltaire. You can call me Miss Vickie if you like, handsome," he camped.

Wagner smiled pleasantly, revealing no hint of his discomfort. "I'm looking for Sarah Rosen." He glanced next door to apartment 1B.

"Sarah? Adore the woman." The stunning transvestite leaned a little closer. Wagner had to admit he smelled good. "But, God, would I like to get my hands on that girl and make her over. She could be an absolute knockout.

She's got it all—she simply doesn't know what to do with it. She a friend of yours?"

"No. Not exactly."

"Hmmm. A cop, right?"

"I just want to talk to her." Wagner added, "She's not in any trouble."

Vickie gave the detective a long, assessing look, shaking his head slowly, his seductive neon-pink smile blinking out. "But you're gonna bring her some, aren't you, honey?"

Sarah was at the bank of elevators across from her office, about to go out on her afternoon calls, when she was approached by her supervisor. Andrew Buchanon was a skinny, thin-lipped, freckle-faced man in his early forties. Six years back, when Sarah was new at the agency, Buchanon, then her colleague, had made a play for her. She gave him the cold shoulder. He hit on her again shortly after he was promoted to supervisor, figuring that his position of authority over her gave him a real edge. Sarah made short shrift of that notion by threatening to file sexual harassment charges against him. A little while later, rumors started circulating around the office that she was a lesbian. Which was fine with Sarah. It kept his cronies from hitting on her. Riding up in the elevator alone with Buchanon once, she'd even thanked him. To his credit, he did look momentarily chagrined.

The same sort of expression he was sporting now.

"Sarah, could you come into my office for a minute?" Buchanon's voice was oddly solicitous. And he couldn't look her in the eye.

Sarah's first thought was that she was going to get canned or laid off, but she changed her mind fast. If that were the case, Buchanon would have been gloating.

"What is it?" she asked warily.

Her supervisor nervously pressed the sweaty palms of his hands together. "Please, Sarah. I'd rather we didn't . . ." He made no attempt to finish the rest of the suggestion.

Something bad had happened. Sarah was sure of that. Whatever it was, all she could think was that she didn't want this jerk to be the one to tell her about it.

As it turned out, she got her wish.

Buchanon silently escorted her to his office, opened the door, and gestured for her to enter. He didn't follow her inside.

Mike Wagner rose abruptly from his chair as Sarah came into the office. He was immediately taken aback.

True, he hadn't expected Sarah Rosen to be a carbon copy of her sister—he considered so much about Melanie Rosen to be unique—but there seemed to be nothing about this woman's physical appearance, style, or manner to even vaguely suggest a blood tie. Not that she didn't have her own appeal. He was reminded of the transvestite's remark about Sarah having it all but not knowing what to do with it. Right on the mark.

Sarah Rosen was dressed abominably in an oversize, faded blue cotton V-neck sweater and an unfashionable multitiered Indian-print skirt that hit her midcalf. Apart from the godawful outfit, though, Wagner had no trouble seeing that she had a lanky, angular, vaguely mannish beauty that was further emphasized by her short, boyishly styled auburn hair. And he was taken by her direct, almost combative brown eyes. Melanie's eyes had been brown, too. But they hadn't been so confrontative.

"You're Sarah Rosen?" She was so different from what he'd expected, Wagner felt the need to double-check.

"Yes. Who are you?" she demanded, folding her arms across her chest. The man did look vaguely familiar, but she couldn't place him.

Prickly like a cactus, was Wagner's assessment. Then he thought about the beautiful flowers that decorated some cactuses. He held off on the introduction, knowing that as soon as he told her he was a cop, she'd know just how bad it was. And he could see that she already sensed it was pretty bad. He found himself wondering in a detached way how she'd take the news. Often he could tell how someone was going to respond, but with this one he wasn't so sure.

"Would you sit down, Sarah?" His tone was soft. He hadn't meant to call her by her first name. It had just slipped out. Maybe because of his feelings for her sister. Or maybe because behind Sarah Rosen's aggressive, defiant facade he sensed a potential fragility.

She made no move. Her eyes furtively darted around Buchanon's utilitarian office, with its dreary, government-issue furnishings, as if searching for an escape route.

But the only escape was via the door she'd entered.

"Please, Sarah," Wagner said quietly, gesturing to the chair from which he had just risen. "Sit down. I'm afraid I—"

She shook her head vehemently. "No," she said sharply, her throat starting to close up, this terrible feeling of déjà vu sweeping over her. Like she was thirteen years old again. Standing in the principal's office at Mill Stream Middle School. Not facing a young man that time. Then it was a middle-aged woman with fluffy salt-and-pepper hair, too dark a shade of red lipstick, and sad, sorry eyes.

It's okay to cry, my dear—

And Sarah, feeling angry and invaded, shrieking— *How the hell do you know what it's okay for me to do?*

Wagner took a step toward her, as if maybe a closer inspection would help him. He couldn't get a reading. He found her face a puzzle. Puzzles had always intrigued him.

She spun away from him as he approached.

"Maybe we should talk somewhere else. How about taking a walk—"

Before he finished the sentence, however, she made a beeline for the door, exited, and headed down the hall.

Wagner, stunned at first by her precipitous departure, took off after her. She beat him down the seven flights of stairs, but he caught up with her when she hit the sidewalk and paused to catch her breath. He kept pace beside her as she turned right, heading north on Van Ness toward City Hall. Long swift strides, arms swinging wide, eyes straight ahead, her backless sandals making a rhythmic slapping sound on the concrete, her long silver dolphin earrings swinging with each step.

At the first corner, she stepped off the curb without looking—right into the path of a delivery van. Wagner yanked her back toward the curb as the van whizzed by with a long, angry horn blast.

Sarah glared after the truck, giving the driver the finger. Wagner smiled, releasing his hold on her. Ignoring him, and still not looking to see if it was safe, she marched across the street.

There was absolute silence between them as they walked for several blocks. He was beginning to wonder if, somehow, she'd already learned the bad news.

"How far are we going to walk?"

She didn't answer him. She gave no indication she'd even heard him.

They were passing a coffee bar. "Say, how about we get ourselves some espresso?" he suggested.

She kept walking, aware of the man beside her only as a shadow she couldn't shake.

Wagner's frustration was starting to get to him. "Sarah, you've got to let me—"

"I don't have to let you—anything," she snapped.

He saw the futility of arguing with her. She'd have to stop sometime.

She turned right onto McAlister. Wagner lit a cigarette, then slipped on a pair of maroon-rimmed aviator sunglasses as they headed into the sun.

Sarah's temples throbbed. She felt like her head might explode. And she knew, without doubt, that it was only going to get worse. What had he started to say back in Buchanon's office? *I'm afraid I—*

Whatever he was afraid of, it was bad. And she didn't want any goddamn part of it.

There was a park just ahead of them behind City Hall, a block of green grass, a few trees, benches lining the paths, most of them occupied by homeless people and derelicts. She headed straight for one of the few empty benches farthest in from the sidewalk and flopped down on it.

Wagner remained standing, regarding her with a curious gaze. The pugilistic glint was gone from her eyes. She appeared oddly composed.

He found the abrupt change in her demeanor unnerving. Also intriguing.

"Tell me now," she said flatly, staring up at him.

No, he reassessed as he sat down beside her on the bench, observing her more closely. Not composure. Defiance. He snubbed out his cigarette on the ground.

"It's your sister." An awkward pause. "Melanie." He scowled. Took off his aviator sunglasses. "She's been murdered. Her—body was found this morning."

At first Sarah seemed not to take it in at all. Then she just shook her head like it couldn't be true.

Wagner's gaze remained fixed on her. She got quite still. He tried to detect tiny fissures in her composure, but none were visible.

"When did it happen? Where?" she demanded.

"Sometime last night. At her house. Upstairs in the living room." He hesitated. "I'm afraid it was very brutal."

Sarah looked away before he spoke his last words, and he wasn't sure she'd heard him. He wasn't sure that he wanted her to—wasn't sure why he'd felt the need to tack on that grisly detail. To spark a response? Some sign of grief? Anguish? Something?

Sarah had heard his last remark. Heard and deleted it. She folded her hands one over the other on her lap. Deep, even breaths. Settle down. *You know the routine.*

A voice from her past echoed in her mind.

"Don't you ever fall apart?" It was Feldman asking. Her Budapest-born shrink with his thick Hungarian accent.

"All the time," she'd answered with a sour laugh. *"I've just learned not to let it show."*

And Feldman scolding lightly, much in the way Melanie chastised her, which was no surprise since Feldman had been Melanie's mentor—*"Letting yourself feel it is the only way you're going to heal, Sarah."*

Well, Feldman, she thought bitterly, if this is the only way to heal, it sucks.

Sarah fixed her gaze on an unkempt woman with straggly gray hair. The woman was dragging along a shopping cart that looked to be filled with her meager life's possessions. She was talking to herself, muttering words Sarah couldn't hear, her facial expressions exaggerated, her voice irritated.

Sarah followed the woman with her eyes as she moved jerkily off. Felt an envy that even in her despair Sarah knew was ludicrous. She could almost hear Melanie say: *"No, Sarah. Not envy. Self-pity. You think no one has it as bad as you, so you want to be in anyone's shoes but your own. Even some homeless schizophrenic's."*

Wagner wasn't sure Sarah Rosen was aware that he was still sitting beside her. Hell, he wasn't sure she even knew he existed. She seemed totally off somewhere. On some other planet.

"I haven't even told you my name," he said, more to get her attention than because he thought she'd give a shit who he was. "It's Wagner. Detective Michael Wagner with the SFPD, Homicide division."

The instant Sarah heard the name, her eyes darted to him, pinning him with a hostile stare. "Wagner? You're one of the cops involved with that killer. Romeo." He was the young detective she'd just barely made out talking with Melanie on that tabloid show the night before. God, was her sister being murdered even as she sat there in her

ratty room watching that prerecorded tripe? Sarah's
knuckles whitened.

"I'm one of the cops trying to catch him," Wagner
corrected. And then he added in a voice thick with intensity, "Now more than ever."

Sarah's head started to spin even as everything oddly
snapped into place. "It was him, then? Romeo?"

"There's always the possibility it was a copycat killing.
But we don't think so. What we think is, Romeo probably
targeted your sister because she was getting too good a
read on him, and he was scared. She was good. She was
damn good. If this hadn't happened—" The rest of the
sentence caught in his throat. "I'm sorry," he finished
lamely.

An inexplicable rage cut through Sarah like a scythe.
She gave a short, harsh laugh. "Romeo. Leave it to Melanie to come up with a name like that for a monster. She
has a warped sense of humor."

Wagner caught her use of the present tense and said
nothing.

"Runs in the family," Sarah went on, talking to herself. "We're all a little warped."

"Did Melanie ever discuss Romeo with you?"

"No, she never did. Though I suppose she would have
if I'd given her the opportunity."

"I don't blame you," he said.

She gave him a curious look. "For what?"

"I mean it probably wasn't a topic—"

"We didn't talk about a lot of topics."

"You weren't close?"

"What does that mean?" she snarled.

Wagner felt stymied. "I'm not really sure. I was an
only child myself."

"Were you close?"

Hadn't she understood what he'd said? "I didn't have
any siblings," he reiterated.

She fixed her eyes on him. "You and *Melanie*." Her

voice was mocking. Like she believed she already knew the answer.

He met her gaze evenly. "We only knew each other for a short time."

"What did you think of her?"

"I thought she was brilliant."

"Definitely brilliant. What else?" she persisted, wanting more.

Wagner resented the role reversal. He didn't care to share his feelings about Melanie. Still, he felt like he owed it to her sister to answer her questions. "Compassionate, dynamic, perceptive—"

"You weren't also her patient, were you?"

He was startled by her question. "Certainly not," he said, looking her straight in the eye. "We just worked together."

"It wasn't meant as an insult."

"No, I know that."

"Melanie thought everyone could benefit from psychoanalysis."

"I'm sure plenty of people could. I just don't happen to be one of them. Anyway, the point is, your sister and I —that is, I met her a couple of months back when she became the psychiatric consultant on our task force. Like I was saying, we felt she had a great deal of insight into the way Romeo's mind works."

"Apparently not enough," Sarah said sourly.

Wagner was trying to contain his anger and frustration, but now it spilled out despite his efforts. "Look, I know this is tough on you. But it's tough on us, too. We've been trying to nab this psycho for months. You think it's easy watching him slip through our fingers time and time again? If you want to know, it's killing me."

"It is, isn't it?"

He couldn't get a reading on what she meant by the remark, either from her tone or her expression. He glanced away, letting his gaze fall on a cast-off newspaper on the next bench. The headline was touting a new tell-all book on Nicole and O.J. Tomorrow, at least in San Francisco, Dr. Melanie Rosen's and Romeo's names would be the ones splashed across the front page. Newspapers, radio, TV. An irresistible lead story. The Romeo task force's own expert consultant turning up as the serial killer's fifth victim. Like Sarah'd said, it didn't reflect real well on the psychiatrist's expertise. Or theirs.

His eyes shifted from the headline, focusing on nothing in particular, deliberately not looking over at Sarah. He wanted to get going, be done with this, with her. Sarah Rosen unsettled him.

"Where is she now?" Sarah asked abruptly.

Wagner gave her a blank look. Then he realized what she meant. "I don't think you should see her."

"I just want to know where she is."

"At the morgue. The pathologist—"

"There'll have to be a funeral," she said inanely.

"It will be a couple of days before we can release—" He started to say *the body* but realized how callous that would have sounded. He didn't feel callous. He wished he did. "Your sister" was the way he finally ended the sentence.

Sarah stared openly at Wagner. He had the feeling that she was noticing him for the first time. Her eyes cruised down his torso, but there was nothing seductive about her scrutiny. Quite the opposite. It felt like a military inspection. Like she was looking for some dress code infraction. Or like his mother, making sure he was clean and tidy before sending him off to school.

She took in the tall, slender detective with his neatly trimmed light brown hair, the gray wool trousers with a perfect crease, blue blazer with no loose threads on any of the shiny gold buttons, no dandruff flakes on the shoulders, cordovan loafers buffed to a soft shine. Michael Wagner wasn't exactly handsome, but his eyes were intriguing, flecked with blue and gray, intelligent and somehow a little innocent, for a cop. She guessed he was in his early thirties, like her.

Finishing her dispassionate survey, she rose abruptly without a word. Wagner, relieved to have the inspection over with, popped up after her.

"Is there anything I can do?" he asked awkwardly.

Her lips curved slightly, but it would hardly be classified as a smile. "They always ask that," she said flatly. "But there never is."

"Who's 'they'?"

Now she did smile, but it had a bittersweet edge. "It doesn't matter."

"I think it matters," he said softly, "but you don't want to talk about it."

Sarah's smile deepened. "She must have liked you."

A redness crept up the detective's neck. "Excuse me?"

Her smile winked out. "Now you've spoiled it."

"Sorry." He found himself suddenly irritated with Sarah. She was playing with him, provoking him even. Why should he think he needed her approval anyway? He wished now that he'd left Sarah Rosen to Allegro.

"Look, this is a hell of a thing," he said, clasping his hands together in front of him, anxious to take off. "Why don't you go home, call a friend, maybe get someone to go with you to tell your father."

"My father," Sarah echoed, turning ash gray. It was the first visible sign that this tragedy had gotten to her. She even started to sway. Wagner thought she might faint. As he reached out to steady her, she regained her balance. Her coloring, however, didn't improve.

"God, I've got to tell my father," she gasped, like she'd just come to the realization on her own. *I can't do this. I can't manage this without you, Melanie. I only know how to be the recipient of bad tidings. Never the messenger. How am I going to tell him? How is he going to bear it? You're the light of his life.*

"Poor Daddy," she said, looking right through Wagner. "He tried so hard to make his girls into his own image. Melanie was his perfect success—I was his perfect failure."

Even as we sit a chasm apart, I feel you penetrating me and I cry out with the pleasure and pain of it. Sometimes I fear that my life is more yours than mine.

M.R. diary

4

After Detective Wagner left her sitting in the park, Sarah debated returning to the office to ask Bernie to drive out with her to Bellevista Lodge in the Berkeley hills. But in the end, she decided to go alone to tell her father the terrible news.

Upon gaining admittance from a ruddy-faced guard, Sarah felt oddly removed driving through the security gates and up the winding road to the exclusive nursing home. She was surrounded by acres of private gardens, topiaries, and well-marked walking trails bordered by groves of cypress and eucalyptus trees. The lodge itself, perched square in the middle of the vast property on the rolling hillside, was reminiscent of a stately but stern English country manor house. Inside were thirty luxurious suites individually decorated with beautifully appointed antiques and the *guest's* personal memorabilia.

At Bellevista, even those *guests* who were bedridden, incontinent, and oblivious to their surroundings or perhaps to their own names, were never referred to as *patients*. As for the staff, a doctor, for instance, might be spotted wearing tennis whites but never a white lab coat.

Sarah had always found the masquerade that went on

at the nursing home jarring. Pretend as everyone there might, the thirty eminent *guests* residing at Bellevista all suffered from varying stages of Alzheimer's disease, and most, if not all of them, would ultimately die there. Several already had "gone on," as the staff would say in hushed tones, since her father had settled into the *resort*. Those deaths had been handled with the utmost discretion, Melanie had once proudly commented to Sarah. What a farce.

Poor Melanie, Sarah thought. There was nothing discreet about her death. And no way to disguise it.

As Sarah pulled into the visitors' parking area to the right of the lodge, she felt her much-prized detachment start to crumple like a used tissue. She turned off the ignition but remained in her car for several minutes, hoping if she sat there long enough, she'd scrape up the courage to face her father with the tragedy.

Would it be worse if he was having one of his *bad* days and couldn't even absorb the news? And if he was able to comprehend what she had to tell him, how would he take it? Inevitably, Sarah was drawn back nearly twenty years to the other monumental loss in their lives. Certainly in her life. The death of her mother. It had shaped her, colored all of her subsequent decisions, invaded her dreams, impacted on her love life—or lack thereof.

No, Feldman. I don't blame her for any of it. Okay, well maybe for dying.

Sunlight angled through the trees and hit the windshield of Sarah's car. She felt the warmth on her face, but her blood ran cold. She felt a stab of guilt thinking about her mother, when it was Melanie and her father she should be thinking about now.

And Romeo. Don't forget Romeo. Now, he, too, however unintentionally, had become a part of her life. Uninvited, unwelcome, unwanted.

It's your damn fault, Melanie. You created this monster. Now I'm the one that gets stuck with Romeo on the brain.

And you know goddamn well I'm lousy at coping with monsters.

She felt a burning sensation on her skin. Only when her hand went to her face did she realize hot tears were running down her cheeks. She hadn't cried in years.

And it wasn't only grief she was feeling. There was more. Guilt? Shame? Fear?

She threw the car door open. Her whole body took on a strange, numb sensation walking across the gravel drive. She had to clutch the thick carved wooden railing as she climbed up to the porch.

The grandly proportioned, aged oak-paneled lobby of the retreat reminded Sarah of nothing so much as one of those stuffy exclusive men's clubs—*sans* the cigar smoke. No smoking anywhere on these premises.

One female *guest* who looked to be in her sixties, primly dressed in a navy gabardine dress with a lace collar, sat in a wheelchair by the unlit stone hearth knitting a red-and-yellow-striped woolen scarf. Catching sight of Sarah, the woman grabbed up her huge length of scarf, protectively stuffing it into her knitting bag.

An elderly gentleman near a window was engaged in a muted conversation with himself. Every few words he'd pause as though listening to a reply, then continue on with what he had to say.

At the far end of the lobby, an attractive middle-aged woman sat behind an antique writing table. Her brown hair was cut stylishly short, and she wore a tailored tweed suit and blue silk blouse. She looked for all the world like a hotel concierge. In reality, Charlotte Harris was the Bellevista's head nurse. The woman's placid oval face filled with not only recognition but sympathy as Sarah approached. She rose from her seat, hurrying around the desk to meet her.

"I'm so terribly sorry," Charlotte Harris said in a hushed voice, slipping her arm through Sarah's.

Sarah felt a flash of alarm. *Sorry? Had something hap-*

pened to her father, too? What little there was left of her family—gone in one fell swoop?

"My father—"

"He doesn't know yet," the nurse hastened to assure her. "Dr. Feldman thought it best—"

Sarah gave Charlotte Harris a sharp look. "Feldman?"

"He arrived ten minutes ago. He's waiting for you. I'll take you."

Reluctantly, Sarah allowed herself to be guided like a blind person through the hushed lobby and down a narrow rose-carpeted corridor. The brass sign on the oak-paneled door read Woodruff Room, giving no clue to the fact that it was in actuality the doctors' lounge.

Dr. Stanley Feldman was alone in the room. As soon as Sarah entered, he rose from a Windsor chair and crossed the gray expanse of the lounge to meet her, taking proprietary hold of her free arm. Having handed her safely over, Charlotte Harris instantly released her grip on Sarah's other arm and slipped away.

They stood there in silence for a few moments. Sarah was enveloped by the familiar scent of fruity pipe tobacco that clung to Feldman's clothes, his skin. Although he was a good two inches shorter than she, Sarah, now as always, had the odd sensation that the noted Hungarian psychoanalyst was looking down on her. In this respect, Feldman reminded her of her father.

But there were no other similarities when it came to their physical appearance. Feldman—in sharp contrast to her tall, refined, classically handsome father—was a homely, almost scrawny little man with kinky graying hair. His face was pitted with scars from what must have been a severe case of adolescent acne. He was a terrible dresser. That day he was wearing an ill-fitting brown suit with worn leather patches at the elbows. Yet for it all, Feldman's charismatic charm was legendary in his rarefied psychoanalytic circle. Even as he neared sixty, his aura and vitality remained undiminished.

Sarah studied Feldman's pockmarked face for any

signs of his response to the tragedy, but as always she couldn't get an accurate reading. Psychiatrists, she thought, would make the best poker players. Feldman would be the ultimate card shark.

"How did you hear?" she asked gruffly. Her throat had gone dry.

"Bill Dennison called me," Feldman said gently, firmly guiding her to one of the chairs that faced each other in front of a large multipaned window framing lush sculptured gardens.

"Bad news certainly travels fast."

"One of the policemen at the scene rang him up. Wanted him to deal with notifying Melanie's patients. Bill phoned me at my office. I told him I'd speak to you." Feldman paused, deliberately waiting for her to take a seat.

She did so, dutifully, even though she didn't feel like sitting. She was too jittery, getting claustrophobic again. As he should well know. Feldman knew far too much about how her erratic mind worked. That was only one of the problems between them, though.

"It's been a while, Sarah."

She laughed sharply. "And here I used to think you always said the right things at the right time."

He sat down across from her, leaning forward, elbow patches resting on his knobby knees. "It's not me you want to attack, Sarah."

"That's better. That's the Feldman I know and love."

"Do you think that will help?"

"Cut the crap, Feldman. My sister's dead. Slaughtered. Nothing's going to help."

"Nothing's going to change the reality, but there are things that can help."

"You bastard!" she spat out as a terrible anger welled up. She could actually hear waves breaking in her head, this awful *whoosh, whoosh*. Before she could stop herself, Sarah lashed out with her foot. The cork sole of her sandal made contact with Feldman's right shin. The psychoanalyst grimaced more in surprise than in pain.

His muted reaction only triggered more fury. Sarah sprang forward in her chair, reached across, and gripped him with both hands by his jacket lapels, shaking him. "Why can't you have the decency to at least *look* the part of the grieving lover?"

He took firm hold of her wrists. "Sarah—"

She shook him harder, slipping off her chair, dropping to her knees. "Admit it, damn it. At least *admit* you loved her."

"Stop it, Sarah," he said sharply.

She couldn't stop. A demon force had seized control. She slapped at his chest, his face, striking again and again. She shut her eyes, but all she could see was a vast canvas of red, a treacherous color, sucking her in. Her eyes sprang open.

Trying unsuccessfully to fend off her blows, Feldman regarded her at first as if she'd gone mad, but then his mouth puckered like he'd just bit into a particularly sour lemon.

She was still slapping him when she was stunned to realize he was crying soundlessly, huge tears tumbling down his pitted cheeks. Her flying hands stopped in mid-air.

Slowly, his arms moved around her. "Sarah," he whispered, his face dropping to her hair.

A strangled cry escaped her lips. She flung herself away from his embrace, crashing into the arm of her chair and landing on the floor.

She struggled to her feet, grabbed on to the arms of the chair, and dropped into it. After a few moments, she looked in awe across at Feldman. The psychiatrist was utterly composed. Even his tears had dried almost miraculously on his face. Her anger turned to envy. And then to confusion.

Had her explosion, his embrace, really happened? Had he really whispered "Sarah," with that same melodic voice she had once heard him whisper *Melanie*? Feldman was giving no hint that any outburst had occurred. But then, Feldman never gave anything away.

"We'll wait a few days to tell your father, Sarah," he said in his firm Hungarian accent. "He's not doing well right now. Besides, you need a little time first to cope with your grief before you have to tackle his."

"What about the funeral? He'll have to come to the funeral, won't he?"

"It depends. It might be too hard on him." Feldman gave her his studied appraisal, an imperious look she'd never managed to erase from her otherwise thankfully faulty memory. "It'll be hard on you, too, Sarah."

"I'll manage." She forced eye contact, knowing how he'd view any avoidance on her part. It didn't help. He wasn't impressed.

"I'd like you to go back on Prozac for a couple of months."

"No," she said fiercely, like he was demanding she swallow poison instead of the antidepressant medication she'd once taken for well over a year.

"Sarah, there's nothing—"

She shot out of her chair. "Fuck you, Feldman!"

He heaved a weary sigh at her invective. Gave her a pitying look. "At least come back to the Institute," he argued. "To do some grief work. You don't have to see me. I can arrange for you—"

"I don't want you to arrange anything for me. I don't need a shrink." She gave him a dismissive glare and started for the door.

"Where are you going, Sarah?"

"To see my father."

"Wait."

"Melanie wanted me to see him, so that's what I'm going to do. I won't tell him what happened until you think I should. I'm just going to spend a little time with him. Then I'm going to go home and—"

Feldman stood and went over to her. Again she

picked up the fruity scent of his pipe tobacco. "And what, Sarah?"

"And slit my wrists. Isn't that what you think I'm going to do? Don't worry, Feldman. I make a point of not repeating myself," she said with a sly smile.

The psychiatrist wasn't amused. "What are you going to do, Sarah?"

"I really don't know." Her throat felt dry, raw.

He rested a hand lightly on her shoulder.

"I thought, maybe one day, Melanie and I would connect," she said, wincing at her own words. *Thanks, Feldman. I was doing fine until you started in on me.*

She yanked open the door.

"I'll call you later, Sarah. If you change your mind about the medication, therapy, anything—"

She turned and fixed him with a cold accusing stare. "But you and Melanie connected, didn't you, Feldman?"

Her father was sitting on a cushioned lounge chair in the solarium on the south side of the lodge, facing out to vibrant green hills dotted with picture-book homes. He wore a pale blue cotton shirt open at the collar, gray wool trousers, and a deeper gray cashmere vest. In the dappled sunlight, shadows falling on his face, he looked to Sarah much like he looked when she was a child. Handsome, commanding, God-like.

When the screen door closed, Simon Rosen glanced over at his daughter and smiled as she entered.

Seeing his pleased expression—a rare occurrence for her at the best of times—Sarah thought with relief that this was must be one of his good days, after all.

As she approached, however, she was quick to see his smile droop, twisting into a frown. How well she knew that look. How it made her insides twist with self-loathing. Still, in a strange way she felt more relaxed. This was what she was used to. It had rarely been otherwise between them.

As she drew closer, his frown intensified. He surveyed her with a look of sheer disgust.

"What in God's name have you done to your hair?" he demanded in that sharp tone that seemed reserved only for her.

"I . . . nothing," she stammered, caught by surprise since she hadn't changed her hairstyle in several years. *He doesn't remember. He's back in another time.*

"Don't hover, Cheryl."

Cheryl? Sarah felt a lump in her throat. He thought she was her mother. He was back in some other time all right, dragging her back there with him. Reminding her that she wasn't the only one he used that curt, disapproving voice with. For years, she and her mother had taken turns bearing the brunt of her father's displeasure and disappointment.

He flicked his head back as he did whenever he was feeling impatient. "Is Melanie home from school yet? Tell her I want to see her the instant she comes in. I don't have a patient scheduled until four."

Sarah's age-old resentment and jealousy shot to the surface. She felt so bitter, she almost blurted her terrible news out right there and then. *She isn't coming home, damn you. She's never coming home again. Your precious Melanie's been murdered. She's dead. You've lost her for good. I'm all you have left, you selfish bastard. How's that for irony?*

His eyes darted around the solarium, then fixed her with an accusatory look. "Where's my appointment book, Cheryl? You're always moving things about. How many times have I told you—?" He stopped midsentence, looking confused and disoriented. He blinked several times, then regarded her with a glassy-eyed stare. "You look familiar." A sly smile lit his face, making him appear breathtakingly vital, almost boyish. "You're my masseuse, right? The girl with those wonderful hands. Would you like me to disrobe, my dear?"

A shudder rocked through Sarah.

Behind her the screen door opened and shut. Her father gave her a dismissive wave as he glanced over her shoulder at the young nurse who had entered the solarium. "Melanie, is that you? Come in here a minute, baby—"

It was almost dusk when Sarah pulled into a parking spot on Valencia, a few doors down from her place. Right behind a Channel 7 news van. As she got out of her car, she saw a crush of reporters and cameramen hovering near the entrance to her apartment building.

Shit. The vultures have descended.

"Miss Rosen?"

She spun around, ready to take a swing, and came face to face with a man about her own height. His dark brown hair was badly in need of a trim, his raw-boned face badly in need of a shave, his clothes badly in need of a pressing. His eyes were gray, melancholy, and rueful. Those eyes sparked a feeling of kinship in Sarah. Maybe that was why she hesitated throwing the punch.

He held up a hand. "It's okay, I'm not a reporter."

"How did you know who I was?"

"My partner described you. My name's John Allegro—"

"Allegro?" It took only a couple of seconds for her to place the name. And the face from the TV show. "Oh, great. The other Romeo cop."

"Look, I'm not here to hassle you. I knew there'd be a circus." He gestured to the reporters, who hadn't yet observed them.

Sarah glanced over at the media people. "I can hear their lips smacking from here."

"Do you want to give them a statement?"

"Are you kidding?"

He smiled. "I didn't think so. Come on. I'll run interference for you."

Allegro, with the assistance of a couple of uniformed

officers, did his best to keep the media at a distance, but the reporters screamed questions at them, shoving microphones, cameras, camcorders as close to them as they could get. Sarah shielded her eyes from the electronic flashes and blinding floodlights, while the detective hurried her through.

"That's enough, boys and girls," Allegro shouted. "Give it a rest. She's not making any comments at this time."

One young man managed to worm his way through the crowd—stocky, ash-blond hair, glasses, wearing chinos, a white button-down shirt, navy cardigan. He waved a paper and pen. "You're Dr. Rosen's sister, right? How about an autograph, Sarah?"

Allegro shoved him away. "Get lost, creep."

He bounded back determinedly. "What's Romeo's secret? Did your sister tell you, Sarah? Was she hooked on lover boy, too? Is that why he sliced her up?"

"Oh God," Sarah gasped.

"You fucking turd—" Allegro lunged for the autograph-seeker, but he ducked back into the throng. Cheers greeted his close call.

Sarah struggled, with trembling hands, to unlock the door. Allegro elbowed her aside and took over the task, two other cops keeping the crowd from closing in on the pair.

Once Allegro got her inside, he followed her down the hall to her apartment. She stood there.

"You gotta ignore them, Miss Rosen. They're showing up everywhere. Romeo groupies. Pathetic little shits who feed off this kind of thing. Get all charged up. Want to be part of the action. Best thing to do is tune them out."

"It's sick."

"You've had it rough. It's bound to get even rougher. I'm sorry." He spoke matter-of-factly but not unsympathetically.

Sarah nodded. She felt hollow, drained, and wired at the same time. And she felt so alone.

She looked over at the detective as he started to turn away. "The deal's no questions, but if you want to come in for a cup of coffee—"

She saw him hesitate, rub his palm across his stubbly face.

"Maybe you want something stronger than coffee," she said.

"I should be the one saying that to you," he said. He leaned a little toward her as he spoke.

She studied the detective. His face was full of visual distractions—the deep grooves at the corners of his mouth, the oddly angled brows, the beat-up nose, those world-weary gray eyes. Allegro appeared to be in his late forties, but he might look a few years younger if he were cleaned up a bit.

"I think maybe you need it even worse than me," she said impulsively.

The corner of his mouth twitched. "This did hit me hard. I liked your sister."

"I think I have a bottle of Scotch—"

"No, that's okay. I'll keep you company, though, if you want to have yourself a belt or two."

"No. I'm not much of a drinker." The truth was, alcohol didn't work on her the way it worked on most people. Instead of helping her forget—drowning her sorrows—booze always intensified her bad feelings.

She turned the key in the lock and opened her door.

Allegro cleared his throat. "Hey, if that coffee offer's still good, though—"

"Sure," she said with a rush of relief.

"Tell you what. I'll even make it."

"Good. I make lousy coffee," Sarah said, letting the scruffy detective in and pointing him toward the kitchen, past her small cluttered living room. She was grateful that he made no comment about the messy state of her place. More than that, he seemed to take it very much in stride. A slob like her.

The phone rang. She jumped. Allegro was at the door

to the kitchen. He turned to her. Their gazes connected. She nodded, and he picked up the phone on the kitchen wall right by the entry.

The caller managed only a few words before Allegro barked, "She's not giving any statements at this time. Don't call her. She'll call you when she's ready." He slammed the phone down. "Let your answering machine take the rest," he ordered, turning off the ringer.

While Allegro was in the kitchen Sarah sank down wearily onto the couch. After a minute she noticed the area rug by the door in her front hall was crooked. The top of a white envelope stuck out from under it. She got up, walked over, and picked it up.

The outside of the business-size envelope was unmarked. The flap wasn't sealed. Probably a goddamn rent increase notice, she thought, withdrawing a single sheet of paper folded in thirds.

It wasn't a rent increase. It was a letter, apparently laser-printed on a plain sheet of stationery.

Dearest Sarah,
    I want you to know you're not alone. No one can share your grief more than I do. No one can understand you better than I can. . . .

There was no closing or signature at the bottom.

God, Sarah thought, crackpot condolence letters starting already. Another Romeo groupie? Maybe the same one who tried to get her autograph outside.

With a shudder of revulsion, she crumpled up the note without bothering to finish it. *Tune the wackos out, like the detective said. Good advice.*

"Milk?" Allegro called out from her kitchen, startling her.

"No," she called back in a voice that sounded foreign to her. Finding the anonymous note had shaken her. The audacity of it. The maudlin creepiness.

"Sugar?"

"Just—black." She dropped the crumpled note on the hall table as the detective entered the room carrying two steaming hot mugs of coffee.

They sat in a taut, edgy silence, side by side on the couch, sipping their coffee. When she noticed the detective had nearly finished, Sarah's anxiety increased. He'd be leaving any minute. Leaving her alone.

She gave a start as she heard Allegro's mug thump down on the coffee table.

"I should go," she heard him say.

"Another cup?"

"No, thanks." He looked over at her, saw that some of the color had drained from her face. "You have someone? Someone you can call to come over?"

She nodded mutely. She could call Bernie. Only if Bernie came, he'd encourage her to "let go." But if she let herself go, she might never be able to put herself back together. *The Humpty Dumpty complex.*

She watched Allegro rise. Start across the room for the door.

"There's something I just thought of—"

He stopped short. "Yes?"

"Melanie. I spoke to her yesterday."

He waited.

"God, was it only yesterday?" She gave him a wan smile. "I was such a shit to her. She called early. Woke me up."

"I'm crabby in the morning, too."

"I'm always crabby with Melanie. I mean—I was. I wasn't ever very nice to her. She didn't deserve that."

"Hey, we always wish we could undo stuff after it's too late. Don't beat yourself up over it."

"Right. No use crying over spilt milk." She laughed, a humorless, corrosive sound. "And I got on Melanie's case for tossing off a homily."

"What was it?"

"I don't remember. What I do remember, though, is that she mentioned she had a date for last night."

There was a charged silence.

"Who?" Allegro asked.

"I don't know. She didn't say who it was."

"How about a guy named Perry? Robert Perry? He's an out-of-work software engineer. About twenty-seven, blond, good-looking."

"No. The name doesn't ring a bell." She hesitated. "That's awfully young. Melanie was thirty-six. I didn't think she went for younger guys. But then, I didn't know much about her taste in men. Except for Bill."

"Dr. Bill Dennison? Your sister's ex?"

"He's in his late forties. They were married for three years."

"Robert Perry's a patient of your sister's."

Sarah stared at him. "Oh."

He hesitated. "Miss Rosen, do you think your sister might have ever crossed the line? As a therapist?"

"Are you asking me if she ever went to bed with her patients?"

"It happens, doesn't it? I mean, you read about it. Priests, lawyers, family doctors, shrinks." He shrugged. "No one's immune from temptation."

Sarah let the charge hang in the air for several moments before responding. "Does that go for cops, too, Detective Allegro?"

"You're pissed."

She regarded him grimly. "Yeah."

"Perry says they were lovers."

"And you think Perry was her date last night?"

"It's possible."

"Then you think he's the one? That Perry's Romeo?"

"We don't have anything on him. Yet." He hesitated, looking uncomfortable. "I'm sorry about your sister."

She nodded.

"I'm not real good at this kind of thing," he mumbled.

"Neither am I," she said flatly.

He reached for the door, spotting the crumpled paper on the hall table. "What's that?"

For him to notice her warped *condolence* note in the chaos that was her home almost made her laugh. "Oh . . . nothing." *Shrug it off. The sooner she started ignoring that kind of crap, the better.*

His gaze lingered on her for a moment, then he gave her his card. "My pager number's on it, too. If you need to reach me. Anytime."

"Detective?"

"Yes?"

"Why does he—take their hearts?"

Allegro stood at the door with his back to her, his head angled down. Finally he turned. His eyes met hers. "I don't know, Miss Rosen. Maybe because the bastard's got no heart of his own."

She stared back at him. "Yes. Heartless. That must be it."

The press once again swooped down on Allegro as he exited the apartment building. Cameras rolled. Flashes went off in his face. Questions were barked and shrieked at him. The detective mumbled another string of no-comments, made sure that creep who'd tried to get Sarah's autograph wasn't still loitering, and elbowed his way to his car.

He pulled out of the parking spot and started down the street, heading back to Homicide. Only, when he got to the Hall of Justice on Bryant just beyond the underpass of Highway 80, he didn't even slow down. He just drove on, zigzagging his way back to his home turf. He pulled up to the curb in a yellow zone right in front of the Bay Wind Grill, a seedy hangout on Polk Street. One of a string of bars in a neighborhood that the tourist commission strongly warned visitors to avoid.

Zeke, the bartender, who looked as dispirited and

run-down as his rancid dark saloon, had a shot of Jim Beam and a beer chaser all ready for Allegro as he got to his usual stool.

He went straight for the whiskey, downing it in one long easy swallow, then followed it with a nice cold Bud.

"Refill?" Zeke asked.

Allegro would have told him to leave the whole bottle, but it was still early and he had to get back to work. Even so, he gestured for Zeke to pour him another shot, figuring he'd clean up a little over at his apartment before heading back to Homicide. He downed the second jigger faster than the first one.

"Must've been one hell of a day," Zeke reflected.

"Yeah," Allegro said, wiping his mouth with the back of his sleeve. "One hell of a day."

When Detective Allegro left, Sarah sat motionless in her chair. Then she sighed, rose, and picked up the crumpled note.

> . . . You mustn't be afraid of me, Sarah. I'll never harm you. We're soul mates, you and I. You are so strong, Sarah. I need your strength. Open your heart to me.

As if the note itself wasn't grotesque enough, the anonymous sender had added a terse postscript at the bottom of the page.

> More later, my love.

Sarah smashed her fist into the paper, then ripped it to shreds. "No, goddamn it, you cretin. You're not going to do this to me. You're not going to fuck with my head!"

She flung open the front door and sprang out into the hall. As if she might actually catch the bastard who'd slipped that garbage under her door. Chase him the hell away from her. She'd been stalked by shadows her whole life. Enough was enough.

The hall was empty and silent. Except for the thudding of her own heart.

. . . that Romeo, as a child, has himself been the victim of sadistic as well as masochistic behaviors. For outlets, he may have sought out animals, playmates . . . seeing nothing wrong with his violent actions . . . a perverse kind of do-unto-others mentality.

Dr. Melanie Rosen
Cutting Edge

5

Romeo hums along with the prelude to *Rhapsody in Blue* as he fries up his dinner. He doesn't usually fuss about his meals, but tonight he's lit the candles on his table, laid out two plates, two wine goblets. One setting for himself. One for Sarah Rosen. She'll be joining him both in spirit and on the written page.

He smiles as he eyes Melanie's diary on the table beside his plate. This is really quite a bonus. A delectable new twist. He feels revived, invigorated, alive with anticipation and expectation. *Melanie, this would please you.*

He slips the sautéed meat onto a serving plate, decorating it with a sprig of parsley, sits down at the table, and opens the diary to one of the marked passages he has now read several times—

> *Sarah has spent so much of her life envying me that she is blind to my envy of her. I project the image of invincibility, but it is all a thin veneer. Sarah has managed to erect a far thicker wall. I've tried to no avail to break through. To get to her damaged heart would take an incredibly adroit miner. . . .*

This other force is there, pulsing like an extra heartbeat inside of me—driving me and holding me back at the same time.

M.R. diary

6

The buzz from the boilermakers Allegro'd had at the Bay Wind earlier that evening was long gone. Back at Homicide at close to midnight, Allegro wrapped up his hand-scrawled report and placed it in the black vinyl three-ring binder right on top of the sheet Wagner had pounded out earlier that evening on his fifteen-year-old electric typewriter—a high school graduation present from his mom.

Allegro flipped through the reports made by the other cops at the crime scene that morning and the autopsy prelims sent over from Kelly's office. Dead twenty-four hours, and already Dr. Melanie Rosen's file was filling up. He slapped the binder shut with a curse. He'd had all he could stomach for one day. He knew Wagner was off doing more legwork on the case, but the only thing Allegro wanted to do now was lose himself in a woozy fog of oblivion.

Jake's Bar, a few blocks from the Hall of Justice, stank of stale cigarette smoke, booze, and cheap perfume. The drone from an off-road auto race on ESPN competed with

Willie Nelson moaning the country blues from the CD jukebox.

Allegro sat at a stool at the far end of the bar and ordered his usual.

A buxom blonde, whose roots were in bad need of a touch-up, sauntered up to Allegro. She wedged her hands on her waist and gave him the eye. Allegro glanced at her, took her in with a silent once-over, then motioned to Freddie, the bartender.

"A Pink Lady for my friend Dee Dee."

"Thanks, Johnny." Dee Dee, a working girl from the Pampered Pleasures Massage Parlor across the street, heaved a worn-out sigh as she slid onto the stool next to him. Not an easy task with that skin-tight black leather miniskirt molded around her ample hips and cellulite-pitted thighs.

"How's it going, Dee?" Allegro asked after downing two shots of Jim Beam in quick succession.

"How does it look like it's going?"

He gave her a closer scrutiny, saw the multilayers of pancake makeup packed especially thick under her eyes. To hide not just the bags but a couple of shiners as well. Still, her eyes themselves were a pretty shade of green.

He took a long swallow of his beer chaser. "You're getting too old for the life, Dee." The bartender was topping off another jigger for him.

She chuckled mirthlessly. "So are you, Johnny. You look like shit."

He knocked down the third drink, but tonight the booze wasn't helping his misery at all. "Yeah, I know."

She gave him a friendly poke. "You still turn me on though, sweetie."

"Gotta count my blessings," he said without any sign of sarcasm.

Dee Dee patted his arm. "Poor baby. Those shits on TV are tearing you and your buddy to shreds. Like you guys are supposed to pull this fruitcake out of a hat or something. I tell you, this is one time I'm counting my blessings, too."

"How's that?"

"Let's face it, Johnny. I'm not exactly Romeo's type."

The bartender set a Pink Lady cocktail complete with paper umbrella in front of the hooker. "Again?" he asked Allegro.

Allegro hesitated. A couple more rounds, and he'd be singing the blues with Willie. "Nah. I'm fine."

Dee Dee smiled. "Cutting back, Johnny? That's good." She plucked the umbrella from her drink and licked off its wet toothpick stem before carefully closing it and popping it into her rhinestone-studded clutch. "For my grandson." Her smile tipped to the left, revealing a missing molar. "Got quite a collection." She took a greedy swallow of her drink. "You want to come over for a late-night snack?"

"Yeah," he said, glancing at his watch to see that it was close to one in the morning. "I could go for something."

"How 'bout I whip us up some eggs?"

He gave her a rueful look. "Do me a favor, Dee."

"Sure, Johnny. Anything. You know that."

"Don't *whip* the eggs. Just scramble them."

Dee Dee got a real chuckle out of that one.

Wagner nodded as he approached the brawny barker with the red-tinged complexion, courtesy of the flashing neon sign overhead. Honey's was one of a string of sex clubs settled into the alleys and streets in and around Ninth Street south of Market. A little after one A.M., and the joint was jumping.

"What's the word, Cal?" Wagner's gaze strayed from the bruiser at the door to the photos of naked women plastered on a brick wall leading into the club. One, poster size, featured a voluptuous brunette sprawled out on a bed. Her wrists and ankles were shackled to the bedposts. Underneath her a sign advertised: "Slave For a Night."

Cal shrugged as he opened the door for a couple of grinning, shit-faced college kids who swayed past Wagner. Raucous noise and sultry strip music blasted out to the street.

"Can't complain, Mike."

They'd been on a first-name basis ever since the detective's days—or more accurately, nights—on Vice. Back then, Calvin Amis had provided Wagner with some useful tips. In exchange, Wagner had overlooked a few of Amis's minor indiscretions with the law. They'd parted company when Wagner moved over to Homicide a little over a year ago. Eight months later, Amis showed up in Wagner's new digs at the Hall of Justice. It was the day after photos of Romeo's first victim hit the newspapers and TV. Turned out Amis recognized the victim, Diane Corbett. Not just in the club, either. In the private back room. Where, for a hefty private club fee, the customers got the opportunity to get in on the act. Everything from bondage to wrestling to kinky fashion shows. He'd spotted her at Honey's on more than one occasion.

Wagner tapped a cigarette out of his pack and into his mouth. "What's the word, Cal?"

"Too bad about your shrink," Cal said.

"Yeah."

"Sure made headlines. And left you guys with egg on your faces."

Wagner scowled as he lit up.

"Maybe that was the idea," Cal said.

Wagner's scowl deepened. "What's that mean?"

"You know. The pervert wants to make you look bad. The worse you look, the better he looks."

Wagner stared hard at Amis. "Funny. She said that once, too. That he gets off on feeling superior to us."

"The shrink?"

"Yeah."

"Got a suspect yet?"

"Following up a few leads."

"Real ugly business."

Wagner took a long drag while Amis folded his thick muscular arms across his broad chest. They stood there in silence, Wagner sizing up the customers coming and going, Amis sizing up the detective.

"So, Mike. You gonna ask me or what?"

Wagner acted like he didn't hear.

Amis rested a large gloved hand on Wagner's shoulder. "I'll save ya the trouble. The only time I ever saw her here was the one time you and your partner brought her over for that little research expedition. And I've talked with some of my buddies in the neighborhood. If your shrink was into getting her jollies that way, no one I know saw her getting off around these parts." He removed his hand and smiled. "Not that you actually did ask." He reached for the gold-painted door leading into the club. "Care to poke around? Ya never know," he said with a faint smile.

Wagner gave Amis a grim look, flicked away his cigarette, and headed over to his car.

"Hope ya catch the freak, Mike," Amis called out cheerfully as Wagner got behind the wheel.

Sarah was drenched in sweat. She sat up in bed and squinted over at her alarm clock. A little past three in the morning. A nightmare. Only a nightmare. It was all right. She couldn't even remember what had frightened her awake.

She started to lie down again when she heard a faint scratching sound. She felt a tremor of the old panic. Monsters in the night. She had always been so afraid of monsters in the night. Monsters crept into the bedrooms of naughty little girls and carried them off to their dark, foul-smelling lairs—

*Now, now, Sarah. Don't cry. It's all right. I'm here.
You've gone and wet your bed again. No wonder
you smell something awful. It's not a monster,
honey. Now go and change your nightie and I'll
change the bed. Yes, I promise. I won't breathe a
word to Daddy. Yes, yes. Or to Melanie. Now come
give Mommy a great big hug—*

Sarah hugged her pillow against her pounding chest,
horrified for a moment that she might have actually gone
and peed in her bed. Feeling a mounting trepidation, she
checked. No, thank God, her sheets were dry.

Water. She needed a glass of water. Her throat was so
parched. She threw aside her blanket and swung her legs
over the side of the bed. As she reached out to switch on
her bedside lamp, she knocked over a half-full cup of cold
tea.

"Shit."

The tea spilled onto the sheet. A nice touch of irony,
she thought. Right color for piss and all.

Once she'd managed to turn on the lamp and the
bedroom was bathed in a soft glow, Sarah felt a bit better.
Monsters scooted away in the light.

She regarded the tea-stained sheet with annoyance.
No way she felt like changing her bed in the middle of the
night. One thing when her mother had been around to
take care of her messes.

She decided to move over to the other side of the bed
until it dried. The sheets could wait until tomorrow.

Tomorrow. Saturday. The medical examiner had
promised to release Melanie's *remains* to the Weinberg
Funeral Home by the next evening. Why in God's name,
when the funeral director had phoned her, had she agreed
to go to Melanie's place and pick out a burial outfit? What
could it possibly matter? It wasn't as if her sister's poor
mutilated body would be on view. No question but that
this would be a *closed* casket. Who would know what she
was wearing? Who would care?

Melanie. Melanie would care.

Sarah got out of bed, issuing herself orders. *Get the glass of water. Do not dwell on morbid thoughts. No point. It won't get you anywhere. Better safe than sorry—*

This mantra playing in her head, Sarah marched into the dark living room and started for the kitchen. Abruptly, she came to a halt.

Something not right. As if the air in the room had changed texture.

Her trembling hand slid up the wall until her fingers touched the light switch. Light flooded the living room. Her eyes darted from corner to corner. She expelled a whoosh of air. Empty. The room was empty. No monsters here.

What about her vestibule? Another letter slipped under her door? *More later . . .*

Nothing there. Relief flooded her. Got herself worked up over nothing.

In the kitchen, shadows from the living-room light played on the walls. Standing at the sink, she grabbed a glass from the drainboard, letting the water run good and cold. Above the sink, behind the window, a dark form materialized. Startled, she lost her grip on the glass. It crashed loudly into the basin and shattered.

A cat. Only a motley gray-and-honey-streaked Tom who'd leaped onto her sill. The cat rubbed his whiskery cheek against the glass, meowing. Looking for refuge from the damp night.

Sarah laughed aloud at her panic. Taking pity on the mangy stray, she reached across the sink to slide the window open. Something clinked against the pane. Her gaze was pulled to the metallic object glinting at the cat's neck. Hanging from a white collar. A bright, shiny gold heart.

Sarah's hands flew to the window shade. She yanked it down, then stood there quaking, the water still running over the shards of glass in the sink.

She could hear the cat meow dejectedly on the other side of the pane.

Call the police. Call Allegro. Get protection.

From what? A scary little cat? *"But, Officer, it was wearing a heart-shaped ID tag!"* He'd think she was nuts. And he wouldn't be the first to make that diagnosis.

Resolutely, she picked the shattered glass from the sink and dumped it into the trash. Right on top of the shredded note she'd thrown in there before she went to bed.

Just night terrors. Tune it all out. Go to sleep.

She's in her classroom. Crouched inside her own cubbyhole. She's wearing pajamas. No wonder she's hiding.

Footsteps approaching. Heart-pounding terror. "Shut up, shut up, shutupppp . . ." Holding her breath, turning blue.

Too late. He sees her. Her teacher. Mr. Sawyer. Oh, he's very angry. Face all red. Red as her pajamas.

Wait, not pajamas now. She's wearing her mother's beautiful satin and lace wedding gown. Mommy will be mad. Not supposed to play dress-up in Mommy's wedding gown.

"Oh now look what you've done," he says with disgust.

He points to a big red stain on Mommy's beautiful wedding gown. Paint. Red tempera paint.

No, no, no. Not paint. Blood. Oozy, drippy, sticky red blood.

"You're going to get it now. That'll teach you. That'll teach you all right."

She is going to get it now.

The media hordes still surrounded her apartment building the next morning. Sarah could see the headlines they were after. SHRINK'S SISTER TELLS ALL—

They'd pounce on her as soon as she stepped outside. And then there was that Romeo groupie. Was he back? Were there more like him out there? Ready to eat her alive? Allegro had muted the ringer on her phone, and she herself had even pulled the wires from her door buzzer. Not that any of it helped. She couldn't sleep, eat, or think straight. Why couldn't everyone just leave her alone? It was hideous how people fed off the pain and suffering of others.

If only she could stay holed up in her apartment until they all found a new horror show and went away. But not today. The mortician was waiting for Melanie's burial outfit. She'd have to run the gauntlet.

Out in the hall she tried to figure an alternative escape route. Back door? And run right into the arms of the press. The roof? Sure, and jump fifteen feet to the next building. What else?

A creaking sound behind her made Sarah's whole body tense. Whirling around, prepared for anything, she felt instantly foolish when she saw it was only her next-door neighbor stepping out of his apartment.

Vickie Voltaire clomped over in his silver mules, tying the sash around his bright pink satin kimono. "Need some help, sweetie?"

Sarah laughed dryly. "Can you make me invisible?"

"No, but I can come close," the svelte redhead said huskily, beckoning her with a beautifully manicured finger.

Unlike the state of siege at Sarah's place, Vickie's studio apartment was as neat as a pin, and as flamboyant and brash as the tenant himself. Midnight-blue velvet curtains with gold tassels. Sheepskin rug dyed a brilliant crimson spread over the ornate filigreed king-size brass bed. Thick rose pile carpeting. Walls a high-gloss persimmon plastered with erotic drawings and posters of some of San Francisco's hottest and sexiest transvestite performers.

"Whatever Lola Wants, Lola Gets" at the Club de Soeur. "Walk on the Wild Side with Wanda" at Junie Love's. And one in particular that immediately caught Sarah's eye—a familiar-looking sultry redhead in a skin-tight red gown stretched across a piano à la Michelle Pfeiffer in *The Fabulous Baker Boys*—"Appearing nightly: Vickie Voltaire at the Club Chameleon."

"That's about five years old," Vickie said, coming up behind Sarah. "Unfortunately the club closed down six months later. I did a great Suzy Diamond. I wish you could have seen it."

"Are you still working the club scene?"

Vickie shrugged. "Catch as catch can, honey. This town is dripping with talent. So once you hit thirty, it's pretty much downhill." He spoke with airy contempt. "I get a few gigs here and there, but most of them are out in the sticks."

He grinned saucily. "I call it my good deed. Bringing a little culture and class to the burbs. The pay stinks, but the crowds eat it up. You should come some time. I'd love for you to see me perform."

Sarah smiled faintly and said nothing.

Vickie's expression was intensely poignant as he reached out and lightly stroked Sarah's cheek. "You poor baby. Here I am prattling on, and you're in such obvious pain. I'm no stranger to pain myself, sweetie. If ever you need someone—"

Vickie's hand, large and still quite male despite the transvestite's fanglike neon pink polished nails, slid from Sarah's face to her shoulder. Sarah was acutely conscious of the weightiness of her neighbor's touch. For all Vickie's overwrought efforts to the contrary, a distinctly masculine aura seeped through the exaggerated feminine glamour. It almost felt like a come-on, but Sarah told herself that was absurd. Then again, Bernie swore that most transvestites weren't gay. They could like screwing women as much as they liked cross-dressing.

"You said you had a plan to get me out of here," Sarah reminded her neighbor.

Vickie's hand dropped away. His bright pink mouth produced an extravagantly girlish smile. "Righto."

He led the way across the one-room studio to a short, narrow corridor, at the end of which was a big closet that doubled as a small dressing room. Inside there was space for a chest of drawers, a full-length mirror, and a dressing table fitted with one of those two-way makeup mirrors, the magnifying side facing out. There was even a window, but a room-darkening shade covered it. The lighting came from a strip of fluorescent tubing on the ceiling. Most of the clothing hanging up on the racks on either side of the space was decidedly feminine, but Vickie directed Sarah to the far end of one rack, where there were a couple of men's suits, a few men's shirts, and several pairs of trousers.

"You can dress up as my date." Vickie winked, tugging the sleeve of a blue gabardine sport jacket. "With your build, short hair and all, it'll be a breeze, lover boy." He took the jacket and a pair of slacks off their hangers, presenting them to Sarah with a flourish.

"From before I came out of the closet," Vickie drawled with a broad grin. "Don't ask me why I keep this stuff around." He gave Sarah a lingering look, the grin replaced by a nostalgic smile. "I guess none of us ever completely closes the door on our past."

For Sarah, who'd spent so much of her life with her back fiercely pressed against that door, Vickie's remark proved unsettling. As did being in a jail-cell-size space with this larger-than-life character whose cheap perfume and heavy-duty hair spray were turning Sarah's stomach. She was beginning to wonder if facing those reporters outside might not be the better choice.

"What's wrong?" Vickie asked a bit defensively.

"Nothing." Sarah camouflaged her lie with a too-bright smile. "This will do fine."

Vickie pursed his lips as if he were debating whether to force the issue.

To Sarah's relief, however, Vickie moved away, plucked some ultrafeminine items from the front of the rack, and said a bit coolly, "I'll dress out there, and you can have this mirror to yourself. Take your time. I always do."

When Vickie exited, Sarah's eyes shot to the closed closet door. It had a hook-and-eye lock. Sarah tiptoed over and dropped the hook in the eye, even as she chastised herself for her paranoia.

In a matter of minutes, she was dressed in Vickie's nicely tailored men's sport jacket and slacks, checking herself out in the full-length mirror. A few tucks and folds since the sleeves and trouser legs were far too long, otherwise there was no question she could pass for a guy, especially from the neck down. But even though her hair was cropped in a butchlike cut, she was certain her feminine features would be a tip-off for the reporters.

She spotted a Stetson hatbox on the shelf. A man's hat. That was what she needed to finish off the disguise.

The unexpectedly heavy hatbox slipped from her grasp and thumped to the floor. The lid popped off, papers spilling out.

Sarah hurriedly knelt down to scoop them up and stick them back into the box when she spotted a photo that had also fallen out. She stared at it.

A voice hissed in her head. *Always sticking your nose where it doesn't belong. Little snoop.*

"How're you doing in there, lovey?"

Crouched, Sarah froze. *Little snoop.* "Fine. A few more minutes." Her voice was preternaturally chirpy.

"No hurry. Just retouching my nails. Take that long for them to dry."

Her gaze remained drawn to the faded five-by-seven glossy photo—an immensely attractive dark-haired young man in a pair of skimpy black bathing trunks towering next to a beautiful fair-skinned older woman with a wild tousle of fiery red hair. Somehow, you could sense the sexual tension. They stood on a sandy beach right by the edge of the sea. While the woman appeared to Sarah to be in her late thirties, she looked exceedingly svelte in a Tahitian-print bikini. The young man's arm was draped around her shoulder, and he was beaming down at her with obvious adulation.

The woman was staring straight ahead into the camera. She had startlingly dark, deep-set eyes, and her mouth, while full and quite sensuous, turned down slightly at the corners, lending a hint of cruelty to her expression.

Sarah flipped the photo over. In small, neat penmanship across the bottom was written: "Vic and Mom—Stinson Beach, '84."

Slowly, she turned the photo round again. Ten years had gone by since it was taken, and there had certainly been stunning alterations in style and presentation, but there was no question that the very handsome man in the picture and her flamboyant cross-dressing neighbor were one and the same. *Did Mom know your secret, Vic?*

A light rap on the closet door made her gasp. "All set, Sarah?"

She quickly tossed the photo back in the hatbox and hoisted it back on the shelf. "Coming."

When the pair exited the apartment building Vickie took center stage in an eye-catching tight black sweater over an amply padded bra, skin-tight coral toreador pants, and black sling-back spiked heels. The transvestite smiled saucily at the crowd of reporters and cameramen, then slipped an arm through Sarah's and giggled lasciviously. "Oh, darling, you say the *naughtiest* things," Vickie said loudly, for the benefit of the media boys and girls.

Feeling her face redden, Sarah kept her head bowed so no one would spot her flush. She needn't have worried. Everyone was too busy either ogling or making fun of the flashy redhead to take much notice of her male companion in his plain blue sport jacket and black chinos. With her close-cropped hair slicked down with gel and no makeup or jewelry, Sarah's charade was a total success. None of the newshounds gave her so much as a second look as they made their way down the street. Vickie, to his delight, got several catcalls.

"Can I give you a lift somewhere?" Sarah asked as they reached her car.

"Thanks, sweetie, but I've only got to go one block. I'm meeting a friend for breakfast over on Delores."

"Well, I guess I'll get going then. Listen, thanks for your help, Vickie. I'll get the outfit back to you—" She flashed on that photo of *Vic*. Felt oddly jarred by it.

"You know what Groucho said," Vickie intoned with a dramatic drawl, leaning closer to Sarah as she pulled out her car keys.

Sarah gave her neighbor a disconcerted look. "Groucho *Marx*?"

Vickie winked coquettishly. "He said that anyone who says he can see through women is missing a lot."

The remark sent a ripple of disquiet straight down Sarah's spine even as she plastered on a phony smile.

If Vickie sensed anything amiss, however, Sarah saw no hint of it. The transvestite bent and kissed her cheek, then flashed a pink-lipped smile of sympathy. "I'm real sorry about your sister, honey. You take care now, you hear?"

The house on Scott Street was sealed off with bright yellow police tape. Media people and curious onlookers jammed the block. Two women in the crowd wore white T-shirts emblazoned with ragged red hearts. In bold red letters under the hearts was printed: **ROMEO'S A HEARTBREAKER.**

Sarah felt her blood curdle. She wanted to tear the shirts right off their backs. The press would love that.

She'd really make their day. And make hers even more of a living hell.

Forcing down her rage and concentrating on her mission, Sarah skulked over to a uniformed cop sitting in a cruiser parked at the curb.

"Excuse me, Officer. I need to get into that house. I'm—"

"Nobody gets in there."

"But I have to get—"

"You have to get official permission, is what you have to get."

"And just how do I get official permission?" Sarah asked acidly.

His glance was bored, weary. "What's your name?"

"Rosen," she said, eyeballing him.

The cop's demeanor instantly changed. "Rosen?"

"That's right. Rosen. Sarah Rosen."

The cop squinted up at her. "*Sarah?*"

It took a few seconds for it to dawn on Sarah why she was being given such a strange look. The cop thought she was a *he*.

"I'm Melanie Rosen's sister."

The cop remained wary. "I'll see what I can do."

So far none of the press seemed interested in her, but Sarah didn't want to push her luck. "Listen, I'm going to grab a cup of coffee up on Union Street," she told the cop brusquely. "How about I check back with you in fifteen minutes or so?"

Sarah was working on her second mug of mocha java in a booth at the back of an upscale coffee bar on Union Street when she spotted Detective Michael Wagner walk into the place and look around. His gaze went right past her at first, showing no recognition.

On his second check, he found her and walked over.

"I'm incognito. My neighbor's idea."

Wagner observed her with quiet scrutiny. "Effective."

Sarah didn't know whether to feel complimented or insulted. "I'd like to go into my sister's house," she said, then shook her head. "Well, *like* isn't really the right word. I have to . . . pick something out for Melanie . . . for the funeral."

The detective nodded. "I understand."

"Is it okay?"

"Why don't you finish your coffee?"

"I want to get this over with." She started to reach for her tapestry tote bag, then remembered she'd left it behind. Hardly the right accessory for the man-about-town. She slipped her hand into her pocket and pulled out a five-dollar bill, laid it on the table.

"How 'bout you tell me what you need? I'll go get it and bring it back here for you," Wagner suggested.

Sarah fingered the bill, staring down at her coffee mug. "You don't want me to go in there, is that it?"

He slid onto the bench seat across from her, folding his hands one over the other on the speckled Formica table. "I'm just thinking about you. The place hasn't been cleaned up yet."

Sarah blinked rapidly several times as she looked over at him. Melanie's voice began playing in her head. A fragment from that last phone conversation they'd had on Thursday morning.

"You can't put your life in order, Sarah, until you put some order into your life."

What about your life, Melanie? I thought your life was in such tiptop order.

"Sarah? Sarah, are you okay?"

She looked across the table. Wagner's clean-cut, handsome face had gone out of focus. She shut her eyes, tried to concentrate on long, even breaths.

"Stay here, Sarah. I'll go by the house and pick out a few different things. You can decide—"

"No," she said stubbornly, her eyes popping open.

"Please, Sarah."

"No. No, damn it."

Wagner leaned forward, hands clasping the edge of the table like he needed to keep it from flying off. "You think it's going to prove something? You think if you go in there and face all that blood, it'll be some sort of an exorcism?"

"Shut up!" she shouted, so loud the customers and waitresses all looked her way.

Wagner rose and reached for her. "Let's get out of here," he said curtly.

She allowed him to guide her out of the coffee bar and over to his silver Firebird parked in a red zone at the curb. He settled her in the front passenger seat and climbed behind the wheel.

He smoothed his hair back as he glanced over at her. "I'm sorry. I was out of line."

She stared straight ahead at the morning traffic moving along Union Street. "You're wrong. I'm not trying to prove anything. I'm just trying to do what has to be done. What Melanie would have wanted me to do."

"What's that?" he asked softly.

"Let's just say—I owe her."

Out of the corner of her eye, she saw Wagner start to reach for her.

"Don't," she said sharply.

Wagner froze midmotion. "I wasn't—I was only—"

"Forget it."

Sarah held it all together until she stepped into the living room. But she wasn't prepared for the macabre scene of her sister's brutal murder.

"Oh God . . ." she whispered. Her body went rigid.

"Come on, Sarah. I'll take you downstairs. You can sit in the waiting room." Wagner was right behind her, careful not to touch her.

"No."

"Why do you want to put yourself through this when you don't have to?"

It was a good question. The answer was, she did have to. For more reasons than she cared to think about. She gave Wagner a resolute look.

"Okay. Okay. Let's do it and get out of here. I'll help you, Sarah."

Wagner guided Sarah across the room past the worst of it—the bloodstained love seat and carpet, the fetid stench of vomit. He tried to block it out himself—that last, awful image of Melanie Rosen.

He sees her not as she looks in death, but in life. When he first set eyes on her. In, of all places, a private sex club nestled in the back of an erotica boutique. The club is windowless, lit by thick, flesh-colored phallic candles on rickety tables that surround a makeshift circular stage where a rousing "slave auction" is in full swing.

She's sitting alone. Pensively studying the latest slave up for grabs—a muscular young Latino on all fours, whimpering softly but with obvious delight while the auctioneer, Brea Janus, digs a stiletto-heeled foot into the base of his spine and opens the bidding.

Emma Margolis, the host of Cutting Edge, *nudges his arm. She's snagged him for an interview for a show she's doing on sex clubs in the Bay Area. And finagled him into escorting her to one of the clubs. "Do you think I should bid on that hunk? It would certainly add some punch to my piece."*

Wagner gives Emma a distracted grunt; his gaze remains fixed on the woman across the way.

"Really, Mike," Emma persists. "Don't you get a little turned on by this stuff? 'Cause I'll tell you the truth—"

Later, while Emma's off interviewing one of the slaves, he corners the auctioneer, asks if she knows the woman.

> *Brea Janus chuckles throatily. "Honey, that's no woman. That's my shrink. Dr. Melanie Rosen."*
>
> *"What was she doing here?"*
>
> *A flush rises on Brea's cheeks. "Making a house call. Doc thought it would be helpful to my treatment for her to see me in my work setting." Her expression turns earnest. "I'll tell ya, Wagner, if you're ever in the market for a shrink, she's the crème de la crème."*
>
> *Before he leaves the club, she slips him Dr. Rosen's business card.*

"You don't seem to be doing much better than me, Mike."

For a moment, Wagner had the crazy notion he was hearing Melanie Rosen's voice. He was startled to see that it was her sister, Sarah, who was speaking. It was the first time he'd noticed how alike they sounded.

Still partially laced into that vivid memory of his first encounter with Melanie, it took him a few seconds to become aware that he and Sarah were standing in Melanie's bedroom. He must really be in bad shape, he thought, because he couldn't actually recall having gotten there.

Sarah could see the anguish and frustration on Wagner's face. Did he feel this miserable about all of Romeo's victims or was Melanie special? She recalled the way he'd sung her sister's praises. Had the detective fallen under Melanie's spell like all the rest of them?

She turned from him, his upset jacking hers up a notch.

"Sarah?"

"God, it could be anyone. A blind date. A lover. A patient. A friend. How will you ever find him? Stop him?"

"We'll get him, Sarah. I promise you."

She shook her head morosely, seeing the helpless expression on Wagner's face. *You're no match for Romeo,* she thought. *None of us are. None of us can stop him.*

She turned away again and stared at her sister's brass

bed. The sight of the box spring—the mattress and bedding having been carted off to a crime lab—was as daunting and disturbing for its sterility as the scene in the living room had been for its grisliness.

"How could such a monster exist?" This from a woman who'd lived with monsters all her life.

And Wagner's strained and ineffectual reply, "I wish I knew, Sarah."

As Wagner pulled up to the curb near Sarah's building later that morning, Sarah was relieved to see that the press ranks had thinned. Then she spotted Allegro leaning against the storefront window of the porno store next to her building.

Shit. She'd been hoping to crawl back into bed for the rest of the day.

Wagner got right out of the car and scooted around to get her door.

Allegro ambled over to meet them, focused in on Sarah. "Just need to ask you a few questions."

Great. Exactly what she felt like doing. Answering pointless questions. Especially given that she was still feeling shaky. And worrying about the dumbest stuff—would Melanie be pleased with the soft lilac silk dress she had chosen for her? With Wagner's help. He'd seemed rather confident about the selection. Had he ever seen Melanie in the dress? Was it her imagination, or had Wagner's interest in her sister been more than merely professional?

Allegro was still wearing the same rumpled suit he'd had on the day before. Sarah wondered if it was his only one. He had shaved, though. But not very carefully. A tiny spitball of toilet paper still adhered to a jag on his jaw.

Seeing the detectives standing together in the street, she was struck by the contrast between them. Her eyes lingered on Wagner for an extra long moment. He really was nice-looking. Did he have a girlfriend? she wondered.

Where is my head at? Am I totally losing it?

"She's been through a rough time this morning," Wagner told his partner. "Maybe you could hold off on the questions—at least let her relax for a while, eat something. We can come back after lunch."

"No, that's okay," Sarah told them. "I don't have much of an appetite. I'd just as soon get this over with. Come inside."

She led the way into her apartment, excusing the mess to Wagner, making it sound like she actually meant to straighten up the place at some point. To Allegro, she didn't feel any need to make excuses.

The detectives remained standing as she pushed aside a pile of newspapers and sat down on the edge of the sofa, folding her hands on her lap and crossing her legs at the rolled-up cuffs of her borrowed trousers.

What must Allegro be making of her in this man's getup, she wondered. Unlike Wagner, he didn't seem the least bit taken aback. Maybe he thought she was a dyke. Oh, what did it matter what he thought about her or her appearance? What did she care what anyone thought?

Her expression turned sulky. She was irritated with herself, with the two cops.

"I'll cut right to the chase," Allegro said, his head pounding ferociously from last night's debauchery. At Jake's Bar and afterward at Dee Dee's place.

"Fine," Sarah replied, her tone cool, distant. But her palms were damp. Emotions collided—fear, sorrow, anger, guilt.

Allegro gave her a knowing nod. She stiffened. *Can he see through me?* He was frowning, but then his face seemed fixed in a perpetual scowl. Like he hadn't had such an easy life himself. For a moment she again felt that disconcerting touch of kinship with him. She wanted to make him an ally. But why did she need one? She'd done nothing wrong.

"Do you have any idea at all who killed your sister?"

It was the obvious question, but when it came, she

stared down at her hands, distressed to see that they were trembling. She quickly slipped them under her thighs.

Allegro asked again, his tone more insistent.

Her eyes shot up. "You mean do I have any idea who Romeo is?"

She looked challengingly at them. Allegro wiped his brow with the back of his hand. Wagner's mouth set into a tight line. Both seemed to find her scrutiny disquieting.

"No. No idea." She answered her own question flatly.

"You told me yesterday that your sister mentioned she had a date on Thursday night," Allegro prodded.

"I also told you she didn't tell me who it was." Sarah could hear the impatience in her voice, sure they could hear it, too. *Don't expect me to solve this murder for you. This is your job. Your responsibility. You fucked up. Leave me out of it.*

Allegro persisted. "And you have no inkling who it might have been? A man or a woman? She never talked about seeing anyone in particular? If not on that Thursday, other times? Maybe one time when you dropped over she had company—"

"I didn't drop over," she said tightly. "We didn't have that kind of a—relationship. Anyway, I didn't particularly like going back to—the old homestead." Never more so, certainly, than that morning. But even before. Awful feelings. Bad karma.

Wagner went over to her, tipped his head down, looked her straight in the eye. But it was more like he was seeing deeper. Sarah squirmed under his gaze. What was it with these guys? X-ray vision?

"Do you blame *us,* Miss Rosen?"

Wagner had called her Sarah when they were alone. Now it was *Miss Rosen.*

"You mean, do I think one of you did it?" she shot back at him, feeling betrayed, frustrated, angry as hell. *Get off my case, Wagner. Don't mess with me. If you think you can push me around, you've got another thing coming.*

Allegro broke in. "No. But maybe you're thinking that

if we hadn't asked your sister to consult with us, she might still be alive." His tone suggested nothing but sympathy.

Still, Sarah felt cornered. "Is that what *you* think?"

"It's crossed my mind," Allegro admitted.

An honest answer. It surprised her. She met his eyes steadily.

Allegro stared back. That surprised her, too.

He gains validation and sexual gratification not only through his victimization of specific women, but through our collective fascination with his lurid deeds.

Dr. Melanie Rosen
Cutting Edge

7

On Sunday morning, Sarah, dressed in a black blouse and a dark print skirt, was escorted from her apartment to her car by a middle-aged uniformed officer, while the ever-voracious press hurled questions, snapped photos, and videotaped her every step. What did it matter to them that she was on her way to her murdered sister's funeral?

As they got to her car, the cop noticed, to his consternation, that the driver-side door was unlocked.

"It's been broken into so often," Sarah said with an impassive shrug, "half the time I don't bother to lock it."

"You really should," he scolded lightly.

Sarah nodded without contrition as he opened the door for her.

"Thanks." She slid quickly behind the wheel and slammed her door. The cop stepped onto the sidewalk, gave a little wave.

Sarah waved back and watched as he headed off back up the street.

It wasn't until she was about to start the ignition that, with a shiver of shock, she saw it. Lying on the dashboard. The sun glinting off its shiny surface. A gold heart. Just like the one she'd seen on that cat the other night. Only she saw now that it wasn't an ID tag but a locket. What a sick, demented stunt. Filled with revulsion and disgust, she shoved the cheap trinket into her glove compartment. Out of sight, out of mind.

Two hours later, after the service at the funeral parlor, Sarah stood by her sister's gravesite in a small Jewish cemetery in the outskirts of Colma, a veritable city of cemeteries south of San Francisco. Of all things to be thinking of at that solemn moment, she found herself reminded of that vile heart-shaped locket. Who could have put it in her car? The same crackpot who'd slipped that letter under her door? A cat lover? A Romeo groupie? Or was this all part of a more sinister plot? What if the *heartbreaker* himself was behind this? What if Romeo was wooing *her* now?

With crazy thoughts like that, no wonder she couldn't focus on her grief.

Liar. That's not the only reason you can't grieve. What about your guilt, Sarah? Huh? What about all those times you secretly wished Melanie would die?

Was this wish-fulfillment? *What do you think, Feldman?*

And you, Romeo? What do you think? How are you doing with your wish-fulfillment?

Where was the monster? Sarah could feel him out there somewhere—an invisible, malevolent presence—savoring the evidence of his success.

She shut him out of her mind—focusing only on Melanie, lifeless in that plain pine coffin, about to be buried beside their mother.

Were Melanie and Cheryl romping together up there in heaven at this very moment? Not very likely. Her mother and sister hadn't shared much happiness together in life. There was little reason to think they would in

death. Melanie, like her father, had never suffered her
mother's weaknesses. They were the strong ones. The
tough ones. Now Melanie was dead. And her father could
barely remember his own name.

Dr. Simon Rosen wasn't present to bid his final fare-
well to his older daughter. He still didn't even know his
darling girl was dead. The physician at the nursing home
feared his weak heart couldn't handle it, and Feldman
strongly concurred. No one had bothered to tell Sarah
about her father's heart condition before this—not even
Melanie, who might have used it to make her feel addi-
tional guilt for not being a more dutiful daughter. Still,
Sarah could guess why Melanie might not have told her.
To avoid a snide response, like: *I didn't even know he had a
heart.* And she could imagine Melanie's quick retort. *He's
not the one who's heartless, Sarah.* Her voice would have
held that familiar mix of frustration, exasperation, and
irritation.

For the first time that day, Sarah's eyes smarted. *I'm
sorry, Mel. I'm really not heartless. It would be a lot easier if
I was.*

She caught Feldman observing her. The psychiatrist
stood on her left, close enough to reach out to her, but of
course he didn't. He wouldn't want to risk setting her off
again. Bad enough when she'd attacked him in private.
This time there were dozens of Melanie's colleagues—and
his—gathered to pay their last respects. What would they
all think if Feldman—who thrived on respect, deference,
reverence—gave the grieving sister a supportive pat on the
back and she punched the shit out of him?

Sarah took some perverse comfort in imagining such
a scene. The distinguished doctor cringing under her
blows. The shock and horror on everyone's faces. Her
one-time psychoanalyst's humiliation. *Come on, Feldman,
wouldn't you rather I expressed my anger instead of holding
it in? Or taking it out on myself? Wasn't that what you were
always telling me? Wasn't it, Feldman?*

"It's called repression, Sarah," he tells her in his thick, melodic Hungarian accent. "You're desperately afraid to look back, to look inside yourself."

She's eighteen years old. Sitting stiffly on the leather chaise in Dr. Stanley Feldman's walnut-paneled consulting room. Her arms are crossed protectively over her chest. "I'm not complaining, Feldman. Why should you?"

"Then why are you here?"

"I slit my wrists. And botched it." Glib. Smiling. But a long-sleeved shirt covers the still-healing wounds.

"So? You want me to help you get it right the next time?"

Anger welling up. "You know what I hate most about you shrinks? You have all the questions and no answers." She's on her feet. Heading for the door. Enough already.

"I can't provide the answers, Sarah. Only you have them—"

It was a cruel lie. She didn't have any answers. She didn't have the answer to why her mother had killed herself—why she herself had tried suicide on more than one occasion—why Melanie had fallen prey to Romeo—or why she was starting to panic that she might be his next victim.

The rabbi, a silver yarmulke on his short gray hair, blue, white and gold tasseled cotton talis over the shoulders of his navy suit, was completing kaddish, the ancient prayer for the dead, at the head of Melanie's coffin. Bernie, on Sarah's right, was sniffling and dabbing at his eyes with a wrinkled blue bandanna-print hanky, even though he had hardly known Melanie.

No shortage of teary-eyed mourners in this crowd. Sarah barely recognized any of them. Close to a hundred —colleagues, friends, and several patients—had turned out for the funeral. A cadre of local and state cops kept the inevitable slew of video cameramen, reporters, photographers, and groupies behind a roped-off area.

Sarah looked across at Bill Dennison on the other side of the coffin, close to the rabbi. Behold the grieving ex-husband. Looking natty as ever. Custom-tailored pinstripe blue suit, double-breasted, European cut. A movie star of a shrink. Just enough character in his handsome features not to be boring. Michael Douglas would play him in the made-for-TV movie if it got made. But he'd probably be pissed not to do the role himself. And do a slam-bang job of it if he got the chance. *Real-life psychiatrist's Emmy-winning performance—*

She spotted the tears in his eyes. What were they about? Hard to tell with Bill. He had such a flair for striking the right pose, making the appropriate response, saying and doing the right things—most of the time. But then no one was perfect. Not even Dr. William H. Dennison.

Maybe she was being too cynical. His tears could be legitimate. But what did they reflect? Loss? Remorse? Guilt over all the secrets he had kept? One of which the two of them shared. Had he told Melanie? Sarah doubted it. And Bill knew she hadn't breathed a word. He knew that much about her. She was the master of secret-keeping.

As soon as Dennison made eye contact, she looked away, catching sight of Wagner and Allegro. The two detectives had distanced themselves from both the mourners and the press, staking out a patch of grass a few feet uphill from the grave site. Wagner stood with his hands at his sides. He wore an Italian-cut blue suit, white shirt, blue-and-green rep tie, and his aviator sunglasses. Because of the bright sunshine or to hide his tears?

Allegro had changed his suit today. So he had two, anyway. This one was no particular improvement. Drab shit-brown, narrow lapels, baggy-kneed from all the times he'd forgotten to pull up on his trouser legs when he sat down. Still, it was less rumpled-looking than the other one, and she observed that he was sporting a decent enough paisley tie. *Had he worn the same outfit to the funerals of Romeo's other discarded lovers?*

Sarah bet Allegro and Wagner were there to do more than pay their last respects. Or shed a few tears. She could tell by the way Allegro kept scanning the crowd, the way Wagner every so often leaned closer to his partner and murmured something in his ear.

Her gaze shifted from the detectives to a man snapping photos off to Wagner's left. She presumed he was a police photographer. He must have been taking shots at those other poor women's funerals, too. Searching for repeat mourners?

Did they also suspect Romeo was here? That this was part of his ritual? Attending the funerals? Savoring the burial of his victims? Feeding off the grief of those who mourned them? A ghoulish prospect. Sick and perverse. And exactly what a demented madman like Romeo would do.

A man behind her began to sob noisily. She glanced around. It was Melanie's patient. Robert Perry. He'd introduced himself to her at the funeral home before the service that morning, barely managing to hold back his tears as he offered his fervid condolences.

The man really was behaving more like a grieving lover than a patient. Could Perry and Melanie have been having an affair, as Allegro had suggested? Hard to believe. More likely it was Perry's fantasy. *Transference,* Melanie and Feldman would have labeled it. Patients were always falling in love with their shrinks. And imagining their shrinks felt the same about them. Part of the process. Expected. Normal.

Was Perry faking it? Sarah recalled the soulful way he'd looked at her when he'd told her how dreadful he felt about Melanie's death. Because she was dead? Or because he had slaughtered her?

A murderous rage flooded Sarah. Her gaze darted to the detectives. Was Perry at the top of their list? Obviously they hadn't found anything conclusive, or they'd have already charged him. But then, they were without a clue that pointed to anyone. Five women murdered. Including their own expert consultant. And the cops were nowhere.

Perry was crying more quietly now. Sarah edgily glanced back at him and saw that he was being comforted by a tall, striking woman who looked to be in her midthirties. Her flawless skin was coffee-toned. She was dressed in a simple gray silk sheath with pearlized buttons that ran all the way down to the hem. She'd left the last two unbuttoned, and Sarah caught a flash of muscular golden calves.

When Sarah's survey returned to the woman's face, she fixed on her short-cropped hair and the hoop earrings. And then it hit her. The woman from *Cutting Edge*. Emma. Emma something. What was a trashy TV journalist doing in the funeral party? How the hell did she get in? Consoling a prime suspect, no less. Hustling Perry for an appearance on her show? Milking him for all the gory details involving his discovery of his shrink's ravaged body? Wouldn't that be a real ratings coup?

Maybe Sarah couldn't mourn, but she had no trouble feeling invaded, outraged, and at the same time powerless to do a blessed thing about any of it.

After the burial service, Sarah was getting into Bernie's specially rigged black Fiat convertible when a shadow loomed over her. She turned around nervously and came face to face with the television anchorwoman.

"I'm Emma Margolis." She reached for Sarah's hand.

"I know," Sarah said coolly. She noticed the woman had a slight gap between her pearly white front teeth, but it didn't detract from her cool, sophisticated good looks.

When Sarah made no effort to take the woman's extended hand, Emma Margolis let it drop back to her side. "I wish I could come up with something less trite than 'I'm sorry,' but the feeling is sincere. I liked your sister very much. We were friends—"

"What do you want?" Sarah asked cruelly.

"I'm with a television magazine show—"

"I know that, too," Sarah cut her off, her features hardening.

Emma Margolis nodded. "Yes," she said, like she understood exactly what was going on in Sarah's mind.

Bernie was already behind the wheel, his folded wheelchair protruding from the narrow rear end of the sports car. He'd heard the brief exchange. "We better get going, Sarah."

Sarah's heart was racing. She nodded, her hand reaching for the door handle.

"Could we talk sometime?" Emma Margolis asked hurriedly as Sarah started to yank the car door open.

Sarah eyed her suspiciously. "About what?"

"About Melanie."

"No," Sarah said sharply. *Let sleeping dogs and dead sisters lie.*

"And about—Romeo."

Sarah white-knuckled the chrome door handle.

Romeo, Romeo. He was assaulting her from all fronts. There was no escaping this monster.

Emma caught hold of the gauzy sleeve of Sarah's black cotton gypsy blouse. Leaning closer, her voice was a whisper in the wind. "He contacted you, didn't he?"

Sarah froze.

"I know this isn't the time—" Emma continued. "But I think we should talk, Sarah. Privately, of course."

All Sarah's rage, confusion, frustration, and festering panic prickled like needles into her skin. Without a word, she yanked open the car door and jumped into the passenger seat. *Got to get away. Escape. Retreat. Before I explode.*

Wagner and Allegro made a fast getaway from the cemetery in Allegro's MG, eager to avoid being accosted by the swarm of reporters ravenous for an official statement. Dr. Melanie Rosen's murder had, indeed, become the biggest news in the nation. The Romeo task force was getting trashed by the media for their ineptitude, while the noted psychiatrist's killer was getting the star tabloid treatment. *Romeo strikes again. Be careful, ladies, or he'll steal your heart away—literally!*

The MG stalled out at the large wrought-iron gate leading from the cemetery to the narrow two-lane access road. The oil light flashed on. Allegro had noticed over a week ago that the car was dripping oil. He'd been meaning to throw in a couple of quarts before he went and blew the engine. Only he kept forgetting. Too many other things on his mind.

"Shit." He thought he'd let it go too far, but on the third try he managed to get the car started again. The oil light flicked off. He gunned the sucker, burning rubber as he made a sharp right onto the road.

"She held up pretty well," Wagner commented, reaching for his seat belt.

Allegro didn't strap in. The driver-side belt had been jammed for a couple of years. What the hell. Live dangerously.

"Yeah. A tough cookie." He knew Wagner was talking about Sarah.

Wagner lit up a cigarette with a shaky hand and glanced thoughtfully over at his partner. "She had her moments." Hadn't they all.

Allegro hooked a left onto the freeway on-ramp, forgot to use his signal making the maneuver, and got an angry honk from the driver he cut off. "Yeah."

"You must have thought about her, huh?" Wagner said after a short pause.

"Who?" Allegro wasn't sure this time if he meant Melanie or Sarah. They'd both been on his mind.

Wagner took a long drag. "Your—wife. Grace."

A muscle in Allegro's jaw jumped. A jab from left field.

"Sorry," Wagner said hurriedly. "I know you don't like to talk about it. I just thought . . . look, John, I know it's been a hard few months for you. First your wife dies, and now—I know she meant something to you. Melanie, that is."

Allegro stared straight down the freeway, driving on autopilot. Grace had been weaving in and out of his thoughts all day. Then again, she managed to sneak her way into his head more days than not. Or more nights, anyway. Sometimes the booze kept her at bay—sometimes it didn't.

There'd been that one brief respite. From mid-February to the end of March, when she'd been at the treatment center in Berkeley. All those blissful days and nights without having her calling, badgering him, showing up at his door at all hours. Okay, maybe "blissful" was taking it too far. But he'd certainly felt less wound up, less worried. Less guilty.

That all came to a resounding end when he went to pick her up at the treatment center. Despite the hospital's strong recommendation that his wife resume outpatient therapy, Grace would have none of it. Told him she'd had her fill of shrinks. Was going to take some R&R in Hawaii instead.

She sounds a little manic, but it's better than when she's depressed. She tells him where she'll be staying so he can get in touch with her if he wants to. He says sure he does. He's lying and he knows she knows it. Part of the game.

Wagner breaks the bad news to him as soon as he walks in the next morning. Grace's super found her. In the alley.

"She must have . . . fallen . . . out her window. I'm sorry. I'm real sorry, John," Wagner says.

He says nothing. Just waits, anticipating the double shot of Jim Beam he's going to down the second he gets to the bar across the street.

At the inquest, Grace's death is ruled a suicide.

Even though she left no note. Even though her plane ticket and hotel reservations were found in her purse. Psychological reports subpoenaed from a host of therapists, including Dr. Melanie Rosen, revealed a history of suicidal ideation and several failed suicide attempts since the death of their son. An open and shut case.

"You think our perp was there?" Wagner asked, expelling a cloud of smoke and bringing Allegro out of his morbid absorption.

Allegro laughed harshly. "Do bears shit in the woods?"

"Perry?" Wagner pressed.

"I don't know."

"You think he was—screwing her?"

"Do I look like a mind reader?" Allegro groused. Then he glanced over at his partner. "Sorry."

"Forget it." Wagner smiled. "Hell, I could do with a drink right about now."

Allegro laughed. "You're the fucking mind reader."

"What do you say?"

"Later. We've got some work to do."

"Perry's wife?"

Allegro nodded. When they'd brought Robert Perry in for questioning the day before, he was still in pretty bad shape, but not so bad that he hadn't thought to bring his lawyer with him. Wagner had asked him where he'd been on Thursday night between the hours of seven P.M. and midnight. Perry conferred with his lawyer before responding.

After a whispered exchange, Perry claimed that on Thursday night, while his psychiatrist, Dr. Melanie Rosen, was being murdered in her house on Scott Street in Pacific Heights, he was sitting two rows behind his estranged wife and her new boyfriend at a movie theater in North Beach. Dug a ticket stub out of the pocket of his jeans to prove it. Even claimed his wife would support his alibi. Seems he

had a brief *encounter* with her at the concession stand.
Couldn't remember the time, but thought it was around
nine P.M. As for his whereabouts for the nights of the
other four Romeo slayings, Perry gave them a dazed look
and said he couldn't remember. Maybe he had a calendar,
Allegro suggested. When they tried to press him, Perry
broke down, and the lawyer demanded they stop brow-
beating his client. Unless they were pressing charges. No,
Allegro had said. They weren't pressing charges. Yet.

"How about we get some lunch before we go chat
with Mrs. Perry?" Wagner suggested, flinging his cigarette
butt out the window as Allegro sped along the freeway.

"You could be fined for that," Allegro quipped.

The detectives stopped for a Sunday lunch special at a
storefront Thai café on busy, chaotic Clement Street back
in San Francisco. Cynthia Perry lived a couple of blocks
away in a walk-up apartment in one of the many row
houses there in the Richmond district, a largely Asian
neighborhood that lay between Golden Gate Park and the
Presidio. This area had become the city's second Chinatown, although with more of an ethnic mix here—Chinese, Japanese, Indochinese, Koreans, and recent Thai
refugees.

The whole time he was eating, all Allegro thought
about was the nice cold Bud he *wasn't* having with his
lunch. Not a good day for drinking. Not only because he
was on the job, either. He was in one of those moods. One
of those can't-get-a-grip moods. If he gave in to it, he
knew he'd end up drinking himself into a stupor. Probably would anyway, once he got home that evening.

Allegro twirled some Pad Thai noodles on his fork.
Instead of popping the food in his mouth, he looked over
at Wagner. "Five fucking funerals, thanks to that bastard.
And we don't have shit." He grouped all of Romeo's victims together, not wanting to single out this last one. Like
he was really fooling anyone. Especially Wagner. Allegro

knew Melanie's death had to be a bitch for his partner, too.

No way they were going to talk about it. About what either of them were going through. They didn't talk about feelings. That was Melanie's territory. *Was* was right.

Get down to business, Allegro admonished himself. Safer. "You see any familiar faces at the funeral home or at the cemetery?"

Wagner shrugged. "A lot of the same talking heads, but that's about it."

Allegro scowled. They'd already put that group of media sharks under a microscope. "Maybe when we go over Johnson's snapshots." He didn't sound too optimistic.

"The creep could have been hiding in the shadows." Wagner stabbed a bamboo shoot from his plate of red curry chicken. "Or maybe for this one he came out of the shadows."

Meaning, as Allegro knew, Perry.

"He still hasn't been able to account for his whereabouts for the other killings," Wagner reminded him.

"Could you, right off the top of your head like that? Could I? Anyway, if Perry had been able to spew out alibis for those other nights, I'd have been even more suspicious."

"You're right there," Wagner conceded. "But we're still going to need an accounting from him. And if we dig up anything solid, we could have his psychiatric files subpoenaed."

"We'll start by having a little chat with William Dennison. He's going to handle Melanie's cases, make referrals, see some of her patients himself. Maybe treat Perry. Under the circumstances Dennison might be willing to bend the rules and fill us in on Perry or any of her other patients that might be a fit. Steer us in the right direction. Could save us a lot of hassle and red tape."

"If Perry's telling the truth—well, it may or may not be in her professional notes," Wagner said awkwardly.

"I think Perry's off the wall myself."

"Right." Wagner hesitated. "But if he isn't, even if there is something about it in her notes, Dennison might not want to let it get out. I doubt he'd want the doc's professional reputation smeared. Which means if there were other male patients that she was—involved with—"

"Let's not get ahead of ourselves, Mike. If it turns out we have to lean on Dennison, we'll lean on him. Hard as we need to. He'll talk if there's anything to talk about."

Wagner nodded as he popped a sliver of chicken into his mouth. "What do you think about Dennison?"

"Not much."

"I mean as our ladykiller."

Allegro gave the suggestion a thumbs-down, hedging his bet by adding, "A real long shot."

"Because he's a shrink?" Wagner countered. "If you think about the doc's profile of Romeo, Dennison has the right fit. He's smooth, intelligent, a real charmer. Smug as they come. And what a great cover. Who wouldn't trust a shrink?"

"Plenty of people," Allegro said with a crooked smile.

"Okay, but plenty would."

"She divorced him, remember?"

"Maybe she had a change of heart. We know Dennison wanted to get back with her," Wagner reflected. "Maybe they did. Maybe he was her date Thursday night."

"We'll get a statement from him, but—"

"But what?" Wagner pressed.

"I'm not holding out much hope there. She didn't seem any too eager to get back with him," Allegro said. "Then again, he was a persistent bastard," he added, recalling a little *scene* outside headquarters about a month back.

He and Wagner are coming out of the building with Melanie at about eleven at night after a long, grueling session. That afternoon, victim number four turned up. Margaret Anne Beiner, a pretty brunette sociology professor at Bay State Community Col-

lege. Discovered in her Sutter Street apartment by a colleague who'd come by for a textbook. The heart beside her on the bloodied bed belonged to Karen Austin, victim number three.

Dennison's leaning against the front fender of his snazzy BMW but starts to approach Melanie as soon as they exit the building. Melanie holds up her hand.

"Go home, Bill. I thought we agreed—"

"I didn't agree, Mel. Why can't we just go someplace and talk? Maybe get a bite to eat?"

"I ate already."

"How about I drive you home then?" Dennison persists.

"John's giving me a lift."

Dennison starts to protest.

"Maybe you should go on home yourself." There's no missing the note of warning in Allegro's tone.

Dennison glares at him. "What are you going to do? Charge me with loitering?"

"Don't start anything, Bill. You'll just embarrass yourself, and you know how you hate to do that," Melanie says coolly.

"Why are you doing this to me, Mel? I thought we—" Dennison takes a step toward her.

Wagner puts a restraining hand on Allegro's arm as he starts toward Dennison. "It's not worth it, John."

"Okay, okay, I'm going," Dennison mutters, backing off. "But I'll call you tomorrow, Mel."

Allegro had no idea whether Dennison did call Melanie the next day. Or if they'd gotten together.

He looked across the table at Wagner, the food remaining on both their plates gone cold. "He wanted her back, all right. Question is, do we know what *she* wanted?"

Wagner wadded up the paper napkin on his lap and threw it onto the table. "We'll never know for sure now, will we?"

I'm burning up. Can't get enough. Can't stop. I cry out for you even as I try with the others. But I lock them out at the same time I'm seducing them.

M.R. diary

8

After the funeral, Feldman held a gathering at his Edwardian house on Nob Hill—mostly for Melanie's colleagues, all of whom had taken the shocking news hard. Feldman had tried to persuade Sarah to come, if only to stop by for a few minutes, but she'd turned him down flat. It had been all she could do to hold herself together during the vigil. Once it was over, her plan was to go home, take a long hot bath, crawl into bed, and stay there for at least a couple of days. *Close the whole world out. Until she got her head together. Ha!*

It was only as Bernie was turning onto her street that Sarah experienced an abrupt change of heart and asked him to drive her over to Feldman's place after all. Bernie was more than a little surprised.

"Are you sure about this, Sarah?"

"I'm not sure about anything, Bernie."

He pulled over to the curb and turned to her. "I know you and your sister weren't all that close, Sarah. And maybe you're feeling bad about that. Thinking there was something you should have or could have done different. It's only natural to feel that way. Up to a point. Don't let it consume you, sweetheart. You loved your sister in your own way. And I know you're hurting bad."

Sarah gave him a pained look. "Don't you dare make me start bawling, Bernie Grossman."

"Why not?" he cajoled softly.

"Because crying isn't going to get me anywhere. I need to stay mad. I need to protect myself."

"Protect yourself from what?"

The letter flashed in her mind. That locket. And that TV woman's remark at the cemetery. *"He contacted you, didn't he?"* How did she know? What made Emma Margolis assume it was Romeo and not some sick prankster who'd been *in touch*?

"I'm confused, Bernie. I'm angry. I'm so goddamn angry. Melanie spent years trying to straighten those fuckers out. And now one of them pays her back by—" She gritted her teeth. "Melanie's dead, and this monster's out there somewhere gloating over it."

"The cops will get him, Sarah. They won't leave a single stone unturned until they do. The best thing you can do is try to put it behind you."

"That means pretending it never happened. Erasing it from my mind. Well, I can't do it, Bernie. I can't run away this time. If I do, I'm done for."

"Done for? Sarah, now you're scaring me. What do you mean, *done for*?"

Her face became expressionless. "Nothing. I'm all worked up. Just take me to Feldman's, Bernie."

He sighed theatrically. "Whatever you say, sweetie pie. I'm here for you. Never forget that. Promise?"

"Promise."

"Want me to go in with you? All those shrinks in one place. I don't know, Sarah. Could be a regular head-fuck fest," he teased lightly as he pulled out and made a U-turn.

Sarah smiled faintly but shook her head. "No, I'm okay." When she saw his dubious expression, she added, "Really," hoping to assure herself as much as him.

He reached over and squeezed her hand. "Can't kid a kidder, sweetie pie. It takes time. We both know that. Rome wasn't built in a day."

"Yeah," Sarah said, but she was thinking—*How long would it take to destroy it? One swift explosion. She could feel a bomb tick, tick, ticking inside of her. She could blow up at any time. Taking along all those close to her as well. The few that were left.*

Fifteen minutes later Bernie deposited Sarah at Dr. Stanley Feldman's posh digs, a stone's throw from Grace Cathedral. He watched her walk tentatively up the stairs of the blue, beige, and white villa, thinking she still might cop out. After she rang the bell, however, she turned and waved him off, like she had things under control.

Bernie gave a little toot with his horn and pulled away.

The psychiatrist looked surprised when he opened his front door and saw her standing there.

"Your poker face is slipping, Feldman." Sarah took her small pleasures where she could. They were like finding a needle in a haystack these days.

He stepped aside to give her entry to his spacious two-story foyer. The walls were done in bold cream-and-bronze-striped paper, the floor in black marble tile with threads of gold running through it. The atmosphere was striking, elegant, and austere all at the same time. Like the man who lived there.

"I'm glad you came." He was observing her now with his far more familiar appraising gaze, tinged today with melancholy.

"A sign of mental health?"

His full lips curved upward a fraction. "If I say yes, I might scare you off."

His almost playful response only served to put her more on edge. Was he trying to humor her? A new tack? Knowing Feldman, he probably wasn't ready to concede defeat. Then again, what did she really know of Feldman? As her analyst, he'd always hidden his feelings and his strategy.

She glanced toward the living room. "Are there a lot—?"

"No," Feldman said. "Maybe twenty, twenty-five. They've come to share fond remembrances of your sister."

Fond remembrances. Sarah's face clouded. It was a dumb mistake to have come. What could she have been thinking?

And then she saw a woman step into the foyer from the living room. Emma Margolis. This, Sarah realized with a rush of cognition, was the driving force that had compelled her to come to the gathering after all. On some preconscious level, she'd felt certain the anchorwoman from *Cutting Edge* would be there. And that the woman would be expecting her to show up.

"Oh, I was just looking for the powder room," Emma Margolis murmured as if she had intruded on a private meeting.

"Ah, directly across from where you're standing," Feldman told her graciously.

Emma Margolis nodded, hung back for a moment as her penetrating eyes fixed on Sarah, then strode gracefully across the foyer and disappeared into the powder room.

What fond remembrances of Melanie had she been sharing? Sarah wondered.

"Do you know her?" she asked Feldman.

"Not very well. Do you?"

"No." Her eyes drifted toward the closed powder-room door, the psychiatrist following her gaze.

They stood there in silence for a few moments, Feldman's expression contemplative, Sarah's tense.

"Would you like to join the others, Sarah?"

Feldman's words took a few seconds to filter through her mind. "In—in a few minutes. I need a little time."

"I understand," he said.

No you don't, Feldman. You never did.

Emma Margolis didn't look a bit surprised to find Sarah waiting for her in the foyer when she stepped out of the powder room a couple of minutes later.

"Do you know your way around here?" the anchor-woman asked without preamble. "A quiet place where we can talk?" There was no smugness in her victory. Sarah appreciated that.

"His library is down the hall."

Sarah led the way. When they stepped into the spacious paneled room, Emma observed dryly, "Well, this *is* a library." She walked over to a gleaming mahogany table that was the centerpiece of the room, ran her hand lightly over its surface.

Sarah remained by the door. "You said you were Melanie's friend." Her tone and expression were deliberately contentious. "She never talked to me about you."

Emma sat down in one of the leather club chairs, crossed her legs. One tawny thigh was partially exposed as her dress fell open to her knee. "She never talked to me about you, either."

"Touché," Sarah said.

The women eyed each other for a long moment, like they were testing the waters. "We both feel awful about this. I know it hasn't fully sunk in for me. Probably not for you either," Emma said softly.

Sarah found it hard to focus. She reached for her glasses. This was one of those times she needed all the clarity she could get. "When did you meet my sister?"

Emma gestured to a matching club chair. "Sit down, and I'll tell you."

Sarah relented, taking the seat.

"Why don't I start at the beginning," Emma offered. "I think it might help."

"You or me?"

The anchorwoman gave her an assessing look. "Both of us, I hope."

"I didn't come here to salve your conscience," Sarah said sharply.

"Give it a rest, honey," Emma said not unkindly. "You're not that powerful."

For some strange reason, instead of making her angrier, Emma's remark struck Sarah as ludicrously amusing. "Powerful is the last thing I feel," she confessed, surprising herself with the admission. Especially to a woman who was a total stranger. And a newswoman to boot.

Emma smiled. A warm, friendly smile. "Ditto."

"You look like you've got your shit together," Sarah said, meaning it. Emma Margolis exuded an aura of cool competence. The woman seemed grounded, connected, self-assured. Sarah felt an old familiar envy surfacing.

"Appearances can fool you every time."

"Yes," Sarah said.

"Your sister knew that better than anyone."

"Anyone except Romeo," Sarah said starkly.

Emma leaned back in her chair, staring past Sarah. A puddle of silence settled around them. Sarah could feel Melanie's presence in the room—like she was reaching out, staking an emotional claim on them both. Sarah sensed that Emma felt the pull as well.

"Tell me about you and Melanie," Sarah said.

"I met her at a seminar she gave this summer at the BAPI—the Bay Area Psychoanalytic Institute."

Sarah knew only too well what those initials stood for. Her father had been on the renowned Institute's board of directors the whole time she was growing up on Scott Street. Feldman had been and still was the president of the Institute. Melanie had trained there. And Sarah had spent more hours there than she cared to remember, having her unconscious prodded and probed. Even her mother had been treated at the Institute for a time. When it came right down to it, she thought sourly, the Institute had been the Rosen family's home away from home.

Emma looked toward a crystal decanter and matching snifters resting on a sterling silver embossed tray on the table. "Do you think Dr. Feldman will mind if I help myself?"

"No. He's big on people helping themselves. He's devoted his life to the cause."

Emma's look grew thoughtful. "You don't like him very much, do you?"

"He was my shrink for a while."

Emma smiled as if that said it all. Sarah surmised that the anchorwoman had also done some time on the couch. She felt a small connection; her guard relaxed a bit.

After taking a long sip of cognac, Emma brought a snifter over to Sarah.

Sarah set it aside. "Go on," she said impatiently. "You met Melanie at a lecture."

Emma sat back down, cupping her drink in both hands. "It was right after the second Romeo killing—well, she hadn't dubbed him Romeo yet. Melanie was giving a talk on the patterns and motivations of serial sex-killers. She wasn't focusing on any specific psychopath, but she did mention him as an example."

"What did she say about him?"

Emma's gaze rested intently on her. Sarah looked away.

"What stands out the most was her comment that Romeo was like a chameleon. She said he might even separate out his different personas so successfully that they existed as completely separate entities. Kind of a Jekyll/ Hyde theory. That when he wasn't committing these horrific and violent acts, he could easily pass for our perfectly normal-seeming next-door neighbor. I remember commenting to Mike Wagner that I had a real normal-seeming next-door neighbor myself. A salesman. Even joked with him that he looked pretty damned normal himself. He wasn't amused."

"Wagner was there?"

"So was John Allegro."

"Why?"

"Like I said, there'd already been two killings in town

with the same MO. The cops were plenty worried they
had the makings of a serial sex-killer on their hands. Your
sister was an expert in the field, so they attended her lecture. They retained her services right after a third woman
was found dead in her Russian Hill apartment—bound,
mutilated—"

"Why were you at the seminar? Were you covering the
murders for your show?" Sarah asked, desperate to cut off
any further gruesome details to remind her of her sister's
corpse.

Emma was slow to respond, seemingly lost in her own
visions. "It was partly professional."

"And partly personal?" Sarah prodded.

Emma nodded. "I knew Diane Corbett. We weren't
close friends, but we were—friendly."

"Diane Corbett?"

"Romeo's first victim," Emma said in a subdued
voice.

"Oh." Sarah felt a wave of guilt. So caught up in
coping with Melanie's murder and its mounting conse-
quences, she'd given no thought to the other survivors.
Poor Emma. Losing two people she knew to Romeo. What
an awful coincidence.

Sarah impulsively reached a hand out. Emma took it.
Squeezed gratefully. Sarah found herself squeezing back.
But only for a moment. Allowing the connection—even
though she'd provoked it—made her uneasy at the same
time it soothed her.

"Did Melanie know Diane? Or any of the other victims?" Sarah asked abruptly. *What if there was some link
among the victims? If there was, wasn't she now linked
through her sister?*

"No. Not that she ever said." Emma paused to ob-
serve Sarah thoughtfully before continuing. "Anyway, all
four of us—Melanie, Allegro, Wagner, and myself—went
out for drinks after the seminar. Actually, it was their idea
for me to invite Melanie to come on the show and discuss
Romeo. She'd talked a lot during the seminar about how

psychopaths have enormous egos; how they relish being in the limelight. She thought Romeo would get off on the publicity and might even contact her or the show. The police were completely stumped in their investigation, and they were gung-ho for any chance to smoke the bastard out. After Melanie's first appearance, we were flooded with calls, faxes, letters begging for more. So we asked her back. She was on four times. The last taping was the very day—"

Emma stopped abruptly. She took another long sip of her drink. The cognac was almost gone. "I cared a lot about Melanie, Sarah. I feel I was in some way responsible for what happened to her."

"Sometimes I think everyone's feeling responsible. Except the one who killed her." Sarah put herself on top of that list.

"I wanted to do whatever I could to help those cops get Romeo. I still do. More than ever," Emma said earnestly.

"Did Romeo contact her?" The moment the words fell from Sarah's mouth, she blanched. "Oh God, what am I saying?" she added with a harsh gasp. "He contacted her all right."

"Not before last Thursday night though, as far as I know. Not Melanie or me," Emma said, her voice huskier. "If he had, we might have nailed the psycho."

Sarah's head was pounding. Squeezing her eyes shut, she began massaging her temples. She felt Emma's hand on her shoulder. Gentle, sympathetic.

"Why don't you try some of that cognac?" Emma asked softly.

"No. It only makes it worse."

"Maybe we should finish this another time."

Sarah tightly clasped Emma's hand again. "You must tell me. What makes you think Romeo contacted me?"

Their eyes met and held. Misery silently shared. A bond established, like it or not. "He contacted me, too. A note."

Sarah clutched the arms of her chair. "What did it say?"

"Just a single ambiguous line. Off a computer. 'She doesn't understand yet, but she will.' "

Sarah gave the woman's face a searching look. "That's all? That's all it said?"

"I found it on my desk in my office at the station. The day after Melanie—" Emma downed the last remnants of the cognac. "He didn't even sign it. He didn't have to. The minute I touched it, I knew it was from him. What I didn't know for sure was who *she* was. Until I spoke to you at the cemetery. That's when it clicked. He's written you, too."

"Someone wrote me. But anyone could have—"

"What did your note say?"

Sarah was perturbed. Why would Emma dismiss even the possibility that someone other than Romeo could be responsible? "It was a warped condolence sentiment. And something about us being . . . soul mates. I ripped it up. Threw it away." She hesitated. "I also found a chintzy heart-shaped locket in my car this morning. The car was unlocked. There are all kinds of crackpots—groupies, as Allegro calls them—hanging around. God, they're even wearing these disgusting Romeo shirts."

"You've told the cops," Emma said. "Showed them the locket."

"No. It would be making a mountain out of a molehill. The police have enough to worry about. Melanie never got notes from Romeo, right? None of the other . . . women did, did they?"

"Are you trying to convince me or yourself?" Emma asked gently.

The pressure in Sarah's head was building. "What makes you so sure it's Romeo?" she demanded. "You don't know. Your note wasn't even signed. You're making a big deal out of nothing. If Romeo's so hot for notoriety, wouldn't he have made sure I knew that he'd written that note, left the locket? Wouldn't he want that kind of crap plastered all over the news? Sure he would."

"Okay, take it easy."

Sarah got to her feet, started to pace. "Take it easy? Now you sound like my friend Bernie. Well, I can't take it easy. I'm bouncing off walls. Everything inside me hurts. I'm so goddamn mad—" She stopped abruptly. In a rare moment of clarity she knew what she had to do. The only thing she could do. If she wanted to salvage her sanity. "Emma, I'm going on your show."

"What? Why?"

"Why? To tell the fucking bastard who murdered my sister exactly what I think of him. I want to tell him what a sick, perverted, loathsome creature he is. God, I'd like to rip his heart out—" A cry broke from Sarah's lips.

Emma reached out to comfort her, but Sarah shook her off. "When? When can I go on?" She needed to set it up fast. Before she lost her nerve.

Emma hesitated. "We got preempted tomorrow night for a football game. Tuesday's solidly booked."

Sarah sensed that the anchorwoman was deliberately putting her off. "Okay, Wednesday," Sarah persisted. "What time?"

"We . . . start taping at two."

"Will the show air Wednesday night?"

"Ten P.M."

"Will you run promos for it during the day? Mention that I'll be on?"

Emma smiled faintly. "You can bank on it. My producers are going to be in shit-heaven. Personally, I still wish you'd give it some more thought, Sarah. Make sure you really want to do this."

"What I really want to do is make it all go away. But I can't." Sarah rose and started for the door. Halfway there, she turned back. "Why were you comforting Robert Perry this morning at the cemetery? What's he to you?" Her tone held a clear note of accusation.

Emma shrugged. "I wasn't much help in the comfort

department. Not my bag. But he was so distraught. I felt
. . . sorry for him. He was hurting so much—"

"Did you know he was Melanie's patient? That he
found her body? That he claims—" Sarah stopped
sharply. What was she doing? It would hardly be a tribute
to her sister's memory to have Emma go on TV and report that Dr. Melanie Rosen may have been screwing her
patients!

Emma was about to say something when there was a
knock on the door. Before either of them could respond,
the door swung open. Bill Dennison stepped in.

"Ah, there you are, Sarah," he said warmly, with the
briefest glance in the direction of Emma. Emma looked
back at him, a hard glint in her eyes.

But Dennison ignored her. "Sarah, Stanley told me
you'd arrived. I'm so glad. I was afraid you'd close yourself off in your apartment and hide away. This is a time
you need to reach out." He was the one, however, who did
the reaching out, giving Sarah a brief embrace.

At his touch, Sarah's heart lurched. *Memories pressing
. . . guilt, fear, shame clamping down on her throat—
choking, gagging.* She forced herself to swallow, but there
was a caustic aftertaste.

"I've got to go." She pulled away and hurried past
him. Racing from the house. Flying down the front steps.

"Sarah, wait," Dennison called. He caught up with
her on the sidewalk.

"Sarah, please." His features were clouded with consternation as he grabbed her arm. "Don't shut me out. Let
me help you."

Slap, slap, slap, slap. Like a rhythmic drumbeat.

*"Stop, Bill. Please . . ." A little girl's voice. A
child's plea.*

*"There's no reason to get so upset, Sarah. I'm
trying to help. I didn't hurt you. We were only
playing."*

Only playing. Only playing. Only playing.

"Stop. Please—" Once again that little girl's voice erupted. A voice awash with panic and terror.

Dennison's expression registered sharp concern. "It's okay, Sarah," he soothed. "You're experiencing an extremely typical post-traumatic stress reaction. Under the circumstances, it's perfectly understandable—"

She wrenched her arm free of his grasp. "How can anything be perfectly understandable when nothing makes any sense?" she cried out, as anger and futility seized her.

She squeezed her eyes shut. To block him out. To block out all the grief and fear. To exorcise the incubus that was penetrating her, growing within her.

> Blackness. And then a singular image floating in the abyss.
> Shimmering. A white silk scarf. Dangling. Shaped like a noose.
> And then a voice—low, seductive, compelling.
> Open your heart to me—your heart—your heart—

"Sarah?"

She blinked several times before she could bring Bill Dennison back into focus. Not that she really wanted to.

He insisted on driving her home. Sarah did not refuse. Capitulation. She hated herself for it.

He pulled his BMW to a stop at a red light on Taylor Street. "I was so worried something like this might happen."

"I'm fine now." She bitterly regretted having given him yet another opportunity to point out the severity of her emotional problems.

"No. I meant . . . Melanie. I begged her not to become embroiled in this case. I told her it was too dangerous."

Melanie. Sarah felt embarrassed, irritated. How typically dumb to think he had any worries about her. It was always Melanie.

Even during their brief and pathetic affair eight months back.

She glanced over at Dennison. His face appeared oddly composed. Or resigned. She remembered the look so well. That last evening back at her place, he'd worn it while he dressed and kept it on as he walked out the door. Quite the switch from the frustration and exasperation etched on his features moments after they'd had sex. Their third and last pathetic go at it.

Funny she had no memory at all of the sex part, only its aftermath. What Sarah did remember, though, she remembered vividly.

She recalled most of all wanting him to get off her right after he was finished. But he refused to budge, even though she'd tried shoving him. Instead, he merely rose up a bit, his elbows digging into the mattress on either side of her breasts as he loomed over her, the tip of his damp, cold, still semi-erect penis pressing against her belly—

"You didn't come this time either, did you?" An accusation. And a verdict. Guilty as charged.

"Don't take it personally, Bill. It isn't you. It's me."

"Spare me that bullshit, Sarah. You use your frigidity as a passive-aggressive—"

"Spare me that bullshit, Bill. Psychobabble afterglow isn't my cup of tea."

There's an unfamiliar intensity in Bill's face that she finds unnerving. "This is no laughing matter," he says.

"Who's laughing?"

"I've treated many women like you, Sarah. If there's anyone capable of understanding you, it's me. I know what you need."

Before she can reply that he doesn't know shit, his mouth clamps over hers, his kiss harsh and savage. Then he roughly rolls her over onto her stom-

ach and begins spanking her. Slap, slap, slap, slap.
Like a rhythmic drumbeat.

"Stop. Please . . ." *A little girl's voice. A
child's plea.*

"Let it go, Sarah. Let it happen. Trust me. You
can pretend not to want it. You can say to yourself,
'Bill made me do it.' "

"Get off of me. Get off. Get off." *She's screaming, close to hysteria.*

He releases her. "There's no reason to get so
upset, Sarah. I didn't hurt you. We were only playing." *He's smiling. No, not a smile. A smirk.* "Melanie never complained," *he adds.*

She's incensed. "We're not the same," *she
shoots back furiously at him.*

That was all she'd thought then. Not wanting to be like
her sister. Needing not to be. Determined not to be.

Now she couldn't stop thinking that Dennison had
thought she and Melanie were alike. *Melanie never complained.* Sarah couldn't forget that glint in his eye. How
rough had Melanie and Bill played? And when was the last
time they'd *played* together? Was it possible that he had
persuaded Melanie to see him again? Could he have been
her date on Thursday night?

Suddenly she was thinking how well he fit Melanie's
profile of Romeo. Handsome, charming, intelligent, alluring. Not to mention a man most women would easily
trust. Would consider a great catch. A chameleon par ex-
cellence. God, she thought, if it is Bill, what an easy time
he'd have of it. Like taking candy from a baby. Only—not
candy.

His arm slipped over the back of her seat. "I'm sorry,
Sarah. I didn't mean to imply—"

"Forget it." If he touched her, she'd punch him. Already her fingers were curling into fists. First Feldman,
now Bill. Like she could somehow slug her way out of this
morass.

The light changed, and he removed his arm, placing both hands firmly on the steering wheel as he pulled away. Fast. A macho show of the power of his fancy sports car.

"I certainly know what you must be going through, Sarah. This is devastating for both of us. I suppose Melanie told you we were getting back together again."

"No."

"Maybe she was worried about how you would take it."

Sarah gave him a sharp look. "Did you tell her about us?"

"No. Of course not." There was a short pause. "I think she guessed. At least that you—well, that you were attracted to me."

Sarah laughed harshly.

"Your sister was exceedingly perceptive, Sarah. Isn't that why she always made you nervous? Why you always took a combative stance whenever you were with her? It was that way even when—" He stopped abruptly.

"Cat got your tongue all of a sudden, Bill?"

"I'm not the one who adamantly refused to discuss our relationship, Sarah."

"Whose relationship?" she asked guardedly, not about to make the same mistake twice.

Dennison sighed. "Yours and mine, Sarah." An exasperated schoolmaster explaining something completely elementary to a particularly doltish student. What had she ever seen in him?

"Is that what you call what we had? A relationship?"

"Sarah, I did care about you. I cared a great deal. I still do. I don't think you ever believed that. I also don't think you could handle it. The wanting was easy—it was the getting that caused you problems."

"How come it's my psyche that always seems to wind up on the couch? You were just as screwed up as I was in that so-called relationship of ours."

He shook his head sadly. "I might have gotten over Melanie with your help. Then again, maybe there was no getting over her." He heaved a sigh. "I like to think, the second time around, she and I would have done it right. It's really my only comfort."

Dennison slammed his foot on the brake to avoid hitting a bare-chested skinhead who darted across Market Street against the light. He blasted his horn, and the punk, now safely on the sidewalk, gave him the finger.

A vein pulsed in Dennison's temple. "Fucking bastard."

Cynthia Perry opened her front door a crack, keeping the chain in place as she scrutinized the detectives' IDs. She was a small woman of Asian descent—Allegro's guess was Korean—glossy dark hair bound with a tie-dye scarf. Pretty. Young. Nervous. Still wearing her bathrobe, even though it was well past three on a Sunday afternoon.

"What do you want?" She spoke without an accent.

Allegro took the lead. "To ask you a few questions about your husband," he said.

"We're separated," she said tightly. "I moved out last June."

"We know that," Wagner said. "Can we come in?"

"I don't have to talk to you, do I?"

"We thought it would be more convenient for you to talk to us here." Allegro slipped his ID back into his pocket. "If you'd rather we brought you down to the Hall of Justice—"

"Look, it's just that it's not a good time. Can't this wait? It's Sunday. My one day off. I've got to clean house, do a million errands. Maybe tomorrow. After I get home from work you could come by—"

"It won't take long," Allegro said flatly.

"Look, I've got company. Really, this isn't such a good—"

"We'd like to talk to him, too," Wagner interrupted.

"Shit," she muttered under her breath, then closed the door to release the chain.

The front door opened directly onto a small, sparsely furnished room—a faded beige sofa, matching armchair, a pair of metal TV trays serving as a coffee table, knotty pine planks supported by bricks under the two windows forming a combination bookcase and entertainment center, the entertainment being a TV and a boom box.

As Wagner and Allegro stepped inside the living room, Cynthia's company padded barefoot out of her bedroom. For a moment, both Allegro and Wagner thought it was Perry. Similar build, same shade of dirty blond hair, same rugged good looks. Obviously it wasn't her husband's physical appearance that had been the cause of their breakup.

"What's this all about?" The boyfriend's plaid flannel shirt was unbuttoned, the shirttails hanging out of his jeans, hair all mussed. He looked like he'd just climbed out of bed.

Wagner officiously flipped open his large note pad and uncapped his pen. "Can we have your name?"

"Why the hell—?"

"They're cops, Sam," Cynthia Perry said wearily. "His name's Butler. Sam Butler. And this has nothing to do with him."

"You two go to a movie in North Beach Thursday night?" Allegro asked.

Cynthia heaved a sigh. "This is about his shrink, right?"

"Whose shrink?" Butler wanted to know.

"Rob's shrink." Cynthia shifted her weight slightly, again sighing with exaggerated weariness.

The boyfriend eyed her suspiciously. "You didn't tell me he saw a shrink."

"I didn't think it was any of your business. Anyway, he doesn't see her anymore," Cynthia said in a dull monotone. "She's dead."

"Dead?" Butler echoed.

The woman hesitated. "Murdered."

Butler took a couple of seconds and then snapped his

fingers. "Hold it. You don't mean the one that was offed by Romeo? The shrink from TV?"

She sagged down into the solitary armchair. "Yeah. That one. Dr. Rosen."

Butler let out a low whistle. "Jesus. Your husband's shrink—"

Allegro moved impatiently. "Can you answer the question, Mrs. Perry?" he interrupted.

Her eyes were fixed on her boyfriend. "What was it again?"

"Were you and Sam here at a movie in North Beach on Thursday night?"

She nodded slowly. "Yeah. I think it was . . . yeah, Thursday. Right, because the show changed on Friday, so it was our last chance to see it. A double bill. A Bruce Lee revival. Sam's wild about Lee."

"*Fists of Fury.* In my opinion, very underrated. And *Enter the Dragon,* undeniably his best work." Butler spoke with the authority of a guy who's seen every kung fu movie ever made.

Allegro grunted. Everyone was a critic. "You pay a visit to the concession stand sometime while you were there?" he asked Cynthia.

She didn't answer right away, but it didn't look to Allegro like she was really thinking about it.

"Yeah," she said finally.

"When was that?" Wagner asked, getting in on the act.

"It was at the break," Butler told them. "Between the two movies. Must have been around ten. *Fists* went on first. At eight. Yeah, close to ten."

"Rob was there," Cynthia said in a washed-out voice. "Buying popcorn. He acted like he'd just run into us by chance, but—"

"But what?" Wagner prodded.

"Let's just say he makes a habit out of accidentally running into me. Especially when I'm with Sam."

Wagner's eyes flicked over Butler. "You saw Perry at the concession stand Thursday night?"

"Yeah, I saw the jerk," Butler snickered, then glanced at Cynthia. "Didn't he make some crack to you about how you shouldn't buy that chocolate bar because your skin would break out?"

"You see him inside the movie theater? While you were watching either of the films?" Allegro asked them.

Butler shook his head.

"He followed us in when we went back to our seats," Cynthia said. "But I purposely didn't look where he sat. And I didn't see him when we left."

"You think he's involved in this wacko business?" Butler was getting nervous.

"Routine questions," Wagner said without inflection. "We've got a few more," he added, focusing on Cynthia. If his voice gave nothing away, his gaze did.

Cynthia pursed her lips. "Do I really have to do this now?"

Allegro heard the pleading note in her voice—surmising that at least part of the reason for her reluctance was that she didn't want to be having this conversation with her boyfriend present. "Maybe we could go into the kitchen," he suggested.

"Don't bother," Butler said, getting the hint. "I've gotta get going anyway."

Cynthia didn't look pleased with this solution. "I thought you said—" She stopped, shrugged, then said laconically, "Right. Sure."

"Honest, Cindy. I've gotta hit the books." Butler turned to the cops. "Going to law school at night. Work in the financial district during the day. A bitch." Buttoning up his shirt, not bothering to tuck it in, he made a beeline for the door, snatching up his jeans jacket from the foyer hook on the way out. "Buzz you later tonight, Cindy," he called back, the door slamming on her name.

Cynthia rolled her eyes. "Thanks a lot. Now he thinks

my husband's some kind of psycho weirdo, and he's scared out of his gourd."

"Is your husband a psycho weirdo?" Allegro asked her.

"No, of course not. Rob's just messed up. Who isn't?"

"Why'd you two split?" Wagner asked.

"None of your goddamn business."

Wagner was undaunted. "Come on, Cindy. Was he into kinky sex? Did he like to slap you around, tie you up, maybe?"

"You're nuts."

"Or did you find out he was getting some on the side?" Allegro suggested. Now that the boyfriend had exited, both cops hunkered down to the task at hand.

She eyed Allegro defensively. "With who?"

"You tell us," Wagner demanded.

She knew when she was licked. "Okay, you want to know, I'll tell you why we split. We were having . . . sexual problems. Rob was into some kinky stuff, but it isn't what you think."

She rubbed her cheeks with her palms. "Jeez, this is embarrassing as hell. . . . He didn't slap me around. He was the one who wanted to get slapped, okay?" Anger flashed from her dark eyes. "Do you get it? Do I have to draw you a picture? He isn't your sadistic serial killer. Rob didn't get off on being the tough guy. He got off on being *helpless*. He's like a whimpering puppy in bed. He used to just cry and beg me to hurt him."

"And do you?" Allegro asked.

Her eyes watered. She didn't answer.

Wagner cleared his throat. "How about sex clubs? S&M—that sort of thing? Shows and—whatnot. A lot of 'em over in North Beach, SoMa. You two ever go to any of those? Have membership in any of the private clubs?"

"God, no," she gasped.

"Rob might have gone without you, though," Wagner persisted.

She shook her head violently. "He wouldn't. He didn't."

"It's a sickness, Cindy." Allegro spoke softly. "An obsession."

Her head drooped, her scarf slipping from her hair so that the dark, straight strands fell about her narrow face like a black fan. "I told him we had to see a shrink."

Allegro was quick to pick up on the *we*. "You both went to see Dr. Rosen?"

"I only saw her a couple of times," she said dully. "We agreed it was Rob who needed treatment. For a while, he seemed to be getting better. We were having some nice, plain vanilla sex. You know. Regular." Cindy flushed.

"Yeah, we know. And then?" Wagner prodded.

"Then he didn't want sex at all." She hesitated. "Not with me anyway."

"Who do you think he did want sex with?" Allegro asked.

Cynthia stared down at her lap. She made no crying sounds, but the tears were slipping down her cheeks. "I don't know for sure."

"But you have a guess," Wagner said, softening his tone so that it was now almost cajoling.

She didn't respond right away, keeping her head bowed, her hair shielding her face from view. They didn't rush her. They could tell she didn't need any further prodding.

When she looked up at them, she absently brushed her hair back from her face. Anguish was written all over her features, her narrow shoulders hunching as she began speaking very fast. As if she was hoping to get it all out and be done with it.

"He used to write Dr. Rosen practically every day. These wild, intense love notes. He left them lying around. I don't think he cared that I read them. Might have even wanted me to. And I don't know if he ever sent them to her or even talked about them at his sessions. I just know I got fed up. It wasn't only the notes. It was—everything. I finally blew up; told him I wanted out. He said I didn't understand, that he still loved me, that one thing didn't have anything to do with the other."

She finally stopped for a breath, gulping in a swallow of air and exhaling, shaking her head. Her face was slick with tears. "She wasn't helping him. She made him *worse*."

She stared from Allegro to Wagner, her expression haunted. "Couldn't she see that?"

There was a lengthy silence, broken by Allegro. "Do you have any of those notes your husband wrote Dr. Rosen?"

She shook her head with disgust. "No, of course not."

"You think he still has them?"

She shrugged. "I haven't been back there in months."

Wagner and Allegro shared a look. Had Perry hung on to them? Had he given or sent them to Melanie? Had Melanie held on to them? If so, they hadn't turned up during the search of her place.

"Been following the Romeo killings on TV, Mrs. Perry? In the papers?" Wagner asked.

"No."

"Pretty hard to avoid it," Wagner pressed.

"I don't watch much TV."

Both detectives' gazes strayed to the TV in the room.

"I mean I've seen stuff just in passing," she admitted. "So ghoulish. Why anyone wants to watch that kind of thing—" She ran her hands up and down her arms.

"Did you know any of the other victims?" Allegro asked.

"No. Why would I?"

"What about Robbie?" Wagner followed up.

"No," Cynthia Perry said sharply. "And he hates when anyone calls him that. Rob. He likes to be called Rob."

"You sound very sure that *Rob* didn't know any of those women, Mrs. Perry. I mean, for someone who hasn't been paying much attention to the killings," Wagner insinuated.

Her lips twitched. "Okay, okay. I saw their pictures in the papers. On the eleven o'clock news. Heard their names. You'd have to be dead not to hear about Romeo in this city. As far as I know, Rob didn't know those women. Why would he? Where would he meet them? He didn't hang out with that kind of crowd. After he got laid off, the only place he hung around pretty much was at home. He hardly ever left."

"He did leave for his therapy sessions," Wagner commented.

Cynthia looked away, her expression unreadable. "Yes, he never missed any of them," she said with a flattened affect.

On their way out, Wagner turned to ask one more question. "Does your husband happen to like Gershwin?"

"Who's Gershwin?"

"A composer. You ever hear Rob listening to *Rhapsody in Blue*? Did you ever see a tape, CD, an album of it lying around the house?"

She shook her head slowly. "He wasn't much of a music lover. He was a TV junkie. He was wild about game shows. When he got laid off from his job, he watched them all the time."

Then as an afterthought, she added wistfully, "It seemed like he knew all the answers."

Romeo, like all serial killers, first locks into the "aura" phase. During this time he separates himself from reality. This is a period of intense visualizing and compulsive plotting . . . creating bizarre parodies of romantic courting. Satisfying, but only up to a point.

Dr. Melanie Rosen
Cutting Edge

9

"*You're breaking my heart, baby.*"

Romeo's eyes tear up. Her plaintive cry fills his head —fills the entire room. A wail of anguish, reproach, disappointment. Ricocheting off the walls and ceiling, vibrating off the furniture, resonating like a vast echo chamber. He can't bear it. Yet there is no escaping her voice. It sweeps over the pores of his skin, leaving festering sores. He lies naked on the bed, soothing these erupting welts with his hands. His hands bestowing light, caressing touches—over his face, down his entire body.

See how gentle I can be? How loving and tender?

The pustular sores disappear, leaving his flesh unblemished. He presses his hand to his heart. The beat is steady, strong. As well it should be.

He picks up Melanie's diary and flips on his CD player. The opening notes of *Rhapsody in Blue*.

. . . *but my suffering, as we both know, is my atonement.*

He smiles. Suffer no more, my sweet. You were right, Melanie. You were different from the others. We did connect in a special way. I put a great deal of time and effort into making that happen. So that it would be perfect for both of us. True and ultimate release from the suffering that was mine as much as it was yours.

His features turn somber. Why then is he still suffering? Why did it fail? Why does that melancholy reproach from his past continue to hound him? Haunt him? Melanie's contrition was supposed to drive that voice out. What went wrong?

His face contorts with rage. Melanie failed him. Like all the others. Bitch. Fucking whore. Cunt. Just like the other cunts.

He can't bear the music now. He switches it off and reviews every moment of his final encounter with Melanie, searching for the mistakes. Hers. His. What he did or didn't do. Where she fell short of his expectations.

Slowly, the visions begin to reconfigure. Now it is not Melanie begging to be the recipient of his gift, his punishment, his salvation. It is Sarah. Sarah is the one he's been searching for all this time. His true challenge. He opens to another page in Melanie's diary.

> . . . that I had Sarah's talent for blanking out the past, for her incisive invectives, for her "fuck you all" attitude. Perhaps if I didn't have to spend so much of my life playing the good doctor— No such strictures for Sarah. All these years trying to play her savior. What a farce.

Romeo closes his eyes. Pictures Sarah so perfectly in his mind. Pictures each of his moves. The letter and the locket were only the beginning. There's so much more.

The fantasy grows. So vivid and clear. The steps he will take. The mistakes he will not make this time.

He becomes utterly preoccupied. Watching her, cruising her, preparing her. He pictures those long lanky legs, the boy/woman body, the tough-girl stance. A fighter. Too tough for Melanie. For all the others. Finally, someone truly worthy of him.

Mmm. That turns him on. A real struggle before she

succumbs. To her own secret yearnings as much as to his. He knows how bad she wants it, even though she's battling against it. He'll open her eyes. He'll awaken her. With Melanie's help. Thanks to all the secrets about Sarah she's so graciously shared with him.

He's beginning to see where he went wrong with Melanie. With all the others. They were too weak. They weren't the challenge he'd envisioned. They gave in too easily, too quickly. They only wanted the pain, not the redemption it would bring them if they were truly chastened. They never really had their hearts in it. Sarah's heart will be perfect.

The music begins playing again. In his head this time. He's coming to the crescendo—

But he's moving too fast. Mustn't get through it too quickly. Cherish the buildup. Cherish every detail.

His cock perks right up. As the fantasy plays in his head, he lies very still, watching with a detached feeling of pride how he grows harder. His magnificent, hard, firm cock. Smooth as the silky strands inside a cornhusk. He can come without even touching himself. Just by imagining what it will be like for him and Sarah. What it will be like afterward.

His eyes flutter closed. Every exquisite detail unreeling. The complex ritual—the pursuit, the courtship, the seduction, the ultimate victory.

He wets his lips like a starving wolf about to feast on his prey. His heart is pounding with the adrenaline rush. She's bound hand and foot. Her breath is coming in shallow puffs. He breathes in deeply. He visualizes his hand moving over her creamy smooth ass.

He raises his hand, then shakes his head. Not a mere spanking for Sarah. A nice, brisk whipping.

She'll cry out with every stroke. A delicious thrashing. *Oh no, it's too much. You can't. No, no.*

But she won't want him to stop. He'll take her over the edge. He'll make her see that this is what she needs. What she deserves. What she's got coming to her.

He'll show her. He'll show her who's in charge. He'll bring her to her knees. He'll make her beg for it. For the agony, the pain, most of all the atonement.

She'll want it, all right. She'll want it more than all the others. And it will be all the sweeter because she doesn't even have an inkling. But she will. Oh, she will.

It will be perfect. This time he's sure. Absolute perfection.

. . . the moments when the shell cracks and I peek inside, waves of panic, disgust, shame, remorse springing out of the crevices like poisonous vipers going for my jugular. God, how Freudian can I get? I suppose the laugh's on me.

M.R. diary

10

Sarah's phone rang on Wednesday afternoon as she was searching under her bed for a missing shoe, cursing because she was running late.

The answering machine came on—first her voice, the beep, then the caller's voice.

"Sarah, it's me. Bernie. Are you there?"

Sarah picked up. "I'm here, but I'm on my way out. As soon as I dig up my other shoe."

"Glad to hear you're getting out. You've been holed up in that grim, shabby apartment you facetiously call home for two whole days. I hope you're not coming back to the office yet, though?"

"No. No, I'm going down to KFRN."

"KFRN? What's—That TV show? I can't believe—"

"Save your breath, Bernie. You're not going to talk me out of it. Now what's up?"

"Just my daily check-in call to see how you're doing."

"How are things over there? Is Buchanon bitching because my paperwork's piling up?"

"Even he's not that big an ass. One of your clients has been calling a lot, though."

"Sanchez?"

"Yep. That guy's got the hots for you, sweetie."

"Oh, stop. What did he say? Did he mention anything about selling his painting?"

"Nope. He just keeps asking how you're doing. Wanting to know when you'll be in. If there's anything he can do for you."

"Well, maybe I'll drop in on him tomorrow. I'll see how I'm feeling."

"Take it easy, Sarah. Give it some time."

"Tell me, Bernie. Just how much time does something like this take?"

Sarah made it to the KFRN-TV station down at the Embarcadero at one-thirty. The receptionist, a reed-thin Generation X blonde wearing a chic red linen suit, sat behind a long glass-fronted counter that reminded Sarah of a cross between a bank and an upscale airline terminal check-in. On the sky-blue wall behind her was a large logo of the Golden Gate Bridge with the station's initials in sun-yellow above it: KFRN.

The receptionist slid the glass window open. "Yes?"

"Emma Margolis is expecting me. I'm doing a segment for *Cutting Edge.*"

"Your name?" The receptionist's voice had a faintly southern tinge.

"Sarah—"

Before Sarah finished, she heard her name being called. She turned to see Emma, looking exotically beautiful in an African-print silk dress and enormous gold-drum motif earrings, step into the reception area. The anchorwoman wasn't alone. Sarah was both surprised and disconcerted to see that she was accompanied by Detective Michael Wagner. She cast the pair a wary look.

When Emma extended her hand, Sarah almost didn't take it. Emma cupped Sarah's hands in hers, squeezed, giving her a reassuring smile. "I wasn't sure you'd come."

Sarah merely returned the smile. It wasn't easy.

Wagner hung back a little, greeting her with a brief nod but a not-so-brief study. Sarah knew she looked like hell. Hadn't eaten much of anything for days. Probably dropped five pounds. Bags under her eyes. And her attire left a lot to be desired. She'd stuck on a pair of gray cotton slacks straight from her laundry bag containing the stuff that she meant to get around to ironing. There was a rip in the seam at the shoulder of her navy blue turtleneck sweater. She hadn't realized it until she was driving over. Not exactly the outfit to wear for her debut appearance on television.

"I'll grab my messages, and then we can all go down to my office," Emma said warmly.

Sarah scowled. Shouldn't they be heading for the studio? Didn't they tape in a half hour?

Emma read her mind. "We've got a few minutes," she said.

"Look, Emma—is this going to happen or isn't it?" Sarah heard the building panic in her voice. *You can do this, Sarah. You must.*

"I gave him my note." Emma said quietly, indicating Wagner. "And I told him about yours, Sarah. And the locket."

The locket. Sarah'd been so absorbed in psyching herself up for this taping, she'd actually managed to put that loathsome trinket totally out of her mind.

"If it makes you feel any better," Emma said, "I agonized for days."

"It doesn't," Sarah said. She had liked Emma—had even stupidly thought she could trust her.

"I did it for you, Sarah. Because I was worried about you. I don't want you to wind up as that creep's next victim."

Wagner spoke for the first time. "Let's talk in Emma's office." His voice was cold, on the edge of anger.

Sarah eyed him warily. "You mean it's either her office or the station house?"

"Mike's not your enemy, Sarah," Emma said, coming to the detective's defense.

"I meant let's talk there instead of here in the lobby," Wagner said with a faint smile.

Sarah relented, falling back on her recollection of how supportive he'd been to her on Saturday morning, when he went with her to pick out Melanie's burial clothes.

The receptionist buzzed them back through the security door. Emma led the way to a corner office at the end of the hall. The space was decorated with framed award certificates for *Cutting Edge* and several rather beautiful Matisse etchings. Her enormous desk, a brass and glass affair, was cluttered with papers, books, magazines, a Powerbook, and piles of computer disks.

"I like working in chaos," Emma said with a jaunty tone that seemed out of character.

She's feeling guilty, Sarah thought. And well she should. *She betrayed me.*

"Let's sit down," Wagner suggested.

Emma obliged, dropping gracefully into one of the gray-green club chairs across from her desk. There was a matching chair beside hers, and against the wall a full-size hunter-green sofa.

Sarah remained standing, confronting Wagner without preamble. "What exactly did she tell you?"

Wagner sat down on the sofa. He was casually dressed today in khakis and a pale beige shirt, sleeves rolled up, an Irish cable-knit sweater slung over his shoulders. He looked more like a college professor than a homicide cop.

"She said you've received some kind of communication from Romeo. And some jewelry."

Sarah squinted down at him. "The letter wasn't signed. And the locket—any sick jerk could have stuck it in my car."

"You don't think it was Romeo, then?" he asked.

"You do?" Sarah challenged.

"Emma says you threw away the note."

"Yes, I tore it up and tossed it in the trash."

"Why?" Wagner demanded, rising to his feet. "You had to know you were destroying what could possibly be state's evidence in a capital crime. Goddamnit, Sarah! Why'd you do such a dumb thing?"

"What's with the third degree, Mike?" Emma cut in. "Sarah's been through hell. Take it easy."

Wagner stood so close to Sarah, she was breathing in the mix of his lemony aftershave and the cigarette smoke that clung to his breath and clothes. She took a step back, not because of the smell but because of the supercharged intensity he was giving off.

"Okay, it was dumb. I wasn't thinking, okay? I just— acted," she snapped, her eyes searching the plain white office ceiling as if the key to coherency was hovering up there.

"Okay, Sarah." Wagner had turned away, but his voice softened. "I understand."

"Bullshit." She didn't want his understanding.

"What about the locket? You didn't toss that, too?"

"No."

Wagner smiled. "Good girl."

"Don't you patronize me," she snapped.

Emma got up from her seat and went over to Sarah. "This is hell," she said sympathetically, putting an arm around her. "But it's not over. You know that, Sarah. It won't be over until they catch the bastard."

It will never be over, Sarah thought with growing despair. If only she could stay mad. Rage kept the rest of her emotions at bay. Rage she could cope with. The rest—

"Any more anonymous letters or gifts since you spoke to Emma following the funeral?" Wagner's tone was less officious now, gently coaxing.

"No. That's why I thought . . . I figured . . . he never did this before, right? Sent stuff to other victims' sisters? Didn't any of them have sisters? Or girlfriends? Or—"

Emma guided Sarah over to a chair. She sank down into it without argument. Emma perched on the arm, taking hold of Sarah's clammy hand. Sarah felt a tug of gratitude toward the other woman. Emma's presence and support helped to ground her a little—made her feel less alone. For an instant she imagined it was Melanie holding her hand. Melanie protecting her. Melanie saying more with a touch than with the torrent of psychological jargon that rolled so easily off her lips.

They'd rarely touched, she and Melanie—a brief peck on the cheek at birthdays and such—always awkward, whether given or received. Obligatory. Ordered.

> *"Give your sister a kiss, Sarah. It isn't every day I have a daughter who gets into Stanford University."* Her father is beaming at his precious daughter. Such pride. Such pleasure. Such adoration.
> *Sarah dutifully touches her lips to Melanie's cool, smooth cheek. "Congratulations."*
> *She smiles like she means it, but she's thinking the whole time*—I hate you for deserting me.

Sarah blinked, disoriented to see the detective squatting down in front of her. And disturbed by the searching way Wagner was regarding her—like if he looked long enough and hard enough, he'd see what made her tick. Well, plenty smarter than him had tried and failed—miserably.

"I'm not saying it is Romeo who's contacting you, Sarah. It *would* point to a change in his MO. As far as we know. But we can't rule out his making a shift for some reason. We have to consider every possibility very seriously. If it turns out Romeo is communicating with you, this could be a major break for us, Sarah. But if he is, this puts you right smack into the middle of this insanity. Not that I'm trying to frighten you. We're going to watch over you around the clock. We're not going to let anyone so much as touch a hair on your head."

"Fine," Sarah said tightly. "But while I'm being baby-sat, Romeo may very well be off seducing his next victim.

Setting her up for a *romantic* dinner for two at her place."
How many more victims before he was stopped?

"Emma and I talked, Sarah," Wagner said. "And we
agree that you shouldn't go on her show."

"Not go on? That doesn't make any sense. Especially
if your theory is right. You haven't got any other leads,
have you? Without me, you've got nothing. Why won't
this help smoke him out? If he *is* communicating with me,
this will really spur him on to stay in touch, won't it?" Not
waiting for his response, Sarah looked up at Emma.
"Shouldn't we be heading for the set?"

Wagner remained adamant. "No. We don't know
what his game is. Where you fit in."

Sarah glared at him. "I'm fitting myself in. How else
do I get at him? Maybe, since you think he's writing to
me, you figure he'll send me his return address so we can
become pen pals. I'm doing this, Wagner. I'm going to
speak my mind—whatever's left of it, thanks to what this
depraved bastard's done. And you're not going to stop
me!"

Wagner was fast losing his patience. "Get this straight,
lady. You're not running this show."

She smiled sardonically. "No. Emma is."

He exploded. "You know damn well what I mean.
You want to do your part? Fine. Turn over the evidence.
Let us do our job."

Emma shot him a look. "Stop playing cop for a minute, Mike."

Sarah checked her watch. "We've got fifteen minutes.
Don't you have to have your nose powdered or something?"

Emma's dark brows furrowed. "Why don't we hold
off for a few days, Sarah? Let the cops—"

"There are other shows who'd welcome me with open
arms. If you don't have the guts—"

"I'm thinking about *you,* Sarah. Your safety," Emma
countered. Her face was stiff.

"And I'm thinking about Romeo. I'm goddamned if

I'm going to make this easy for him. Let him have every-thing his way. He's not going to win anymore. I won't let him. I don't know what his game is either, but I do know I've always felt a victim—my mother's child—weak, inad-equate. Always ineffectual. Always hiding. Always scared. Scared of my own shadow. And I'm tired of it. I've got to do something, or I won't be able to live with myself. Can't you understand that?"

Emma's features filled with sympathy. Wagner's too. But Sarah didn't want their sympathy. She wanted them to help her fight back.

"Melanie challenged him," Sarah told them defiantly. "Told him—told everyone—what she believed made him tick. Well, now it's my turn. She thought she'd psyched him out, but she was too analytical. I'm planning a more direct, in-his-face approach."

Wagner shook his head. "This is nuts—"

"You didn't think it was nuts when Melanie appeared on the show," Sarah countered caustically.

"I wish to God now she never had." His eyes skidded off her face, and everyone fell silent.

"Maybe she should go on, Mike," Emma said finally. "This could smoke him out, like Sarah said."

"That's what worries me," Wagner groused.

"And if it isn't Romeo, but some crackpot bugging her," Emma continued, "then letting Sarah have her say will be cathartic for her, if nothing else."

"Face it, Mike," Sarah persisted, "I'm our best shot right now—"

Wagner's features darkened. "*Our?* Whoa—"

He was cut off by the buzz of Emma's intercom.

She reached over and punched the button.

The receptionist's voice crackled through the speaker. "They're paging you on the set, Ms. Margolis."

"We're heading over there now, Gina."

Wagner started to argue, but Emma cut him off. "Do you have any better ideas, Mike?"

"You mean," the detective said sarcastically but resignedly, "do I have any worse ones?"

A scrawny young woman in jeans and a tank top unceremoniously put Sarah in a swivel chair at the desk to Emma's right. She thrust a tiny lapel mike at her and ordered her to pass it up under her sweater so the wire wouldn't show. Then she clipped it to the neckline.

Sarah barely had time to orient herself before Emma slid into her seat, clipped on her own mike, and gave Sarah's hand a reassuring squeeze. An instant later, Sarah saw the red light flash on in the camera in front of Emma. A chubby man, wearing headphones with a mike fitted to it, pointed to the anchorwoman. Cool and composed, Emma began speaking—well, reading off the TelePrompTer fitted over the camera lens.

"Welcome back from the break, folks. As promised, tonight we have a very special guest with us. Miss Sarah Rosen. All of us here on *Cutting Edge* share her sorrow over the brutal slaying last Thursday night of her sister, Dr. Melanie Rosen. Many of you, I'm sure, tuned in to watch our show when we featured Dr. Rosen's expert commentaries on the very killer who later took her life."

Emma folded her hands on the desk. Behind her, on the wall, was a bank of televisions. Sarah stared at the studio monitor in front of her. All that showed on the screen was Emma Margolis, making it look for all the world like the anchorwoman was alone at the desk. It was a weird feeling. Like she—Sarah—didn't exist.

"Romeo." Emma deliberately paused, staring straight into the camera. "I don't know about the rest of you, but that name curdles my insides."

Sarah glanced at the TelePrompTer. Saw that those words weren't printed there. Emma'd ad-libbed them. When Sarah looked back at the monitor, the screen was filled with a close-up of Emma's face—her expression a study in anguish and loathing. Sarah could feel her own already-shaky composure start to crumble. It got worse when she saw the red light flash on in the camera in front of her. Now the monitor showed the two of them seated at the desk. Sarah blinked nervously, seeing herself for the first time on the screen. She looked dreadful. Maybe she shouldn't have nixed the makeup. But she wasn't here to look good. Or to give a *performance*. What then? If only she knew. If only there was something *she* could read off the TelePrompTer.

Emma was concluding her prepared introduction. "Sarah Rosen is here tonight because, enraged and overcome by the senseless, savage murder of her sister, she feels a desperate need to speak out. To speak out to the killer himself. To speak directly to—Romeo. I'm sure all of you out there applaud her courage. I know I do." Emma glanced over at her, smiled supportively. "Sarah—"

Suddenly, Sarah found herself staring into the blank TelePrompTer of the camera now close on her, its Cyclops red light beaming. The set was totally silent.

She folded her hands, damp palms together, on the desk. Then she slipped them back down to her lap. A glance at the monitor, and she saw that only her face now filled the screen. Even though Emma was, in real life, still sitting right next to her, Sarah felt as alone as she appeared to be on the TV screen.

She panicked. Should she run? And then she thought of Romeo. Sitting out there later tonight. Watching her when the show aired. Feeling so fucking proud of himself. Plotting his next depraved seduction. Had he already set it in motion? *Was he courting her? Was Wagner right? Melanie hadn't been enough for him? He had to have her sister, too?*

Her fist slammed down on the desk. "You're depraved!" Sarah rasped into the camera. "The lowest scum of the earth. Do you even know it? Do you know what a monstrous creature you are?" Her cheeks were hot, her throat constricted. "My sister was on to you, wasn't she? She saw through that phony front that those other poor

women you slaughtered couldn't see. That's why you had
to kill her, isn't it? Because she got too close. Because she
knew what you really are. Because you were afraid you'd
finally be exposed, you coward! And what about me? Am I
getting too close as well?" Sarah was shaking with rage. "It
can't go on! You've got to be stopped! Coward . . . coward—" Now both fists came down on the desk. She just
kept banging. Even as they cut to a station break.

Wagner stopped Sarah as she headed for the exit door
from the studio.

"Are you okay?" he asked.

"Pretty pointless, huh?" Sarah was embarrassed and
drained by her on-air outburst.

He smiled. "No. It was powerful. Like Emma said,
cathartic if nothing else."

"The catharsis hasn't hit yet." But Wagner's warm
smile made her feel a drop better.

"Let me give you a lift home," he offered.

Sarah backed off. She didn't feel that much better. "I
have my car." *Don't crowd me, Wagner. I've got enough on
my plate without you to deal with.*

"Sarah, don't close me out. I want to help you."

"Like you helped Melanie?" she shot back at him, the
anger springing up from that never-empty well inside her.
Jabbing each word. Like sticking pins in a voodoo doll.
"What do you think? Practice'll make perfect?"

He let out a weary sigh. "We want him stopped, too,
Sarah."

She felt herself being tugged apart. This was too
much. Despite all she was going through, she couldn't
dismiss a rumbling undercurrent of attraction toward Michael Wagner. Not that she imagined it going anywhere.
She'd never let that happen.

But before she could recover, the receptionist slid
open her window and called out, "Miss Rosen. Someone
called from your office and left a message for you."

Puzzled, Sarah went over and got it. Glancing from the note to Wagner she saw his clear concern. He obviously thought Romeo had already responded to her outburst. "It's from Bernie. A guy I work with," she told him. "Why don't you go ahead? Something must have come up at the office."

"You sure you don't want me to wait? Walk you to your car?"

"It's broad daylight, for God's sake. People all around. I really don't think Romeo's going to leap out of a doorway and carry me off."

"I know you still don't think he's behind those *special deliveries,* Sarah. But just so you also know, we're not taking any chances. I've arranged for a twenty-four-hour watch on you. One of our boys will be parked at your building when you get there. You are going straight home from here?"

"Yes."

"Okay. I'll drop by your place a little later. To pick up that locket."

Sarah was in the middle of dialing her office number on the wall phone when she remembered that the locket was actually in her car. But Wagner was already out the door. Oh well, she'd give it to him when he came over later.

Bernie picked up on the second ring. "Thank God you called back, Sarah."

"What is it? What's wrong?"

"Where are you?"

"I'm still at the TV station. Bernie, you sound so upset. You're scaring me."

"Well, that makes two of us. Something came in the office mail today. Actually, it was with the mail, but there was no postmark on it. Don't ask me how it got slipped into the pile."

"What? What was it?" Sarah's tone drew the young receptionist's attention. She turned her back to her.

"It looked like your typical condolence card. You've

gotten quite a few. Only this one was addressed to you care of me. So—so I opened it. Sarah, it was a valentine. A red heart."

Sarah had to lean against the counter for support. "What . . . did it say?"

"There was one line. It said—*'Did you look inside the locket?'*" He hesitated. "And then—at the bottom . . . *'Romeo.'*"

She shut her eyes—dizzy. Like she was fast losing altitude. When she crashed, she wouldn't hit earth but collapse, instead, into the outstretched arms of a madman. *How could she have been so naive? Stupid, stupid girl. You never know what's coming.*

Bernie was practically hyperventilating on the other end of the line. "What locket? What's going on, Sarah? I called the cops. After I stopped shaking. I spoke to that Detective Allegro. He's sending someone right over here for this note. Sarah—what the hell is going on?"

By the time Sarah stumbled out of KFRN and made it to the parking lot around the corner, she was shaking so badly, she could feel the tremors in her fingertips, the soles of her feet, her scalp.

She leaned heavily against the passenger-side door before opening it, trying to catch her breath and swallow down her panic at the same time. She shook her head violently. He had started this. If she fell apart now, he'd finish it.

Yanking open the car door, she flung herself onto the passenger seat, her eyes fixed on the glove compartment. She felt queasy. Remembered that she hadn't eaten any lunch. When had she last eaten? She couldn't remember.

Open the glove compartment, Sarah. You were gutsy enough when you were staring at that camera. Yeah, but that was before you really believed this was Romeo's doing. Come on, come on. Didn't you really know all along? Why do you always lie to yourself?

She didn't see the locket on first sight. What if he'd already come and taken it? Where would it turn up next? Was he wooing her or driving her crazy? Was there any difference?

Frantically shoving papers, wrappers, and other crap aside, she finally spotted the locket. The gold heart. *Taking on life. Throbbing. Odoriferous. Oh God—*

"Sarah."

She was so startled to hear her name, she nearly hit the inside roof of her car.

"You!" she gasped.

Wagner bent down, gave her a close scrutiny, his expression uncharacteristically tender.

Sarah found it almost painful to look at him. She returned her gaze to the locket in the glove compartment. She went to reach for it, but he grabbed her wrist. Then he pulled out a tissue from his pocket and carefully retrieved the small locket. "It's got to be dusted for prints."

"It's from him. I know that now." Her voice sounded alien. She wished it didn't belong to her. No, she wished she didn't belong to it; could escape it. Escape everything. *You are your mother's child. And don't you forget it.*

"I know," Wagner said soberly. "I just spoke to Allegro on my car phone. He told me about the note your friend Bernie got. I was hoping I'd catch you here. I knew you'd be . . . upset."

Her eyes shifted from Wagner to the locket in his hand. "There's . . . something inside."

That information had been relayed to him already. What remained to be seen was *what* was inside.

He was still watching her closely. "You want to do this now?"

Sarah couldn't tear her gaze from the little gleam of gold in the tissue. The locket was no longer a mere trinket. Some crackpot's bizarre joke. It could have been her own heart lying there in the palm of Wagner's hand. And yet the amputated organ still pounded painfully inside her chest.

"Open it," she commanded him raspily.

Without a word, Wagner pulled out a second tissue from his pocket. He slipped the catch on the locket and opened it.

Sarah thought she was prepared, but when she saw what was there, tears stung her eyes. On the right side of the heart was a miniature photo of Melanie. Melanie as a beautiful vibrant teenager. Smiling brightly for the camera. Looking radiant. Full of life. Sarah immediately recognized the shot. It was from Melanie's high school yearbook.

And the photo on the left side of the heart? Sarah recognized that one, too. A sad-looking little girl. Eyes downcast. A grimace on her lips. She remembered precisely when that picture of her had been taken. Right after one of her humiliating dance recitals—

"Smile, Sarah."

"I'm trying, Daddy. I'm trying." A child's voice thick with desperation.

Bernie showed up at Sarah's door twenty minutes after she got home from the station. At first she thought he'd come over to make sure she was okay. But one good look at his strained expression, and she knew that was wishful thinking. *Oh, what she wouldn't give for some wishful thinking that turned out to be real.*

"What happened? Don't tell me I got more—mail."

Bernie raised his eyes to the ceiling. "It doesn't rain, but it storms."

Sarah shot him a bleak, drained look. *How many more terrible things would there be before this nightmare ended?* "What is it?"

"Dr. Feldman called me at the office five minutes after I hung up with you. I tried to call you back, but you'd already left the station."

"Feldman called you?"

"Looking for you. Unfortunately, he chose this day to tell your father about your sister. He wants you to get right over to the nursing home. He said he'd wait for you there."

Sarah didn't move. She felt incapable of moving. She had to force herself just to breathe.

"I'll drive you."

She shook her head.

"I wasn't asking permission," Bernie said firmly.

A flicker of a smile graced her lips. "I love you, Bernie."

"I know that, sweet stuff."

Wagner watched his partner pace agitatedly up and down the aisle between the rows of squad-room desks.

"I don't like it," Allegro grumbled.

"Which part?"

Allegro threw him a look. He was ripping mad. "Any of it. All of it. How could you let her go on that goddamn show?"

"What did you want me to do? Arrest her?" Wagner snapped. "What's the crime? Anyway, she thought it was some crackpot until—"

"We should bring her in and read her the riot act. Withholding evidence, obstructing justice—"

"Shit, John. That's not going to work with her. It'll only make her hold back more from us."

Allegro snatched up the plastic Baggie containing the heart-shaped note and the envelope it had come in. "No postmark. No one down there at state rehab has a clue how it got mixed in with the regular mail. I left Corky there to question every single person in the building." He looked with disgust down at the locket in its own plastic pouch. "You think there'll be more?"

"Don't you?" Wagner said grimly.

Allegro was staring at the locket. "Did Sarah say where he got the photos?"

"She's pretty sure the one of the doc is from her high school yearbook. Cut from a group photo of the lacrosse team or debating team or swim team. The doc was a team player. I've already sent one of the boys back to her place on Scott to see if he could track the yearbook down."

"Odds are, Romeo swiped it," Allegro said. "What about the one of Sarah?"

Wagner shrugged. "From the family album. Also presumably at the doc's place. No albums there now, as far as we know. But if we don't succeed at first—"

Allegro motioned to one of the uniformed cops who'd just walked into the squad room. "Miller. Get this stuff over to forensics. Tell 'em we want something on this shit *yesterday*." His voice was savage.

Wagner watched as Miller took the items from him, gave a little nod, and took off.

"Maybe we'll get lucky this time out," Wagner said.

"Right. And maybe fucking hell'll freeze over." Allegro threw open the Melanie Rosen case binder. Flipped to the Lab Notes section toward the back of the thick book. Right on top were the latest reports from the crime lab and the medical examiner. "We've got squat. No prints here either. No bloody drips or tracks, even though he's got to be covered with the stuff."

"Could be he's naked when he does 'em. Or has a change of clothes, shoes handy." Wagner perched on the corner of his partner's desk.

Allegro kept reading the report. "Sperm sample confirms same blood type as the others. DNA workup's gonna take a few weeks, but it'll be a match—bet on it. So we know it's still one doer. Now all we need is to find the fuck."

"I still think Perry's our best shot. Anything new come in on him?"

"*Nada*. No connection with the other victims that they could dig up. They showed Perry's photo around, but no takers. We may be off on the wrong track."

"Who else? Assuming it's someone we know the doc knew. And quite possibly someone Sarah knows, too."

"There's always the doc's ex. Could be he had this demented scheme for offing his wife, and the others before her were just to throw us off the track."

"How would that explain his little communiqués to her sister?"

"Maybe he's just your everyday psycho in shrink's clothes."

Wagner smiled faintly. "You don't like him much, do you?"

"Do you?" Allegro countered harshly.

Wagner's smile broadened. "Not much."

"Then again, we're not talking a personality contest here," Allegro said.

"No question Dennison's a real sharp cookie. And you know the old saying, John. Every cookie crumbles. Eventually."

Allegro laughed harshly. "Eventually, huh? Yeah, tell that to Sarah Rosen. I'm sure she'll find that real comforting."

"I've put a round-the-clock on her." Wagner popped a cigarette into his mouth and lit it, a few feet away from the no-smoking sign nailed to the squad-room wall.

Allegro walked over to the coffeemaker, grimaced at the grimy pot. "I guess that's about all we can do until he makes his next move on her."

"Sarah's a real tough number to figure out." Wagner paused, idly shuffling reports on his desk. "In some ways she's a lot like her sister."

"She's a mess. How's she like Melanie?"

"I'm not sure if I can put my finger on it. Funny, the first time I met Sarah, I thought she and the doc were complete opposites. Appearancewise, certainly. Personalities, too. There's this hard edge about Sarah. But she's almost working *too* hard on it. Like inside she's going in all directions at once. The doc, on the other hand, always seemed to know exactly what she was doing and why. Cool, clear-headed, take-charge."

"So far I don't see the similarities," Allegro deadpanned.

"Yeah, I don't know that Sarah does either. She pictures herself as the loser, her sister the big success. But Sarah surprises you. Well, she surprises me. Just when you think she's finally gonna fold, next thing you know she's popping out into the center of the ring, swinging for all she's worth. Maybe she's not going to win, but she's not going down without a fight."

Allegro poured himself a cup of the morning's left-over sludge.

"I have this feeling about the two sisters," Wagner said slowly.

"What's that?" Allegro tossed a heaping tablespoon of sugar into the muck, thinking he'd like to add a few shots of whiskey to it, too.

"Don't laugh," Wagner said, "but the only way I can put it is that they both seem to be more than the sum of their parts."

Allegro raised a shaggy brow. "You mean they don't add up?"

Wagner nodded slowly, then grinned. "Hey, I was a philosophy major in college. What do you want?"

Allegro sat back at his desk, brought the mug to his mouth, and drank the overly sweet, stale coffee without noticing how lousy it tasted. He reached for the task force's Romeo file. Flipped to the section marked "Victims," his gaze drifting to the series of crime scene photos of Romeo's five victims grouped together on one page.

Diane Corbett, Romeo's first known victim. April 22. Her photo was in the upper-right-hand corner. A tall, athletically built lawyer who specialized in bankruptcies. Found in her Green Street apartment by her landlady, she'd been dead at least forty-eight hours. Jennifer Hall's picture was beside Diane's. A curvy blond stockbroker whose friends all described her as a real "go-getter." Her husband of ten years was the one who discovered her mutilated body. He'd come home a day early from a business trip to surprise his wife on her birthday. Jennifer Hall turned thirty on June 9. That date got to be engraved twice on her tombstone.

Karen Austin's photo was right under Diane's. Romeo's third victim, she was a reed-thin redhead with freckles everywhere. A financial adviser for a firm on Union Square. Her boss "thought the world of her." She'd just gotten a big promotion. The whole office had celebrated two days before she was killed. August 21.

Then came Margaret Anne Beiner, the pretty, petite, brunette sociology professor, murdered September 16. You could see the crystal wineglasses and the untouched pork roast on the dining table in the far corner of the photo. And the bloodstained knife she'd intended for carving the meat.

And finally there was Melanie. The obscene shot of her ravaged body on that blood-drenched caramel-colored sofa. Melanie Rosen's photo was the only one Allegro couldn't bring himself to linger on.

He shut the book, his mind going back to that evening late last February when he'd gone to her office to discuss his wife's extended hospital commitment—

> He's in a chair across from her, legs crossed, trying to conceal the bulge in his trousers as she sits behind her desk.
> "Will you visit her while she's there?" she asks.
> "I wasn't planning—that is, we are separated."
> Melanie rises from her chair, comes around her desk, leans against it. He's disturbingly aware of her flowery perfume, her long, lovely legs crossed at the ankles. He feels his prick thickening up even more. Starting to ache.
> "I think it will be best for both of you if you don't go and see her."

He smiles, relieved. Now he doesn't even have to feel guilty. Just following doctor's orders.

She smiles back. Like she knows what he's thinking. Not just about Grace.

"Are you hungry, John?"

A cruising glance at him, the smile still there. Caught and returned. "I'm not much of a cook, but it'll taste good. I promise."

Beads of sweat. Fuck. Spell it out, why don't you? "Is it—kosher?"

"Are you Jewish?" Her tone faintly mocking.

He's not sure she isn't setting him up—that this isn't some sort of test. Like she wants to see for herself if John Allegro is the shitty husband his wife surely made him out to be.

She makes no move, letting him think it over, but he knows that she knows she's already won. Not like he thinks he's on the losing end of the deal by any stretch of the imagination.

He follows her upstairs, enjoying the seductive swing of her hips as she precedes him.

She deposits him in the living room, brings him a whiskey without even asking first if he wants one. She knows. She sits down beside him on the sofa, watching him drink it in one long gulp. Then she takes the glass from him.

She's staring blatantly at his crotch now, and he feels both turned on and uneasy. She's got the edge here. She's in control. There's a part of him that's pissed. Not as big as the part of him that's burning up inside.

Her lips are parted. She murmurs something. He can't hear. He has to move closer.

She says it again, whispering it in his ear. This time he hears her loud and clear.

■   ■   ■

Sarah and Bernie were stuck in a bottleneck on the Bay Bridge. He was gaping at her. "Sarah, you're crazy."

"So what else is new?"

"Why didn't you tell me that maniac wrote to you?" he demanded. "Sent you gifts—"

"Gift. Only the locket. So far. And I am telling you. Before this afternoon, I didn't know who'd sent them."

"But going on that television show. Challenging him. Do you realize what you're getting yourself into?"

"What choice is the bastard giving me?"

Bernie seemed at his wit's end. "And you think confronting him on the air isn't going to make the whole situation worse?"

"Don't you get it? I'm in it up to my ears already." Sarah didn't mean to take her anger out on Bernie, but she welcomed the emotion back, praying it would keep her mounting hysteria under wraps. "I'm thinking of going on again, if you must know," she added defiantly. *Turn the pursuer into the pursued.*

"You're all worked up, not thinking straight. I'm not going to argue with you now. I'll trust that those detectives will see to it that you don't go sticking your neck—"

"Those detectives? Allegro? Wagner? They're less than worthless. Five women are dead, Bernie. One of them is my sister. And it looks like Romeo's planning on making me number six unless I . . . do something," she finished desperately.

Bernie's sigh was heavy with exasperation and apprehension. "Sarah, I'm not going to have a single worry-free moment from now on—until this animal is caught. Will you at least move into my place for the time being? Thinking of you alone in your rat hole of an apartment—"

"Check your rearview mirror."

"Huh?"

"See that black sedan two cars behind us?"

Bernie angled the mirror. "Yeah."

"He's been following us since we left the house."

Bernie blanched. "You don't think—"

"Relax. It's a cop. I've got a full-time bodyguard, courtesy of the SFPD. So you don't have to worry about me."

"I still wish you'd stay at my place. I've got plenty of room. And it would give you a chance to get to know Tony."

"Don't tell me. He's already moved in?"

"You're so cynical when it comes to love, Sarah."

"I won't argue with you there, Bernie."

Thanks to the heavy traffic, it was well past six when they got to the Bellevista Lodge. Bernie rolled his wheelchair up the ramp into the main building with Sarah a few feet behind him.

How had her father taken the news of his beloved Melanie's death? Would he blame her? Accuse her? Wasn't everything always her fault in the end? Hadn't her failure as a daughter, a sister, brought on all this tragedy? If she'd been less defensive, less jealous, reached out more, couldn't she have somehow saved Melanie?

"If you didn't spend every waking minute thinking only about yourself, Sarah," her father says tightly, "this never would have happened."

She is ten years old, and she is standing inside the door of her father's den in their Mill Valley house.

"I didn't mean—"

"You never mean," he cuts her off. "Nonetheless, your sister now has a cast on her arm."

"I didn't break her arm," she mutters truculently. "She fell off her bike."

"Did you or did you not pester your sister to bike over to your friend Lily's house—"

"Bonnie."

"What?"

"Bonnie. Not Lily. I left Gordo at Bonnie's

house." *Gordo is her favorite stuffed animal—a gangly-armed monkey with matted mud-brown fur. Sleeps with him every night. Drags him around with her. Her father tells her that it is time to wean herself from her transitional object. She wishes he wouldn't call her beloved Gordo a transitional object. She hates it when he uses his psychiatrist words on her.* Narcissistic, anal retentive, passive-aggressive. *She doesn't know what any of them mean. All she knows is they always make her feel ashamed.*

He pins her down with that accusatory stare. She squeezes her legs together. Not just because they're shaking but because she suddenly has to go. What would he do to her if she made wee-wee on his beautiful Persian rug?

"I thought we had a long discussion only a few weeks ago, Sarah, about my preferring that you did not spend time with Bonnie."

"I haven't really." She tries to defend herself. "I hardly ever see her."

"That brother of hers is nothing but a trouble-maker."

He's talking about Bonnie's fourteen-year-old brother, Steve. Sarah has a crush on Steve. She stupidly told Bonnie. Bonnie'd giggled and said, "Too late. Your sister's already got dibs on him."

She wants to tell her father that she didn't have to pester Melanie to bike over to Bonnie's house. It was a great excuse for her sister to get to see Steve. But she can't tell that to her father. He'll be even angrier. And then Melanie will be angry at her, too. Very angry.

"Sarah, you're not listening to a word I'm saying."

At first she thought it was her father's voice. Then she realized the tone was no longer harsh and judgmental. It rang with concern. Bernie's voice. He was holding open the door to the rest home. She'd come to a full stop a few feet away. Like someone had spread Krazy Glue on the soles of her sandals and she was stuck to the spot.

"You don't have to do this, you know," he said softly.

She shook her head. "It's not that. It's just—God, Bernie, things are—coming back to me. . . ."

"What things?"

She dropped her hands to her sides, tried for a smile. "Flashes from the past." Bernie knew all about her limited recall of her childhood—her *amnesia*.

"Bad stuff?"

"Is there any other kind?"

Feldman was waiting for her in the lobby this time. He popped out of a chair as soon as they entered. Sarah could see from Feldman's expression that he hadn't anticipated she'd bring someone with her. Another ex-patient at that. When Bernie was struggling through his master's degree, he'd had a bout of depression, and some shrink at a drop-in clinic had wanted to put him on Prozac. Given Bernie's history of drug dependency, he was scared stiff to take the stuff. So he decided to get a second opinion from a big-wig. He chose Dr. Stanley Feldman, of all the shrinks there were to choose from in a city with a glut of them. To give her ex-shrink his due, Sarah had to concede he was able to help Bernie through that rough time with a brief period of crisis intervention and without having to put him on meds.

"How is he?" Sarah asked the psychiatrist immediately after Bernie and Feldman exchanged a subdued greeting.

"Let's talk in the doctors' lounge," Feldman said. "Bernie, why don't you get a soda or something? There's a little café down the hall on the left. Sarah will meet you back here."

Bernie shot Sarah a look.

She gave him a faint nod, and he wheeled himself off.

Feldman led Sarah in the opposite direction, back to the Woodruff Room, where they'd had that fracas last Friday. Was it really only six days ago? It felt like a lifetime to Sarah.

There was a goateed physician reading the paper in there, but as soon as he made eye contact with Feldman, he set the paper down, rose, and exited without a word.

"Well?"

Feldman motioned to the chair vacated by the doctor. Sarah sat down this time without arguing. Feldman took a seat across from her.

"Well?" she pressed, hating how shrinks always took their own sweet time. Part of their *shtick.* Keep the basket cases squirming. Heighten their anxiety. The more on edge the better. Break down their resistance.

She had to remind herself she wasn't a patient. Anymore.

"Your father overheard two of the nurses talking this morning," Feldman said impassively. "Melanie's name was mentioned, and from what I could gather, there was some reference made about what a terrible thing it was that had happened. No details were spoken, fortunately. Your father confronted them, and they attempted to cover up, telling him it wasn't his daughter Melanie that they were talking about. But his disease is such that paranoia plays a key role—"

"How was it paranoia?" Sarah retorted. "Those nurses *were* talking about his daughter. He wasn't being paranoid."

Feldman smiled faintly. "It's rare I've seen you ever come to your father's defense."

"I'm not defending him," she said acerbically. "I'm challenging you."

"Ah," he said with one of his sage nods.

"Go on," she snapped, loathing that knowing look of his. That was another thing about shrinks. You could never just say something and that was it. Everything got analyzed, dissected, interpreted. Used against you. It was that way with Feldman—her father—Melanie.

"Your father became quite agitated. He struck one of the nurses."

Sarah squeezed her hands together. An image flashed in her head—a hand coming at her—but she erased it instantly. *Did old shrewd eyes notice? Wouldn't let on if he did. Poker-faced to the bitter end.*

"I was called," he continued. "By the time I got here, Simon had calmed down. He was finishing his lunch, and when I walked over to his table in the dining hall, he recognized me immediately. I decided that it would be risky to delay telling him any longer. Even though those nurses had received serious reprimands—"

"Jesus, Feldman, for a Freudian you sure do a lot of talking."

"I assumed you'd want all the details," he said calmly. "I told your father shortly after he finished his lunch. We went back to his suite, sat together in his sitting room and —I told him." Feldman bowed his head and paused for a moment like he was saying a silent prayer.

Sarah felt light-headed. Still hadn't eaten anything. Still no appetite. Maybe she'd just melt away. *That would cheat Romeo, all right.*

Feldman lifted his head. Something wavered across his face—sorrow? Regret? Pity? For whom? Her father? Melanie? Himself? Her? She knew better than to ask him. Ask a shrink a question like that, and all he'd do was twist it around and throw it back in your face.

"How did he . . . take the news?" she asked instead.

"This happened to be one of his more lucid periods. Still, he had trouble at first absorbing it," Feldman went on slowly, his accent seeming to grow thicker. A lump in his throat? "He got to his feet, walked over to a framed photo of Melanie he keeps on his desk. I think you know the one. She must have been seventeen or eighteen at the time. She's on your father's sailboat, at the wheel. One hand pitched over her eyes shielding them from the sun. She looks so lovely in that shot—so full of life."

Yes. All Melanie's pictures were full of life. Until Romeo stole her picture. Her heart. Her life.

"I know the one. He took it that summer after Melanie graduated," Sarah said tonelessly. He'd kept the gold-framed photo on his desk at his office at Scott Street, and he'd brought it—as well as a number of other favorites—all of Melanie—with him to the rest home. As far as Sarah knew, he'd brought none of her along. None that he kept on display, anyway.

Feldman sighed. "Your father held the photo up to the light almost as if it were an X ray, stared at it, and then quite suddenly broke down and sobbed. We sat together for a time. I poured him a glass of iced tea, he drank it. Calmed down some. Wanted to take a walk around the grounds. I joined him. He stopped after about ten minutes and sank down onto a bench, asked me if it was really true that she was gone. I simply told him yes."

Sarah said nothing. Feldman nodded. "We returned from our walk, and he sat down in the solarium. Picked up a book he'd been reading. I stayed with him. Twenty minutes later, he put the book down, called out to a nurse who was attending to another patient nearby, and asked her if Melanie had arrived yet. He wanted to know why she was so late."

Tears slipped down Feldman's acne-scarred face. A reminder, once again, that he was human after all. Or was this a trick? If she saw him break down a little, maybe she'd risk it, too. *Wrong, Feldman.*

He quickly took out a linen handkerchief from the breast pocket of his ill-fitting blue serge jacket and blew his nose.

"We all shed our tears," he said softly.

As if that were all that could be done. As if tragedy were merely something you cried over and that somehow absolved you. Saved you. *Surely Melanie had cried that hideous night—*

"—some paranoid ideation," Feldman was saying. "Thinking the nurses were deliberately keeping him from seeing her. He became quite belligerent."

Sarah wasn't listening. Romeo had wedged himself firmly in her head. Working his way down.

Feldman stopped abruptly, keenly scrutinizing her. "You're very pale, Sarah. Let me assure you, your father is not in any physical danger."

Well, that exempts one Rosen, anyway.

"I gave him something to settle him down, and he slept. He awoke a couple of hours ago. The instant he saw me, he started to cry like a child. Remembering. He'll forget again. And then it will come back, most likely only for brief moments. It's going to be that way for a while."

Sarah felt terribly disoriented. Wanting to confide in Feldman, tell him her fears, her secrets. Wanting him to soothe her, comfort her, take her in his arms. The desire struck a discordant note—

She's rushing into Feldman's waiting room. Sees his door ajar. Relieved to hear faint voices from his office. She'd been afraid he'd gone for the day. Her appointment isn't until Wednesday. But she can't wait. She's had a dreadful fight with her father. The worst since she's been home from college. Terrible, ugly things were said. And then he slapped her. Hard. Across the face.

She hopes the redness from that slap is still visible on her cheek. See, Feldman. See what a monster my father is. Is it any wonder I hate him?

She hesitates near the psychiatrist's door. Who's he talking to? Not a patient or his door would be firmly shut. And then she recognizes the voice of Feldman's visitor. It's Melanie.

Bet he likes her better. Bet she doesn't keep secrets from him. Bet she's *his* favorite, too.

Silence now. What's going on in there?

She peeks in through the crack. Sees them.

Feldman and her sister. Entwined in each other's arms. Hears him murmur, "Melanie."

She races out of the waiting room. Fighting for breath on the street. People passing by staring at her. She dashes into an alley and pukes.

"Are you feeling sick, Sarah?"

"What?"

"You're clutching your stomach," Feldman said.

She immediately dropped her hand to her lap.

"What exactly did you tell my father about how Melanie died?" Sarah asked, refusing to be the focus of this encounter.

"Only that there'd been a terrible accident, and that her death was instantaneous. He didn't ask me for any details. Unlikely that he will. Too much already for him to absorb, considering both his mental and physical condition."

"You mean his heart?"

Feldman nodded. "He's being monitored, but thank God, so far, so good."

"He'll probably outlive us all." Sarah felt the dizziness set in again. Continuing her free fall. Hard to breathe. Spinning. Nothing to grab on to.

Feldman gripped her arm. The dizziness stopped instantly, replaced by an even more disturbing sensation of exhilaration.

He quickly released his hold on her, even stepped back. Like she might take another swing at him.

"You should be seeing someone for grief work, Sarah," he said with his special brand of subdued persuasiveness. "It's only making it worse for you to hold everything inside."

And what about you, Feldman? What about everything you're holding inside?

"He wants to see you, Sarah."

She heard Feldman's voice but not what he said.

"Your father, Sarah," Feldman said. "He's been asking

for you since he woke from his nap. Do you feel up to seeing him now?"

"You're sure it's me he asked for?"

"You're all he has left, Sarah."

She laughed harshly. "Ironic, isn't it, that it's me he's stuck with in the end?"

Feldman sighed sadly. "Sarah, Sarah. Make peace with him. For your sake, if not for his. Your father may have been a brilliant and distinguished analyst, but do not imagine for an instant that I am blind to Simon's faults as a parent. I know he always favored Melanie. That you lived in your sister's shadow for a long, long time. That when you lost your mother, you felt betrayed and abandoned because you saw her as your only ally. That you've tried desperately to bury all the pain and the hurt you felt growing up because you were terrified those feelings would destroy you. But what's happening now, Sarah, is that all of those emotions are bubbling to the surface. You're feeling very vulnerable now, and to make matter's worse, your complex defense systems aren't working for you."

"I'm holding my own."

Feldman dismissed her lie with a shake of his head. "Had it not been for this terrible tragedy, you might have gone on as you were, blocking out your past—denying the truth."

She rolled her eyes.

Feldman was unswayed. "What truth, you may ask."

"I didn't ask," she said dryly.

"The truth that you are not escaping your past, Sarah. You're trapped in it. You can't let go."

"Is the sermon over, Father Feldman?"

"You can't let go until you know what it is you're letting go of."

"Is that the crap you told Melanie? To let go? Did you know what it was she needed to let go of, Feldman? Did you know what she kept locked inside of her?" It was all Sarah could do not to hurl herself at him again.

"We're not talking about Melanie."

"No, but we're both thinking about Melanie. Because *neither* of us can let go of Melanie, can we, Feldman?" It wasn't a question, it was an accusation.

Feldman could have tried to plead not guilty. But he didn't.

Her father was in the parlor of his suite, in an armchair by the window overlooking the sweep of meticulously manicured gardens. Sarah's first thought on seeing him after little less than one week was that he seemed to have physically shrunk. His features were gaunt, his shoulders slumped, his arms hanging limply over the sides of the chair.

Then she saw the heart monitor he was hooked up to.

When she closed the door, he continued staring out the window, not turning to see who had entered even though she cleared her throat so he would know he was no longer alone.

"Dad?"

He didn't answer her.

She hesitated near the door.

"You wanted to see me, Dad?"

"It's cloudy out."

She glanced out the window. "Yes."

"Do you think it's going to rain?"

"I think it might."

"You always argued about putting on a raincoat when it rained."

"I still don't wear one."

"Remember that bright yellow slicker?"

Sarah wrinkled her brow, trying to remember. A bright yellow slicker? Yes, she could picture it. Like the one worn by Maine fishermen.

"That was Melanie's," she said in a hushed voice.

"Yes. Melanie's," her father echoed.

Melanie's name hung in the air. He turned and

looked at her. His eyes, so like Melanie's in both shape and color, even in intensity. "Is she really dead, Sarah?"

A muscle in her cheek jumped. She wanted to run over to him, bury her head in his lap, and—and what? Beg him not to blame her for being the one to survive? Beg him to love her instead? Beg him to let Melanie's death bring them closer together?

Feldman's exhortation reverberated in her head. *"You're all he has left, Sarah."*

But what about me? Who's left for me?

"I asked you a question."

The sharpness of her father's voice startled her.

She immediately felt weak, her knees wobbly. "Yes. Yes, Melanie's dead." No anger in her tone, no sorrow, no passion. *Feel nothing. Safer that way. Much safer.*

He looked away again, staring out the window. She'd expected wailing, thrashing about, fury, despair. It wouldn't have surprised her to see him leap from his chair and attack her. *Your fault. Your fault. You never listen. You never do anything right.*

To her surprise—dismay?—he didn't budge. He didn't even seem aware that she was still there. Was that it? Was her presence no longer required? Far be it from her to overstay her *welcome.* She reached for the doorknob.

"I think it's raining now," he said in a flat voice.

She stopped in her tracks, looked back over her shoulder. Raindrops splashed on the glass. "Yes."

She saw his eyes close. She felt a shudder of alarm. What if he were having a heart attack? No. He was being monitored. If anything were wrong, a doctor would come running.

She started toward the door.

"Don't forget."

Her father's voice stopped her midstep.

"Your yellow slicker. In the hall closet."

Sarah sighed. For her, release came from eradicating the past. For her father, it came from clinging to it.

"Good night, Dad."

"And close the door quietly, Melanie. You don't want to wake your mother."

Romeo's unable to find appropriate outlets for his anger, sexual desire, fears. He can't control them; they control him. But he's adept at keeping that hidden. He revels in his duplicity.

Dr. Melanie Rosen
Cutting Edge

11

She's in a field of daffodils. A man comes up be-
hind her, plucks one of the yellow flowers, puts it in
her hair. The sun is in her eyes as she turns. But
she can make out his smile. She's so happy. She
cannot remember feeling so happy.

"Lie down with me," he says seductively, "and
I'll tell you my secrets."

His large, comforting hand touches her shoul-
der. She finds her body letting go, sinking, falling.
To her horror she slams down onto something hard
and cold. Metal. Gray metal. Gray everywhere.

Where is she?

And then she knows. A morgue. Gray metal
slabs circle her. Trapping her.

She is naked, shriveled like a prune. He is pin-
ning her down, flattening one breast so that it dis-
appears under his big dirty hand.

Oh God, not dirty. Bloody. It's covered in
blood. The only color in the gray room. So red.

Can't see his features in the shadows, but the
menace emanates from them, curling around her.

"Tell me your secrets, Sarah."

Liar. Never intended to tell her his secrets. Only wants hers. But, if she gives them to him he will destroy her.

His mouth is at her breast. Slowly, he draws in her nipple between his hot, moist lips.

Ooh. Feels good. The anchor of fear begins to lift. He doesn't mean to harm her.

Can't feel the cold metal now. Only warmth. Mmm. Nice. Nothing to be scared of, silly.

"More?" he asks. So considerate. So generous.

"Yes, please." So polite. So aroused.

He smiles. The faceless man with the big, friendly smile.

And then the shock of pain. Excruciating. Her whole body writhing with the agony of it.

He has bitten her nipple off.

And he doesn't stop there. He is munching away at the tissue of her breast, gnawing right through the bone—

A muted sound. Faint banging. At first Sarah thought the disturbance was part of her dream, but then she realized she was awake. In a panic, she yanked up her nightshirt, checking her breasts. Nipples still there. She inspected for tooth marks. The nightmare was too real and even more gruesome and lurid than the ones preceding it. Especially as it had started so well, lulling her into a false sense of well-being.

The banging continued. Now she realized someone was knocking on her door. Probably a goddamn journalist. She covered her ears. She wouldn't answer.

The knocking didn't stop. Then she heard her neighbor, Vickie, shouting to her from the other side of the door.

"Sarah, if you don't open up, I'm going to call the cops!"

Drawn and disheveled, Sarah reluctantly made her way to her front door and unlocked it.

"I heard you screaming. You scared the bejesus out of me." Vickie standing there. Hands on his hips. Skin-tight black velvet jeans. Metal-studded leather belt. Scooped neck, bright pink fuzzy angora sweater.

Sarah frowned. Screaming? She'd been screaming?

"A—bad dream," she mumbled, looking away. "What time is it anyway?"

"A quarter after eleven. A.M."

Sarah looked surprised.

"Now you tell me what day it is?" Vickie challenged.

Sarah smiled sardonically, but it was really a delay tactic. She had to think. Oh God, Thursday. It was Thursday. The one-week anniversary of Melanie's murder.

Vickie wagged a manicured finger at her. Today his nails were painted a fluorescent pink to match his sweater. "You look awful."

Sarah's hand absently moved to her chest. Feeling achy. "I think I'm coming down with the flu or something. . . ."

"I saw you on that show last night. It was positively heartwrenching." Vickie put his fingers on his ruby lips and flushed. "I'm sorry. That was so—so tactless. But you know what I mean, Sarah."

"Yes."

"Look, sweetie, I'm not a shrink, but I really think it won't do you any good, holing up here in your apartment, brooding. Let me take you out for lunch. Well, brunch. Whatever. I'm afraid you'll have to borrow one of my suits again. Now that you're a TV star, the reporters are parked on our doorstep again."

"Shit."

"No problem. We fooled them before. Come on next door, and I'll help you get decked out."

"No, I can't keep avoiding them. I'll just give them a brief statement. Make them happy."

"That's right. Tell it like it is. So where do you want to go for lunch? My treat."

"I can't."

"Why not?"

"I've got this client I really need to check on." Sarah thought of Hector Sanchez. He'd called her at home last night. After *Cutting Edge* had aired. She hadn't picked up, but it was obvious from the message he left that he was anxious and disturbed.

"I'm busting my buns begging you to get your feet wet, and you turn around and decide to jump right off the high diving board. Really, Sarah, I don't think you want to start back to work so soon."

"Vickie, you've been a big help. Work's the very thing I need now. Honestly. Getting back into my routine. Putting—putting this all behind me."

Putting it behind her. That was a laugh! There was no routine, no *anything* as long as Romeo was on the loose.

The plainclothesman outside Sarah's building did his best to keep her from being trampled by the press, but he was no match for them. They bombarded her with sly questions, poked her with microphones, shoved camcorders in her face.

"Why'd you appear on *Cutting Edge*?"

"How close were you and Melanie?"

"Do you know who Romeo is?"

"Are you going on TV again?"

"Will you be making the rounds of the talk shows?"

"Did Melanie tell you anything?"

"Do you really think Romeo picked Melanie because she was on to him?"

"Are you working with the cops now?"

"Do you feel this is a personal mission?"

Sarah faced them coldly. Her features were like stone. "All I can say is—all I'm going to say is—next time it won't be so easy. I just want Romeo to know that. I want him to know there is one of us he can't seduce."

■   ■   ■

Sarah got to Hector Sanchez's studio a little past noon, only to find that he wasn't home. She considered driving over to her office, but she didn't feel ready to face the sea of curiosity-seekers and well-wishers at rehab quite yet. Instead, she took a long walk, stopped in a coffee shop, and ordered a cup of coffee. Then, realizing she did have to make an effort to eat something, she added a corn muffin to her order. When it came, she managed to take only a few bites of it. Washed down with her mug of coffee and two refills.

At around one-fifteen, she headed resolutely back over to the artist's studio. At least he wouldn't be able to see what a mess she was.

She forgot about the acuity of Sanchez's other senses. She'd barely managed a hello before the artist was on the alert.

"You're not doing so good, Sarah."

Sarah had to smile at her client's canny remark. "I knew dropping by to see you today would cheer me right up, Hector." She glanced around the studio looking for the seascape Sanchez had painted.

"It's gone."

Sarah laughed. "What is this? Second sight?"

"Vibrations," he told her with a crooked grin.

She shuddered.

"Seriously, Sarah. I'm real sorry about your sister. And when I saw you—well, heard you anyway—on that show last night, I broke down and cried."

"How'd you know I'd be on?" She heard the paranoia in her voice and softened it. "I didn't think you went in much for TV."

"I don't usually. But ever since your sister—well, I've been keeping an ear on the news. Hoping, I guess, to hear that they caught him. Supposedly, the cops are saying they're checking out several important leads."

"They don't confide in me," Sarah said tersely.

His voice softened. "This must be torture for you, Sarah."

"That about says it."

"Wanna do a little pot? Might help you some."

"I'm your rehab counselor, Hector. I don't do pot with my clients. I don't do pot, period. And you're supposed to be staying clean, too."

"You need some vices, Sarah."

She laughed harshly.

"Okay, if I can't offer you some first-rate pot, how about a cup of java? It'll have to be instant, though. My espresso maker's on the fritz."

"No, thanks. I'm javaed out. How about telling me what Arkin said about your seascape?"

Sanchez smirked. "That's my big surprise for you. He took the thing off my hands not thirty minutes ago. After telling me I was the best fucking blind artist he'd ever come across. Jeez, I wonder how many other fucking blind artists the guy knows."

"What Arkin's telling you, you jerk, is that he thinks you're a *great* artist. Oh, Hector, that is fantastic news."

"Yeah, yeah," Sanchez conceded. "Hey, he even took me out for lunch. I told him to order me the most expensive dish on the menu." He snapped his fingers. "Jeez, I'm so blown away by everything that's happened, I almost forgot." He moved with ease across the room he knew by heart, picking up a rectangular package from the waist-high counter that divided the painting studio from his living area. "Arkin found this lying on the floor outside my door. With your name on it. Can you believe that?"

Sarah froze.

Sanchez gave the box a little shake. "Sounds like candies. What do ya think? Maybe one of my neighbors's got a crush on you. There's this dude across the way who's got a hot new babe over there every other day. If it's him, forget it. He's not your type. Funny, though. Arriving today. Like lover boy knew you'd be showing up." Sanchez held the plain-brown-paper-wrapped package out to her. "Well, you gonna take it? Find out if there's a card inside? 'Cause if you're waiting for me to read it to ya, Rosen—"

She didn't say a word, didn't make a move. Couldn't.

"Hey, Sarah. That was a joke. What's going on? What's wrong?" His tone switched from teasing to anxious.

She just kept staring at the package Sanchez was waving in the air.

"Sarah, you're spooking me. Say something."

She stepped a little closer, still not able to bring herself to touch the thing. But she saw the label pasted on the front of it. Her name computer-printed across it. Same Helvetica font as his letter.

"You gonna take it, Sarah? What? You think it's a bomb or something?"

Yeah, it's a bomb all right.

She snatched the parcel from his hand. Then she sank onto his wooden stool a few feet away.

"Sarah, I'm really worried about you."

"Nothing to worry about. I'm okay." She tried her best to sound as if she meant it. She wouldn't start dragging her clients into her personal hell.

"Hey, I'm not stupid." Sanchez found his way over to her, took hold of her arm. "Come on, Sarah. Talk to me. Let me help you. You gotta know how I feel about you. And don't give me any of that crap about me being your client. Hey, I'm about to become a world-famous artist, babe. I won't be needing your services anymore. As a counselor, anyway."

Sarah clutched the package in her hand. Hard to breathe. As if Romeo were sucking the air right out of her. Telling her he was here. He was everywhere. There was no escaping his demented seduction. No matter where she went—what she did—how many cops they had watching over her—he was determined to worm his way to her heart.

"I'm sorry I had to put you off until this afternoon, gentlemen." Bill Dennison's voice was clipped and formal as he stepped out of his Chestnut Street consulting room and greeted the detectives in the waiting room. Like Melanie's reception area, the decor here was neutrally attractive—the requisite magazines on the end tables, the comfortable, well-spaced upholstered chairs, even similar Japanese prints on the wall. Wagner had commented to Allegro while they were waiting that maybe the two shrinks had shopped at the same art gallery.

"This has been a devastating time for me," the psychiatrist went on. "I'm still reeling from the shock of it." In contrast to Dennison's emotional language, both cops noticed that the handsome, immaculately attired psychiatrist looked quite composed.

"All the more reason," Wagner remarked, "that you'll want to cooperate with us in any way possible."

"That goes without saying," Dennison said emphatically, gesturing for them to step into his office.

"No couch," Allegro commented as he surveyed the traditionally styled room, a cherry Queen Anne desk tucked into one corner, four brown leather camelback armchairs resting on a russet, blue, and cream Persian carpet in a circle facing the center.

Dennison smiled. "I'm not a psychoanalyst, just your garden variety shrink. I prefer looking my patients right in the eye."

Funny, Allegro thought, since the shrink wasn't making great eye contact with him. Maybe it was something he reserved strictly for his paying customers.

"Why don't we get straight down to business," Wagner broke in officiously.

Dennison was most apologetic. "Yes, of course. I would have gladly given you more time if I could. But I've had to squeeze in all the patients I had to cancel first because of the funeral, and then, naturally, it took me the early part of this week just to pull myself together enough to see anyone. Including a few of Melanie's patients. It takes so much concentration. I feel if I can't give myself fully—"

"You happen to catch your ex-sister-in-law on the tube last night?" Allegro interrupted.

"On television? Sarah? What on earth—"

"She sent a message to Romeo on that show *Cutting Edge*."

Dennison stared at Allegro in disbelief. "My God. And you let her? After Melanie—" He sank down in one of the leather chairs. He pressed his fingers against his temples, then brought his hands down to his lap. Allegro noticed he was wearing a thick gold wedding band.

Wagner leaned forward. "Have you gone through Dr. Rosen's case files, Doc?"

Dennison sighed. "I assume you're particularly interested in the records on Robert Perry. I must tell you, so am I. I saw him at nine this morning for an evaluation. He's in very bad shape."

"What does that mean?" Wagner asked.

Dennison hesitated. "I can't breach patient-doctor confidentiality. Even telling you I saw him—" He threw up his hands. "This is an impossible situation."

"You may be treating a serial killer, Doc," Allegro said soberly.

"You may be treating the psycho that killed your ex-wife," Wagner added, with an edge.

Dennison heaved a sigh. "Don't you think I know that? Don't you think I dissected every word, every gesture, every expression on the man's face while he sat right there in that seat?"

"And what did you conclude?"

Dennison eyed Wagner. "There's no question that Perry displays an abnormal—even a pathological—transference to Melanie."

"He told you they were lovers?" Allegro asked. His face was pale.

The psychiatrist looked away. "Patients often fantasize. . . ."

Wagner stretched out his legs, crossed them at the ankles. "It isn't always fantasy though, is it, Doc? Shrinks have been known to—" He knew he didn't have to finish the sentence.

Dennison gave him a cold look. "We're talking about one of the most respected psychiatrists in this community. Oh, I know you read in the paper all the time about unethical therapists sleeping with their patients, but as far as Melanie is concerned, I can assure you she would never breach one of the most sacrosanct rules of the profession. Utterly unthinkable. So you can skip any further questions in that arena, gentlemen."

The two cops shared a knowing look. Just as they'd predicted.

"What did it say in her records on Perry?" Wagner kept his voice deliberately laconic. "Did she discuss Perry's *fantasies* about being her lover?"

"That's just it," Dennison said icily. "There aren't any."

Wagner leaned forward in his chair. "Fantasies?"

"Records."

"Are you telling us she didn't keep any records on Perry?"

Dennison shook his head. "I find that hard to believe, Detective. Melanie was meticulous about taking notes on patients. Extensive, detailed notes. She had a wonderful gift for writing. Melanie always strove to be the best in everything she did. If Perry's file isn't there, it's because someone wiped it out. Perry himself might have gained access to it, or—"

"Are you saying you think Perry killed Dr. Rosen?" Wagner asked.

"I'm raising it as a possibility. You obviously have strong reason to be suspicious. On the other hand, he could have managed to gain access to his record sometime prior to Melanie's murder. I understand his wife's filing for divorce. He may have been worried she'd subpoena his therapy records. He told me she's accused him of stalking her." He paused briefly. "Of course, someone else could have erased the file."

"Someone else?" Wagner asked.

"Romeo, Detective. Romeo could have scanned through her files after . . . murdering her, seen Perry as a likely candidate, and figured erasing his file would make him your prime suspect. As Melanie remarked to me on more than one occasion, Romeo clearly enjoys throwing the police off track." Dennison half smiled. "But I'm sure you've already figured that out yourselves."

There was a chilly silence.

"What about her other patients?" Allegro asked curtly.

"I've gone through the rest of her current cases. The records appear to be completely up to date and untampered with. I can tell you that nothing about any of these individuals raised my suspicions that one of them might be a serial killer. I also took a look at the files on the patients she terminated during this past year. She kept them all on her hard drive. Again, nothing troubling." His gaze rested on Allegro. "Obviously I can't be sure other files weren't wiped out as well as Perry's."

Allegro had to make a concerted effort not to squirm. Did Dennison know about Grace? Had Melanie consulted with him about her? Had his risky effort to conceal his wife's treatment been a waste?

"It will take some time to check the patients on file against the names in her appointment book to see if all are present and accounted for," Dennison went on.

He now looked from one cop to the other. "A time-consuming and, at the moment, an impossible task since all I have is Melanie's daily calendar sheet, and that only covered this past month. I looked for her appointment book in her office yesterday when I was finally allowed admittance, but I couldn't track it down. The officer who accompanied me inside didn't know anything about it. Told me to ask you. Was the appointment book confiscated by your people?"

Wagner looked over at Allegro. "You see it?"

Allegro shook his head. "No. All I saw was that calendar sheet." Silently, he cursed the day his wife had sought Melanie's help. If Melanie hadn't treated her, he wouldn't have had to mess up the investigation by stealing that appointment book with Grace's visits in it. And, he'd discovered to his chagrin, a record of his solo visit to Melanie's office right before his wife's commitment.

Wagner tapped a cigarette out of a pack of Camels, saw Dennison frown, and got the message. He popped the cigarette into his pocket. "I can see why Perry might destroy his file if it contained incriminating evidence, but why swipe the appointment book?"

"Maybe it also contained notations of personal appointments. Like for the night she was murdered," Dennison suggested.

"Are you going to treat Perry?" Allegro asked.

The psychiatrist hesitated. "I'm torn. Even the thought that I might be treating the man who did this to Melanie—" For the first time, Dennison lost his composure. His lower lip started to quiver; he shielded his face with his hands.

"I'm sorry," he mumbled.

"Yeah," Allegro said.

Dennison slowly lowered his hands from his face. Again, his gaze focused on Allegro. "We were going to take another shot at it, Melanie and I."

"A shot at what?"

"At marriage, obviously. We were talking quite seriously about it."

There was absolute silence in the room.

Dennison rose abruptly, checking his watch. "I'm afraid I have to be over at the Institute for a conference in fifteen minutes. Anyway, there's nothing more I can tell you, gentlemen."

"There is more one more thing," Allegro said, rising. Dennison was already at the door, clearly eager to show them out.

"What's that?" the psychiatrist asked impatiently.

"Where were you on the night Melanie was murdered?"

Dennison's composed features darkened. He glared at Allegro. "Melanie? And did she call you John? On those nights you so gallantly gave her lifts home from the Hall of Justice?" He bared his teeth without smiling. "She was out of your league, Detective."

Allegro stiffened. Wagner had to step between them to keep his partner from slugging the shrink.

"You didn't answer the question, Doc," Wagner said. "Where were you last Thursday evening? Maybe you dropped by your ex-wife's place that night to *discuss* the wedding plans. Only maybe she changed her mind. Or maybe you just had the *fantasy* that the two of you were going to get back together again. Tell me something, Doc. What happens when the rug gets pulled right out from under a fantasy? Couldn't it make someone go berserk?"

"You want to play shrink, Detective, I suggest you take a few advanced classes in abnormal psychology. First of all, I wasn't suffering from a fantasy that Melanie and I were going to get married again. Less than two weeks before she was murdered, we had dinner over at Costa's, a restaurant down on the Embarcadero—one of our favorites—and we talked to the manager about a date for a wedding reception in one of their private rooms sometime next month. They were booked, but they thought they might get a cancellation, and they were going to get back to us."

His gaze shot over to Allegro, a faint smile of victory on his lips. "You can check with Marc Santinello. He's the manager at Costa's."

Allegro added it to his notes.

"Secondly," Dennison said, "on Thursday night I was attending a seminar at the Institute. That's the Bay Area Psychoanalytic Institute. Dr. George Ephardt was lecturing on the diagnosis and treatment of sexual dysfunctions. It started at seven, but I had an emergency call, so I got there a bit late."

"How late?" Allegro asked.

Dennison's nostrils flared. He wasn't enjoying this interrogation. "I'd say it was about seven forty-five," he said with forced evenness. "The lecture ended at nine-thirty. Then there was a video that ran about a half hour, after which there were questions and answers. We broke a little after eleven."

Wagner opened his mouth to follow up.

"No, I didn't ask any questions," Dennison said, beating Wagner to the punch. "Afterward, I joined a few of my colleagues for coffee. There's a little coffee bar directly across from the Institute. Figaro's. You can confirm that with Stanley Feldman."

Allegro arched a brow. "So Dr. Feldman was at the lecture, too?"

Dennison nodded. "I assume so. He was the one who arranged for Ephardt to speak. I admit I didn't actually see him until we all gathered at Figaro's, but he certainly participated in our lively discussion about the lecture. If you'd like the names of the other psychiatrists who joined us, or the waitress who served us—"

"We'd like the names of the people you sat next to at this seminar," Allegro said. His face was still grim.

Dennison hesitated. "I didn't really pay attention. I was in the back on the aisle. There was a woman on my right, furiously taking notes. Very absorbed in the lecture. I didn't know her."

"Can you describe her?" Allegro asked.

Dennison pursed his lips. "Blond. Young." A brief pause. "Very nice legs." He gave the detectives a sheepish smile, but it only lasted for an instant before he turned appropriately solemn.

"Anyone else who saw you there during the seminar?" Allegro tapped the pad with his pen. "Once it got rolling? Once you were sitting on that aisle seat way in the back?"

A muscle twitched in Dennison's jaw. "I'll have to give it some thought."

"You do that," Allegro told him.

"For chrissake, you can't honestly think I'm this madman," Dennison exploded. "Even if you could somehow imagine a scenario where I might kill my ex-wife, what the hell reason would I have had for killing those other poor women? Don't tell me you think I had the *fantasy* of marrying all of them, too?"

Allegro's lip curled. "You're the shrink, Doc. You're the one who knows all about *fantasies*."

Sarah left Sanchez's studio swiftly, got into her car, and drove off. The plainclothesman, parked at the curb eating his lunch, hurriedly tossed aside his sandwich, started his engine, and took off after her.

Twenty minutes later, Sarah found herself in Chinatown. Pulling carelessly into a spot, she began walking through the crowded streets, ending up on Waverly Place, a busy narrow alley that ran parallel to Grant Street. She was halfway down the bustling market area when she came to a rather nondescript building. She stopped in her tracks. A jolt of déjà vu. Vague. No solid recollection of having ever been there before, yet a certainty that she had. A long time ago. The hurting time. The time she'd been so successful at burying. Or so she'd thought.

She spotted the long narrow stairway just beyond the open door, the small sign posted outside. Yes, she was beginning to remember. The field trip to Chinatown with her seventh-grade class. A few months after her mother's death. Not long after their move to Scott Street.

Her classmates are pouring into the souvenir shops and odd-smelling little bakeries. She's bored, so she wanders off, finds herself on Waverly Place. Sees the sign on a building indicating a Buddhist temple upstairs. Her curiosity peaks.

At first, the vivid colors overwhelm her. The gleaming black lacquer, the gold enamel, and especially all the bright red paint on the altar.

She takes in a deep breath. Smells nice. Reminds her of the eucalyptus trees around her old house in Mill Valley. Another family lives there now. Another shrink, his wife, two young daughters. Eerie. Like clones.

She sits on one of the red silk floor cushions. In a minute the tears begin to flow. No sound escapes, but her lips are moving. She is not offering a prayer. She is begging for forgiveness. But she knows no one is listening.

The memory dissolved, and Sarah found herself once again climbing up those steep stairs to the temple on the second floor.

She'd thought it odd that first time to find a house of worship, especially one so splendid, situated above a shop. She'd even commented on it to the Chinese man who'd allowed her admittance to the sanctuary.

Here we are closer to nirvana, he'd told her. She'd liked that answer.

She pressed the buzzer as she'd done on that day so long ago. What had compelled her to be so bold then or now, she couldn't say for sure. A need for sanctuary? A yearning to escape into another world? A secret daring?

A diminutive Chinese man with a scraggly wisp of a goatee, a thinning pate of silvery hair and a loose-fitting black linen jacket and trousers opened the door.

"Would it be all right—?"

He nodded, motioning her to come in, then disappearing through a rear door moments later.

The temple was precisely as she remembered it. Tears flooded Sarah's eyes. The large plain room with its piercing red, gold, and black lacquer paint, the incense that smelled like eucalyptus burning at the exquisitely carved altars. The red cushions on the floor. Such simplicity and serenity. Such a contrast from the ramshackle exterior of the building.

She could be safe here.

After sitting quietly for only-the-gods-knew how long, Sarah took the package from her tote, steeling herself.

She tore off the wrapping. Hector had been right. A box of candies. Expensive ones at that, the top of the box sheathed in shiny gold foil. She lifted the lid.

Chocolates. In six neat little rows. In the shape of hearts.

Sarah's own heart rammed against her chest.

There was more. A sheet of paper folded in quarters on top of the chocolates. She gritted her teeth as she unfolded the communiqué. This time she wouldn't be stupid enough to rip it up.

Only this wasn't another *love letter* from Romeo. This was a photocopy of a page from what looked to be a personal diary. Sarah instantly recognized the handwriting on the page. It was Melanie's.

She stared down at the sheet. Not seeing the words. Not wanting to see the words. Black lines on a white page. Blood pounded in her ears.

These are Melanie's private thoughts. He stole them from her. I shouldn't read this. I don't want to read this.

There was really no question, though, that she would. That she had to. As Romeo had to have known she would.

Sometimes I imagine you coming up behind me when I'm doing my face in front of the bathroom mirror. I'm naked, putting on some lipstick. You grab me and hoist one of my legs up roughly, my foot going right into the basin. You bend me over so that my lipsticked mouth is pressed right up against the mirror clouded now with my hot breath and a red smear as you take me violently, slamming me into the sink as you ride me.

Sarah had to stop. Her heart was pumping wildly. And she was appalled to realize that her nipples were hard. That, for all its repugnance, her sister's masochistic fantasy had aroused her. And in doing so, horrified her.

She forced herself to resume reading.

> It is the cruelty, real or perceived, blatant or subtle, that is the driving force that propels me—that I find irresistible, intoxicating. I arm myself with rationalizations, justifications. I put it down to primitive need. I need the release, or else the pressures build and I'm afraid one day I'll explode. But all the time I am thinking—is anyone on to me—do they suspect? I fear discovery, but I'm so good at the game. I'm always so good at the game.
>
> Of course, there's Sarah. I am my sister's keeper as she is mine. Lucky for me she doesn't know it.

I am my sister's keeper as she is mine. Yes, Sarah thought. It was true. She and Melanie were linked by more than blood. She couldn't fully grasp what that link was—was not at all sure she wanted to—but she could not turn away from its existence. And from the stark understanding that was now so clear. To understand Melanie was to understand herself—to peel away her sister's layers was to expose her own.

Sarah could feel memories long buried beginning not only to take shape but to inflate inside of her. The prayer room was spinning, the piercing colors of the temple merging, melting into gray. Everything gray. Gray like that awful morgue in her dream.

The fragrant scent of incense vanished. Obliterated by the smells of gardenias and talc, and that ephemeral but repellently sweet medicinal odor that used to make her wrinkle up her nose in displeasure. Like overripe fruit turning rancid.

You know, Sarah. You know what that smell's all about. You remember, a voice whispered in her head.

She takes in a deep breath. She can smell it clearly now. That special peach liquor Mommy likes so much. In that amber bottle—squat at the bottom with a long tapered neck. There are so many bottles. Tucked away in Mommy's secret hiding places.

She's home early from school. Melanie's off playing lacrosse. Daddy's at work. She's hoping she and Mommy can garden.

She stands in the hall at the bottom of the stairs. Calling out. No response. She trudges up the stairs. Mommy's sprawled on her bed, eyes shut, her long blond hair all tangled and matted.

She sees the empty amber bottle on the floor beside the bed. She picks it up, leaves the house and buries the bottle deep inside the trash can out back. I'll never tell, Mommy. I'll never tell. I promise, Mommy. I can keep a secret.

When Sarah opened her eyes again, she half expected to still be entwined in the memory. She looked around the temple to reorient herself, grateful to find that the room had stopped spinning. She straightened in her seat, only then remembering the sheet of paper that had fallen to the floor. She picked it up and stared at the deeply troubling passage from her sister's diary—and at the long-buried images that were starting to surface.

The keys are beginning to turn, Melanie. Is this what you feared? And Romeo—is this what you wanted? To make me revisit all the pain and heartache of my past? To drag me back to hell so I won't have the strength to fight you?

Her hand jerked. The box of chocolates fell off her lap, tipping over. Another sheet of paper spilled out as well.

Romeo's postscript—

My sweet Sarah,
    Can you feel my warm breath, Sarah? Can you feel my adoration and devotion? Can you

feel my tongue wending its way in all your hot, moist crevices? Making you burn up inside? Initiating you to the exquisite pleasures only I can give you? I know what you're suffering. What you need. I know you're saving yourself for me. Because only I can understand.

Be patient, Sarah. It's only a matter of time.

Soon, Romeo

P.S. You looked beautiful on television. But not nearly as beautiful as you look in the flesh.

An overwhelming sensation—malignant, loathsome, perverse—tore through Sarah. She began to sweat. There was a terrible tugging in her groin. Romeo's questions became more than grotesque words on a piece of paper. *Can you feel my tongue wending its way in all your hot, moist crevices? . . . Initiating you to the exquisite pleasures only I can give you?*

She could hear the monster's cunning, seductive voice, feel his vile imprint on her flesh. Worse, feel him pervading her very being. No question about it now. Melanie hadn't been enough for him. She should have known. Hadn't she?

A shuffling sound behind her made her gasp. She spun in time to spot a shadowy figure slipping out the door of the temple. The light streaming in from the hallway outside made it impossible to see who it was. But she felt a shaft of ice inside. *It's only a matter of time.*

Someone had been there, watching her. Her police bodyguard? No, he wouldn't have snuck off like that.

Romeo?

She sprang up from the floor cushion and raced out of the temple. *Get him. Get him before he gets me.*

But when Sarah hit the alley teeming with pedestrians, she faltered. Who was she looking for? How would she ever spot him? Was it even someone she would recognize? Someone she knew? Or was she imagining things? It could have been nothing more than a local worshipper up there.

And where the hell was that cop when she needed him? Had he spotted Romeo, too? Gone after the killer himself?

She kept on searching the crowds, brushing past Asian-Americans with their grocery carts and shopping bags, many with little children in hand. No one seemed to notice her. Frustrated and irritated with herself for having been so spooked, she was beginning to buy that this was a case of her runaway imagination.

And then she saw a familiar face in the crowd. Her heart nearly stopped. There—ducking into a Chinese herbalist shop diagonally across the street from where she stood.

Sarah dashed across the narrow street, missing a delivery boy on a motorbike by a hairsbreadth. An elderly woman with wispy gray hair, bundled in a threadbare black wool coat, scolded her as she got to the other side. Sarah was oblivious.

A bell tinkled as she burst breathless through the door of the shop, its shelves lined with huge jars of exotic herbs, an altar behind the counter lit by red candles.

At first she didn't see him. Was there a back entrance? Had he already ducked out? Was he leading her on a wild-goose chase? Or worse—into a trap?

Then he stepped out from one of the aisles and leisurely idled up to the counter that ran along the far wall of the shop. His back was to her, but he turned to face her as soon as she shut the door, the bell above it jingling again.

Perry smiled hollowly, without any expression of surprise at seeing her. Like he was expecting her. Wanting her to find him. He was wearing worn blue jeans and red hightop sneakers. A brown leather bomber jacket over a black T-shirt. His blond hair looked as if it had been combed with his fingers. Except for the casual attire and that he needed a shave badly, he appeared much like he had at Melanie's funeral. Bereft. Little boy lost.

He placed a hand to his forehead. "I've been having these terrible headaches," he said as if she had asked. "There's a Chinese herb that I've heard can do wonders."

The Asian druggist who stood behind the counter smiled obligingly, turning to remove a jar with a hand-written Chinese label from a shelf behind him. He took a scoopful of dried-out greenish flakes from the jar and slipped them into a small brown paper bag, then set it on the counter for his customer. Perry picked the bag up. "How much?"

"One dollar and forty-nine cents," the clerk replied with a thick Chinese accent.

"A bargain, don't you think?" Perry asked Sarah.

"If it works," she heard herself saying.

Perry paid in quarters, left the penny change on the counter, and crossed to the door, where Sarah remained rooted to the spot.

"Do you like plump buns?"

Sarah was speechless at what she took to be both a ludicrous as well as a blatantly lascivious question.

"The pork buns at Li John's are the best. We're not that far."

A laugh spurted out of Sarah's lips.

Perry looked wounded.

"Why are you following me?" she demanded. If he'd followed her here, why not earlier that day to Sanchez's studio? Giving him ample opportunity to leave that package in front of her client's door while Sanchez was out having lunch with Arkin. Had he been trailing her since Melanie's murder? He could have been lurking in the shadows when she went to see Sanchez last Friday morning. Saturday to Scott Street. Sunday, she saw him at the funeral. But had Perry been near her apartment earlier that day? Had he gone by her car, left that demented *gift* on the dashboard?

Perry leaned toward her. She recoiled.

"I was just going to open the door for you." There was a hurt expression on his face. "If you don't want to get something to eat, we could go sit down on a bench or something and talk."

She nodded. Yes, talk. As long as they stayed out in the open, what could he do to her? And if she managed to get anything out of him—anything incriminating—she'd get him arrested.

He opened the door. She motioned for him to go first. Staying on guard. Watching her back. Protecting her *buns*!

Perry stopped at a water fountain, tapped some of the herbal headache remedy into the cup of his hand, filled it with water, and swallowed it down, grimacing. Then he joined Sarah on a bench in Portsmouth Square, which was little more than a small grassy knoll built over an underground garage on Clay Street on the edge of Chinatown. Close by, elderly Chinese men were playing mah-jongg at bridge tables. The click of their tiles mingled with the squeals of the children romping in the bright yellow and red pagoda-style playground behind them.

"Have you been following me all day?" she demanded.

"No. No, I haven't been following you at all. I couldn't believe it when I saw you going up to that temple. In fact, I was so sure I was imagining things, I went up there to see—"

"You just happened to be here in Chinatown?" Sarah said sourly.

"Yeah. Just like you happened to be here. Maybe it's fate."

That wasn't what Sarah would have called it.

"I have been wanting to talk to you." Perry rested his hands flat on his knees, his sneakered feet planted several inches apart on the ground. He was staring down at them, head bent. "I was going to wait—you know—until a little more time had passed."

"What did you want to talk to me about?" Sarah asked in somewhat the same careful, guarded tone she used to use with her father and Melanie.

His expression was a study in earnestness as he lifted his head and looked at her. "About Melanie, naturally. I think about her all the time. She didn't deserve this."

Was he saying that those other poor women did? That anyone did?

He stared at her intently. "I never even knew she had a sister until I read about you in the papers." His lips quivered. "Then I saw you at her funeral and on TV last night. Don't think this is awful of me, Sarah, but it helped knowing you're in as much pain as I am. It's something we can share."

We're soul mates. . . .

She could see the sooty hollows under Perry's eyes. The naive expression on his handsome boyish face, arrestingly pale.

"You can't imagine how much I miss Melanie," he continued. "She made everything feel so right. Not just the sex part. Do you know what I mean?" He gave her a strange private smile.

Sarah felt sick inside. She nodded.

Perry accepted her gesture as permission to explain. "She took away the anger and the shame. She taught me not to be anxious."

"How often were you—with her?" Melanie wouldn't have been the first shrink to screw a patient, but she'd always given the impression that her professional life was sacred. Then again, things weren't always as they seemed, to quote Emma Margolis.

Perry smiled guilelessly. "You mean how often did we make love? Not as often as I would have liked."

Robert Perry's ingenuousness repulsed and fascinated Sarah. Was he putting her on? Was this the *chameleon* in top form?

Perry lightly massaged his temples. "Mmm. My headache's going away. Those herbs really do work." He looked off in the distance, his hands pressed together now as if in prayer. "I visit her grave every day. To be close to her and to—to force myself to accept that it's real. That she's really gone."

He shut his eyes; tears started to stream down his cheeks. Sitting there in the early afternoon sunshine, his blond hair glistening, his head bowed, sorrow etched in all his features, he made a very poignant figure. A superb con job?

"It wasn't Melanie that awful morning," he said in a strained whisper. "That's what I kept telling myself over and over when I—when I saw her. It was such a nightmare. I'll never get the image out of my head."

"No," Sarah said in a low voice. "I don't suppose you will."

A blanket of silence fell over them both. Sarah gazed off at the mah-jongg players.

He shifted around uneasily. "The cops think I did it. They made me come down to Homicide. They wanted to know my blood type. When I said I didn't know, they asked if I'd take a blood test. They even asked if I'd volunteer to jerk off into some goddamn jar so they could have my sperm analyzed. I would have done it. Just to get their asses off my back. But my lawyer said no way. Not unless they were going to press charges against me, which they can't do because they have nothing to stick me with. I wasn't anywhere near Melanie's place the night she was killed." His agitation was escalating, his face reddening, his eyes wild.

"And I never knew any of those other women. I'm not some freak," he snarled. His ferocity jarred Sarah. "I'm just a guy trying to find my way. And Melanie was my guide. Now—now I'm lost."

Whether or not Robert Perry was Romeo, there was no question in her mind that the man was unstable. No question of why he'd been in therapy. Only a question of just what kind of *therapy* her sister had been administering.

Perry abruptly popped up from the bench. "I've got to go now, Sarah. But I want to thank you."

"Thank me?" Great. She was trying to get the goods on him, had come up with zip, and to top it off, he was thanking her.

He smiled winsomely. "I feel a little better. Talking about it helps. I wish Cindy would give me the same chance."

"Cindy?"

"My wife. We're . . . separated, but I'm hoping Dr. Dennison will help us get back together."

"You're seeing Dr. Dennison?"

"Oh, yes. I saw him this morning." His smile took on a wicked twist. "I feel it's what Melanie would have wanted me to do."

After Perry left her, Sarah drove straight from Chinatown to the Hall of Justice, to the Homicide squad room. The instant John Allegro saw her, he sprang out of his chair and rushed over.

"Why the hell did you give your bodyguard the slip in Chinatown?"

"I didn't give him the slip. He must have lost me. If you can't do any better—"

"Okay, okay. Let's not argue. We won't lose you again. That's a promise." His features were set.

Sarah surveyed the drab, fluorescent-lit squad room, lined with rows of desks. This was where Melanie had sat that last day. Where she'd seen her later that night on *Cutting Edge.* Her final glimpse of her sister.

"Sarah?"

Sarah shook her head to clear it, slipped her hand into her tote, and brought out the latest letter from Romeo. "There's a box of chocolate hearts, too. I left them behind at the temple." She gave him the location. As for the disturbing words from Melanie's diary, Sarah could see no purpose in sharing her sister's intimate, masochistic fantasies with Allegro. Or with anyone else, for that matter. It would be a terrible betrayal.

Allegro reached for a tissue from the box on a nearby desk and used it to gingerly grasp one edge of the sheet.

He read in silence, his features grim. When he was finished, he inspected the paper itself, then looked silently across at Sarah. As if he knew she was holding back on him. As if it showed. She turned her head away, feeling vulnerable and exposed. And guilty.

Such a familiar litany, she realized. Self-condemnation, self-recriminations. Years of it. A whole lifetime. Blaming herself. For what? For everything bad that had ever happened. And yet never remembering half of what the bad stuff was.

When I tell you that it hurts, you say the hurt is love. Inseparable. Inevitable. To lose that love—that pain—would be worse than death itself.

_____

M.R. diary

12

It was raining hard when Sarah pulled into a parking space across the street from her apartment building. As she stepped out of her car, she saw the unmarked police sedan that had followed her from the Hall of Justice pull into a space at the curb. The plainclothesman cut the engine and the lights, staying put behind the wheel. Allegro, who'd ridden shotgun, stepped out the passenger-side door.

"Hold on," he called out as she started to cross the street.

Sarah stood there in the rain, waiting for him to walk over.

"Give me a break, Allegro. I'm beat. You want to talk to me some more, talk to me tomorrow."

"You haven't eaten."

"I'm not hungry."

"Sure you are. So am I. What's good around here?"

"Nothing."

He glanced down the street at a storefront restaurant called Dos Amigos. "Mexican?"

"Get lost, Allegro."

"Yeah, I'm not wild about Mexican either. Me, I'm a

nut for Thai food. Could eat it three, four times a week. Maybe you know a good Thai spot? Nothing pricey. Neither of us is exactly rolling in dough."

"What? This is Dutch?"

He grinned. "Okay, Rosen. I'll treat. That make your day?" He gave a damn good imitation of Clint Eastwood's Dirty Harry. Looked the part, too, wet and scruffy.

She laughed. Now who would have thought anyone would extract a laugh from her that day?

"You're a smooth operator, Allegro. I never would have guessed."

"You sure know how to cut a fellow down."

"You're just getting your feet wet."

"You know what they say. If you can't stand the wet, get out of the rain."

They settled for a Vietnamese restaurant down the block, since it had started to rain even harder and neither one of them was dressed for the turn in the weather. The place was empty, and the young Vietnamese fellow who was holding down the fort, hoping to close up shop early, didn't look too thrilled to see a pair of customers walking in.

He showed them to the worst table in the place, right next to the swinging doors leading to the kitchen, slapped down a couple of menus onto their plates, and pulled out an order pad from his back pocket.

They'd barely glanced at their menus when he asked them if they knew what they wanted.

"Yeah," Allegro said. "I want you to get lost for about ten minutes, then come back for our order." There was a sharp contrast between the detective's easy smile and his biting tone.

The guy muttered something in Vietnamese under his breath as he stalked off.

"I don't think he likes you," Sarah said.

"Everyone can't be your friend, I guess."

She set the menu aside. "Was Melanie your friend?" she asked pointedly.

Allegro mulled her question over. "Not really."

"Could you be a little more ambiguous?"

"Let's say we were on friendly terms. How's that?"

"You mean you were screwing her."

"That's what *you* mean, Sarah. What I mean is that we had a decent rapport. We saw a lot of things the same way."

"Is that right?"

Allegro didn't much care for the way Sarah Rosen was eyeballing him. "I gather you and your sister saw most things differently."

Sarah shrugged off the question. "Why don't you just spit it out, Allegro? I took you for a no-bullshit kind of guy."

"Okay," he said. "I'm worried about you."

"I'm touched."

"Cut the crap, Sarah. I saw your debut performance on that show last night. What did it get you? Another sick mash note—"

"*Mash* note? You sure got a twisted perspective on romance, Detective."

"And a goddamned box of candies."

Sarah folded her arms across her chest. "Chocolate *hearts*."

His eyes were unreadable. "For starters, I'm nixing any more TV appearances."

"How do you know I was thinking of making any more appearances?"

Allegro gave her a long look before answering. "Because you want to follow in your sister's footsteps. Or think you need to."

The waiter started over to their table. Allegro's fierce glare stopped him in his tracks. He walked off again.

Sarah slapped her hands on the table. "You want him, don't you?" she challenged.

"Yeah, I want him," Allegro said. "And I'm going to nail him. Without your help."

"Bullshit. You haven't got a clue. You got nothing out of that letter he sent me the other day, or the locket, right? Or anything else, for that matter."

"We're making some headway," he hedged.

"If you were, you wouldn't be wasting your time trying to bribe me with a free meal that I don't even want."

"You're wrong."

"About which part?"

Allegro grinned. "Who doesn't want a free meal?"

"What about Perry? Are you going to pick him up?"

"We're going to question him again, that's for sure."

"Do you think it's him?"

He squinted at her. "Do you?"

"No. But I hope I'm wrong."

The food arrived within five minutes—barely warm. To Sarah's amazement, she was ravenous. Gobbled up several bites of a greenish chicken curry. Allegro didn't even taste his pork and noodle dish. He was watching her. Waiting.

After another bite, she set her chopsticks down. "I do think Perry was telling me the truth. About having some kind of sexual involvement with Melanie. You think so, too, don't you?"

"Maybe."

Sarah laughed dryly. "Come on, Detective. I give an inch, you give an inch."

He stared down at his untouched food. "Yeah," he said finally. "I think so, too."

"Change how you feel about her?"

He lifted his bleak gaze to Sarah's face. "No."

"You're not really surprised."

He rubbed the back of his hand across his dry lips. "No."

"Funny," she said, her turn to look away. "I sure as hell was."

She drained her glass of water, set it down, and downed half of his. He leaned toward her. "Talk to me, Sarah."

He didn't say it with a demanding tone. Maybe that was why she abruptly slid her plate away and said, "Let's get the hell out of here if we're gonna talk."

Allegro was already on his feet. "Yeah, the ambience is crummy." He couldn't comment on the food since he hadn't sampled so much as a bite of it.

Sarah let him grab hold of her hand as they ran down the street in the downpour. They were soaked by the time they got to her apartment. Corky, the cop on the four P.M. to midnight shift, took up position in the hallway outside her apartment door. Allegro brought him out a chair from Sarah's kitchen.

"You still have that bottle of Scotch lying around?" he called out to her when he came back inside.

Sarah stepped out of the bathroom and gave him a questioning look but nodded. "I'll dig it up in a minute."

She finished toweling off her hair, then tossed the towel over to Allegro—the only clean one she had left. Her pile of dirty laundry was oozing out of her hamper.

Allegro was slipping off his drenched suit jacket, looking for a place to dump it, when the towel landed at his feet.

She eyed the shoulder holster he was wearing, the gun tucked tidily inside it. She made no comment about his being armed.

"You can hang your jacket in the bathroom," she told him. "I'll hunt down that Scotch."

He retrieved the towel from the floor and headed for the bathroom while Sarah went off to the kitchen. She vaguely remembered that the booze was on a shelf in her broom closet.

A few minutes later, Allegro stepped out of the bathroom, running a pocket comb through his hair. Sarah was already in the living room. Pouring Scotch into a couple of juice glasses she'd scrounged out of the sink and rinsed out.

"I thought you didn't drink," he said.

"I don't. Usually. But these are unusual times." She took one of the nearly full glasses, handed him the other. "Let's skip the toast, okay?"

Allegro was working on a refill, Sarah nursing her first Dewars. They were sitting on her sofa. So far, their promised talk had not materialized. Sarah took a long swallow of her Scotch.

"Want me to top you off?" he asked, reaching for the bottle on the cluttered coffee table.

Sarah gave him a skewed look. "Trying to get me drunk, copper?" Half a juice glass of booze, and she was feeling the effects. A little light-headed. Woozy. Not unpleasantly so. Maybe it was the company.

His eyes met hers. "You can stop me anytime."

For some reason his response made her edgy. Shifted her out of her mellowing mood. Maybe she didn't believe that telling him—or any man—to stop *anything* counted for much.

His eyes were still on her. More unnerved, she set the glass down. He did the same with the bottle. And smiled, like he was showing her how well he read body language.

"What the hell do you want from me, Allegro?"

"What the hell do you have to offer?"

Where was the man coming from? What was he after? Neither his deadpan delivery nor his expression gave anything away. Sarah wasn't about to give anything away either. "Nothing," she countered defensively.

Allegro's glass was still half-full when he set it down on the table. Not a good time to get himself smashed, he decided. He already had plenty of a buzz on. He'd downed his first drink greedily.

"You know what you're getting yourself into," he said.

It was a pretty open-ended remark. Could mean a lot of things. Because she certainly felt that she was getting into a lot of things. "I think I do."

"Well, that makes one of us. You tell me what you hope to gain by picking up where your sister left off."

Her eyes shot to the detective. Talk about cryptic statements.

Allegro, too, realized there were several ways Sarah could interpret that remark. He smiled awkwardly. "I'm talking about you appearing on the TV show."

"I know what you're talking about," she lied. "And you're wrong. I'm not picking up where Melanie left off. I'm no shrink. I just want to let the bastard know in no uncertain terms that I'm not—"

"Not what? Not scared of him? Like hell you're not."

Sarah's features hardened. "Scared or not, he's coming. He's trying, in his inimitably warped fashion, to seduce me—"

"He's been damn good at it up to now."

"Which only makes him feel all the more powerful," she argued. "Well, I'm going to show him I'm powerful, too. Even more powerful."

"Going to show him? So you are planning a repeat television performance. Shit," Allegro cursed. "Don't I have enough problems here?"

"I'm not your problem," she snapped.

"The hell you aren't."

"Don't push me, Allegro. I've got to do this my way."

"Jesus. Any minute now you're gonna break into song."

She laughed harshly. "Believe me. The last thing in the world I feel like doing is singing."

He leaned in a little closer. He was getting too close—physically, emotionally. "The last thing in the world I feel like doing is finding your mangled body—"

"Stop!"

Allegro shuddered. "Sorry." He took another swig of Scotch, looked idly around. "You always live alone?"

"Changing the subject?"

"Yeah."

"I've had a couple of overnight guests now and again. Basically, I like my privacy."

He gave her a level look. "Don't you ever get lonely?"

Sarah decided that being with Allegro was like having a cavity filled, the dentist's drill hitting a nerve just as the Novocain was wearing off. She retrieved her glass of Scotch from the table, started to bring it to her lips without answering—liquor was an anesthetic, after all—but the detective capriciously snatched it from her hand.

"I really don't want you plastered," he said, returning her glass to the table.

"And I really don't want you on my case."

He half smiled, leaning back against the sofa, their shoulders almost, but not quite, brushing. "You got a boyfriend, Sarah?"

"You making a pass, Allegro?"

He grinned. "I'm making conversation."

"You're not too good at it."

"Yeah, I know," he said with surprisingly boyish candor.

Sarah found herself smiling even though there was no denying that Detective John Allegro was having an unsettling effect on her. Stirring up a vortex of dread and longing—she never seemed to manage one without the other. Probably why she always avoided situations like this one. Until tonight.

What the hell was going on with her? First she'd been attracted to Wagner, and now to Allegro. Great timing. Getting schoolgirl crushes while the psychopath who'd raped and murdered her sister was stalking her, sending her jewelry with pictures from her past, chocolate hearts, demented *mash* notes.

Then again, maybe it did make sense. She was feeling more vulnerable and alone than she had felt in years. And incredibly frightened. For all her fiercely held independence, she still desperately craved solace. A secret desire to be held, protected. Loved? No, that was going too far. Love was a manipulation. A lie. Lust was more honest. Lust only messed with your body, not your mind.

At least it wasn't hard for her to understand why she felt a physical attraction for Michael Wagner. He was sexy in a clean-cut way, age-appropriate as her sister might say. Might have *said*—

But John Allegro—at least ten years older if not closer to fifteen, shopworn, unpredictable, complicated, dangerously inquisitive. A man whom she imagined—much like herself—had his own long list of toxic miseries. Yet she couldn't shake the erotic charge he triggered. A shocker. Not only because of who'd evoked it but because that kind of feeling was rare for her, no matter whose finger was on the trigger. Yet there she was, not only feeling aroused but finding a sexual fantasy taking hold.

> *They're in her bedroom. No light. Tonight she isn't afraid of monsters lurking. He's there with her. Smiling tenderly. Telling her there's no hurry. Telling her they'll do only what she wants.*
>
> *And she believes him.*
>
> *As he slowly undresses her, he tells her how beautiful she is, how desirable, how sweet and pure and good—*
>
> *She's naked now, but not feeling exposed. This time it's different.*
>
> *She feels daring, even brazen, as she flicks the tip of her tongue over his nipples. He groans softly. The sound thrills her. She is even guiding his hand—*
>
> *Feldman's voice intrudes. Whispering psychoanalytic detritus—even now, when she's on the brink of fulfillment.*
>
> *"You're drawn to this man because you see*

*him as a father figure. This is not true attraction,
Sarah. It's merely transference. It is really your father's love and approval that you're seeking."*

*Sarah's pissed. Why must Feldman ruin every-
thing?*

"You married, Allegro?" The question popped out. *To hell
with transference.*

He smiled. John Allegro didn't look half bad when he
smiled. Took a few years off his face—softened some of
those hard edges. *Handsome and incredibly desirable, like
in her fantasy.*

"You thinking of proposing?" Now his smile was a
broad, calculated grin.

"No. I think you'd be a hard man to live with," she
answered with more honesty than she'd intended. Eradicating any lingering fragments of her sexual fantasy. Just
as well, she told herself. Fantasies had their dangers.

Allegro was jarred. He'd expected a snappy retort. Instead she was treading on some very touchy territory.

"My wife thought so, too." He reached for his drink.

Sarah didn't need to be a shrink to understand John
Allegro's hankering for booze at that particular juncture.

"Thought? As in past tense? Did you split up?" she
pressed, in part because she was curious, in part because
she much preferred playing offense to defense.

Allegro took a greedy swallow of the Scotch, then
cuffed the glass in his hands. "She's dead."

"I'm sorry."

Allegro nodded, the lines on his face deepening. He
stared down at what was left of his drink.

It felt to Sarah like the room had been suddenly
drained of air. "Death is a bitch. Any way it comes."

"Yeah."

"Do you want to talk about it?"

Allegro rubbed his hand slowly over his scruffy chin,

stirred despite himself by her tender tone. He hadn't really wanted to talk about this. Or had he?

His extended silence made Sarah uncomfortable. "Look, you don't have to—"

"Yeah, I'll talk about it. Why not?" The words started pouring out. "Grace jumped out of a seventh-story window in her apartment. Last April. We were separated at the time. She'd just been released from a six-week-long stay in a psychiatric hospital. It had supposedly gone quite well," he added acidly.

"So you're not a fan of psychiatric intervention either."

Allegro thought about Melanie. How could he not think about Melanie? "Shrinks help some people. The good ones."

"Shrinks or patients?"

He said nothing.

"You think Melanie was good?"

Allegro eyed her speculatively, not sure what feelings were behind her question. Had Melanie told her about seeing Grace? Or him? Shrinks were supposed to keep stuff like that confidential. "I'm sure she must have been. She had a great reputation."

"Did you love her?"

The question was disconcerting, to say the least. It showed on his face.

Sarah smiled wryly, which ticked him off. That showed, too.

"I meant your wife, Allegro. Not Melanie."

His eyes narrowed into slits. She was deliberately playing mind-games with him. "Uh-uh," he said, wagging a finger in her face. "You don't give a horse's ass about how I felt about my wife. You just want to lay into me a little. Why is that, Sarah?"

When she didn't respond, he smiled acerbically. "You'd be good in a ring, Sarah. You throw lots of solid little jabs in the right spots. You duck and weave when the jabs come your way. But you'd never make it to the final round. Not with a pro. One time you wouldn't see the blow coming. And when it struck, you'd go down for the count."

A current of muted fear spread through her body. She knew Allegro was referring not only to himself but to Romeo as well.

"I might surprise you." She forced a cocky tone. Instinctively, she reached for her drink again.

Just as he'd done before, Allegro made a grab for her glass before she got it to her lips, this time spilling a little onto her lap as he snatched it from her hand.

Sarah's body stiffened. "Look, Allegro, I'm a big girl. I can—"

Allegro's palm clamped over her mouth midsentence. Sarah froze. What the hell was he doing?

"Sarah, listen to me." Allegro's voice was low and urgent. "I heard something. Don't make a sound. I'm going to check."

She gave him an anxious look, then nodded, going limp as he removed his hand from her mouth. Her eyes were riveted on him as he pushed himself off of her and rose from the couch.

What had he heard? She hadn't heard anything.

Shuddering, she burrowed into the far corner of the sofa, hugging her legs, knees pressed against her chest. Trying to make herself smaller. Shrink herself into invisibility.

She watched Allegro cross the living room, surprised to see this broadly built man move with almost a dancer's grace. He really was a study in contrasts.

While she remained frozen to the spot, straining to hear the sound he'd claimed to hear, he made a quick check of the rest of the apartment—her bedroom, kitchen, the bathroom.

When he stepped back into the living room, he gave her a reassuring nod. She forced a weak smile, but she was far from comforted.

He headed over to the front door.

Corky, the cop on guard outside in the hallway, shot to his feet as the door opened.

"You see or hear anything out here?" Allegro barked at him.

"Not really."

"What the hell does that mean?" Allegro snapped.

Corky shifted nervously from one foot to the other. "Some chick came in a few minutes ago. I—uh—had a couple of words with her. You know—what was she doing here, that sort of thing. Lives in the building. Right next door to Miss Rosen." He pointed to Vickie's apartment.

"She was alone?"

The cop nodded.

"No one else?"

Corky shook his head.

"And you didn't hear anything unusual?"

"Traffic outside, that sort of thing. Nothing unusual."

Allegro rubbed his jaw. "Let's just take a little look around. Check outside, especially out back behind the building. I'll nose around the hallways."

Corky gave a thumbs-up sign and headed off without delay. Allegro stuck his head back in the apartment. "Sarah, come lock this door. Don't open it for anyone but me. Got it?"

She sprang up from the sofa. "Let me go with—"

He shook his head. "Stay put. Nothing to be afraid of. Be back in a few minutes."

"John—" she called out as he started to close the door.

"It's probably nothing, Sarah. Best to play it safe, that's all."

Romeo is sublime at the charade. He is quite brilliant and cunning . . . his macabre acts seem perfectly reasonable . . . making him all the more dangerous.

Dr. Melanie Rosen
Cutting Edge

13

As Allegro left her apartment, Sarah had a powerful impulse to run after him. But she knew he'd only turn her back around.

He called to her from the other side of her door. "Lock it, Sarah. And put the chain on."

She crossed the room and did as he ordered, hovering against the door as if somehow that would keep her closer to him. Safer. But already she could hear his footsteps fading.

She must have stayed plastered to that door for a couple of minutes before she heard a light rapping sound coming from what seemed to be her bathroom.

"Oh God," she gasped in terror.

"It's me, Miss Rosen. Officer Corrigan. I'm outside by your bathroom window. It's cracked open."

What was her window doing open? She'd been unable to budge it since the day she'd moved in. Jammed solid.

"Miss Rosen? Can you hear me? You okay in there, Sarah?"

"Yes, yes, I'm okay," Sarah called out as she headed on rubbery legs for the bathroom. It was faintly lit by the cop's flashlight beam coming in from the window over the bathtub. She flicked on the light switch, pushed aside Allegro's wet sports jacket, which he'd thrown over the shower rod. Reaching across the tub, she pulled up the white plastic blinds she'd hung over the window so she'd have privacy when she bathed.

"Looks like it's been jimmied," Corky said, his flashlight beam fixed on the sill. The young cop had climbed up onto a metal garbage can outside in the alley, allowing him to reach her ground-floor window. "Marks on the sill. Sure does seem like someone was trying to get in. The garbage can was right under the window. You keep it here?"

"No, of course not."

"Right." He swung his flashlight up and down the narrow alley between her house and the back of an empty tenement that faced onto Albion Street. "Must have got scared off. No one here now."

Sarah's heart thumped so hard against her rib cage it hurt. She shut her eyes and she could see blood moving in waves across her closed lids. *There was her mother. And Melanie. And her. All of them floating on a red sea.*

"I better go get Detective Allegro. He'll want to check this out. Don't touch anything, okay?"

Someone had been trying to get inside her apartment. It could have been any common criminal. The area was teeming with them. But Sarah knew it was Romeo. Brazenly showing off. Right under the cops' noses. Doubtless taking a perverse pleasure in his daring. Dare for dare.

She pictured a shadowy figure sneaking in through the window, lurking in the tiny bathroom, waiting until Allegro left—waiting to show himself—

Closing her eyes, she tried to bring the figure into focus. Robert Perry fit. He was a perfect suspect. Stealthy, perverse, obsessive—but obvious. He didn't impress her as being all that clever or audacious. More desperate and pathetic.

So if not Perry, then who?

Another image flashed in her head. Clear and sharp this time.

Bill Dennison.

She shuddered. Crazy for him to keep coming to mind. Crazy to let their pathetic excuse for an affair color her feelings about him. Besides, if he did have this dark compulsion to hurt and torture women, as Romeo surely did, he certainly wouldn't have stopped at a mildly kinky spanking that last time they were together. It was idiotic to think that Dr. Bill Dennison, a man whose profession it was to treat just such warped characters, could be this hideously deranged maniac.

A shuffle of footsteps outside her window made her tense up. She let out a whoosh of breath as Allegro appeared at the other side of the bathroom window.

"You must have X-ray hearing, Allegro," she said, trying to sound glib. And brave.

He merely grunted, all business now. Corky came up behind him and handed up the flashlight. Sarah watched him shine the beam all along the sill, careful not to touch it.

"You want me to call for the boys to come and dust for prints?" Corky asked.

"Yeah. And go door to door—every apartment facing this back alley. See if anyone saw somebody." He glanced in the window at Sarah. "You okay?"

"Just great."

"Sit tight. Chances are we scared him off, but Corky and I'll have another look around."

"I don't think he scares too easily," she said.

"It could have been a run-of-the-mill B&E, Sarah. Some junkie, most likely."

"Why don't you say it?"

"Why don't you go back to the living room and pour yourself another drink?"

"Come on, Allegro. Say it. I asked for it. I went on Emma's show and challenged him. Go ahead. Say it."

"You said it for me. Go put up a pot of coffee. It's gonna be a long night."

She nodded but remained rooted to the spot. A familiar numbness was setting in, overriding the panic—everything.

"Do it, Sarah." Not a request now. An order.

His trenchant demand got her moving. She went to the kitchen and made the coffee, stared at the drips of dark brown liquid as they began falling into the glass carafe. It looked strong. She'd probably put in too many scoops. She hadn't really counted them out.

So hard to concentrate on something so mundane. Her heart was still beating hard. And she could feel a burning sensation in her chest. She opened a cupboard in search of some antacids, then remembered she'd stuck a pack of them in her tote bag.

But when she got halfway across her living room, she came to an abrupt stop. All the blood rushed from her face. On the floor of the foyer just past the front door of her apartment, its edges touching her rug, was a white business-size envelope.

How long had it been there? She hadn't looked in that direction when she'd left the bathroom and gone to the kitchen to make the coffee.

If Romeo had slipped it under her door moments ago, he could still be out there in the hall. If she raced over and threw open the door, she might come face to face with him. No more wondering who it was. She'd know. It would all be over.

Over.

There was a sharp rap on her front door. Sarah stiffened.

The knock sounded again.

"Sarah, it's me. John." A brief pause. "Allegro."

She sprang the rest of the way across the room for the envelope, shoving it under the rug. Still protecting Melanie's privacy. And honor. Then she threw the door open and flew into his arms.

"It's okay, Sarah. I didn't see anyone." He could feel her whole body trembling as he tried to comfort her with his embrace.

"He was here. I know it."

He drew back and looked down at her. "Did you see someone?"

"No, but—" *Show him. Even if it is from Melanie's diary again. Show him. Show him.*

"But what, Sarah?" he pressed.

She clung to him. Yes, she'd show it to him. As soon as she'd read it first. She owed Melanie that much.

"I called in for backup. We'll comb the whole area. Don't worry, Sarah. If he's around here, we'll get him."

She couldn't stop shaking. An image surfaced—*She's standing in the hallway of their house, wearing her mother's white wedding gown, holding something in her hand. Something live and pulsing. A heart. A bleeding heart. Melanie's heart. No, no. I didn't mean it. I swear. I didn't. I didn't.*

"You didn't what, Sarah?"

She gasped. Was he reading her mind? Was she losing it entirely?

She jerked away from him. "Nothing. Nothing."

He made no response. Instead he started across the room.

"What are you going to do?" she demanded.

She followed on his heels as he headed for the phone on the wall inside the kitchen entry, flipping open a small address book he'd pulled out of his back pocket.

He checked a number and began to dial. Sarah came closer. She could hear the phone ringing. After ten rings, Allegro hung up. "No answering machine."

"Who did you phone?"

He gave her a long level look. "Perry."

Before she could say anything, he cut her off. "All it means is he's not home. Or even just that he's not picking up. He's still probably being hounded for interviews. The press knows he discovered . . . Melanie. Could be he's decided not to answer the phone."

Sarah snatched the receiver. Her turn to dial. She hesitated even though she knew the number by heart. Wrestling with herself. Telling herself this was nuts even as she began to punch in the numbers.

A pickup after four rings. She held the phone from her ear so that Allegro could hear.

"Bill Dennison here. Well, actually I'm not here at the moment, but if you leave a message of any length, I'll get back to you as soon as I can."

Sarah hung up. Allegro stared at her.

"I know," she said. "It doesn't mean anything. Nothing means anything." Bitterness as well as frustration and fear crept into her tone.

Their eyes connected. The faint sound of sirens filtered into the room.

"What makes you think it could be your brother-in-law?" Allegro demanded.

"Ex-brother-in-law. Nothing. I can't think straight. Can't you see that?"

"Sarah . . . there's something you're not telling me."

That was a laugh.

"We had an affair. If you could call it that."

His eyes narrowed. "You and Dennison?"

She nodded. *Why am I telling him this?*

"What would you call it?" he asked.

"Lunacy," she said. "I always seem to end up with Melanie's hand-me-downs." *Was John another of them? Was this the real reason she was attracted to him?*

There was a drawn-out silence.

"Is that coffee ready?"

Sarah laughed dryly, partly to conceal her own discomfort. "Throat suddenly parched, Detective?"

Allegro's gaze remained solidly fixed on her. "Let's stop fucking around, Sarah. Ask me straight out."

"Were you and Melanie lovers?"

He didn't flinch. "No. Did I want to be her lover? Yes and no." He smiled. "Ambiguous enough for you?"

Before she had a chance to say that it was more than enough, there was a knock at the door. Only then did Sarah realize the sirens she'd been hearing before in the distance were now wailing loudly outside her windows.

Allegro tipped his forehead against hers for the briefest instant, but the contact felt electric to Sarah.

"Later." He left her and headed for the door.

Talk about ambiguous.

A fever of activity. Uniformed cops and detectives everywhere. Combing the area, checking for prints, questioning tenants. Media close behind—thirsty for news. Desperate to catch a breaking story.

Vickie showed up at Sarah's door moments after being questioned by the police. "Do you really figure it was him? Romeo?"

Despite her neighbor's bouffant hairdo, the exaggerated makeup and the silky, ultrafeminine floral lounging gown, Sarah kept flashing on that photo of the handsome and surprisingly masculine-looking *Vic* standing on the sand with his arm around his pretty mother.

"I really don't know," Sarah answered guardedly, picturing *Vickie* sans the highly styled long red hair—which, on close scrutiny, she observed was a wig—the expertly applied cosmetics, the garish costume. The years since that photo was taken had added some lines to the face, a bit of softness under the chin, but there was no question that this statuesquely striking *she* would still make an imposingly attractive *he*. Vickie, Vic. Like a chameleon—

Sarah's mind was racing. When Corky saw Vickie come in, wasn't it right after Allegro had heard the sound of her bathroom window being jimmied open? How easy it would have been for Vickie to give the window a try and then realize it was making too much noise. Or better still, what a cleverly staged event to set Allegro and Corky off on a wild-goose chase, leaving the hallway empty long enough to dash out of his apartment and slip that envelope under her door.

Sarah blanched. Now that her suspicions about her neighbor were mounting, the envelope she'd so impulsively shoved under her foyer rug zoomed back into her memory with sonic speed.

"Darling, you're white as a sheet," Vickie crooned. "Here, let me help you—"

Sarah recoiled as Vickie reached out for her. The very thought of being touched—

"No, please. I'm fine," she insisted, and saw a wounded look flit across the transvestite's face. Was it really hurt feelings, or was it the actor's touch, concealing some darker, more sinister emotion?

This is nuts, Sarah told herself. She really was going crazy. Twisting everyone's appearance, words, deeds into something malevolent and treacherous. First Perry, then Bill, now Vickie. She thought of that surge of panic when John Allegro's hand had clamped over her mouth.

"Well, I'll go then," Vickie said, then vamped a smile. "Gotta get my beauty sleep, ya know."

To squelch her free-floating paranoia, Sarah deliberately took hold of her neighbor's arm. She gave it a friendly squeeze. "I'm sorry. Guess I'm a bit unnerved by all this."

Now Vickie's smile appeared thoroughly genuine. "I'd feel exactly the same way if I were in your shoes."

Sarah's gaze reflexively fell to Vickie's large feet. Vickie grinned. "Yeah, I know what you're thinking. These big old hooves of mine aren't likely to squeeze into your itty-bitty sandals."

Sarah heard the ring of envy in the husky voice. Did Mother have small feet, too? And what about Romeo's victims? Melanie had worn a size 6N. *Sure, Rosen. The common thread wasn't that all the murdered women were young, successful, professional women. It was that they all had small feet. Brilliant. Romeo's a transvestite with a foot fetish!*

"I'm off, but if you need anything, honey—"

"Thanks, Vickie. I'll let you know if I do."

As the door closed, Sarah remained in the foyer, a vein pulsing in her temple, staring down at the rug that covered Romeo's latest communiqué. She hugged herself tightly, recalling how good it had felt, if only for the briefest instant, when Allegro had held her close. And then there was that fantasy of the two of them together—unfinished, cut off. Leaving her frustrated. Unfulfilled. The story of her life.

Usually, it unnerved her to dwell on her mostly unrequited and always unsettling sexual yearnings. Now she saw it as a delay tactic. Avoidance. John Allegro was a convenient distraction. A way to divert her mind from the man—the monster—who was intent on claiming it. Romeo. Permeating her space, her thoughts, her body if she wasn't very careful. He stuck so close, she could smell his demon stench. Like unwashed armpits. Unwashed crotch.

The odor was repugnant. She imagined it impregnating her skin, contaminating her. And there was nothing she could do to stop it. Powerless. Defenseless. Alone.

Unless she trusted John. Then she wouldn't be alone. She could put her faith in him. He would protect her. Not only because it was his job. There was something drawing him to her. As much as whatever it was that drew her to him. *Screw you, Feldman. You're all wrong. John's not my father substitute. He's nothing like my father. Finally I find someone decent, caring, sexy. I'm not gonna let you louse it up this time, Feldman.*

Her hand trembled as she retrieved the envelope. Even before she opened it, she made up her mind. As soon as the other cops cleared out and she and John were alone again, she would show him this latest message from Romeo. No matter what was in it. The other one, too. And then he'd know about Melanie's deep dark secrets.

And what about my own?

Her phone rang. Startled, she shoved the envelope into her skirt pocket. She let the answering machine pick up, but when she heard Michael Wagner's voice after the beep, she hurried over and grabbed the receiver.

"I'm sorry," Sarah said.

"For what?" Wagner asked.

She was flustered. "I mean—I'm here," she said inanely.

"I'm glad to hear it."

"I don't understand."

"I was worried about you. You're okay then?"

"Yes, I'm okay. Someone tried to break in."

"I know. That's why I'm calling."

"I thought you'd be here," Sarah blurted. Flushing, she added hastily, "It might have been—"

"Yeah, I know," he said. Romeo's name remained unspoken. "I'll be there within the hour, Sarah. I'm en route from Ledi."

"Ledi?"

"It's a town south of Sacramento."

"Oh."

"My old hunting ground."

"Hunting ground?"

"Where I grew up. My stepdad still lives there. It was his birthday, today. I drove up to have dinner with him. Funny how things always seem to happen in one place when you're off someplace else," he mused.

"Not for me," Sarah said soberly. "I always seem to be in the place where it's happening. I'd be a lot happier if I were somewhere else."

There was silence on the other end of the line.

"Sorry," she said.

"You say that a lot."

"No, I don't."

"Is John there? Allegro?" he asked.

As if she needed clarification. As if she hadn't already begun thinking of him only as John. "Yes. No. I mean he's not right here in the apartment, but I can get him."

"Don't bother. Just tell him I'll get there as fast as I can."

Sarah glanced at her watch. It was ten after eleven. John had certainly been right about one thing—it would be a long night.

His place. A bleak little studio a few blocks from the club. Smelly mattress on a grimy floor. It wouldn't have mattered. Not if he'd been able to come through with what I needed. But he was lousy. Not an ounce of subtlety. Kept saying, "I fuckin' thought this was what you wanted, baby," as he walloped me. He didn't get it. Didn't get it at all. None of them do.

But you.

M.R. diary

14

*L*osing it. Headed over to the Mission District last night. Told myself I wanted to drop in on Sarah. Never got there. Went into this scuzzy neon-lit club down an alley off of Sixteenth. Hadn't been there before, but I'd heard about it. One of the secret pluses of my trade.

The place reeked of beer, sweat, pot. Couples grinding into each other against mud-colored walls. Serious boozers at the bar. Wasted, naked women with bags under their vacant eyes gyrating wearily on a stage to some dreadful industrial rock.

The show was just about to begin. The dancers shuffled off the stage, the lights dimmed, and when they came up again the first couple came on. The woman was dressed in a cheap gold lamé body suit with a rhinestone-studded dog collar around her neck. She was led in on all fours by a blond, blue-eyed surfer dude in a pair of black bikini briefs. Carrying a big black whip. Wearing an evil smile on his face. Stroking the thick handle of the whip before he got down to business.

Later, I saw him in a booth way in the back.

He wasn't watching his competition on stage. He was staring openly at me. Dark eyes. Leering. Slimy bastard.

His place. A bleak little studio a few blocks from the club. Smelly mattress on a grimy floor. It wouldn't have mattered. Not if he'd been able to come through with what I needed. But he was lousy. Not an ounce of subtlety. Kept saying, "I fuckin' thought this was what you wanted, baby," as he walloped me. He didn't get it. Didn't get it at all. None of them do.

But you.

Allegro's expression as he read Melanie's diary entry was too complex for Sarah to analyze. For a moment she actually thought he was about to break down and cry. The next moment his features went hard and hollow, like he'd sucked in all of his emotions.

What was he feeling? Thinking? Sarah needed to know. But she was afraid to ask.

Instead, she shared her own responses, her tone full of remorse, anguish, and—try as she might to conceal it—disgust. "This isn't my sister. I never knew this—this woman at all. She is wild, destructive, out of control."

This excerpt was far worse than the other. That first one had merely expressed her sister's disturbing fantasy, her troubling emotions. This one revealed that she'd acted on those feelings. "I can't fathom any woman begging to be demeaned, beaten. Least of all Melanie."

"Maybe the beating wasn't really what she was after." Allegro's voice was strained.

"Meaning what?" What did he know about her sister that *she* didn't know? How much had Melanie shared with him? Just how close had they been? Terrific. Here she'd believed she was keeping secrets about her sister from Allegro: maybe it was really the other way around.

And you were going to trust him. You stupid little gullible idiot. You always get everything wrong. Smarten up.

"Meaning, I don't know what," Allegro said, sounding angry and defensive. "I'm not the shrink. Ask your friend Feldman."

Sarah winced. Ask Feldman. Right. That sanctimonious son-of-a-bitch probably did have the answers. *Hoarding them.*

Again she could see Feldman and Melanie embracing in his office. A sight she'd banished from her mind for close to fourteen years. Now she was living it all over again. Tormented not only by what she'd witnessed but by her fevered imaginings of what had happened after she'd fled. Had Melanie shared her masochistic cravings with Feldman—like maybe she had with Allegro—with all the guys? Had it turned Feldman on? Had things gotten down and dirty up there in his office while she'd been in the parking lot puking up her guts?

Yes, of course they had. She could picture the whole scenario perfectly. Couldn't make it go away. As if she'd stayed and watched it—the entire disgusting episode.

Locked in each other's arms. Faces slimy with sweat. Loud, raspy breathing. Uncontrolled panting.

"Doyawanit? Doyawanit?" He's taunting her in a jeering whisper, his penis now jutting straight out. Oh, it's so big, so hard.

Melanie's begging. "I wanit. I wanit."

Feldman laughs harshly. Now he's got her where he wants her. Now he can call the shots. She'll do everything he says if she knows what's good for her.

She knows. She wants.

He throws her roughly onto his head-shrinking couch. She lies there, spread-eagled, limp as a rag doll. Breathless.

Oh yes, she wants him. She's caught in his spell. She's his for the taking.

Look at the way his eyes are seething. That lewd smile on his thin lips.

He descends on her. Savagely tearing off her blouse, her skirt, her lacy bra—

"Nowait, nowait, nowait—"

There is terror in Melanie's eyes.

Sarah can see it, hear it, taste it way back in her throat. Rancid, vile. But she's mesmerized.

He flips her over like a pancake, uses his tie to bind her wrists behind her back, flips her back again.

"Is this what you fuckin' want, baby?" he whispers huskily all the while he is ramming her.

And she is crying still. Only now it's with abandon, "Yes, yes, yes—"

Why was she doing this to herself? Wasn't it bad enough that true memories were surfacing? Why create gross fantasies? Why invent a barbaric scenario of bondage between Melanie and Feldman? Was her unconscious telling her Feldman was as good a candidate for the part of Romeo as anyone? Why not add him to her mounting list of suspects? Why not, indeed?

"Are there any others?" Allegro's voice seemed to be coming through a long tunnel.

"Others?"

"You've gone this far, Sarah."

No point in holding back the other missive from hell. She got it out of her tote bag, mutely handing it to him.

Allegro read it, then looked back up at her. "I know this is painful for you."

She was having trouble focusing on his face. It was an amalgam of smudged, cryptic shadows. But she was acutely aware of his presence. The way his large frame took up so much of the space on the sofa they shared. His boozy breath. A whiff of peppermint. Breath-freshener to hide the alcohol?

And Romeo lurked on the other side of her locked

door, crouched like a tiger, growling deep in his throat, licking his chops—listening, watching, waiting for the right moment to prey on her, as he'd preyed on the rest.

"Melanie was obviously obsessed with this man she was writing about. This *you* she keeps writing to. The one who gave her what the . . . others couldn't," she said in a faint whisper. "It must be Romeo."

"It's certainly possible," Allegro said tonelessly, tucking the diary excerpts into his trouser pocket.

Sarah winced. It was like he was taking away what little she had left of her sister. Another betrayal. *Wouldn't that be your diagnosis, Feldman? But what about your betrayal? I saw the two of you—I saw you.*

"Talk to me, Sarah," Allegro had to say it twice.

"You'll think . . . I'm nuts."

He smiled. "I'm partial to nuts. Go ahead."

"I was thinking of Feldman. What if it's him? What if he's Romeo?"

"What makes you think so?"

It was only because Allegro's tone was so nonjudgmental that she dared go on. "Feldman and Melanie could have been lovers. Not that his screwing Melanie makes him Romeo."

"It doesn't *not* make him Romeo either," Allegro pointed out.

She looked away. As easy as it had been to picture her ex-shrink and Melanie as lovers, it felt absurd to consider Feldman as this psychopathic killer who raped and tortured women, ripped out their hearts.

Wagner phoned Emma Margolis a little after one in the morning. Despite the late hour, she picked up on the first ring.

"Guess I didn't wake you."

"Who can sleep?"

"Look, I just got to Sarah Rosen's place. There was an attempted break-in. John and I want her to hang out somewhere else for a while. She said she'd check into a hotel, but I—"

"You drive her right over here," Emma said emphatically. "She can stay with me as long as she likes."

"Good," Wagner said with a nod at his partner, who stood nearby. "She's throwing a few things into a bag now. We'll have her there in twenty minutes."

"I'll be waiting with some Valium at the ready. Think I'll take a couple, myself."

"You're sure you want to stick your neck out?"

"Maybe if I'd stuck it out sooner . . ." Emma let the rest of the sentence trail off. "Yeah, Wagner, I'm sure."

It was close to two A.M. Allegro and Wagner sat in the basement cafeteria of the Hall of Justice. After dropping Sarah off at Emma's, Wagner'd driven back to headquarters to find his partner at his desk poring over the Romeo files. He'd dragged him out of the squad room for a coffee break wrap-up to the long day.

The cafeteria smelled like a Chinese restaurant. No big surprise. During the day, the largely Chinese staff behind the counter dished out everything from egg rolls and fried rice to Szechuan shrimp and lo mein.

Wagner saw Allegro watch him finish off a large piece of apple pie. He smiled crookedly. "Didn't eat much for dinner."

Allegro remembered Wagner had spent the evening in Ledi visiting his stepdad.

"How's the old shit doing?" Allegro asked after pouring extra sugar into his coffee. *The old shit* was Wagner's pet name for the guy.

"Once a bastard, always a bastard," Wagner said, lighting up. "Gave me grief because the transmission went on that Corolla I picked up for him last year at the police auction. Didn't even bother to open the birthday gift I brought him. Pissed it wasn't booze. Like he doesn't have a big enough supply of his own. He was half in the bag when I got there."

Allegro scowled. Reminded him too much of himself in his serious drinking days. Could be that was why he'd chosen to sit around the caf with Wagner, drinking rank coffee. His way of staving off that bottle of Jim Beam waiting up for him like a seductive but dangerous lover back at his apartment.

"Why do you bother going out there if he's such a drunken prick?"

Wagner shrugged. "My mom was always big on birthdays. And on Joe. God only knows why. Still, I guess I do it for her. Would have made her happy that I went. Dumb, huh?"

Allegro grunted.

Neither had any real interest in drinking the sludge. Or talking about Wagner's drunken stepfather.

"What do you make of the break-in?" Wagner asked.

Allegro scowled. "I suppose on the plus side, he's taking more risks. The more we nudge him out of the woodwork, the better our chance to nab him."

"We're not doing the nudging. Sarah is. You don't think it's an accident any more than I do, that he makes this move the night after she goes on television and puts him down."

Allegro eyed his partner over the rim of the mug. "Sarah say anything when you drove her over to Emma's?"

"She's pissed we haven't nailed the perp. Told her I was pissed, too."

"That makes three of us."

"We gonna tackle that creep Perry again tomorrow?"

Allegro nodded. "Dennison and Feldman, too."

"Definitely Dennison. You know that garbage he was spouting about a wedding reception? I had a talk with the manager at Costa's before heading out to Ledi this evening. Dennison brought it up with the guy while the doc was powdering her nose. When the manager dropped by the table to congratulate her, he told me she acted like she didn't know what the hell he was talking about. I'd say Dennison was putting the cart way before the horse." Wagner paused. "Or planting an alibi for himself."

Allegro smiled faintly. "I'd have bet money she wouldn't go back to him."

"But Feldman? That old geezer—Romeo? I can't see it."

"He was her mentor, or whatever you call it. Sarah was the one who mentioned him as a prime candidate."

Wagner rolled his eyes. "Feldman and Melanie lovers? He's not exactly a dreamboat. I'd say he was downright ugly."

"You're a guy."

Wagner grinned. "True enough."

"Melanie consulted with him on some of her patients. Maybe she talked to him about Perry. Or some of her other wackos who might fit the bill." Allegro rubbed his face. His stubble scratched his palms. "Looks like tomorrow's gonna be a busy day."

Not that they'd been sitting around twiddling their thumbs up till now. The Romeo task force had been doubled since Melanie's death. They worked extra shifts, checking alibis of the known suspects, questioning their fellow workers, friends, family members for leads, clues, suspicions. Making the rounds of sex clubs, showing pictures of the five victims. Anytime someone recognized one of the women, out came the police photographer's photos of the suspects. Were any of these guys seen with the victim? Had any of them ever come around to the club on their own?

Allegro had gotten one of his men out of bed not twenty minutes ago, ordering him to try to track down that creep Melanie'd written about in that diary entry. The guy she'd picked up in that bar in an alley off Sixteenth. The guy who'd worked her over.

Allegro's throat went dry. Picturing Melanie in that

scummy fleabag room with that fuck. Then picturing that bottle of booze on his bureau.

Emma Margolis folded down the poufy floral print comforter. "It's pretty decent as sofa beds go. I bought it for Douglas's folks," she told Sarah.

"Douglas?"

"My ex. His parents threw a party when we split."

Sarah fought back a yawn.

Emma smiled apologetically. "Anyway, if Doug's obnoxious parents slept on the sofa bed without complaining, it must be damn comfortable."

Sarah managed a small smile in return. "I'm sure it is."

Emma frowned. "I'm prattling. I never prattle. I hate prattlers."

"You're upset," Sarah said softly.

"I'm not nearly as upset as you must be." She fiddled with the tie of her pale blue flannel bathrobe. "Did you bring something to sleep in? I could lend you a nightgown. Or pajamas. Whatever." She shoved her hands into the deep pockets of her robe. "I'm mothering you, aren't I? Making a nuisance of myself."

"No." The truth was, Sarah was touched by Emma's concern. It had been a long time—

"Listen, sleep as late as you want tomorrow. I'll be here most of the day."

"Don't you have a show to tape for tomorrow night?"

"I'll go in around one, and I should be home, bar any catastrophes, by four. Oh, just so you know, my number here's unlisted so you don't have to—worry about any calls from reporters or—anyone."

"He never calls. I don't think he will."

"Why is that?" Emma asked.

"Because he's afraid I'll recognize his voice."

Emma gave her an edgy look. "You sound convinced he's someone you know. Any ideas?"

"Is this for your Romeo segment on tomorrow night's show?" Sarah asked warily.

"Fuck, Sarah. Don't you get it?" Emma shot back. "I've lost two friends to that maniac. I'm wracked with guilt morning, noon, and night, that somehow I contributed to their deaths, failed to do something I should have done. I feel sick inside. Sick and scared. I want to stop him, too. I want to stop him before he adds you to his list." With that, she spun on her heel and headed out of the room.

"Wait. Please."

Emma stopped. "You want something?" Her voice was gruff.

"No. Yes. I'm sorry, Emma. I didn't mean . . . I don't know what I'm saying anymore. Or thinking, half the time." It was so damn hard to let her guard down. To let anyone in. To risk caring.

Sarah sat on the edge of the bed. Her fingers smoothed the yellow flowers on the comforter. "It would be so easy to cave in. And maybe in the end, I will. So much is happening. Sometimes I know that he's already won, that I'll be his next victim, that none of this will make the slightest bit of difference."

"Sarah, wait a sec—"

"John Allegro thinks I went on your show because I want to be like Melanie. But it's not that. Before Melanie was . . . murdered, I went about my merry way—my way, anyway—content not to know anything about my sister's life. Or examine my own, for that matter. But now the not knowing is eating me up alive. And the scraps will be Romeo's for the taking."

"Don't say that, Sarah. There's a cop parked right this minute outside the building. You'll have police protection until that psycho's caught."

"*If* he's caught. I can't sit here waiting, Emma. I've spent thirty-two years waiting, hiding, and letting my life happen to me instead of doing something about it. You told me that you and Melanie were friends. She talked to you, right? Not just on the air."

Emma nodded.

"About why some women were fascinated with the whole—sexual deviance thing?"

"Well—we did all get into a conversation about sado-masochism one time."

"All?"

Emma stared down at the floor. "It was after the last taping. Down at Homicide. We sat around afterward. Melanie and I, Allegro and Wagner. We got into talking about whether it was only having low self-esteem that attracted some women to S&M. Melanie said it also had to do with guilt. And with this overwhelming need to be punished because of what some women viewed as shameful acts or even what they considered despicable thoughts. . . ."

"Go on."

Emma sighed. "I think Allegro said something about how he figured, for some women, S&M was a way to have guilt-free sex. You know, if you're forced to submit, you can't be blamed for really enjoying it. He made me mad. I said he was full of shit. Wagner agreed with me. I was sure Melanie would, too. But she didn't. She sided with Allegro, saying how so many girls are raised to feel sex is something bad, that they can only let go if they believe someone else is making them do it. I could dig that. What shocked me, though, was—"

"What?"

"Melanie sort of tossed out as how some women just plain old got turned on by rough sex. That they *wanted* to be naughty, dirty, bad."

Sarah could feel her heart pounding in her chest.

"I told her the feminists could have her strung up for a theory like that."

Sarah watched her face closely. "It upset you."

Emma asked hollowly, "What do you want from me, Sarah?"

"I want to understand. Don't you see—I desperately

need to understand, Emma." She hesitated. "Along with those demented notes and *romantic* little gifts of his, Romeo's been sending me pieces of Melanie's diary."

"Oh God."

"You knew about her diary?"

"I knew she kept one. She told me one time it was her only outlet for getting out all of her uncensored feelings. And her fantasies. She said I ought to keep one, too." Emma smiled faintly. "She could be very bossy."

"Did she ever share any of those fantasies with you?"

Emma didn't answer.

Sarah took her silence for a *yes.* "And you had similar fantasies? Did you tell Melanie about them?"

"I didn't have to. She already knew."

"I don't understand."

"About a year ago, I was doing a piece on alternative sex in the Bay area. I interviewed some dominants, submissives, fetishists, as well as some of the cops who worked Vice. That's how I met Wagner. I talked him into taking me and my cameraman to one of those sex clubs." Emma hesitated. "I saw your sister there, Sarah."

"You saw Melanie—"

"It's not what you think. She wasn't cruising or anything. Mike told me the owner of the club was a patient of hers and had asked her to come."

"Did you and Melanie ever talk about it?"

"Later. Once we got to be friends. After she told me she'd spotted me at the club, I confessed to her that the scene there had turned me on."

"Did it turn her on, too?"

"She didn't say. Frankly, we ended up talking about our exes."

"She talked to you about Bill Dennison?"

"A little. I told her I'd been in therapy with him for a while."

"You saw Bill?"

Emma grimaced. "I quit after two months. There was something about the kinds of questions he used to ask me about my sexual fantasies. And when I told him I'd gone to that sex club and got turned on, he really started pumping me for details. He made me feel uncomfortable. Like he was getting off on it. Which I told him straight to his face. He called it projection. I called it bullshit and quit." Emma wore a far-off look. "Maybe Dennison was right after all. Maybe it was projection. There was stuff going on. Stuff I couldn't bring myself to tell him."

"What stuff?"

Emma began wringing her hands. Her forehead puckered. "That wasn't my first visit to—" She avoided looking over at Sarah. "I'd already been to another club a couple of times before. That was really how I got the idea to do the piece in the first place. I'd met this woman at my health club—a lawyer—a few months before—" She fell silent. The grooved lines at the corners of her mouth and the pained look in her dark eyes bore witness to the strain of what had abruptly switched from recitation to confession.

Sarah's gaze was fixed on Emma. It came to her like a puzzle piece snapping into place. "She was the one, wasn't she? The friend you told me about at Feldman's after the funeral? The first woman Romeo killed. Diane something. Colman? Corman?"

"Corbett," Emma said dully. "Yes. Diane talked me into going that first time. Not that I was hard to convince. Doug and I had split. I was feeling pretty down. I was curious. Diane made it seem no worse than going to watch male strippers." She toyed nervously with the sash of her robe.

"Was she right?"

"No. It was—more than that. I almost walked out that first time, because when I saw what was going on, I panicked. But Diane made a big point of convincing me everything that was going on was strictly consensual. That we were all adults and coercion was definitely taboo. That nothing would happen that I didn't want to happen."

"Was that true?"

"Yes. It was true."

"Where was this place?"

"A club in the burbs. Out in Richmond. A real hole in the wall. Diane's ex-boyfriend had taken her there once. That night, we were both strictly onlookers. There was this male bondage skit, then two transexuals had a wild wrestling match. We had a good laugh on the drive home. I agreed to go back with her the following weekend."

"And were you strictly onlookers when you went back the second time?"

Emma looked away. "Let's just say that neither of us laughed on our way home that night."

. . . the murders must all conform
to his dark, sadistic fantasy . . .

Dr. Melanie Rosen
Cutting Edge

15

Romeo is restless. He hears a constant hum in his ears as he prowls the derelict streets of SoMa. The hum is good. Keeps thoughts from intruding. Keeps him in check. If the hum stops, he's in trouble.

Don't get sloppy now. You're almost there. Almost home free.

Shit. Thoughts are sneaking in. God, he wants her. The fantasy alone is not sustaining him. He can't get her out of his mind. He can smell her, taste her. Seeing her on TV the night before almost drove him mad. Seeing her need for him. Hearing the secret hunger in her voice. So palpable it fills his pores.

You're teetering on a tightrope, but I'm there to catch you when you fall, baby. Don't be scared. It's going to be so good, Sarah. You don't know how good.

He pictures them in her apartment, the table set for dinner. He'll bring along the candles as well as all the other accoutrements. But those will come later. Melanie rushed things along. That was her problem. She was too eager. Too trusting. Too desperate. Like the others.

Sarah will fight him. That alone gives him a rush.

Ultimately, he will open her eyes. Open her mind. Open her heart. To the truth.

Sarrrahhhh. Sarah. Oh God it's going to be so glorious. You can run but you can't hide, Sarah. Not from what's inside you. Inside me. We're one, baby. We are one big hurting mass. Together, we can erase all the pain.

There's an awful gnawing sensation in the pit of his stomach. He needs something. But what?

Who the fuck's he kidding? Wanting Sarah's burning a hole in his brain. But he can't have her yet. Ruin the perfect seduction. It's all going so well.

But he's so fucking edgy. Needs a temporary release. He'll drive himself nuts if he doesn't do something.

He stops at an all-night drugstore, makes a purchase, then heads over to an address he's been to often enough that he doesn't have to flash his membership card to the brunette in black leather at the door.

He surveys the scene. Close to five in the morning, and the place has the high-voltage frenetic energy of a big city ER.

The backdrop of the stage is glowing with sparks of computer-orchestrated flames. Heart red. A naked blonde's in a straight-back chair, stage center. Her wrists are cuffed behind the chair. Her head is forced back by a choke collar around her neck with a chain running down to the handcuffs. A bruiser of a guy wearing only a black cowboy hat and a skimpy black velvet jockstrap is leering down at her, whip in hand.

"Spread 'em wider." The whip snaps close to the chair.

She quakes as she parts her legs, but she's not scared. Can't fake it for shit. A lousy put-on. No question she's loving every minute of it.

From where he's sitting, Romeo's got a bull's-eye view of her crotch. She's shaved. Like a newborn baby. Her lips down there are lipsticked cherry red.

He turns away in disgust. A ravaged-looking druggie at the bar, dressed in a see-through lacy white blouse and hot pink miniskirt with tattoos snaking up her thighs, is giving him the once-over. He wastes a brief smile on her, but he knows she won't do. He always can select the right one. Like Melanie said on TV, he can pick up their vibes.

He cruises the murky terrain. Takes a couple of minutes before he spots her. Over at a wobbly little table near the fire exit. She's sitting with some creep in a leather jacket, but her eyes are fixed on him. She tilts her head slightly, smiles.

Yes, she'll do for a diversion. Get him through the night.

And tomorrow night? What then? He pushes the question from his mind. He'll deal with tomorrow, tomorrow. If things get bad enough, he has someone tucked away for just such a rainy day.

A nod from him. A wink from her. She leans over, says something to her companion, then gets up and saunters in his direction. A nice swish of the hips.

He steps out of the club first. They meet up outside. A quick embrace.

"My place, hon?" she asks.

He shakes his head. They go down the street to a fleabag hotel. The halls reek with the stench of urine and sweat. The room itself doesn't smell much better. And the decor's straight out of a bad dream.

As soon as the door closes, she turns to him. "What's in the bag? You bring me a present?"

He pulls out his new purchase from the drugstore—an enema.

She takes a step back. "I don't know about that—"

"Take off your panties."

"I'm not really into hot lunches, baby."

He smiles tenderly. "If you're a good girl, you won't have to have one."

Last night I imagined you were sitting on the chaise in my bedroom watching me making love with a faceless man. In the end, they are all faceless. . . .

M.R. diary

16

Sarah slipped out of Emma's at eight-fifteen the next morning. The fog was thick and oppressive. Impossible to see so much as a foot in front of her.

Was he waiting out here for her? Spying on her?

You're the sneaky little spy, Sarah. Always sticking your nose where you shouldn't—

"Miss Rosen?"

She gave a little yelp of alarm, then saw the cop who'd been on guard duty the previous night, stepping out of the gray haze. Dressed in khakis, a navy crew-neck sweater, white sneakers.

"Anything wrong?" he asked, approaching her.

"No. No, I was just— Look, would you mind giving me a lift? Over to North Point Street, Officer Corrigan?"

"Corky will do. Sure. No problem. Save me having to follow you in this pea soup." And risk losing her again, she was sure he was thinking.

Ten minutes later, the cop pulled up right in front of the whitewashed Bay Area Psychoanalytic Institute.

The receptionist in the main lobby checked the over-size schedule book, which was open to Friday, ran her finger down one column, and informed Sarah that Dr.

Feldman was seeing a patient but had a free hour at nine
A.M. Sarah checked her watch. He'd be out in twenty minutes. She started to walk up the curved staircase in the
center of the lobby to the psychiatrist's office on the second floor when she heard her name being called.

Bill Dennison, smartly dressed in a navy suit, attaché
case under his arm, strode over to her. "I'm glad to see
you here. I've been worried about you, Sarah. I was hoping you'd get back into therapy."

"What are *you* doing here?" she asked warily.

"Supervising a couple of residents. Just finished a session. Let's find a quiet spot so we can talk."

"I can't. I have to—"

He glanced at his watch. "What time's your appointment?"

"Nine. But it's not—" She didn't want him to think
she was back in therapy. That she needed to be. But he cut
her off.

"You've still got about fifteen minutes." He gripped
her arm. "Come on. Please, Sarah." He flashed her a be-
seeching smile. It took her back to a time when a smile
like that from him had sent her pulse racing with anticipation.

He guided her over to a couple of easy chairs in an
empty corner of the lobby. "I've called several times since
—since the funeral, but I always get your machine."

"Funny," Sarah said. "Last night I called you and got
your machine."

Dennison scowled. "Last night? I was home. When
did you call?"

"A little after eight."

"There was no message on my machine."

"I didn't leave one," Sarah said.

"I must have been out walking Monk. I'm truly sorry
I missed your call. But I'm glad you phoned me, Sarah. I
was beginning to think we were . . . washed up."

Sarah gave him an incredulous look. What the hell
was he talking about? They *were* washed up.

"I meant as friends," Dennison quickly clarified. "Even though we stopped being lovers, I never wanted us to stop being friends, Sarah." He studied her intently. "We should be helping each other through this tragedy."

"I'm managing."

"Are you? Is that why you went on the Margolis show the other night?" He shook his head slowly, several times. "That's always been your problem, Sarah. Either holding everything in or letting it all out in a big explosion. Never facing what's between those two extremes."

"And what exactly *is* between them, Bill?"

"Whatever it is, you can't find it alone. You have to allow yourself to connect with someone, Sarah. Therapy is certainly one way, but if you keep yourself isolated the rest of the time—" His hand sprang out and captured hers. "Let me help you, Sarah? What if we start, say, by having dinner together one night? Tonight, if you like. How about if I pick you up—"

Sarah pried her hand free of his grasp and jumped to her feet. "It's almost nine. I have to go."

He got up, too. Blocking her way. "All right, Sarah. I won't rush you. But I want you to know I'm here for you."

He was smiling down at her again. A *wooing* smile?

Minutes later, when she entered Dr. Stanley Feldman's small, private waiting area on the second floor of the Institute, Sarah felt like she was stepping into a time warp.

Her eyes fell on the door to Feldman's consulting room. Closed shut now. He was seeing a patient. A woman? Young? Pretty? Troubled?

Was Feldman comforting her? Holding her? Stroking her? Were they having sex right there on his couch?

Was she nuts? Had her surprise encounter with her ex-brother-in-law/ex-lover totally unhinged her? Was her paranoia running rampant? Or was this merely a textbook example of projection at its finest? The truth being that she secretly wished she was the one in Feldman's arms. Wouldn't that be Feldman's analysis? That she was projecting her own desires onto this patient? Just as she had onto Melanie? That because she'd quit treatment so abruptly, she'd never worked through her transference feelings toward him?

Feldman was standing at the open door of his consulting room silently observing her.

She gave him an edgy look.

"I'm glad to see you, Sarah. Come inside."

She hesitated. "I'm not here for the reason you think I'm here."

"All right," he said pleasantly. "We can talk about why inside."

"I want answers."

"First, you'll need to ask questions."

She smiled wryly. "Point for you, Feldman."

"I don't want to match points, Sarah." He stepped aside, waiting patiently.

Steeling herself, she took long determined strides until she'd got past the threshold. Anything less assertive, and she might not have made it. She hadn't set foot in that office since the time she'd spied him and Melanie locked in each other's arms nearly fourteen years ago. Heard him whisper *Melanie*.

As soon as Feldman shut the door behind him, she whirled around. "I want to know about my sister."

"Sit down, Sarah." He gestured to one of a pair of upholstered chairs across from his desk, taking the black leather swivel chair behind it.

At least he knew better than to suggest the infamous black leather chaise, which stretched between two beige-draped windows to her left.

She remained standing. Assessing the space. Little had changed. Still the same classic English drawing-room furnishings, the same carved desk with the "No Smoking Please" plaque. Still no paintings on the paneled walls. In other words, nothing to distract his patients.

Feldman folded his hands on his desk, his expression seemingly benign. "What is it you want to know about Melanie?"

"Whatever she told you," Sarah countered defiantly.

Feldman leaned forward slightly in his chair. "Whatever she told me? That's quite vague, Sarah. I imagine you have specific questions."

"Yes, you're right. I do have specific questions."

He nodded, again waiting for her to proceed.

His composure was infuriating Sarah more and more. "God, you're so cool, Feldman. No one would ever guess, would they?"

"Guess what?"

"How screwed up you really are," she charged, the fine line between reality and fantasy wavering wildly. *Was Feldman Melanie's lover? Melanie's killer? Was it so far-fetched? Feldman was cunning, brilliant, charismatic. Far more so than Bill Dennison. Didn't he make the perfect psychopath?*

"You've been very angry at me for a long time, Sarah." He didn't seem disturbed by this. Merely an analytic observation.

"Oh no, you're not going to play your mind-games with me anymore, Feldman. Not that game or any other game. Maybe I'm messed up, too, but not like Melanie. Not like *you.*"

"You said you came here for answers, but you seem to have them all already," he said, his inflection not changing one iota.

"Not all. But some, Feldman. More than you can guess."

"I have no doubt of that."

"Funny how I used to think you could read my mind. Know everything I thought and felt."

"You gave me a lot of power."

"Not anymore," she said emphatically.

"Talk to me about what's troubling you, Sarah."

"I told you. That's not why I came here."

"Isn't it? Even in part?"

"Stop it."

"I saw you on television Wednesday night. It's obvious how stressed you are. And it's not just Melanie's murder. I suspect memories are filtering back. That's it, isn't it? The trauma of Melanie's murder has forced open some doors you've kept locked tight for a long time. The remembering is frightening you. Making you think you're going crazy. I think the very opposite is true, Sarah. However tragic the catalyst, it's making you finally come to grips with your past. I know you don't believe it yet, but you're embarking on the road to recovery."

"The road to recovery?" She laughed harshly. "I'm lucky if I live through the month."

"If you're feeling suicidal, Sarah—"

"I'm not talking suicide. I'm talking *homicide.* Romeo wants me."

She stared across the desk at the psychoanalyst. Not even a muscle twitched on his face. No change of expression whatsoever.

"Now why don't you look surprised, Feldman? Because you already know all about Romeo and his yearnings? Or do you merely think I'm delusional? Or projecting? Maybe you think I *want* Romeo to want me. A death wish? A kind of suicide?"

"It's more important what *you* think."

"What did *Melanie* think? Tell me about that, Feldman. Tell me about Melanie and her death wish. Tell me why she was so messed up, Feldman!"

"What makes you so sure she was?"

"You think she wasn't? You think it's normal to want to be mauled, humiliated, raped? You think her need for pain was healthy?"

"Where does all this come from?"

"Where? Right. Play dumb, Feldman. That's real clever."

"Whether you believe it or not, I'm in your corner. I

want you to come out a winner. I always have. You used to believe that."

"I used to believe in Santa Claus, too," she spat out acidly.

"Sarah, I'm at a loss—"

"Melanie kept a diary. Romeo's been sending me excerpts from it. Do you want to know what my sister wrote about? Or do you already know?"

He didn't say a word.

"She craved pain, Feldman. She got off on being beaten. She found it irresistible. Intoxicating. She picked up scumbags in bars and did it in seedy hotel rooms. Begging for them to hurt her." Sarah gasped for breath. "Dr. Melanie Rosen. Who would have guessed, Feldman? Huh? Who would have guessed? Tell me."

Oh, what a look he gave her. Anguish, pity, despair. And something else. A knowing. It was the knowing more than anything that filled Sarah with dread. She had come for answers, demanded them. Now there was no question but that he had the answers, and she wanted desperately to flee without hearing them.

She sprang up and headed for the door. Feldman started for her.

"Don't. Don't touch me," she warned. "There's a cop waiting out there in the receptionist's office. All I have to do is shout, and he'll come running. I'm under constant police protection, Feldman."

"I'm much relieved to hear that," he said, having stopped a few feet from her.

"Are you?" She could smell that potent pipe tobacco —like rotten fruit—on his clothes. It repelled her.

"I'm not the enemy, Sarah. I wish you could believe that."

Sarah wasn't listening. She was on her own track. "Don't think for a minute, because of your position, that you aren't on their list of suspects."

"I've made it extremely clear to the police that I'll do everything in my power to assist them."

"And does that mean you're going to tell them everything you know?"

"Sarah, whatever I may know, you know much more."

She shook her head violently. "I don't. It isn't true."

"It's crucial that you talk about what you're remembering, let yourself piece together all of the threads. Face the answers, Sarah. About Melanie. About yourself. Otherwise, it's like participating in a cover-up. The most damaging kind of cover-up because in this case you're concealing vital knowledge from yourself, knowledge essential for your recovery. In effect, Sarah, you are your own enemy. Conceivably more dangerous to yourself even than this pathological serial killer. The police can protect you from him. They cannot protect you from yourself."

"Then you don't think Romeo can outsmart the cops, Feldman?"

"I hope to God not."

"He outsmarted Melanie, though. He pulled the wool right over her eyes. Just like he did with the other women. They thought they were so smart—so in control. But deep down they weren't in control at all. And he knew it. He used that knowledge to seduce them. Those women were all victims because they wanted him to prey upon them. Does that surprise you, Feldman?"

"About the others, no. About Melanie . . ." He hesitated, clasping his hands tightly together.

"You had no hint before this that Melanie was sick? That she was so completely masochistic that she went in search of abuse?" Sarah didn't realize she was screaming at him.

"I don't accept that term, Sarah. Masochistic personality disorder isn't even considered a diagnostic category anymore. No one really wants pain. Even those who come to believe they do. There are reasons, Sarah. Reasons why Melanie learned to link pain with pleasure. Reasons why she felt driven to submit to abuse. You mustn't hold Melanie responsible for these feelings, these self-destructive actions. You mustn't hold Melanie responsible for her own murder."

"I don't."

He smiled. "Good."

"But you're another story, Feldman."

His smile winked out. "So you blame me for her death. You think that I could have done something more—"

"Or done too much."

"Meaning?"

"Meaning?" she echoed harshly. "Meaning the way the two of you carried on. Right here. Right in this very room. You didn't even remember to close your goddamn door. I saw you, Feldman. I saw you all over Melanie. I saw the look on your face. Greedy, lascivious, disgusting. And she let you. She let you—" *She's seeing them again. Locked together. Only Feldman's face won't come into focus. Just Melanie's. Oh, the look of rapture on her sister's face. She's loving it. Sheer ecstasy.*

Slowly the lover's face becomes clearer. Only . . . only it isn't Feldman's face she's seeing. It's her father's—

Sarah called Bernie from a phone booth near the Civic Center. As soon as he heard her voice on the line, he launched into an anxious harangue. "Sarah, Sarah. I've been worried sick about you. I didn't sleep a wink. Not a wink. My eyes are positively bloodshot. Are you okay? Where'd you go last night? Where were you all morning? I rang you at least a dozen times. God, if I hear that damned answering machine one more time—"

Sarah could feel the tremors running through her hand as she gripped the phone. "I spent the night at Emma's."

"Emma who?"

"Emma Margolis."

"Oh, *that* Emma."

"Bernie, can I crash at your place for a few days? I

need to get my bearings." *Bearings. If only it were so simple. Not that it had ever been simple in the past. Her whole life had been a pretense. A brittle pretense that was now crumbling all around her.*

"I need someplace that's—neutral. Do you know what I mean?" *Get some distance. A respite.*

"Do you even have to ask me, sweetie? What should I make for dinner?"

Sarah managed a tremulous smile. "Nothing with grape jelly."

"Huh? Oh. Grape jelly. Right." Bernie chuckled. "Which reminds me. You don't have to worry about 'three's a crowd.' Tony moved out. We're still seeing each other, but we decided we were rushing things a little. Okay, okay, *he* decided."

"I'm sorry," Sarah said softly. *Never count on love. She'd tried to warn him. Should have tried harder. Not that he would have listened. Melanie wouldn't have.*

"I'm fine with it. Honest," Bernie said with forced earnestness. "And now I can devote myself fully to your every need. I know, I know. Pot roast. I'll make a nice pot roast. My mother's recipe. Of course, Mom'd have conniptions if she knew I stuck it in a microwave instead of cooking it on the stove for twelve hours, but who has time these days?"

"Thanks, Bernie."

"What for? The pot roast? You think I don't know that you're only going to pick at it? Like you pick at everything?"

"I'll eat. I promise," she said, feeling pathetically grateful for any morsel of nurturance—edible or otherwise. Even if she didn't think she deserved it.

Once again Feldman was whispering in her ear: *Why aren't you deserving, Sarah? What have you done that's so terrible?*

"Where are you now, Sarah?"

"I wish I knew."

"Poor little girl lost," Bernie cooed.

Sarah gripped the receiver like it was her lifeline. "I'm so scared, Bernie."

"Of Romeo?"

"Yes. But that isn't even the half of it. I had quite a morning. First a run-in with Bill Dennison. Then I had this intense, crazy session with Feldman. Talk about a dumb idea."

"Why dumb?"

"Because now I'm even more confused. It's hard to think. Oh God, I can barely breathe." She flung open the door in the phone booth and quickly gulped in some air. It only made her dizzy.

"Sarah, tell me where you are, and I'll come get you. I'll drive you back to my place. I'll tell Buchanon I'm sick."

"No, it's okay," she said, getting a grip on herself. "There are . . . things I've got to do. Everything's running together, Bernie. Kind of like doing the laundry so you get all the colors bleeding into the whites. I need to separate them out. Otherwise there'll be no getting rid of the stains—"

Robert Perry folded his hands across his chest, giving Allegro and Wagner a belligerent sneer. He was still in his pajamas at ten-thirty in the morning. "I didn't even have to let you in here, did I? I mean, you don't have a search warrant or anything, now do you?"

"We aren't doing any searching," Allegro said, casting his eyes around the spare but attractively furnished and tidy living room. Wicker sofa and two matching chairs divided by a bamboo coffee table, a large tatami rug on the oak-planked floor. A wood and rattan-trimmed bookcase housed an old TV, VCR, a ministereo, beside which were a few tapes and a dozen CDs. Interesting, since Perry's wife had made a point of her husband not being much of a music lover.

"We just want to ask you a few more questions, Robbie," Wagner said conversationally.

"She's the only one who calls me that," Perry snapped.

Wagner asked, "Who's that? Dr. Rosen?"

"No. Cindy. Cindy's the only one who calls me Robbie. Even though she knows it bugs me. I was once dumb enough to tell her it was what my mom always used to call me. And that I hated it." His face crumpled. "Jesus, you talked to her. You went and talked to Cindy, didn't you? You fuckers. You talked to her about me and Melanie." He slumped down on the sofa.

Wagner sat down beside Perry. Allegro remained standing near the bookcase. On the shelf below the TV, VCR, and stereo was a half-row of paperbacks—mostly men's action/adventure yarns—and a stack of magazines. The one on top of the pile had its cover torn off, but the *Golden Gate Magazine* masthead was visible on the first page. The last issue, Allegro guessed. The one that had featured Melanie's face on the cover. The issue that went on sale a few days after Melanie's murder. *Had Perry torn her photo off because he found it too painful to look at? Or had he stowed it away in a special scrapbook?*

"Your wife did most of the talking." Wagner leaned back against the sofa, stretching his legs out and crossing them at the ankles.

Perry turned his head sharply. "What's that mean? What did she say? I've called her a hundred times, but she won't talk to me. I begged her to come with me to see Dr. Dennison. I just want things to be right again between us. Why won't she give me another chance?"

"Maybe she's just the jealous type," Wagner said sardonically. "First you hit on your shrink, now you're after her kid sister."

Perry's face turned red. "I never hit on Melanie. It wasn't like that at all. But you wouldn't understand. You couldn't begin to understand what she meant to me."

"And does Sarah mean as much to you?" Allegro asked evenly.

"Sarah?" He squinted. "You're off the wall. There's nothing between me and Melanie's sister."

Wagner looked him straight in the eye. "So why have you been following her around?"

"You mean yesterday? In Chinatown? That was a chance meeting, that's all. An accident. I go to Chinatown a lot."

"You go to Valencia a lot, too?" Allegro asked.

"Valencia? I don't know what you're talking about."

Wagner's turn. "Where were you last night? After seven o'clock?"

"I was home. Here. I was here all night."

Allegro smiled faintly. "I don't think so."

"Wait. Wait, I was out for a while. What time'd you say? Around seven? Yeah, I was out then. I went to get a bite to eat. I'm a lousy cook."

"Where'd you go?"

"Where? Just some joint in the neighborhood."

"Which joint is that?"

Perry squirmed. "Well, it wasn't exactly in the neighborhood. I don't even remember the name of the place. Or what I ate for that matter. I was out walking, and I started to get hungry—"

"So first you took a stroll. Then you got something to eat. And then what did you do, Robbie?" Wagner asked. "Drop by Sarah's place, maybe?"

"No. I don't even know where she lives. I came back home. I was in by eight-thirty, nine at the latest. Look, she was the one that came looking for me in Chinatown. She wanted to talk to me."

"She says you wanted to talk to her."

"Okay, so it was mutual. I thought, being Melanie's sister, she'd understand. But—she didn't understand any more than you jerks. Nobody understands. Nobody—" His voice became a snarl.

Wagner leaned forward. "Not even Melanie? Was that

what triggered it, Robbie? That not even your shrink could understand? Or was it that Melanie understood too much?"

Perry's expression turned wary. "Don't think I don't know what you're trying to do. But it won't work."

"What won't work, Robbie?" Wagner asked in a deliberately insinuating tone.

"Stop calling me that, you cretin! You can't turn something beautiful into something cheap and ugly. What Melanie and I had together was pure and special. She made me whole. She made me feel reborn. I wouldn't have hurt a hair on her beautiful head." Perry was looking straight at Wagner, but his blue eyes had a glassy, faraway cast to them.

"Cindy didn't think you were much of a music lover," Allegro commented nonchalantly. He was fingering a CD. "She was sure you never even heard of Gershwin."

Wagner sat bolt upright in his seat; his eyes were glued to the cover of the CD. "Jesus Christ . . ." It was Gershwin's *Rhapsody in Blue.*

Perry was instantly on guard. "She played it for me once. Asked me what I thought of it. I wanted to impress her, I guess. I told her it was one of my favorites."

"Wasn't it?" Wagner's gaze skewered their suspect to his seat.

"No. No, I told you. I'd never even heard it before."

"Where was this? In her office or upstairs in her apartment?"

His Adam's apple bobbed. "Upstairs."

"Before or after?"

Perry gave Wagner a shaky look. "Before or after what?"

"You tell us."

"It wasn't before or after anything. She just brought me upstairs one afternoon after our session and played it for me. That was all. Oh, I know now it's connected to Romeo. That he . . . he plays it for . . . them. But I didn't know back then. It wasn't in the papers yet."

"I thought your sessions were in the morning. Friday morning," Allegro said.

Perry glared at him. "Melanie got a morning opening a couple of months ago. She asked me if I wanted it. I did. I liked seeing her first thing in the morning."

Allegro smiled condescendingly and studied the CD's glossy cover. "And what did Melanie do? Give you this as a little token of her affection?"

Perry shook his head in a hangdog fashion. "No. I bought it. After . . . after—"

"After what?" Wagner asked sharply.

"After she was—after he—killed her." Perry's reply was a choked whisper. "I don't know. I read that it was probably the last thing she was listening to. I thought it would make me feel . . . closer to her."

"Just to Melanie? Or to *all* of them, Robbie?" Wagner insinuated cruelly.

The color bled from Perry's face. Both cops could see he was losing it even before he started screaming at them.

"I never even played that CD! I couldn't. It hurt too much!" he shouted at them. "Look, it's still sealed with a little gold tab."

Wagner eyeballed Perry. "What about Melanie's heart, Robbie? You got it on ice? Until you get to exchange it for a nice, new fresh one, you little shit?"

Perry sprang to his feet, arms flailing. "You wanna search my place, check my freezer? Go ahead and look. Fuck what my lawyer said about a warrant. Go on, you fucking bastards!"

Allegro gave a nod to Wagner while Perry stood in the middle of the living room, his face bled white with rage, his arms crossed over his chest. A couple of minutes later Wagner returned. He shook his head.

"Now, get out of here. Get the fuck out of here. If you show your fucking faces here again, you better have that warrant." Perry's fists were clenched, his eyes blazing with hatred.

The two detectives ambled over to the door. Wagner smiled. "Be seeing you again, Robbie. Real soon."

Emma Margolis reached Wagner on his car phone shortly after they left Perry's apartment.

"Sarah's gone," she began anxiously. "She left the house before I woke up."

"We've got someone keeping a close eye on her," Wagner said. "She went to see her old shrink."

"Feldman?"

"Yeah. Right now she's browsing in a bookstore over on Geary."

Allegro took the phone from his partner. "How'd things go last night?"

". . . Okay," Emma said. "As well as can be expected."

"Right. Well, I'll probably drop by your place later. When she gets back."

"You're not going to badger her with questions, I hope." Emma made the statement a warning.

Allegro caught Wagner's faint smile. "Just need to . . . tie up a few loose ends. Look, I gotta hang up. We're paying another call on a shrink ourselves. Dr. Dennison."

"Wait, John. Before you hang up. That reminds me."

"What?"

Emma hesitated. "There's something I forgot. Until last night. Something that might be important. When Sarah and I were talking, it came back to me."

"Yeah?"

"It's about Diane. Diane Corbett. Romeo's first—"

"What about her?"

"I think she might have seen Dennison for therapy. That is, I'm not sure, but I did recommend him to her. It was when I was still in treatment with him. Before—"

"Before what?" Allegro asked.

"Before I quit," Emma finished abruptly, clicking off.

■   ■   ■

William Dennison edgily plucked an invisible speck of dust off the sleeve of his dark blue suit. He was clearly unhappy getting the third degree. First about his relationship with Sarah Rosen and now these questions about Diane Corbett.

"To be honest, I forgot. It was a year ago or more. And I only saw her once or twice."

"Which was it?" Allegro asked. "Once or twice?"

"I don't really remember. It was only for an evaluation."

"You kept notes, didn't you?" Allegro pressed. "Why don't you check?"

Dennison glanced at his watch. "I've got a patient in fifteen minutes. And I like a few minutes to—"

Wagner approached the psychiatrist's desk, putting a hand on top of his computer. "Corbett. Diane. Look it up. Won't take more than a few seconds."

"I cannot simply hand over my notes. They're confidential."

"Corbett's dead, Doc. There's nothing to protect. We can get a court order. Or you can save us a lot of time and bother," Allegro said.

Dennison stared down at his keyboard. "I remember now. I only saw her once."

"The notes, Doc. You can give us a verbal rundown. Like last time. We don't have to pass any papers. For now."

The psychiatrist's face was stiff with irritation as he typed in the name. Corbett, Diane. When her file came up, he gave the single-spaced writing on the screen a cursory glance. "She didn't say very much. Nothing that would be of any help in your investigation—"

"Let us make that call," Allegro said. "Run it by us."

Dennison's jaw clenched as he gave the screen a closer scrutiny. "Diane Corbett. 2253 Green Street. Date of Birth: 5-18-63. Single. Law degree from Stanford. Bankruptcy specialist for Markson, Hyde and Remington. No steady boyfriend at the time of the interview, but she did say that she'd recently broken up with a man she'd been dating for a few months."

"Grant Carpenter?" Allegro asked.

Dennison looked up from the screen. "Yes. She didn't say why the relationship ended. Should I continue?"

Allegro nodded. He'd interviewed Carpenter shortly after Corbett's murder. The guy had refused to say much except that neither he nor Diane had ever viewed the relationship as anything but casual. When pressed, he did admit he and Diane had "dabbled in a bit of alternative sex," as he called it, even confessing that he'd taken her to a private "social club" out in Richmond a couple of times. "Nothing too heavy," he'd told Allegro. "Just some light erotic torture." Carpenter would have been the ideal prime suspect, except that he had a solid alibi for the night of his ex-girlfriend's murder.

Dennison continued reading from the screen. "One older brother in Idaho, a college professor. She didn't say what he taught. Parents deceased. Father, an insurance agent, died of a heart attack when Miss Corbett was eleven. Mother, a homemaker, died of breast cancer at the age of fifty-two. Miss Corbett was twenty-three at the time. I indicate in my notes here that she did show some affect when mentioning her mother's death. A glimmer of sadness. Otherwise she was rather cool and guarded throughout the fifty-minute evaluation."

He scrolled down. "Not much more here. No drugs. Light drinker. A glass or two of wine or a beer every now and then. Not a problem."

"What brought her in?" Allegro asked.

"She reported periodic bouts of depression, but couldn't say what provoked them. Nor could she give even a ballpark date for when they began. She worked out regularly in a gym. Felt it helped some with the depression. I made a note that she didn't volunteer any information, waiting instead for me to ask her questions."

"Did you find her attractive?" Wagner asked casually.

Dennison shot him a disdainful glance. "I really can't recall."

Wagner tapped his fingers on the top of the psychiatrist's monitor. "Nothing in your notes about her appearance?"

"Why don't you just step around and read them yourself," he said with disgust.

Wagner obliged, Dennison sliding his chair several feet away to give the cop access to the screen.

After a few seconds, Wagner looked over at Allegro and then at the psychiatrist. "This all you've got?"

"She was quite resistant. I wasn't able to obtain very much."

"Sure something didn't *accidentally* get deleted?" Wagner asked.

A muscle jumped in Dennison's jaw. "If there was an *accident,* why didn't the whole file get deleted? I have absolutely nothing to hide. What? You want to charge me with taking lousy case notes?"

"Maybe you want to explain why you withheld the fact that you treated Romeo's first murder victim," Wagner countered evenly.

"I didn't treat her. I saw her for one fifty-minute evaluation. And as I already told you, I completely forgot that I'd seen the woman."

Allegro got in on the act, grabbing on to an arm of Dennison's chair and leaning down close to his face. "Even when you saw her picture splashed all over the television and every newspaper after her murder? Didn't the name ring a bell? Didn't her face? I mean those *before* photos. *Before* that pervert turned her into a horror-show freak. Like he did the others after her. Like he did your beautiful, beautiful Melanie. The love of your life. The woman you claim was going to marry you again."

Dennison threw his hands up like a boxer about to go down for the count. "You bastard," he muttered hotly. But his ruddy complexion had gone green.

"Now what kind of a diagnosis is that?" Allegro taunted.

"Okay, boys," Wagner said, stepping into the fray. "Let's take it back a few paces."

Allegro straightened. He moved a couple of steps away from the psychiatrist's chair. His face was white.

Wagner glanced benignly over at Dennison. "No secret here that all three of us are especially upset about Dr. Rosen's murder. But right now you can help us, Dr. Dennison, by focusing back on Miss Corbett. Is there anything else—anything that you might have overlooked putting in your notes—that you might have discussed during that evaluation?"

Dennison absently smoothed back his hair, working hard at regaining his composure. "No. Nothing that I can recall," he said evenly.

"You ask her any questions about her sex life?" Allegro asked.

Dennison glowered at him.

"Wouldn't that be something you'd discuss with a prospective patient during a psychiatric evaluation?" There was no hint of insinuation in Wagner's voice.

Dennison relented. "I think she might have mentioned having some sexual hang-ups—"

"Did she elaborate at all? Anything you can dredge up from your memory, Doc? You never know what might give us a lead." Wagner assumed a respectful, tempered tone. The tried and true good cop–bad cop routine.

Dennison compressed his lips, looking like a man hard at the work of thinking. "Actually, I remember now that she said she didn't feel comfortable talking about anything to do with sex." The psychiatrist looked chagrined. "I should have made a note of that in her file. I imagine I wasn't as thorough as I usually try to be because I had the impression she wouldn't be coming back."

"And why is that?" Wagner asked.

"I recall her mentioning something at the end of the session about possibly feeling more comfortable being seen by a woman. I imagine I told her I could make a referral if she liked. I believe we left it that she'd think it over and call back if she wanted one. She didn't call back."

"Would you have recommended your ex-wife if she had?" Allegro asked.

Dennison's caution immediately returned. "I always give patients three referrals and suggest they talk with each of them before deciding." He enunciated every word in a careful, controlled manner.

"And would Dr. Rosen have been one of the names?" Allegro persisted.

"Yes," Dennison replied warily. "Is there some reason why she shouldn't have been?"

"Did you also recommend your ex-wife to Emma Margolis when she quit treatment with you?" Wagner asked laconically, again moving into the driver's seat.

Dennison blanched. "How did you know—?"

"That she saw you for therapy, too?" Allegro finished off the psychiatrist's question. "Emma told us. She told us quite a few things."

Dennison shot to his feet, his face infused with color. "I don't know what she may have told you, but since Miss Margolis is very much alive, I am not about to engage in any discussion whatsoever of her case," he said caustically. "Now, if you don't mind, I really must get ready for my next patient, gentlemen." He squeezed out the brush-off between clenched teeth.

Allegro made no move to leave. "Did you treat or evaluate any of the others, Doc?"

Dennison looked blank. And then he got it. "I never had any contact whatsoever with those other women," he said contemptuously.

"Except for your ex-wife, of course."

Dennison glared at Allegro. "Is that all?"

"Oh, we're just getting rolling, Doc. Next, I want to know where you were last night." Allegro had crossed the room. Pretending interest in one of the Japanese prints that hung there.

"What is this? Sarah asked me that same question when I ran into her at the Institute this morning. Now you. What the hell happened last night?"

"How about you tell us?" Wagner said.

"I have no idea. I was home most of the evening. Except for about a half hour after dinner when I was walking my dog." Dennison looked greatly relieved when his buzzer rang. "That'll be my patient," he said dismissively.

Sarah showed up at KFRN at five minutes to two. Emma looked surprised and slightly disconcerted as she hurried from the set into the reception area. "I'm so glad to see you, Sarah, but I'm about to start taping tonight's show. . . ."

"So am I," Sarah announced with forced brightness.

"What? You want to go on again?"

Sarah smiled faintly. "Emma, Emma . . . think of the ratings."

"I'm thinking about *you*."

"I'm sorry. I know you are," Sarah said, instantly contrite. "That's why you have to let me do this. Last time I went on, I couldn't be sure I was his next target. Now I'm certain of it. This is my only direct access to him—"

"Sarah, do I have to remind you that only last night that maniac tried to break into your apartment? This is an insane cat-and-mouse game you're playing here."

"Let's not talk about cats."

"Huh?"

"Forget it. Sick joke."

"This is no time for jokes, sick or otherwise, Sarah."

"Two minutes, Emma. That's all I'm asking for."

It was strange how connected to Romeo Sarah felt when she sat there this time, staring into the blank Tele-

PrompTer-fitted camera. Like the empty screen was Romeo's face. Unreadable, mysterious, fathomless.

Yet there was this connection. There was no other way to describe it, hideous though it was. She had to face that. Accept that they were linked. Somehow turn it to her advantage. Otherwise she was doomed.

The instant she was cued, she just started talking. Talking to Romeo. As if he were listening at that very moment, even though the show wouldn't air until ten o'clock that evening.

"My sister believed that you grew stronger and more powerful with each killing, but she was wrong. You're running scared, Romeo. I can even pick up the scent of your fear. You try to fight it, pretend it away. But you can't fool yourself. You can't fool me. That business last night. You never meant to break into my apartment. I see that now. Another silly, childish stunt. Like waving a sign. 'I'm out here, Sarah.' For a minute, I believed you really did have the guts to show yourself—cops be damned. But deep down in your own rotting heart, you're scared shitless of exposing your true self. You can only keep up the act for so long. I know all about the lies. I know all about pretending you're one person when you're someone else altogether. Try as hard as you might, the cracks start to show. I'm going to be looking real hard, and soon I'll see them. I will. You may have hid them from the others, but you can't hide them from me."

After the taping segment, Emma blinked back tears as she hugged Sarah. "We'll have to bleep the *shitless* when we air it."

Sarah managed a small laugh, but she felt bewildered and drained. Her explosive eruption in front of the camera had caught her completely off guard.

"Would you prefer going out for dinner tonight, or should we eat in?" Emma asked. "If you want to hang around here, I'll be finished in about an hour—"

"I decided to spend a couple of nights with a guy I know."

Emma's eyes widened. "A guy?"

"A friend. We work together."

"Was the sofa bed a problem after all?" Emma asked dryly.

"It was nothing you said, Emma," Sarah said earnestly. "I think you're terrific. It's just—look—let's just say everything's a jumble. But I'll call you tomorrow." She reached out and squeezed Emma's hand. "Promise."

"Sarah, take care of yourself. Don't take any chances. I think what you said on camera to him—about being scared—you're probably right. But who's to say what he'll do if he does start coming unglued?"

It was a good question. For a change, Sarah was without an answer.

Gina, the receptionist in the KFRN reception area, called out to Sarah as she and her trusty bodyguard were heading for the doors.

"Excuse me, Miss Rosen. A package arrived for you."

Sarah's eyes darted to Corrigan. He held up a hand to stop her from moving. As if she could move.

"I'll take it," Corky told the receptionist. Before turning over the box, gift-wrapped perversely in shiny white paper sprinkled with tiny crimson hearts, Gina glanced at Sarah, who managed a faint nod.

"Who delivered it?" he asked, slipping on a pair of latex gloves before taking possession of the box. Not that there was much point to it, Sarah knew. The receptionist's prints were all over it. And others, no doubt. The only prints unlikely to be there were Romeo's.

The receptionist frowned. "A kid. Just a delivery boy from the florist downstairs."

Corky set the box on the counter, carefully tugged at the white ribbon, removed the wrapping, and lifted the lid.

"What is it?" Sarah asked huskily.

Corky gingerly folded back the crimson tissue paper. "A wreath. It's just a heart-shaped wreath."

Sarah forced herself to look at it. The wreath, grapevines twisted into the shape of a heart, was dotted with tiny dry red roses, Queen Anne's lace, and everlasting.

She saw the small white gift card. Reached for it. Corky beat her to it. He held it up for her with his gloved hand. Four words.

Heart of my heart.

In Romeo's mind, sex and killing are entwined. They equal power, revenge. Does he feel any remorse? Yes. But not for his victims. For himself. Because it's never enough to drive off his secret demons.

Dr. Melanie Rosen
Cutting Edge

17

Wagner was off tracking down all possible links—professional or otherwise—between Dr. William Dennison and any of the other Romeo victims. Allegro had a quick bite, then headed over to the Institute for his three P.M. meeting with Dr. Stanley Feldman.

Feldman was thumbing through some papers while Allegro took a seat across the desk from him. He pulled out his tape recorder. "Do you mind if I tape our interview, Doc?"

Feldman seemed to hesitate.

"My partner's the better note-taker."

"Fine," Feldman said, although he didn't sound like he meant it.

"It's my understanding that you were Dr. Rosen's consultant," Allegro began benignly.

The psychiatrist nodded distractedly.

"How often had the two of you been meeting, say, for the last year?"

Feldman shrugged. "Once or twice a month. It depended."

"On what?"

"On our schedules. On whether there were any pressing problems."

"With patients?"

"Yes," Feldman replied icily.

"So Dr. Rosen didn't routinely discuss all of her patients with you?"

"No. Only a handful. As I said, Detective, problem cases. Melanie didn't have that many. She was an expert therapist."

"Was one of those problem cases Robert Perry?" Not that Perry was the only patient of Melanie's on Allegro's mind. There was also his wife. Had Melanie ever discussed Grace with the shrink?

"Robert Perry? No."

"She never discussed him?" Allegro didn't attempt to hide his incredulity.

"Actually, Melanie discussed very few male patients with me over the years. She seemed to have more difficult issues with female patients."

"You do know Perry was the one who found her body."

"I saw it on the news."

"He claims to have had a sexual relationship with Dr. Rosen."

Allegro saw the psychiatrist's body stiffen. "It's certainly not uncommon for patients to imagine having an intimate relationship with their doctor. It's a part of what we call transference. A patient may develop an intense, almost desperate need to see the therapist as a lover, someone who is giving, nurturing, won't abandon him."

"Then you don't believe Perry and Dr. Rosen could have been sleeping together?"

"I believe that he believes it."

"Maybe it was part of some sort of sex therapy."

Feldman's face darkened. His accent thickened. "If your purpose in coming here, Detective, is to get me to help you to in any way smear Dr. Rosen's exemplary reputation—"

Allegro leaned forward in his chair, his eyes hooded, his features menacing. "Get this straight, Feldman. I'm here fishing for any possible lead to the maniac who's left five murdered women in his wake. And he's gonna leave a sixth and more after that if we don't nail him fast. I'll ask any questions I have to to nail this bastard. And you're gonna answer them. Do I make myself clear, Doc?"

Feldman shut his eyes for a moment and took a deep breath. "Don't you think I want you to find this psychopath? I was extremely fond of Melanie. She was a lovely and gracious young woman and a fine psychiatrist. What happened to her is a tragedy."

"You were more than her consultant, right?"

"What are you implying, Detective?"

"Melanie was never your patient, was she?"

"No. Never."

"So there were no restrictions about the two of you socializing. You could have dated, couldn't you?"

Feldman gave Allegro a glacial look. "Did Sarah tell you her sister and I were having an affair? Is that why you raise this nonsense? Well, Sarah's wrong."

"Why would Sarah think she was right?" Allegro asked without missing a beat. "You think maybe it was just her overwrought imagination? Like it was just Perry's imagination?"

"Don't mock the power of imagination, Detective," Feldman said archly. "Fantasy is often the only retreat for a person in a great deal of pain."

"So you think Sarah's in a great deal of pain?"

Feldman fixed a hard gaze on Allegro. "Don't you? Her sister was brutally murdered a week ago. Her mother committed suicide when she was a young girl. Her father has Alzheimer's and barely recognizes her. Yes, I would say Sarah Rosen's extremely distraught."

"Her mother committed suicide?"

"Cheryl Rosen hung herself in the attic of their home while the girls were at school and Simon was here at the Institute." The psychiatrist said it impassively. He folded his hands together. "Sarah took it hard. She and her mother were extremely close."

"Why'd she kill herself?"

"Cheryl had severe emotional problems. I really can't elaborate."

"Or won't?"

The psychiatrist made no response.

"You worried Sarah's going to follow in her mother's footsteps?"

Feldman's eyes rested at a spot somewhere over Allegro's shoulder. "She has made attempts in the past. Once after her mother died. And once when she was in college. Both a result of clinical depression. I tell you this in the strictest confidence, Detective Allegro. And only because I know the police—and Sarah—are concerned that she may be this psychopath's next target."

"And how do you know that?"

"Sarah told me when she came here to see me this morning."

"She told you? Everything? Including Melanie's diary entries?"

Feldman exhaled with a shudder, answering Allegro's question.

"What did you think?"

The psychiatrist shook his head sadly. "I never suspected that Melanie was so deeply troubled. She hid it quite successfully. At least—from me."

"You never had a clue?"

Feldman started to shake his head, but stopped. He stared off across the room. "In all the time I knew Melanie, there was only one occasion when I saw her decompensate—fall apart. And that was only for a few minutes."

"When was it?"

"Sarah began treatment after she cut her wrists at college and was brought home. Melanie came in for an appointment because she was extremely concerned about her own relationship with Sarah."

"What exactly was Melanie concerned about?"

"Sarah's hostility. Melanie was doing her best to reach out to her, but Sarah continually rejected all of her efforts."

"Why was that?"

"Sarah resented Melanie. She felt Melanie was her father's favorite."

"And was she?"

"Melanie and her father were very much alike. And Melanie was following in Simon's footsteps. That pleased him."

"What you're saying is, Sarah was right. Melanie was the apple of Daddy's eye."

"You could put it that way," Feldman said.

"Okay, so Melanie came to see you to discuss Sarah's resentment toward her. And she broke down?"

"Yes." Deep grooves bracketed the corners of Feldman's mouth as he spoke. "Melanie and I were discussing Sarah." He stopped, a frown adding new furrows across his forehead. "She was sitting in the chair you're sitting on now. We'd been analyzing what might be making Sarah feel so hostile to her. Next thing I knew, Melanie curled up in a fetal position. I must confess, I was quite taken aback. This was extremely atypical of her."

"What did you do?"

"I hurried over, knelt down beside her, and touched her shoulder. 'Tell me what's wrong, Melanie,' I said."

"Did she?"

"She shook her head, her hands covering her face. I told her she didn't have to be so strong. I thought our discussion had triggered a delayed grief reaction to her mother's suicide. I was trying to give her permission to deal with her own feelings of loss and rejection. 'Don't hold it all in,' I told her."

"What did she say?"

Feldman lifted his hands, palms up as if in supplication, then clasped them together. "She began muttering incoherently. I couldn't make any of it out."

"And then?"

Feldman shrugged. "An instant later she'd pulled herself together, smiled wistfully, and got up to leave."

"What did you say to her?"

"Nothing. I was at a loss for words. An unfamiliar predicament for me." Feldman looked away. "I can still see her standing there, facing me, trying desperately to regain her composure. But all of her vulnerability was so patently obvious, and I felt this tremendous sadness. Quite instinctively, I extended my hands out to her, feeling that it was important for us to make some kind of a connection. Instead of taking hold of my hands as I'd intended, she completely surprised me by stepping into my arms and clinging to me. Whether or not you believe it, this was the only physical contact we ever shared. If anything, Melanie, like her father, always held herself slightly apart. As if she never felt comfortable with too much intimacy."

"And has your impression changed now that you know about those diary entries?"

Feldman sighed heavily. "No. Sadly, it's been confirmed."

"I don't get that," Allegro said.

"Those words reveal a deeply disturbed young woman, Detective. What she was driven to achieve wasn't intimacy."

"What was it then?"

Their eyes made contact. "Self-destruction," Feldman said bluntly.

"And what about Sarah? Two suicide attempts. You figure she's on the same track?"

"I think Melanie's murder has brought Sarah to a crossroads, Detective Allegro. I believe she's desperate not to give in to her depression and her sense of futility. Fighting it with all her might. And in doing that, she's discovering that she has more strength and determination than she'd ever realized."

"Did you see her on *Cutting Edge* the other night?"

"Yes, actually I did. Quite an astounding perfor-mance."

"Performance? You think she was acting?" Allegro challenged.

"We all have to do some degree of acting to survive, don't you think, Detective?"

"You're the shrink."

Feldman smiled enigmatically. "That's precisely what Sarah would have said."

"She thinks you could be the psycho waiting on that crossroads, as you put it."

The psychiatrist's smile vanished. "Did she tell you that?"

"Not in so many words," Allegro hedged. "Anything to it? You can save us an awful lot of time and trouble—"

"I understand that you have to consider every possi-bility, Detective. So I'll save you the time and trouble. Believe me. I am not Romeo."

Allegro shrugged. "I'd like to believe you, Doc. And maybe I will get around to it. But we're a ways from that point. So let's start with Romeo's first victim. Diane Cor-bett." He flipped open his black vinyl pad, reading from his notes—"If you could tell me where you were between the hours . . ."

Emma Margolis heard her phone ringing as she unlocked her front door at four o'clock that afternoon. She made a dash for it, picked up the receiver, and barked a brusque greeting. There was no response on the other end of the line.

"Is anyone there?" she asked impatiently. And then, thinking it might be Sarah, she quickly altered her tone. "I'm sorry if I sounded abrupt."

"Am I calling at a bad time?" a man asked, his voice unfamiliar.

Emma went cold all over. Who had her unlisted num-ber? "Who—who is this?"

There was no answer.

"No," she said, replying to the caller's question while at the same time trying to squelch what she told herself was unwarranted panic. "This isn't a bad time. May I ask who's calling?" she repeated, but this time careful to sound unthreatening.

"You gave me your card at Melanie's funeral, remember? Told me I could call. You were so kind to me that day. The only one, really, who seemed to understand what I was going through."

Every muscle in Emma's body tightened. "Robert Perry?" *Or should she have said "Romeo"?*

"You do remember." Perry said, his voice brightening.

"Yes. You were so distraught."

"It doesn't seem to be getting any better." His tone went flat. "The cops are making me feel even worse. They keep pestering me. Do you know they actually went and talked to Cindy?"

"Cindy?"

"My wife. We're separated, but I'm still in love with her. Cindy's refused to come with me to see Dr. Dennison, but I'm trying to get her to go in for an appointment on her own. If he could explain to her—"

There was an abrupt silence. The newshound in her made Emma want to pounce, but she had the good sense to realize that this might not exactly endear her to Perry. Then again, did she want to endear herself to him?

"I can imagine that this is a very difficult time for you," she said quietly.

"You do understand."

"I miss her, too," Emma said.

First there was silence, and then she could hear soft sobs on Perry's end.

"Could we meet for a drink or something?" he asked finally.

"When?"

"Anytime, really. I'm not working. I was laid off. I

know I should be looking for another job, but then I tell myself that it really doesn't matter. I don't think I could concentrate on work now anyway."

"No, I suppose you're right."

"So can we meet?"

"Where were you thinking?" Emma asked cautiously.

"Actually, I'm not far from your apartment."

How did he know where she lived? Her business card had her unlisted number but not her address. He must have followed her home from the station.

She jerked up to her feet. "I was just on my way out," she lied. No way she was going to have a cozy tête-à-tête with him alone in her apartment. "Give me—say fifteen minutes. There's a little neighborhood tearoom on California near Laurel. The Upper Crust."

"All right. You will show up?" He sounded anxious.

"Of course," Emma said. She checked her watch. "I'll be there at four-fifteen."

She started to hang up.

"Miss Margolis?"

She brought the receiver back to her ear. "Yes?"

"Can I call you Emma?"

"Yes."

"Good. You are coming as a friend, aren't you, Emma? I mean, this isn't for TV, is it? I know you do that show and all, but our conversation will be . . . off the record, won't it? Just between friends?"

She hesitated. "If that's the way you want it, Robert."

"I very much need someone I can confide in. Could be you do, too, Emma," he added.

She could feel her pulse pounding at her temples. "What makes you say that?"

"The way we connected at the cemetery. You're hurting, too. And you don't think anyone understands. But I do understand, Emma. I know we understand each other in a special way."

While Emma struggled with a response, the phone went dead.

∎   ∎   ∎

Sarah had a stack of books on sexual homicide and serial killers on the table in front of her, determined to get at the root of what made a creature like Romeo tick. Although it was after four and she'd been sitting in the library at the Civic Center for well over an hour, all she'd managed was to make it through a couple of chapters of one of the books. Extremely upsetting.

She focused in on a page in the open book on top of the pile. *Probing the Mind of a Serial Killer: Sex, Lies, and Obsession.*

She read a few paragraphs and had to stop. The words started to blur. She pressed her hand down on the page as if somehow through osmosis she could absorb what was printed there. At the next table, Corky glanced her way, then quickly returned to the boating magazine he'd ostensibly been reading the whole time they'd been sitting there. She'd asked him that morning if they ever gave him a day off. He'd told her he'd put in for the extra shift. That he was taking a personal interest in the case. She wondered now if he was bored with his assignment.

Face it, Sarah. You disappoint all the men in your life in the end.

> "And what exactly are you doing snooping around, Sarah?" *Her father's face is etched in granite. He towers over her.*
>
> "I heard Mommy moaning upstairs. I thought she was feeling sick. That you'd want to know."
>
> "Your mother isn't sick, Sarah. She's drunk," *he says sharply.*
>
> *She feels the tears building. But she knows she mustn't cry. He'll think she's looking for sympathy, and that will make him even angrier.*
>
> "On the other hand, Melanie is sick. That's why she came down here to me. Your mother is obviously in no condition to deal with a sick child."

"Melanie's sick?"

"Wipe that look off your face, young lady."

What look? What does he see on her face?

He grips both her arms tightly, shaking her so hard, she feels her teeth rattle. "I will not have you being a Peeping Tom, Sarah. Do you understand? Do you?"

One hand releases her. She thinks it's a reprieve. Until she sees his hand raised—

Sarah nearly jumped out of her skin when she felt a hand press lightly on her shoulder.

"Relax. It's just me."

Sarah spun nervously around, taken aback to see John Allegro standing behind her.

"What are you doing here?" He'd been spying on her. Prying into her most secret thoughts.

"Want to go get some coffee?" he asked amiably, ignoring her curt question. "Or something stronger? You look like you could use it."

She was having trouble catching her breath. "You scared the hell out of me."

"I'm sorry. Next time I'll drop a book on the floor first. Or on my toe, if you like."

"Your charm's wearing thin, Allegro."

"It must be the atmosphere."

She saw him give a faint nod to Corky, who immediately put down his magazine, rose with a friendly smile, and headed for the exit. Then, without comment, Allegro closed the volume she was reading.

She eyed him warily. "You're not planning to give me a lecture."

"A lecture?"

"About the TV segment I taped this afternoon."

He gave the back of her chair a little pull. "No, I'm not going to give you a lecture. Because I'd only be wasting my breath, right?"

"Right." She gave him a bleak look. "You know about

the . . . wreath." It had been picked up at the studio and was now at the police lab for analysis.

Allegro nodded.

"It was from the florist downstairs. How did he . . . manage it?"

"The florist claims he found an envelope on the counter after he finished with a customer. Inside was a fifty-dollar bill and a laser-printed order for a heart-shaped wreath to be sent up to you at KFRN at two o'clock. With an enclosed note saying—"

Sarah shot up her hand to stop him. She didn't want to hear that hideous sentiment aloud. "And the florist didn't see anyone slip into the shop? Or the customer? Or anyone else?"

"No. The SOB apparently got in and out without being spotted."

"A wreath. You get them for . . . funerals." She stared down at the closed book in front of her. "Does he really think I could find these *gifts* romantic? Or is he just trying to drive me crazy before he zeroes in for the kill?"

"Sarah, you've got to take a breather from this or you'll drive yourself crazy. Hey, I've got an idea," Allegro said. "Let's take a drive up the coast. Do us both good to get away for a couple of hours."

"I already have plans with . . . someone."

"I thought you didn't have a boyfriend."

"Huh?"

"Someone? Sounds like a male."

"I never said I didn't have a boyfriend."

He squinted at her. "Didn't you?"

"Why the third degree, Allegro? Anyway, it's Bernie."

"The guy from your office. The one in the wheel-chair?"

Sarah nodded. "He's a good friend." *Maybe the only friend I have.* "I'm gonna camp out at his place for a few days."

"Why'd you leave Emma's?"

"The bed was lumpy." She saw the perplexed look on his face. "Forget it. An inside joke."

"Come on. Let's get out of here." Allegro's free hand was already on her arm, helping her out of her seat. His touch set off a panic alarm. She banged into the table, the book on sexual offenders tumbling to the floor.

Allegro bent down and picked it up, giving the title a quick glance before setting it back on the table. "Wouldn't it be good to leave this all behind for a little while?"

Good? There was nothing in the world she wanted more.

"So let's go."

"What about Bernie? He'll worry."

"Give him a call. Tell him I'll drop you off at his place later this evening." He gave her a jaunty smile. "I know this great little French restaurant in Tiburon. You'll love it."

"How do you know I'll love it? How do you know what I love or don't love?"

"You have something against coq au vin?"

Sarah had to smile. John Allegro did have this way about him. Not that she wasn't still cautious. She sensed that he had plenty of his own secrets. And that he put a lot of effort into concealing them. Like her. Was that the heart of the attraction? That they both were so damn good at keeping secrets?

"Tell you what," Allegro said with a boyish wink. "This time around you pick up the tab if that'll make you feel any better."

Robert Perry's brows knitted together. "Don't you like Darjeeling?"

Emma immediately lifted the teal-blue bone china cup to her lips. "No, it's fine."

"Are you sure you don't want a pastry or something to go with it?"

"No, this is fine. Really."

Perry refilled his own cup from the matching blue teapot, then gave the tiny storefront restaurant yet another survey. Two middle-aged women sat across the room near the lace-fringed window, and a young mother with her little girl in tow was at the counter buying some loose tea and scones.

"She's real cute, isn't she?" Perry said, his eyes on the child.

"Yes."

"Cindy wanted kids. She came from a big family. Six girls and two boys."

"What about you?"

He shrugged. "You mean wanting kids? I don't know. I always told Cindy I wasn't ready. I still feel like a kid myself. I'm only twenty-seven. I have this kid sister. Hannah. A real screwup. We don't see much of each other. She got involved with the wrong crowd in high school. Got into drugs and booze. Messed her head up. My mom finally threw her out when she caught her stealing from her purse. I didn't blame her."

"What about your dad?"

Perry's expression clouded. "What about him?"

"Did he agree with your mom? About your sister?"

He laughed harshly. "They didn't agree on anything. He used to beat Mom up."

"Your sister?"

"Her, too—why are you asking me all these questions? You're not working with the cops or anything? I know they're keeping tabs on me. Probably got binoculars fixed on us right now. Or are you wearing a wire or something?"

"I was just trying to get to know you, Robert. You said we could be friends. Friends know stuff about each other."

"I don't know anything about you." His mouth twisted into a grotesque smile. "Well, that's not quite true."

"What do you mean?" Emma asked uneasily.

"I know you've got a good heart."

The tea spilled over the rim of the cup in Emma's hand, staining the beautiful white lace tablecloth.

Allegro and Sarah were stuck in the rush-hour traffic jam going over the Golden Gate Bridge. The windows were rolled down, and she was staring out at the bay, watching the sailing sloops working against the stiff wind.

"Better?" he asked.

She turned to him. "Better than what?"

He smiled. "Better than sitting in that stuffy library."

She leaned forward and switched on the radio. The five o'clock news was in progress. "*. . . tomorrow for the latest update on the Whitewater scandal. Now turning to local news, San Francisco's DA, Lawrence Gillette, made a statement today, announcing that the police are accumulating important leads as to the identity of the serial killer known as Romeo. With five notches already on the brutal murderer's belt, including that of the noted police consultant involved in the investigation, psychiatrist Dr. Melanie Rosen—*"

Allegro flipped the radio off, cursing under his breath. Sarah rubbed her hands up and down her arms as if she could somehow scrub through her skin and erase the pain beneath it.

A car cut in front of Allegro. He blasted it with his horn.

Sarah glanced over at him. "You're angry about my taping tonight's segment."

Allegro tugged at his tie. "I'm angry about a lot of things."

"Me, too," she said.

"And scared?"

"Yes."

"Me, too."

"You're not supposed to admit that," she said.

He smiled, maneuvering the car into the left-hand

lane because it seemed to be moving faster. "If I'd said I wasn't scared, would you have believed me?"

She found herself smiling back. "No."

Their eyes connected. "You look pretty when you smile."

"You flirting with me, Allegro?"

"I'm complimenting you, Rosen. You have a problem with that?"

"If I said no, would you believe me?"

His smile broadened. "No."

Emma Margolis walked the four blocks from the tea shop back to her apartment. When she turned the corner onto her street, she was stunned to see William Dennison leaning against his car at the curb in front of her building. She stopped in her tracks as the psychiatrist glanced her way. He straightened immediately and started toward her. Emma crossed her arms and waited for him.

"What are you doing here, Bill?"

"The police came to see me again today. You told them you saw me for therapy."

"So? You're the one who's bound by confidentiality, not me."

"And you told them I saw your friend Diane. They were under the impression I'd deliberately withheld that information from them. They also made some other extremely disturbing insinuations. Wanted to know if I'd treated any of Romeo's other victims."

"Look, I've had one hell of a day, Bill—"

He blocked her way. "You think my day's been a bed of roses?"

They stared each other down for several moments.

"Look," Emma said, "I'd ask you to come up for a drink or something, but last time I tried that—"

"Last time you tried that you were my patient," Bill said.

"And what am I now?"

The moment was laden with ambiguity. Then, without a word, Emma started for her building, Bill Dennison walking beside her.

Lorraine Austin was a plump woman in her midfifties with washed-out blue eyes full of grief. "As far as I know, Karen was never in therapy," she told Wagner. It was a few minutes before the five-thirty closing, but she'd hung the "Closed" sign on the door, and since she was the only one on that day, they were alone in the shop. "Then again, a daughter doesn't tell her mother everything. Even though we were very close. . . ."

She pressed her index finger hard against her quivering lips, battling tears. "I keep wondering when I'll finally stop crying. There's nothing worse than losing a child. Nothing in the world."

Karen Austin had been Romeo's third victim. A financial adviser for a European banking group with offices off Union Square, Karen had worked only a few blocks from the upscale jewelry store where her mother was a saleswoman.

When Wagner and Allegro first interviewed Lorraine Austin shortly after Karen's murder, they'd asked her about the men her daughter had been involved with. According to her mother, the only man Karen had ever been serious about was a fellow she'd met in graduate school at the University of Colorado in Boulder in the late eighties. The old boyfriend had been followed up. On the night of Karen's murder he was in a hospital delivery room in Boise, Idaho, filming the birth of his second child.

Mrs. Austin also told them during that first interview that she and her daughter used to meet for lunch at least once a week. When asked what they'd talked about, she'd said they'd chatted about work, movies, fashion, and the trials and tribulations of being single women—Karen never having married and Lorraine having divorced when her daughter was seven. Wagner teased his partner after

the interview, saying that Mrs. Austin had been giving
him the eye. Allegro hadn't been amused.

"Do you have a new lead, Detective?" Mrs. Austin
asked now. "I keep hearing on the news—"

"I'm really not at liberty to discuss any details of our
investigation. But I can tell you that we're making progress."

Mrs. Austin's brow furrowed. "Those tabloids are disgusting. What they're saying about Karen and those other
poor women. I don't believe for one minute that my
daughter would have in any way encouraged that madman
—that she would ever want any man to—to dominate
her," she finished weakly. "She wasn't like that at all. She
was very strong. Very independent. He tricked her. All she
wanted was to be loved. Is that a crime?"

"No, of course not," Wagner said quickly.

"You really should do something about what the press
is saying. Not just those filthy papers either. It's all over
the news. Even that woman psychiatrist he went and murdered. I saw her on television. I heard what she said even
before—before Karen—saying how the victims were doing
—disgusting things sexually. Not my Karen. Never. She
was a good, decent girl."

"I'm sure she was," Wagner soothed. "Now, about
William Dennison—"

"I told you. I never heard Karen mention his name."

"What about Robert Perry? Dr. Stanley Feldman?"
Wagner took photos of the three suspects from his pocket.
"If you could take a look at these—"

Lorraine Austin's eyes brimmed with tears. "You
worry when you hear about these awful things happening
to other girls. I remember after that second girl was murdered, I warned Karen to be very careful, but I never really
thought it would happen to her. You never do think it'll
happen to someone you love."

Wagner reached across the glass-topped counter and
patted the woman's hand. "No, Mrs. Austin. You never
do."

She managed a tremulous smile. "And these men you're asking me about—"

He handed her the photos. She glanced at Feldman's, then Perry's, finally Dennison's. She seemed to study that one more closely.

"That's William Dennison," Wagner said. "Lot of people call him Bill. Karen might have. Or Dr. Dennison."

She stared at it for several moments. "He looks so sad."

"It was taken at—a funeral."

Mrs. Austin's head jerked up. "Not Karen's?"

"No."

She continued studying the photo. "A psychiatrist, you said."

"Yes. That's right."

"You really think Romeo might be a psychiatrist?"

"These are just routine questions. All I'm asking is if your daughter knew Bill Dennison in any capacity, Mrs. Austin. She might not have been a patient of his, merely a date, or a friend."

"Karen never mentioned him to me. Or these others," she said, checking the other photos.

"And none of them look familiar to you? You never saw any of them with Karen? Or maybe when the two of you were at a restaurant, you might have noticed one of these guys at another table on a few occasions—"

"Are they all therapists?"

"Two of them are."

Mrs. Austin frowned. "If she were going for therapy, I know she would have told me. I'm not saying she was never down. Aren't we all sometimes?"

"What got Karen down?"

"Nothing to do with sex."

"I know how terrible this must be for you," Wagner said softly. "Believe me, Mrs. Austin, no one feels anything but sympathy for the women this psycho murdered so mercilessly. And for all the loved ones they left behind."

Now it was the victim's mother who gripped Wagner's hand, squeezing it tightly. "I feel so alone. I miss her so much. She was a lovely girl. You would have liked her."

Wagner smiled sympathetically. "I'm sure I would."

Once again her eyes fell on the photos she still held in her hand. "I suppose Karen might have dated any one of them. Like I said, a daughter doesn't tell a mother everything," she repeated forlornly.

Allegro pulled off crowded 101 and headed east into Sausalito, where they'd take the twenty-minute ferry ride to Tiburon. There was still a fair amount of traffic, but it was no longer stop and go.

Sarah said, "You know that book I was reading back at the library—the one on sexual homicide."

"Yeah?"

"The author's a psychologist who works with sex offenders. He wrote about what turns a person into a killer."

Allegro glanced over at Sarah. She was talking about the book he'd picked up from the library floor. Melanie had actually referred to it during her consultation with them. He chose not to mention that to Sarah.

"He hasn't always been a killer," Sarah went on, almost as if she were giving a school report. Her hands were clasped dutifully on her lap, and she sat very erect. "He becomes one. Bad things happen in his childhood. An accumulation of abuse, pain, isolation. Rage, most of all. The feelings gather inside, building up. And then one day something sets him off. Like a trigger that's just been waiting to be released. An event occurs that enrages him or causes him extreme anxiety or depression. Could be a girlfriend breaking up with him or a wife walking out on him. Or it could be he was feeling stressed out because of something that happened to him at work, or bummed out because he got fired."

"Two of those fit Robert Perry like a glove," Allegro

commented. "His wife walked out on him right around the time the murders started. And he got laid off just a short time before that."

"You're pretty much convinced it's Perry?"

Allegro turned onto Bridgeway, Sausalito's main drag that hugged the bay and led to the ferry terminal. "I think it's quite possible. You don't?"

"I'm having trouble not thinking that every man I know—including you and Wagner—is Romeo. Everyone but Bernie. And only because he's gay and in a wheelchair." She shook her head. "That's not true."

"You suspect Bernie, too?"

"No. I mean it's not only what I said. I love Bernie. He's one of the few people I've ever really trusted. He's my best friend." In time, Sarah thought, she and Emma might become quite close. A substitute for the older sister she'd lost?

Her eye caught sight of a couple ardently kissing in front of an art gallery, oblivious to everyone around. She felt a pang of such aching envy, tears stung her eyes. And then came the anger. Why did her life have to be besieged by pain? What she would give at that instant to change places with that carefree young woman. *Oh, Sarah,* she could hear Melanie saying with her familiar heavy sigh, *you imagine everyone else on this planet has it easier than you. The reality is, we all have our crosses to bear.*

Only a few weeks ago, Sarah would have been quick to mock what she perceived as Melanie's self-righteousness. Not anymore.

"So what should we talk about?" Allegro asked her.

"Anything meaningless."

Allegro grinned. "Tall order."

Something about the way he said it made Sarah laugh. Or it might have come simply from her desperate need for a feeling of normalcy. Even if it wasn't real.

They ended up not talking at all for a while, which suited Sarah fine. How rare to find a man who knew when to shut up. Surprisingly, she found herself relaxing a bit, enjoying the bay breeze, this little jaunt, even the company.

Oh, this is nice. See, Feldman. You're wrong. The past with all its grief, confusion, anguish, and fear hasn't choked every ounce of joy out of me.

Later, on the ferry chugging toward Tiburon, they leaned against the deck railing, shoulders almost but not quite touching, looking out at the sailboat-studded bay. Sarah's thoughts drifted to that couple kissing in front of the art gallery. Then she thought about how it had felt, the night before, after that near break-in at her apartment, to cling to John, to feel him holding her. It had felt good. Under other circumstances—

She glanced his way. *Did he really think she was pretty?*

My fingers close around you, and I see the light click off in your eyes. I feel a desperation so intense that I imagine myself being devoured by it. You are my private agony, my mystery, my life.

M.R. diary

18

Sarah sat beside John Allegro on a porch swing outside the quaint inn where they'd feasted on a marvelous candlelit French dinner. The first decent meal she'd eaten in ages. And he'd picked up the sizable tab, after all.

She glanced over at him, experiencing an inexplicable sense of contentment. She had no real idea what her feelings were for John Allegro, beyond a budding physical attraction, but she found herself enjoying the fantasy of being in love with him. The fantasy being as close to the real thing as she'd ever gotten.

Naturally, she could hear Feldman's familiar whisperings. *This is only another attempt at denial, Sarah. Your way of trying to find safety when you are feeling desperately unsafe. It won't work. You can only keep the terror at bay for so long. And we both know it's getting harder and harder. Your secrets are starting to spill out, and there's no shoving them back in—*

"I wish we could stay here forever," she blurted.

Allegro didn't look her way as he said, "I don't know about forever, but we could—" He hesitated.

"We could what?" Sarah pressed.

Their eyes connected. "We could stay the night, if you want. There are—rooms. Upstairs."

"Rooms?"

"It was just an idea. I forgot about your friend. Gary, is it?"

"Bernie."

"Right. Bernie."

"I could call him again."

"Do you want to?"

"Do I want to what?"

"Call him?" Allegro rubbed his jaw. "Stay here?"

"Detective, I believe you're blushing."

"Hey, don't go getting the wrong idea, Sarah. I'm not putting the moves on you. I did say rooms, not room. I only thought—"

"What did you think?"

"That's a loaded question. You don't want to hear everything I'm thinking."

"Would you tell me if I did?"

He smiled. "No."

Impulsively, Sarah leaned toward him, her face only inches away. "That's all right, John."

"Jesus," he whispered as he cupped her chin and brought her mouth to his.

For all her wanting that kiss, the instant his lips made contact with hers, Sarah felt a surge of panic and abruptly jerked away. If she was using John Allegro to distract her from her terrors, she could toss in bad judgment on top of all her other failings.

Allegro was immediately apologetic. "That was dumb. Look, Sarah, I know what you must be thinking—"

"No you don't, Allegro. Really you don't."

"We can go back to the city. I'll take you to Gary's. Bernie's."

"Is that what you want to do?"

"I want to do whatever it is you want."

"And if I don't know?"

"I think you do."

Sarah was silent for several moments. Then she whispered, "I'm nothing like Melanie."

Allegro stared off into the shadowy night. "I know that."

"You wanted her. You were attracted to her."

"Yes." No point denying something he'd already admitted.

"So then why didn't you have sex with her? Did she turn you down?"

"No."

"Then why?"

"I don't know if I can explain it."

"Try."

He leaned back in the porch swing, pressing his hands together between his thighs. "I guess in part it had to do with Grace."

"Your wife?"

He nodded. "There was this desperation about Grace. There were times when I'd be leaving for work, and she'd follow me to the door, hovering there, watching me walk down the hall, and I'd think—she'll stay in suspended animation until I get back."

"And you felt the same way about Melanie?" Sarah asked incredulously. Whatever her sister's failings, Sarah did not see the correlation between her driven, fiercely independent sister and Allegro's nonfunctioning wife.

"In a strange way, yes," he answered. "As I got to know your sister, I began to feel as though there were two Melanies—the one who maneuvered her way adeptly through life on automatic pilot, and then the other Melanie."

"The one hanging in suspended animation? Desperate for you to set her life back in motion?"

Allegro turned his head and looked unwaveringly at Sarah. "Desperate for someone."

Sarah turned away, staring off into the darkness. *Yes, desperate for someone, all right. The "you" in those diary fragments.*

"All I knew was, I couldn't give Melanie what she needed," Allegro was saying.

Sarah turned back to him, her expression awash with accusation. "Couldn't or didn't want to?" *Yes. Put the blame on him. Put the blame on all of them. They all failed Melanie. Just like they'll all fail me in the end.*

Allegro smiled darkly. "That's what I like about you, Sarah. You cut straight through the bullshit. Maybe you're right on target. The truth of it is, I hate feeling manipulated. I hate feeling inadequate even more. I could have screwed your sister," he said bluntly, "but it wouldn't have left either one of us satisfied. And even worse, I would have gotten myself tangled up again in a situation that was only going to fuck up my life even more than it already was."

"And what about me? Am I fucking up your life, too?"

His expression was as piercing as a blade. "I don't know yet. There's no getting away from the fact that we're both dragging along a lot of baggage. But—" He stopped abruptly.

"But what?" she demanded.

His features softened. His hand reached out and lightly stroked her cheek. "But you are getting under my skin, Sarah," he whispered.

His touch, light as it was, soaked into her skin, slid across her muscles, easing and tensing them at once. This time, when their lips met, she didn't pull back. For a few moments she was even able to fully give herself to the kiss, keeping her usual panic at bay, imagining she and John were no different from that pair of lovers she'd seen kissing back in Sausalito. The pure thrill of it. The intoxicating, even centering sensation of being wanted, desired. Being the one who was cherished. Time slipped away. This was everything, this moment. Filling her universe—

She climbs on his lap. Straddling him. Wanting him. Aching. Predatory. Pinning herself on him.

"Yes, yes, yes . . ." he's panting in her ear.

A flurry of panic. Lethal shadows on the walls. "I don't know. I don't know."

"It's all right, baby. I promise you. I promise. I promise—" He's kissing her all over. Taking charge now. His hands circling her waist. Lifting her. Up and down. Up and down. She's powerless. She must surrender.

"Yes, yes, yes." Her voice now. No guilt. No fear. No demons. No betrayal. If only she can make it last.

But it was ending even as the thought entered her mind. That old familiar bad feeling was taking her over—that feeling like she was coming together and breaking apart at the same time. *Got to stop. Got to stop before it's too late. Before he chews me all up and gobbles me down. Isn't that what they all do? Ravage and destroy? Tear out your heart?*

Sarah gasped, flinging herself away from Allegro.

His hand darted out. He gripped her arm. "Sarah, it was only a kiss. Take it easy." There was an edge to his voice.

Only then did she realize her fists were clenched and she was about to pummel Allegro. She stopped midmotion, catching her breath, shaken to realize they were still on the swing, fully clothed, side by side.

Only a kiss. Yes, she realized now. That was all it was. And a rather chaste one at that. All the rest an illusion. Fantasy love. Fantasy lovemaking. Dumb to imagine she was capable of the real thing.

But it had felt so real. Like it was actually happening. Wish-fulfillment? Projection? The image of her sister embracing Feldman flashed in her mind—how Feldman's features had evaporated before her eyes—a new face taking on form and substance. Her father's face. Or was that pure fantasy, too? Was she flipping out?

Allegro still had a firm hold on her arm. She didn't want him to touch her now. She wanted to bolt, but she forced a *that was nice* smile. Not that she really thought she was getting away with anything.

Exhaling a breath that was clearly tinged with exasperation, he muttered, "Let's just chalk it up to lousy timing." He dug his hands into the pockets of his jacket as if to demonstrate he would not accost her.

Sarah felt like shit. Well, it was a nice fairy tale while it lasted. But then, so many fairy tales had their dark sides. No one knew that better than she did.

She rose abruptly to her feet. "I guess we should be getting back. Bernie will be worrying."

"Right," Allegro said, resignedly getting up and following her as she hurried down the steps from the porch, the empty swing rocking slowly back and forth, a thick nighttime fog rolling in from the bay.

"I kept some pot roast on the stove," Bernie said by way of a greeting when she showed up at his place at nine forty-five that evening.

She gave him a wan look. "I think I may throw up."

"Well, I guess I don't have to ask if your date went well."

"It wasn't a date," she snapped.

"I was joking. What is it, Sarah? Come sit down and talk to your old pal, Bernie." He wheeled himself into his ersatz Greco-Roman living room, a remnant of a brief affair with an interior decorator. Expertly maneuvering his chair around several little Neapolitan tables studded with marble sculptures and other pseudo-classical objets d'art, he parked himself beside a burnt umber velvet wing chair, patting the overstuffed cushion.

Sarah slumped into the chair and dropped her head into her hands.

"Want some aspirin? Tums? Hot milk and honey?" Bernie asked solicitously.

"Bernie, either I'm going nuts or having false memories or—" She couldn't bring herself to finish the sentence.

"False memories?" Bernie rubbed his beard. "You mean remembering something traumatic that happened in the past, only it turns out you imagined it? Made it all up?"

Sarah nodded. "How do you ever know for sure if you really remember something or if it's just a figment of your screwed-up imagination?"

"I suppose if the person who caused the trauma admitted it."

"He . . . can't."

"What about witnesses?" he asked innocently.

Sarah's stomach cramped. *Why'd you hit me? I didn't do anything wrong. I didn't. I didn't.*

Bernie wheeled himself closer, taking hold of Sarah's hand, their knees practically touching. "What is it, sweetheart? You can tell me."

Sarah let her head fall back against the chair. She stared up at the ornately plastered ceiling. "What if—what if the only witness is—me?"

"The only witness to what?"

She hugged herself tightly and shut her eyes. "I think I saw them. Melanie and—" How could she say it aloud?

Bernie didn't understand. "You saw Melanie and Romeo? Is that it, Sarah? You think you know who did it?"

Yes, she thought. In a way she did. Because Romeo wasn't the beginning of Melanie's sad saga, merely the tragic end.

"I'm not talking about Romeo," she said bleakly.

"Who are you talking about, then?"

How to begin? Impossible to even let herself really accept it, allow the memory to truly take on depth and clarity, much less blurt it right out.

"I've been having these terribly upsetting visions. They started right after Melanie was murdered. Really, right after Romeo started contacting me. Triggered these awful . . . flashes. And they're getting worse by the day.

This morning at Feldman's, there was this particularly horrible nightmarish image—"

"Feldman?"

"Not really to do with him. Although in a way—I guess you could say he was the catalyst."

"What was it you saw?"

Bernie was moving too quickly. The images—incubating on the surface of her memory all day—made her flinch. "I've begun to remember this incident from my past. It was when I was thirteen. Just a short time before . . . my mother died." *Killed herself. Strung herself up by a clothesline in the attic. Died* sounded so much more *chaste.*

"Go on," Bernie coaxed gently.

"I'm not truly sure any of it's real, Bernie. It could have all been some terrible nightmare I've been carting around in my unconscious for years. Or some of it may actually have happened, but the rest . . ." Her mind raced ahead of her words. Seeing more than she wanted to see. A film running in her head, no matter how hard she tried to turn off the projector.

Bernie was still holding her hand. "Tell me about the part that you think might have actually happened."

She smiled at him. "You would have made a good shrink, you know that, Bernie?"

"I'll settle for being a good friend."

Her smile took on an edge of seduction. "If you weren't gay—"

"Yeah, yeah. Enough with the delay tactics."

His knowing remark quickly sobered her, but she was glad he hadn't let go of her hand. Giving her some much-needed courage.

She told him about that night when she was thirteen and she went down to the den to tell her father that her mother was sick. How angry he'd been. How he'd told her Melanie was the one who was sick.

"I remember now," she went on. "My parents had this big blowup over my tap dance lessons. I'd begged my mother to let me quit. I hated them. Finally, she agreed. Told the teacher. Then came home and told my father. He was furious. It's the only time I can recall my mother actually standing up against him. Standing up for *me*." She shut her eyes. "Three days later she hung herself."

"Because of the argument with your dad?" Bernie sounded incredulous.

"I don't know. I don't know why she did it."

"Okay, go on. So you went down to the den—"

"What if this is all some . . . delusion? Maybe I am cracking up. Feldman's probably right. I should go back on Prozac. Or something. Romeo's fucking up my head. As if it needed any help."

"What happened when you got to the den, Sarah?" Bernie coaxed.

She kept her eyes closed. She wasn't in Bernie's apartment anymore. She was in that downstairs hall in her old house in Mill Valley. She was in her fire-engine-red pajamas. "When I first got to the door, I was frightened. He'd be mad if I woke him. I just opened the door a crack to check if he was asleep. I could see inside—"

She stopped abruptly, her breath coming in short, quick puffs.

"What did you see, Sarah?" Bernie asked gently.

"I—see them. Oh, God. I see them. Daddy and— Melanie." Even her voice had altered. It was the voice of a frightened little girl.

Tears began streaming down her cheeks, but she kept on talking. Not even aware that she was talking. As if she were there again. All she was conscious of was what she was seeing. "Melanie's back's to me. She's on Daddy's lap, facing him. On the big fold-out sofa bed."

She cowered in the chair. Her arms shot protectively across her belly. "She's naked. Mellie's naked. I see her nightgown lying on the floor . . . the white cotton one with the lace on the cuffs . . ."

She could see his face now. Her father's face. But not looking like him. Not like any way she'd ever seen him look. Neck arched back, purple veins protruding. Mouth yawning open. Eyes rolled back in his head. Large hands wrapped around Melanie's narrow, naked waist. Lifting her up and down, up and down, up and down.

She squeezed her eyes shut, but the awful, hideous image wouldn't go away. She jammed her fists into her eyelids. *Still there. Still there.*

"Let me get you some water. Something," Bernie pleaded.

But Sarah was clutching him now. "It happened, Bernie. It really happened."

"Yes, Sarah. Yes."

Bernie's confirmation fell over her like a blessing and a curse.

"He saw me. At the door. It was horrible. I felt like his eyes would burn a hole right through me."

She'd thought the look on her father's face before had been hideous, but this was worse. The look of sheer disgust—no, revulsion—hatred. "I can see him. Towering over me. In his gray flannel robe. Pulling the tie around his waist. The funny way he smells." Her eyelids flickered open. "He was so mad, he struck me. Hard. Right in my belly."

Bernie's eyes flooded with tears.

Clutching her stomach, Sarah slipped off the chair to the floor, sobbing, her head dropping onto Bernie's lifeless legs. "Oh, Bernie, Melanie was sixteen. I think maybe it wasn't the only time. I think maybe . . . down there in that den in our Mill Valley house. All those nights when Momma was passed out cold upstairs. I hated when she drank. Because then I knew he'd be sleeping there. And that Melanie—Melanie—"

Other images and sounds bombarded her. It felt as though her mind was being ransacked, violent, sensory flashes tossed around her head helter-skelter. She struggled for breath. "And it didn't stop then, Bernie. Even after—after Momma died and we moved, I remember now the noises at night. Awful sounds. Cries. Moans. I'd put my pillow over my head. I never got out of my bed. I never went to check. I didn't want my father to—to catch me snooping again. But sometimes I could hear them. I could hear them having sex."

Spasms ripped through her. Her whole body started jerking. Bernie was terrified she was having some kind of a traumatic seizure. If she hadn't been clinging so fiercely to him, he'd have wheeled to the phone and dialed for paramedics. As it was, all he could manage was to stroke her back, clinging to her, trying to find words that would soothe her awful pain. "I know how terrible this is for you, Sarah. But it's good you're remembering. You know what they say about the truth setting you free. I believe that. I really do. Let it go, Sarah. . . . Let it go. . . ."

Little by little, the convulsions began to subside. So did her sobs. She was experiencing an exorcism.

"This is Romeo's doing," she said in a raspy whisper. "He's the one that forced open Pandora's box. If he hadn't sent me those pieces from Melanie's diary, I might have gone on denying what happened till my dying day."

"What pieces?" Bernie asked. "You told me he was writing to you, sending you bizarre little gifts. You didn't say anything about Melanie's diary."

"I was afraid to show them to anyone. And—I was ashamed about the things—she'd written. Now I'm ashamed I felt that way. That I didn't understand. That I didn't realize . . ."

"You didn't know then, Sarah. You'd blocked it out. It's certainly easy enough to understand why."

She gave Bernie a bleak look. "This is what Romeo wanted. To make me remember. Make me suffer. He knows the truth. Melanie wrote about me in her diary." *I am my sister's keeper, as she is mine.*

"Feldman looked shocked when I told him about Melanie's diary." After a brief pause she added, "Or else he was putting on a great act."

"Why would he—? Oh, Sarah, surely you don't think Feldman—"

"Who better than a shrink to plot out these intricate mind games?" she demanded. "Of course there was still another shrink in Melanie's life. Bill. Knowing about Melanie and my father would have driven Bill to distraction." Her eyes fixed on Bernie's. "Or worse."

"Bill Dennison, a brutal psycho serial killer?"

"All the nights I cried myself to sleep, longing for him —just once, even—to make me feel as if he wanted me."

"Dennison?" Bernie knew of Sarah's brief affair with Melanie's ex, although she hadn't gone into any of the details.

"No," she said. "My father."

"Did your father—ever?" Bernie asked tentatively.

"What are you saying?" she cried hoarsely.

"I'm not saying anything, Sarah. I was only asking. That's all. We don't have to talk about it."

She flung herself away, wild-eyed, furious. "There's nothing to talk about. My father *never* touched me. *Never*. Not in that way. *Never*. I disgusted him. How could I ever compare to Melanie in his eyes? Is that what you think I wanted? You think I used to wish it was me? That I wanted my father to have sex with me?" She was raging, her face ugly and beet-red, her hands clenched into tight fists.

"Look, if it'll make you feel better, go on. Take a punch at me. Go ahead. Let it fly."

That stopped her cold. She almost laughed, it was so ludicrous. "Are you nuts, Bernie?"

"What I'm trying to tell you is, I'm your friend, Sarah. I love you. And I wasn't saying your father molested you, too."

She sank heavily back into the wing chair. "I bet that's what Romeo thinks, though. That Melanie and I both—" Her mouth gaped open; her eyes widened.

"Sarah, what is it?"

"Maybe that's it. What if Romeo thinks we were *all* victims of incest? Not victims, though. That somehow we're to blame. That we're the *sinners*. That he's our redeemer."

Bernie gaped at her. "Jesus, Sarah, you may be on to something here. You've gotta call that cop pal of yours, Allegro."

"Tell him? Tell him that my father sexually abused my sister? Tell him to check with the fathers of the other victims and see if they were involved in incestuous relationships with their murdered daughters?" Hysteria bubbled up in her throat. She turned away.

"All you have to do is tell him that Romeo may think it, not that it's necessarily true, Sarah," Bernie argued. Easy for him to remain calm and rational.

"I don't see how it would help much in their investigation," she said stubbornly.

"It could help a lot. It gives the cops another aspect of Romeo's personality to consider and check into. Hey, maybe he was abused as a kid, himself. You know, he identifies with his victims and hates them at the same time. And hates himself, probably."

"I don't know, Bernie." But even as she protested, she recalled quotes from sexual offenders she'd read in that library book—

My father started molesting me when I was seven. When I threatened to tell on him, he beat me within an inch of my life. . . .

After my dad left, my mother made me sleep with her. We had sex the whole time I was in high school. . . .

My older brother raped me when I was eleven and then started calling me a queer. . . .

Bernie could be right. A lot of sexual psychopaths had been raised in violent and abusive homes.

"What do you know about Dennison's family life?"

Sarah shrugged. "Not much. I only met his folks once. At the wedding. They live in Manhattan. His father's an internist, I think. His mother—I don't know anything about her."

"And Feldman?"

"Feldman? Nothing. Except that he was married and his wife died young. I think it was a car accident."

"And his folks?"

"He grew up in Hungary. That's all I know. Maybe I should call him up and ask him. Say, Feldman, I was just wondering. Did your daddy ever play hide the salami with you? Did you ever hide your salami in your mommy?"

"Shit. Talking of phoning, I almost forgot."

"What?" Sarah asked distractedly.

"Emma Margolis called a couple of times. She wants you to call her back."

Sarah frowned. "I should call her. She's probably worried about me. I was pretty upset after the taping today." Even before getting that wreath.

She checked her watch. It was a few minutes past eleven P.M. She'd missed the airing of Emma's show. Not that she thought she could stomach sitting through it. Traumatic enough having made it.

"What about your pal—Allegro? You gonna call him and tell him your theory?" Bernie asked as Sarah rifled through her cluttered tote bag for the slip of paper on which she'd jotted down Emma's unlisted home number.

"I'll call him, too, but it's not something I can explain over the phone."

Bernie grinned. "Guess you'll have to make another date with him."

Sarah shook her fist at Bernie, but this time there was a faint smile on her face. Okay, so she wanted to see John again. Strangely enough, given all that had happened, she was actually feeling a flicker of hope.

She called Emma first but had to settle for her answering machine. After the beep, she left a brief message saying she was fine and that she'd try her again in the morning. She tried John next at the home number he gave her the night before.

No one answered there either.

The satisfaction is short-lived. The sense of frustration inevitably resurfaces, escalates. Because he never can get it right. He never can get at the original rage, the original pain.

Dr. Melanie Rosen
Cutting Edge

19

Romeo drums his fingers lightly against his lips as he watches Sarah on TV. *"You can't fool yourself. You can't fool me."*

"Such intensity. It's quite beautiful. Incredibly moving. It's true. I can't fool myself. Or you. Deep down, you know. You know the true me. And the true you. You're just waiting for me to strip away the facade. For both of us," he says. "Isn't that true, Emma?"

"Please," Emma Margolis pleads, her face twisted by terror and pain.

"Please what?"

"Please untie me." Emma's voice is a whimper. The silk restraints are digging into her flesh, even though she stopped struggling once she realized it only tightened the binding.

Romeo's eyes remain fixed on the television. He's totally absorbed. *"Like waving a sign. 'I'm out here, Sarah.'"* He feels an incredible rush. "Yes, I'm here. So close, Sarah. So very close."

He's sitting on the sofa bed in Emma's guest room—where Emma told him Sarah slept the night before. He presses the pillow she'd slept on to his face, breathing in her scent. The predator sniffing out his prey. ". . . *cracks start to show. I'm going to be looking real hard, and soon I'll see them. You may hide from the others . . .*" He smiles. "You're trying, baby, but you're still not looking hard enough. Or maybe you are and you're just not ready yet. Soon, Sarah."

He stretches out as the segment he taped on Emma's VCR an hour ago ends. He gives Emma a cursory glance. She lies naked at his feet, her bound body leaving her in a contorted and wholly vulnerable position. He is still fully clothed, but his fly is unzipped and he is idly stroking himself as he picks up the remote, rewinds the tape for a few seconds, then hits *play*.

"*My sister believed that you grew stronger and more powerful with each killing, but I think she was wrong. I think you're scared. Sometimes I think I can even pick up the scent of your fear.*"

He hits *pause* and smiles sardonically at Emma. "Do you smell my fear?"

He hits *play*—begins stroking himself again. Watching the screen intently. Breathing her in. Her words. Her voice. Her image.

"*Sometimes I think I can even pick up the scent of your fear. You try to fight it, pretend it away. But you can't fool yourself. You can't fool me.*"

"Sarah's right about one thing, Emma. I am getting tired of the pose. Romeo is my true identity. The authentic me. Everything else is a lie. We all need to reunite with who we truly are. Some of us need help. Enlightenment. That's what I did for Melanie and the others. That's what I'm doing for you tonight, Emma. Helping you strip away the lies. So that you can connect with the true Emma. The cockteaser. The whore. The sorceress. The sinner. Isn't that true, cunt?"

"Yes," she whimpers, quaking with fear.

He grins. "You're a liar. You would say or do anything now, wouldn't you?" Smiling obscenely, he extends his bare foot. "Lick it then. Suck on it deep and hard. Give it your very best effort, baby."

Emma begins to cry even as she obediently draws his toe past her raw, cracked lips.

He watches her ministrations impersonally. What this boils down to, in the end, is another diversion. Definitely better than the last one—that little slut from the club. She wasn't worthy of his absolution. He knew that well before he claimed her heart.

He frowns. Melanie had been so much more satisfying than the others. He'd actually believed she might be the last. That she would be his redemption—as he was hers. That he would be able to keep her heart miraculously untarnished. Pure. In the end, her heart proved no better than the others. Now he saw that Melanie, too, was capable only of taking, not giving.

He knows that things are moving faster than he'd planned. Frustration building. Getting out of control. Sarah's right. The cracks *are* starting to show.

He knows it will be exquisite with Sarah. He's finding it harder and harder to postpone turning the fantasy into reality. There's this terrible pressure. This urgency. Her televised pleas to him are so tantalizing he can barely contain himself.

He'd hoped Emma would stave off some of his mounting frustration. But she's proving a disappointment. Destined to fail him. Like all the others. Still, he must finish what he's begun. If only for Emma's sake.

As he strokes his prick, Emma is already a fait accompli. He is thinking about Sarah. His delicious vision of their final evening together. Only Sarah is special. That is absolutely clear to him. And there hasn't been anyone that truly special in his life in such a long time.

He lowers the volume on the television so that Sarah's voice is a whisper. The strains of *Rhapsody in Blue* can be heard from the living room. *Her* favorite piece. His homage to the one woman who truly understood him. Totally adored him. To let her know she is always there with him, a part of him. That he is doing all this for her.

"You're breaking my heart, baby."

Romeo squeezes his eyes shut as her familiar cry resonates in his head, drowning out Sarah's televised voice, the music. *I'm sorry. I didn't mean to break your heart. But you shouldn't have broken mine.*

Sorrow mixes with rage, as it always does. It didn't have to happen the way it did. If only she'd been true to him. If she hadn't said all those terrible things to him that last day. *Why did she hurt him so? When he reached out for her, why did her face fill with such contempt? That beautiful face. How hideous it turned.*

His mouth twitches. *You never really loved me. You only said you did. You used me.*

Hatred stings the back of his throat. *You fucked me good. You got what you deserved, you bitch, you whore, you cunt.*

He swats away the tears from his eyes. *No, I didn't mean that. I love you. I'll always love you. That's what this is all about. I'm trying so hard to make it up to you. I'm doing everything I can. I want your forgiveness. Your love.*

He hits *pause.* Sarah in *freeze frame.* Her image floods him with hope. With love.

He feels full of himself. In utter control. Everything's back on track. All's right with the world.

He slides down to the floor beside his captive, yanking her head up by her thick, dark hair. She is drooling saliva and blood. Her face is so bruised, she's almost unrecognizable. "How about another glass of champagne, Emma? Just to show there are no hard feelings."

He reaches for the Perrier-Jouët, filling both their glasses. Beside the bottle rests a carving knife from Emma's kitchen, its finely honed steel blade reflecting the light cast by the flickering candles.

The phone rings.

You are as good as dead. I mourn and celebrate in the same breath.

M.R. diary

20

"How do you feel?" Bernie asked solicitously when Sarah, wearing one of his borrowed pajama tops, shuffled into his kitchen the next morning.

She poured herself a cup of coffee from a glistening carafe. "How do I look?"

"Like hell."

"I feel worse."

"Of course you do," Bernie said. "But it's good that you remembered—what you did, Sarah. In the end—"

She scowled. "You know what I feel the most right now? Fury. At my father. At Romeo. At John."

"John?"

"Allegro. And Mike Wagner and the rest of their *brilliant* task force."

"I'm sure they're doing everything possible, Sarah—"

"It's not enough. There's got to be something more. Something more I can do. Goad him on until he can't be satisfied with his notes, his candies, his lockets. Get him so worked up, he has to shed his skin. Show his true colors. I'll go on Emma's show again on Monday. And every day after that. I'll keep this up until he has to respond. It's a battle of wills, Bernie." She stared past her friend. There were so many battles to fight. So many scores to settle. And now there was another name right up there with Romeo at the top of her list. Simon Rosen.

Outside Bernie's building thirty minutes later, Sarah spotted Corky leaning against his unmarked car at the curb, having a smoke. He saw her, ground out his cigarette, and said, "Good morning."

She glanced cautiously up and down the street. Would there ever come a time when she wouldn't be watching out for monsters?

"Don't worry. All quiet here," Corky assured her. "Not even the press has tracked you down here yet."

Sarah nodded. She was sure, now that she'd done those segments on *Cutting Edge*, they'd all be the wilder for a piece of her.

"Would you mind giving me a lift again, Corky—"

"Where to this time?"

"Berkeley. The Bellevista. It's a nursing home. I want to visit my father."

When they drove up to the Bellevista about twenty minutes later, Corky asked if she wanted him to come in with her.

"No. This place is as tight as a drum. Not because they're worried about break-ins, but break-outs. I'll be fine."

Fine. An overstatement if ever there was one.

"Well, I'll be right outside here, Sarah," he promised, brushing her shoulder with his hand.

Charlotte Harris, Bellevista's head nurse, gave Sarah a startled look as she marched into the lobby and started directly for the elegant staircase. The nurse left her desk and rushed over. "I'm sorry, Miss Rosen, but visiting hours aren't until eleven—"

"I need to speak to my father now," Sarah said adamantly, stepping around the woman.

Harris followed on Sarah's heels. "You appear to be upset, Miss Rosen. I'm sure you wouldn't want to get your father agitated—"

"Wouldn't I?" Sarah was already four steps up.

"Please, Miss Rosen. Come back at elev—"

"I'm going to see my father right now."

"But that isn't possible."

"You'd be amazed at what's possible," Sarah said, halfway to the second-floor landing where her father's suite was located.

"I really must insist, Miss Rosen. Your father is a very sick man."

"Tell me about it."

Sarah's savage response left the head nurse aghast. "I am afraid I am going to have to take steps, Miss Rosen. I simply can't allow your father to be disrupted—"

"If I make a scene—which I promise you I will if you don't get off my butt, Miss Harris—think of how disruptive that would be, not only to my father, but to all of your *guests* here."

Tight-lipped, the nurse finally backed off. "You will have to take full responsibility for the outcome of your rash action, Miss Rosen."

"Don't we all have to take responsibility for our own actions, Miss Harris?"

When Sarah stepped into the parlor of her father's suite, she found him sitting in his favorite armchair near the window, reading the newspaper. He was dressed in a tailored dark suit, starched white shirt with the requisite gold cuff links, paisley tie, highly buffed cordovan oxfords. Seeing him dressed as if for work, Sarah felt hurled back in time.

"Am I disturbing you?"

He glanced up at her. "Has she arrived?"

"Who?"

"My first patient." He checked his Rolex watch. "Seven minutes late." He started to rise. "Transference issues."

"No. No, your—patient isn't here, Dad. I just came in to talk with you."

His eyes narrowed. "Do I know you?"

"It's me—Sarah. Your daughter."

"My daughter?" Caution shifted to confusion. He sat back down, staring at her. "Why are you up so early, baby? Is something the matter? Tell Daddy. Are you sick?"

Sarah bit back tears as she shook her head.

He smiled at her, patting his knee. "You know you aren't supposed to disturb me when I'm working, Mellie. But there's always time for a little snuggle. Come sit on my lap. Just for a few minutes."

"It's not Mellie, Dad. It's Sarah. Mellie's gone." She tasted ashes.

He didn't seem to hear her. He was still patting his thigh. Slowly, Sarah approached, dropping to her knees before him. "Why, Dad? Why?"

Her father closed his eyes as his hand fell lightly on her cheek. He stroked her spiky hair, not criticizing or even commenting now about her haircut. "It's all right. It's all right, baby," he murmured.

Sarah, too, closed her eyes, tormented as much by what she had remembered as by what she had yet to face. Fear bubbled like hot lava through her veins as another image she'd denied for so long popped to the surface.

She's sitting on the top step of the curved hall stairs a few hours after the dance lesson blowup.

The front door opens. Melanie comes bursting in, her book bag slung over her shoulder. Daddy greets her in the foyer. They hug. A warm, friendly father-daughter embrace. Sweet, innocent. Loving. Sarah feels a keen pang of envy.

> "What? No kiss?" he says as Melanie tries to wriggle free.
>
> Melanie dutifully pecks his cheek.
>
> "A chicken could do better than that."
>
> "Okay. If I give you a big kiss, will you let me go over to Jenny's for supper? Her mom invited me. Jenny and I are working on a physics project—"
>
> "Oh, so now your kisses are a bribe?"
>
> She sees Melanie throw her arms around her father, kissing him full on the mouth. Hears her giggle as he releases her. "Jenny's waiting for me outside in the car."
>
> "Not so fast, Mellie. Your mother's in one of her states again. Worse than usual. So I'm going to be camping out in the den tonight."
>
> A wilting look flickers across Melanie's face. And then it's like someone else possesses her: this smiling, seductive girl-woman whom Sarah doesn't recognize.
>
> "I'll be back by ten. I'll tuck you in."
>
> "Promise?"
>
> "Promise," Melanie says brightly, sealing the promise with another movie kiss.

"This simply will not do."

Sarah's eyes popped open. Her father was staring at her with consternation, trapping her excruciatingly between the past and the present.

Shame shot through her. "I'm sorry." No sooner were the words out than she felt a surge of fury. Why the hell was she the one apologizing? Hadn't she come here to drag those very words from her father's mouth? Wasn't this visit her attempt to get him to finally acknowledge what he'd done to Melanie? To admit he'd molested his own daughter—and to offer even a kernel of remorse for his terrible sin?

"Sorry doesn't cut it, young lady."

Sarah got to her feet so that now she was the one

looking down on him. "No, it doesn't. It's too late for sorry, Dad."

He wagged a finger at her. "I demand to see the nutritionist. I know for a fact she approved two eggs a week for me. And I have not had a single egg in ten days. I've been keeping count."

Sarah glanced at the breakfast tray on the table beside her father. Remnants of scrambled egg clung to the otherwise empty plate. Hopelessness swept over her. She walked to the window and stared out over the plush green lawns. Behind her came the rustle of the newspaper as her father resumed reading. She felt frustrated, disgusted, sick at heart.

"What do you want, mister? It isn't time for lunch, is it?"

At the sharp sound of her father's voice, Sarah turned around to see who he was talking to now. She expected a security guard, there at Charlotte Harris's request to toss her out—so she was taken aback to see John Allegro standing at the door. One look at the detective's expression, his pasty complexion, his even more rumpled than usual appearance, and she knew something dreadful had occurred.

"What—?"

He motioned for her to leave the room with him. "Let's talk outside."

Her gaze shifted to her father. Simon Rosen was removing tiny slips of crumpled papers from his jacket pockets, muttering as he carefully sorted through them. He seemed oblivious to both her presence and Allegro's. He didn't so much as glance her way as she passed by him.

As soon as they stepped into the hall, she turned on Allegro. "What's happened? Tell me."

Not responding, he took her arm, guided her to the staircase, down the stairs, past Charlotte Harris fretting away in the lounge, and out the front door. Corky was gone. Allegro's beat-up red MG was the only car in the visitors' lot.

She freed herself from Allegro's hold and came to an abrupt halt on the gravel path. "Tell me, damn it." Even as she made the demand, she knew a part of her didn't want to be told. It was more bad news. No question of that. And she was already drowning in bad news.

The story of *A Christmas Carol* flashed through her mind. She felt a bit like Scrooge, dragged around by the ghosts of her past and present, having her face shoved into the horrors she'd so assiduously avoided.

And what of the ghost of her future? Maybe she'd have no need of that one.

"It's Emma Margolis," Allegro said.

Sarah stared at him, not comprehending. "What about Emma?"

He was watching her closely. "Her cleaning lady found her this morning."

"Found her?" Sarah's thoughts were in a whirl.

Allegro reached out. Sarah backed away, stricken. "No. No. No."

"She's dead, Sarah. Murdered."

Emma. He got to Emma. One of the few people she ever let herself care about. Who'd cared about her. Who she'd trusted. *That'll teach you, Sarah. That'll teach you, all right.*

Her fist slammed down on the hood of Allegro's car. "How could you let this happen?" she screamed.

"Sarah—"

"He can do whatever he wants, can't he? You can't stop him. None of you. You're all a bunch of incompetent assholes."

"Sarah, I know how you feel—"

"You don't know anything!" She was trembling all over, feverish. A few faces appeared at the windows of the nursing home, peering out at them.

"We're going to get him. I swear to you, Sarah."

"Shut up. I don't want to hear your lies anymore. He killed Emma. He killed my sister. He's going to kill me.

And you want to know something: It'll be a relief. This hell I'm living will finally be over."

He grabbed her so roughly, she stumbled against him. "Don't talk like that. Do you hear me?" he shouted. "Something's going to break. This time, something's going to break. We've got every available man on the job. Nothing, no one's going to be overlooked. We're going to bear down on this bastard. We're going to get him."

"Bullshit, John. You'll never beat him. Emma. Poor Emma. I should have guessed. I should have put two and two together. Especially after talking with Bernie."

"What do you mean? What should you have guessed?"

"Where were you last night? I called you. After—after I tried to reach Emma."

"Your message was on her machine. We heard it this morning."

"That's not what I asked. *Where were you?*"

He frowned. "I stopped off for a drink after I left you at Bernie's."

"A drink?" She became aware of that minty scent of freshener on his breath. Had he hit the bottle that morning, too?

"A few drinks, okay? More than a few. I got plastered. I do that sometimes," he countered defensively.

"It's none of my business," she mumbled.

Allegro sighed heavily. "I'm sorry. It's been rough. I'm gonna do better. So why did you call?"

She glanced back at the rest home, catching a glimpse of her father at his window on the second floor. He was staring down at her. Once again, as on that night years ago, their eyes met and held. That night a terrible pact was formed. And now she had to find the strength to sever it completely.

"He raped her," she said, her eyes never wavering from her father's face. "My father raped my sister. She thought it was love. But it wasn't love. It was never love. It was rape. He was the one who first put her into bondage.

Enslaved her. He didn't need silk scarves. He was far more clever. And insidious. Melanie never had a chance."

Allegro's eyes lifted, and he stared up at Dr. Simon Rosen, but he didn't say a word.

"I caught him right in the act. Only I blocked it out until—" Her hands flew up to her face. "I should have done something." *Now you're going to get it. This'll teach you.*

"Sarah, you were a child. There was nothing you could do." He reached for her, but she shrank away. Repelled by the thought of being touched. *I don't deserve comfort. I don't deserve tenderness or pity. Anyway, even if I did, I wouldn't trust it.*

The tears spilled over and ran down her face. But she wasn't crying for herself. She was crying for Melanie. And for Emma. "If abuse is hell, John, what do we call its aftermath?"

Allegro gave her a stark look. "Purgatory."

She shook her head. "No. It's called death."

Once more, she lifted her eyes to the window. Her father was gone.

"Let's get out of here." As she spoke those words, she knew this had been her last visit. She would never come back. She would never see her father again.

They sat in the MG in the parking lot and talked. Sarah had her head pressed against the side window. "If only I'd stayed at Emma's place last night, maybe—"

"Don't do that to yourself, Sarah."

But the voice in her head wouldn't stop. *It's all your fault, Sarah. You have no one but yourself to blame. This is your doing. If you'd minded your business—*

"Emma was a good, decent, caring woman. Even if she was messed up."

"Messed up, how?"

Sarah hesitated. "She was into S&M."

"How do you know that?"

"She—she talked about it—the other night," she said, then felt guilty for revealing still more secrets.

"Please, Sarah. It could be an important lead. You've got to tell me."

Sarah knew Allegro was right. She should have told him right away. Maybe if she had, Emma'd still be alive. *It's all your fault. . . .*

"She went to one of those private S&M sex clubs."

"I know Mike took her to a sex club once for a piece she was doing for her show. I don't think that means—"

"She went before that. With Diane Corbett. To a place in Richmond. A couple of times."

"Jesus," Allegro muttered under his breath. "What was the name of the club?"

"She didn't say."

"That's okay. We'll find out. It's something, Sarah. You did good."

She told Allegro her theory that Romeo might believe that all the women he murdered were incest victims.

"Did Emma say anything about having been molested as a kid?"

"No, but it might explain why she was drawn to S&M. Don't abused children learn to connect sex with shame, guilt, and surrender? Doesn't it make sense that you might spend your adult life driven to re-create the pain, humiliation, submission because it's—all you know?"

He was silent. She couldn't tell what he was thinking.

"John, if Romeo's after me, he obviously thinks I was molested, too. That I'm into wanting to be dominated. Punished. Even though it isn't true," she hurriedly added. "None of it."

"Maybe there was something in Melanie's diary."

She gave him a sharp look. "Like what? You think my sister made something up about my having been molested?" First Bernie. Now John. Wasn't it traumatic enough that she'd witnessed the incest?

"I only meant that she might have written something about the fact that you'd seen her and your father——"

"What makes you think Melanie knew I saw them together?"

"I'm a detective, Sarah. I make deductions. I figure if you saw her, chances are she saw you."

"That's not possible—but she must have heard my father laying into me in the hall for spying on them. Only I wasn't spying."

"I'm sure you weren't, Sarah."

"I think Romeo might have been an abused child, too."

Allegro sighed. "So did Melanie. We've got the whole team looking into the backgrounds of all our suspects to learn whatever we can about their childhoods."

Sarah stared out the window. So strange to see people casually going about their affairs. A routine, normal day. Doing errands, hurrying off to their jobs, getting together with friends or family—

She closed her eyes to block them out. Too jealous. "I was so sure I was going to be his next target."

"Yeah, so was I."

"He's moving so fast now. Melanie last week. Now Emma eight days later. He's getting more bloodthirsty, John. More desperate. I did this."

"Don't, Sarah."

"Going on TV. Challenging him. I thought . . . I thought . . ." Her voice snagged, then broke. "Oh God," she sobbed, "what have I done?" Even with her eyes closed, the late morning light seemed to burn through her lids.

"What about . . . Melanie's heart? Did he . . . leave it at . . . Emma's?"

He gave a tight nod.

Sarah's face was a landscape of suffering. She'd been so sure Romeo was saving Melanie's heart for her. *Did you really think you could outsmart this monster, you silly girl?*

Allegro reached across and touched her arm. In a gesture that laid bare her vulnerability, she took his hand and pressed it to her cheek. "I liked Emma. You and Mike did, too," she said.

"Yeah, but it's more than knowing the victim; more than liking her. It's this goddamn helplessness we're both feeling. Hell, that everyone working on this case is feeling."

Sarah knew all about helplessness. She'd written the book on it. *No, not me. Melanie's the one that wrote the book.*

"Look, Sarah, I hate leaving you like this, but I've got to get back to Emma's apartment. I sent Corky off to your friend Bernie's place. He'll stay with you. I wish it could be me, but we're working against the clock. And I want to get someone on your lead about the Richmond club. You never know what little piece of information could break a case wide open."

"Thanks for coming out here to tell me. It means a lot—" She wanted to tell him it was much more than appreciation. That she was touched by his caring. And that she wished they had stayed in that lovely romantic inn last night. That maybe her fantasy feelings for him were becoming real. She wanted to tell him all those things. But she couldn't.

"I knew how upset you'd be. I just thought I should be the one," he mumbled.

"I'm sorry about calling you an incompetent asshole before."

He smiled faintly. "I've been called worse."

"I want to stay with you, John."

"Sarah—"

"Please."

It was pure mayhem on Emma Margolis's block. Plainclothesmen, uniformed cops, reporters, photographers, cameramen, and swarms of gawkers fighting for space on the sidewalk and the street. Allegro couldn't even get close to Emma's building. The street in front was jammed with a half-dozen cruisers, the medical examiner's hearse, media vans.

"Keep down," Allegro told Sarah as he double-parked half a block away, "or they'll swarm around you like locusts."

Sarah slid down as best she could in the tight confines of the sports car. Wagner, who was in a powwow with a couple of uniformed officers outside Emma's building, spotted the MG and made a gesture for Allegro to sit tight. A minute later, Wagner left the cops and jogged over. He looked both surprised and appalled to see Sarah crouched in the passenger seat.

"What's she—?"

"It's okay. She won't go upstairs."

Wagner, bending over the driver's-side door, looked across at Sarah. His expression softened. "You holding up?"

She nodded. "You?"

"Yeah," he said brusquely. Sarah could see frustration etched deep in his features.

"We've got a lead, Mike. Thanks to Sarah," Allegro said.

Before he got to tell him about the club in Richmond, Wagner jumped in with his news. "Then we may actually have two whole leads. A neighbor of Emma's, a Margaret Baldwin, saw Emma late yesterday afternoon in a tea shop a few blocks from here. The Upper Crust. Seems it's a popular spot with the neighborhood ladies. Emma was there with a guy. We showed Baldwin some pictures. She didn't hesitate a beat when she got to Perry's snapshot. Swears he's the one she was with. Not only that. When Emma left, Baldwin—who was at a window table—noticed that while they parted company outside the shop, Perry hung around on the street for a couple of minutes, then took off in Emma's direction."

"Let's pick him up," Allegro said.

"Already in the works. This time with a search warrant."

"Anyone else see anything?"

Wagner pointed to a pale pink stucco building across the street. "There's an elderly woman lives on the first floor, a Mrs. Rumney, who says she saw a couple going into the building around five. Her eyesight's not too good, but she's pretty sure it was Emma because there are no other black women living in the building. Couldn't tell us much about the guy, though."

"What he was wearing? What about height? Hair color?" Allegro's voice was strained. "Jesus, Mike, did she see *anything?*"

Wagner lit a cigarette. "Thinks he was tall. Caucasian. That he was wearing a sport jacket, but she's a little colorblind, so she's foggy on what color it was. Pretty foggy in general."

"She wasn't foggy on the time of day," Sarah pointed out.

"Only because it was right before she took her five o'clock medicine," Wagner said.

"You think it was Perry?" she asked.

Wagner eyed Allegro before answering her. "It's a strong possibility."

Sarah wasn't convinced. "Why would she invite him up to her apartment? Wouldn't she be wary if he'd followed her back to her place?"

Wagner scowled. "Emma took risks. Especially if it meant a scoop for her show."

"It was more than a ratings game for her," Sarah said, bristling.

Wagner wore a chagrined expression. "I know it. I didn't mean it that way."

"Why don't we see what Perry has to say for himself?" Allegro gave Sarah's shoulder a squeeze.

"I was going to drive over to his place now," Wagner told them. "Rodriguez and Johnson are meeting me there with the warrant."

Allegro glanced at Sarah, then back to Wagner. "We'll follow."

Wagner's expression made it clear he didn't think it was a bright idea to bring Sarah along, but he didn't say it. Instead, he asked about the lead they'd uncovered. Allegro told him about the Richmond club.

"Don't know it," Wagner said. "But I'll get someone on it pronto."

Robert Perry didn't come to the door despite repeated knocking. "We've got a warrant!" Wagner shouted. "If you don't let us in, Perry, we're going to use force."

"Maybe he's out," Rodriguez suggested.

Sarah had a bad feeling. "I don't think so. Break the door down, John."

Allegro gave her a searching look. Then, retrieving his gun from his shoulder holster, he nodded to Wagner and Rodriguez. "Let's get in there. Johnson, you stay out here with Sarah."

Johnson, a short, barrel-chested, twenty-year man with gremlin eyes, didn't look happy to land the baby-sitting job. But since Allegro was running the show, he reluctantly trudged over to Sarah.

As Wagner and Rodriguez heaved their full weight against Perry's door, several neighbors popped heads out of their apartments. Allegro waved his badge at them. The doors all slammed closed before he had to utter word one.

On the fourth heave, the door gave way. The armed cops burst into the apartment. When Rodriguez darted back out a minute later with the bad news, Sarah's fears were confirmed.

"Dead?" Johnson asked.

Rodriguez shook his head. "Still had a pulse when we cut him down. Found him dangling from the skylight in his bathroom. Allegro's calling the paramedics."

"Cut him down?" Sarah's voice was a harsh whisper.

"Yeah, the bastard tried to hang himself."

She felt a powerful jolt. Like she'd touched a live wire. Another hanging. Another suicide. One that had succeeded. *Oh, Mommy. I'm sorry, sorry, sorry—*

"Looks like we got our boy," Johnson said, holstering his gun. "Rather off himself than face the music."

Rodriguez's mouth curled. "Talk about music, he had a portable CD player in the bathroom with him. Guess what he was playing."

"Wait. Don't tell me," Johnson said. "*Rhapsody in Blue.*"

"And get this. What do you suppose he used to string himself up? A white silk scarf."

The other cop whistled.

Sarah slipped past them. Through an open door, she saw Perry sprawled out on a carpeted floor. Wagner knelt beside him, administering CPR.

Allegro came up behind her. "You knew he'd try this."

"I suspected." Her face was expressionless.

"How come?"

"Intuition."

Allegro didn't get it at first. Then he remembered Feldman telling him about Sarah's two suicide attempts.

She glanced back into the bedroom. "Is he going to pull through?"

"Probably. Although my guess is he's going to wish he hadn't."

Sarah saw the packages Allegro held in his latex-gloved hand—two clear plastic evidence bags. One held a white silk scarf, and the other a shiny silver CD.

Johnson came in from the bedroom. He, too, was carrying something encased in plastic. "Bingo. A videotape. Got *Cutting Edge* written on the label."

She winced; the light streaming into Perry's living room suddenly felt too bright.

"Are you okay, Sarah?" Allegro asked hurriedly.

"There's no question then? That he's the one? That Perry's Romeo?"

"Looks that way. I found something else by his bed," he said.

Sarah felt like she was suffocating. "What?" Melanie's yearbook? Her diary?

"A scrapbook. Stuffed with clippings about each of the victims."

"Nothing . . . else?"

He slipped an arm around her shoulders. "Not yet. Once we get Perry squared away, the crime scene team will turn this place inside out."

"John, promise me something."

Before she could say it, he was nodding. "If we find the diary, I'll make sure it isn't pawed over."

She pressed her cheek against his for a moment. He needed a shave as usual, but the prickly sensation felt oddly comforting.

"He's turning blue!" Wagner shouted from the bedroom. "Where the fuck are those medics?"

Even as they're telling themselves they are aroused by being hurt and debased, on some level the victims all secretly share a feeling of shame, worthlessness, inadequacy. And so does Romeo. Whether receiving or giving the pain, suffering is the bond that ties them.

Dr. Melanie Rosen
Cutting Edge

21

Robert Perry was in a coma in intensive care at San Francisco Memorial. Allegro and Wagner were sticking around, hoping to get a statement as soon as he regained consciousness. If he regained consciousness. Sarah waited with them. Needing to hear the confession from Perry's own lips.

They were sitting it out in the ICU waiting room. Close to six P.M. Rodriguez showed up from headquarters. Rolling his eyes, he gestured to Allegro and Wagner to step out into the hall.

Sarah's gaze flitted anxiously from one detective to the other.

"I'll see what's up, John," Wagner said, rising. "You stay with Sarah."

A minute later, Wagner returned alone to the lounge.

"What?" Allegro asked impatiently.

Wagner was clearly reluctant to speak in front of Sarah.

"Did they find Melanie's diary?" she demanded.

"No. Seems they didn't find her . . . heart either."

Sarah could only stare at Wagner, incredulous.

Allegro squinted at him. "What are you talking about?"

"The lab just finished running prelims on the heart found with Emma's body. Couldn't have been the doc's. Wrong blood type."

Sarah felt like her own blood was draining out of her. She barely heard Allegro demand, "Who the fuck's heart was it?"

And Wagner's weak response. "No idea."

Mike Wagner led Sarah to the street via a rarely used side entrance of the hospital at six-thirty that evening. She'd hoped to get a ride back home from Allegro, but he'd been ordered by his chief to keep post on the still-unconscious Perry and to make a statement to the media —not about the unidentified heart from the Margolis murder scene, though. That was being kept under wraps until the cops found out who it had once belonged to.

Sarah'd tried to convince Allegro to let her stay with him, but he stiffly ordered her out. He wanted her gone before the questions started flying. The press would be breathing down her neck soon enough.

"I'm taking you for something to eat before I get you home," Wagner said, lighting up as they headed down the path. She'd called Bernie earlier from the hospital to tell him she was going back to her apartment since Perry had been caught. Despite niggling doubts, she was desperate to believe Robert Perry was Romeo. That it was over.

"What do you feel like eating?" Wagner prodded.

"I'm not hungry," she replied dully.

"Keep me company then. I'm starving," he said as he helped her into his car.

Fifteen minutes later they were sitting in a green-trimmed vinyl booth at Salt & Pepper, a fifties-style diner on Geary. Wagner ordered a fried egg sandwich, chocolate milk shake, and a side of fries.

"You obviously don't have a cholesterol problem," Sarah said dryly.

"The milk shake's for you."

She bristled a little. "If I'd wanted something, I would have ordered it."

"Playing hard to feed, huh?"

She frowned.

"Hey, that was a pretty decent joke, Sarah. I was just trying to put a smile on your face." He sighed. "Guess neither of us feels much like smiling right now."

"Do you think he'll make it, Mike?"

"Doc seemed reasonably optimistic."

"I keep thinking there's some other poor woman out there who we don't even know—"

"Don't think about it, Sarah. There's no point."

Another diner dropped coins into the jukebox against one wall; a love song churned out. The only tune in Sarah's head was *Rhapsody in Blue*.

Wagner pulled out a cigarette, but a passing waitress pointed to a no-smoking sign on the wall. He glowered at her but moved to stick the cigarette back into his pack. It broke apart in his hand, and he shoved it into his pocket.

Sarah watched his tense, jerky motions. "This has been a nightmare for you, too."

"Hopefully it's over now."

"Hopefully? What does that mean?"

"Just what it says."

"You're not sure it is Perry."

"We have enough to hold him for now, but even with what we got at his place, we don't have enough incriminating physical evidence yet to bring him to trial and guarantee a conviction. Of course, if we get a DNA match, we're in business. But that'll take weeks. Maybe longer. Unless Perry decides to make life easy for us and confesses."

"How do you stand it, Mike? Doing this kind of work?"

Wagner straightened out the fork and spoon on his napkin. "Somebody's got to do it."

"Seriously. Is this what you always wanted? To be a cop?"

"Not always."

"What did you want to do?"

"You won't laugh?"

"Do I look like I'm capable of laughing right now?"

"Okay, but not too many people know this, so don't go blabbing it around. Not even John knows."

"Your secret is safe with me," Sarah said, raising her right hand. "Scout's honor."

"Well, when I was a kid—mostly when I was in college—I seriously thought about being a singer."

"A singer? You sing?"

"See, I told you."

"I didn't mean to sound so surprised," she apologized. "I mean, why wouldn't you sing? Opera? Pop?"

He shrugged. "This is a dumb conversation."

"There's nothing in the world I'd like more right now than to sit here and have a dumb conversation, Mike."

Their eyes met in shared understanding. "Well, I was in this a cappella group at Sacramento State. And I had singing leads in a couple of musicals. Then there was a girl I was dating at college whose dad owned a small nightclub in town. She got me a gig there on weekends. One time an agent dropped in, heard me, and offered to represent me. Thought he could get me into some of the Vegas lounges."

"Did he?" Somehow, she couldn't picture Mike Wagner as a Vegas lounge crooner. A high-class lawyer, maybe.

"No. My mom wasn't too keen on it. She wanted me to get my bachelor's degree. I did keep on singing at local clubs until I graduated, though."

"How'd you get from gigs to guns?"

Absently, he tapped out another cigarette from his pack and lit it, managing to get in a couple of drags before their waitress returned with his order and told him to put it out. He dropped it in his water glass.

As the waitress grabbed the glass and stomped away, he slid the milk shake over in front of Sarah and put the French fries in the middle of the table.

"My stepdad was a cop. He pushed for me to go to the Academy when I graduated Sacramento State. And since I was at loose ends, I just kind of went along."

"And your mom? How'd she feel about it?"

He smiled. "She thought I'd look real nifty in a uniform. Actually, she was pretty sick at the time, and I mostly wanted to stick around. Funny how things worked out. I really dug the training. Graduated from the Academy first in my class."

"Your folks must have been very proud of you."

Wagner stared down at the fried egg sandwich he hadn't yet touched. "Actually Mom died about a month before I graduated. And my stepdad was on probation from the force for showing up drunk for duty one too many times. It was either AA or turn in his badge. He tried AA for a few months, but the booze won out in the end." He gave her a quick glance. "I guess that's why I worry about John."

"John doesn't drink when he's on duty, does he?" She tried to sound only casually interested in his answer.

"Not anymore. But he's been through some rough times. Losing his kid must have been hell for him. I didn't know him back then, but from what I heard when I moved over to Homicide, after his kid died he really started hitting the bottle. He was still on shaky ground when I teamed up with him. Having seen it all before, I guess I got on his case a lot. John's the best partner I've ever had."

Sarah stared at the milk shake. "He never told me he had a kid."

"A boy. Died of spinal meningitis when he was ten or eleven."

"How long ago was that?"

"Maybe six years ago. He only mentioned it to me once. When he was good and drunk. Never talked about the kid after that. Then again, John isn't much of a talker."

"No. I suppose not."

Wagner took a bite of his sandwich and washed it down with some of Sarah's water since the waitress had never brought him a fresh glass of his own. "What gives with the two of you?"

Sarah, who'd been about to sample that milk shake after all, stopped short. "Me and John? Nothing. What makes you think anything *gives* between us?"

Wagner reached for the catsup next to the napkin dispenser. "You mind?" he asked, gesturing to the fries.

"Anyway, it's none of your business," she said defensively. Had John been blabbing to his partner? Not very likely. Wagner had said it himself—John wasn't much of a talker. Certainly not the type to kiss and tell.

"Here's what I'll do. I'll put catsup on half—"

"If you've got something to say, Wagner, spit it out."

He tipped the bottle, swatting the bottom until the catsup started to flow. "From what I know, John hasn't dated much since his wife—" He glanced her way.

"He told me about her suicide." Sarah knew it was foolish, but she felt like she'd scored a point. Making up a little for his not having told her about his son dying.

Wagner set the bottle down, wiped off the top, slowly screwed the dented white cap back on. "Did he tell you she once filed charges against him?"

"Charges?"

"It was a couple of months after John and I were teamed up. They were still living together, but from what I gathered, it had been a marriage in name only for a while. John talked about wanting to find his own apartment. I even tagged along with him to check a few places out when we were on breaks."

"What kind of charges?"

"She claimed he beat her up."

"I don't believe it. John told me she was a very unstable woman." Now that she knew about the death of their son, it wasn't hard to understand. Or sympathize. With both of them. "She probably knew he wanted to leave her. She must have felt desperate."

"I saw her, Sarah. She came down to the squad room the next morning to press charges. She had a black eye and a swollen jaw. John took off after her when she left. I guess they talked. Next day she dropped the charges."

"Did John admit he'd beaten her up?" There must be another explanation. His word about what had happened, against his wife's.

"I never asked him," Wagner said. "As far as I know, neither did anyone else."

The way he said it made it clear to Sarah that he didn't think it would be a good idea for her to ask John either.

Wagner dropped Sarah back at her place a little after eight P.M. A plainclothesman was still posted outside. Since the police hardly had an airtight case on Perry, orders remained in force to keep a close watch on her until they were sure they had their killer.

Sarah was standing at her apartment door about to slip her key in the lock when the front door to the building opened, and a tall, extremely handsome, dark-haired man dressed in a stylish gray suit stepped into the hallway. Seeing the stranger, she felt a knife-prick of panic, especially when he headed directly toward her. Wagner wasn't the only one who had some lingering doubts about whether they were holding the right man. Still, the cop outside must have checked him out.

"Sarah," the stranger exclaimed, coming right up to her. "I just heard the good news on the radio. You must be so relieved that they finally caught that madman. You've got to tell me all about it. Is it true you were there when they nabbed him and then held a bedside vigil for hours? Is he really going to pull through? I heard he was brain dead."

While Sarah still didn't recognize the man, she did know the breathy voice. "Vickie?" She was so startled, her door key slipped from her hand.

He blushed as he knelt and picked it up for her. "Oops, my getup. Dinner with Momsy tonight. She won't admit it, but I know it's not the cross-dressing that really bugs her. It's that I look better in dresses these days than she does."

Sarah didn't know what to say.

"Why don't I go slip into something more comfortable and then bring you over a bite to eat? You look like you could use it. I've got a terrific leftover meat loaf. I'll make you a big fat sandwich."

Sarah couldn't stop staring at her neighbor. Vickie was so handsome. So completely masculine. So much, she saw now, like that photo of him she'd unearthed in his closet the other day.

"What do you say? If you don't like meat loaf, I've got these simply incredible frozen gourmet pizzas. I could zap one in the microwave—"

Sarah had trouble finding her voice. "No. Thanks. I ate at the hospital," she lied.

"Hospital food. Yuck." Vickie grimaced. "I know. I'll bring you something to settle your stomach."

Sarah was beginning to feel unnerved by Vickie's persistence. "Really, I'm beat. All I want to do is climb into bed and get my first decent night's sleep in weeks."

"You must be so relieved that it's finally over." Vickie's gushing voice was in sharp contrast to his virile looks.

"Perry hasn't been officially charged yet."

"Naturally they can't read him his rights and throw him in the slammer until he comes to," Vickie said. "But according to that news flash I heard driving back, he strung himself up with one of those white silk scarves he used to tie up his victims. How positively symbolic."

Sarah's key turned in her lock. "I really don't want to talk about it now, Vickie."

"God, I sound just like those dreadful reporters that must have been swarming around you all day."

She smiled weakly. "No comment."

Vickie grinned. "That's the ticket."

"I don't mean to be rude, Vickie, but I'm exhausted. I've really got to hit the sack."

Before she could slip inside her apartment, however, Vickie placed a hand on her cheek and gave a caressing stroke. "Well, hopefully your nightmares will stop now. Pleasant dreams, sweetie."

The combination of the transvestite's masculine appearance, his parting remark, and that unsettling touch clung to Sarah as she shut herself inside her apartment. The place was even more of a mess than usual, and a foul odor emanated from the kitchen. The garbage had been sitting for days. Wrinkling up her nose, she tied up the plastic trash bag, hoping she'd remember in the morning to toss it out. Maybe she'd even clean the place a bit, she thought as she headed for her bedroom. *"You can't put your life in order, Sarah, until you put some order into your life."* Melanie had said that to her in their last conversation.

After taking a hot shower, Sarah smoothed out her rumpled bed, shaking out the cover so that crumbs and dust flew up into the air. As she climbed in, she thought again of Robert Perry lying in a coma in his hospital bed. If only she could be sure he was Romeo. If only she could stop thinking about Melanie's missing heart. And now Emma's stolen heart. Two hearts still unaccounted for. Why? Why break the pattern?

Lying in bed, Sarah kept thinking about her encounter with Vickie, her mind starting to swim with a new possibility. What if there'd been no eyewitnesses before now because, instead of a *man* entering the victims' buildings on the nights of each Romeo murder, a *woman* had? Or someone who looked convincingly like a woman? It was perfect. Brilliant. All it would take was a quick change

—no sweat for a drag queen like Vickie—and suave, handsome *Vic* would show up for his date.

And there was something else. Wouldn't Vickie be likely to know the underground sex club scene? Hadn't he told her he'd *performed* in the burbs? Why not at that club where Emma had gone? Or maybe he'd just hung out there. Not in drag. Picking up women. *Vic* was strikingly handsome. A man someone like Emma, Diane Corbett, the other victims, even her sister might well find very appealing.

Still, Perry was a far more likely Romeo. The guy was unbalanced for sure. Probably had a multiple personality disorder. He'd simply never allowed Melanie to see a hint of the part of him that was *violently* deranged. That part only surfaced when he was Romeo.

She turned out the light, pulled the covers up to her neck. She lay there willing herself not to think of Romeo, not to think of poor Emma, her father and Melanie, John's battered wife, the son he'd lost, or John, for that matter. What she wouldn't give for a nice old-fashioned stupor.

Wagner looked up from the report he was reading as Allegro strode into the squad room at 9:40 that evening. "We got another problem, partner."

Allegro shrugged off his jacket and tossed it over a chair. Then he leaned his palms flat on his desk. "Do I want to hear this, Mike?"

"We got a guy and his girlfriend out in the hallway—" Wagner paused to check the name on the report sheet. "Fred Gruber and Linda Chambers. They saw Perry's photo on a CNN news flash while they were having drinks at their local bar about an hour ago, and they're both willing to swear Perry's the guy who sat right in front of them at a movie house in North Beach on the night Melanie Rosen was murdered."

"Probably a pair of drunks."

Wagner shook his head. "Tested them. And the girl-friend even describes the little tiff Perry had with an Asian woman at the concession stand. This Fred Gruber and his girlfriend both claim Perry returned to his seat and sat through the entire second feature. Gruber swears he re-members because Perry was there in the seat right in front of them and kept twitching the whole time."

"Shit."

"Ready for more good news?"

Allegro glared at Wagner. "No."

"Perry wasn't wearing a jacket the other day when he and Emma were at that tea shop." Again Wagner referred to a sheet of paper on his desk. "I was going over Rodri-guez's report. He was the one who interviewed Margaret Baldwin, the neighbor who saw them at the Upper Crust. She says Perry was wearing one of those off-white Irish cable-knit sweaters. I phoned Mrs. Rumney, the old lady in the building across the way. She's sticking by her story that the man who went inside with Emma was wearing a sport jacket. Now she thinks it might have been brown. Or gray. Oh, and she thinks the man she saw is taller than Perry."

"How the fuck does she know how tall Perry is?"

"I showed her the photo of him at Melanie's funeral. He was standing right next to Emma. Well, she says that she didn't really make anything of it this morning, but now that she thinks about that picture, she recalls that Perry and Emma were practically the same height. And she's right. She insists the man she saw go in that building with Emma was several inches taller than Emma."

"And you said she was foggy?"

"Come on, John. You never thought it was going to be this easy, did you?"

"Easy?"

"You know what I mean."

The phone rang. Allegro snatched it up. "Yeah?" He listened for a few seconds. "Okay, we'll be right over."

"What's up?" Wagner asked as Allegro grabbed his jacket.

"Perry's conscious. Wants to make a statement."

A woman, her face in shadow, sits at the edge of her bed. She has long blond hair that glistens even though the room is dark. She wears a pale yellow chenille robe, the sleeves barely skimming her fragile wrists. She places her elegantly tapered hand delicately on the child's back. "There, there," she repeats over and over in a lilting singsong voice. "There, there."

The child is sobbing into her pillow. She thinks she will suffocate if she doesn't turn her head. She doesn't. She wants to suffocate.

"There, there." The golden-haired woman croons her comfort to the child. She doesn't know the child is suffocating. To death.

Sarah woke with a start, gasping for breath, her own face buried in her pillow, tears streaming from her eyes. She lifted her head instantly—as if she thought she'd actually been suffocating herself.

So much for believing she'd gotten past her tauntingly alluring suicidal tendencies. Was she really so far gone that if Romeo didn't do her in, she was going to take the matter into her own hands?

"No. I don't want to die!" she cried out into the silent room, flinging off the covers. She hadn't suffered through and survived all this misery and anguish to give her life up so easily now.

Her nightgown was drenched in sweat. She pulled it off, then sat naked on the edge of the bed, clutching herself. *Oh God, it doesn't feel over yet.* Shadows still enshrouded the walls. Panic and desperation continued to bleed from her skin. Letting back the memory of her father molesting Melanie hadn't staunched the flow.

She bent forward so that her head dropped over her knees, her small breasts squashing into her thighs. Why was she still afraid? What other terrible memories were lurking there in her unconscious? Why couldn't she just remember, instead of being tormented by broken fragments? Struggling to pry the lid open with one hand, while fiercely pressing it down with the other.

She checked her alarm clock. Eleven-fifteen. She'd been asleep for less than twenty minutes. Now she was wide awake again. And chilled as the sweat evaporated from her naked skin.

She slipped out of bed and started for her bureau to pull out a fresh nightgown. Instead, she snatched up her plaid cotton robe. She'd make herself a cup of hot milk to help her relax and, hopefully, fall back asleep. As she was putting on her robe, the robe that the woman had been wearing in her dream flew back into her mind. The pale yellow chenille robe.

Sarah's breath caught. She remembered that garment vividly. A birthday gift. Given to her mother on her final birthday. The year she turned thirty-eight. Sarah remembered her mother opening the box, looking first for the birthday card. There wasn't any. Just one of those little freebie enclosures tossed in. *To Cheryl, Happy birthday. From, Simon.* Not even *Love, Simon.* Not even his handwriting. Her mother had taken the garment out of the box without a word, without a hint of emotion. Sarah could recall only one time when her mother had worn that pale yellow chenille robe instead of her favorite one—the white seersucker with the pink flowers. It was coming back to her.

A knock on her door shattered the memory she'd been grasping for. Sarah tied the belt on her robe and stepped out of her bedroom, flicking on the light in her living room.

"Who is it?" she called out cautiously.

"It's me. Vickie. Are you awake?"

Sarah rolled her eyes. "No."

"Please, Sarah. I think this could be important."

"Can't it wait until tomorrow? You woke me from a dead sleep," she lied.

"There's something in front of your door."

Sarah's breath caught.

"A parcel. With your name typed on it."

Sarah's hand went to her chest. She could feel her heart pounding. She hesitated.

"Sarah?"

What if this was a clever ruse to get inside?

"Are you all right, Sarah?"

"I'm not dressed, Vickie. Just leave it. I'll get it in a few minutes." How could there be a parcel? Who could have gotten by the cop outside? Unless her next-door neighbor . . .

"Okay," Vickie drawled.

Sarah tiptoed to her door, pressed her ear against it, listened as Vickie's footsteps disappeared back down the hall. Then she heard the front door to the building slam shut.

Cautiously, Sarah cracked her door and peered out. No one in sight. She dropped her gaze. The parcel wrapped in shiny white gift paper—the size of a large box of candy—was on her doorstep as Vickie had said. She drew the door open a little wider so she could retrieve it.

"Sarah, I am truly worried about you."

Sarah shrieked when she heard Vickie's voice.

"Now, don't be angry at me, honey. You sounded so weird, I wanted to make sure you were okay. I was starting to think maybe you were being held at gunpoint. Or knifepoint, I should say. What if that Perry character isn't Romeo, or what if he escaped from the hospital, I said to myself, and he was in your apartment this very minute. I swear, I was ready to dial 911."

Sarah could only stare in panic at Vickie. He was back in drag—skin-tight gold lamé toreador pants, a black leather bolero jacket over a bright red corsetlike top, and huge gold spiked heels. He bent down and lifted the package to his stuffed bosom.

"You're probably wondering why I'm all dolled up at this hour," Vickie drawled. "I was on my way out. A friend of mine called. She's opening at the Vanguard tonight. First-night jitters—so I told her I'd come over and hold her hand. I was passing your door and I saw this—" Vickie extended the small package.

Sarah's eyes were fixed on the gift-wrapped box.

"Aren't you going to open it, Sarah? Do you want me to—"

She snatched it from Vickie's hands. "No. No, thanks. You better go. Your—your friend will be waiting."

"Fuck my friend. She couldn't possibly be in a worse state than you, sweetie. There must be something I can do for you. You're as white as a geisha."

"Please, Vickie. I'm fine." She thought of the cop outside. Must have dozed off. Or God knew what. She would be long dead before he even knew anything had happened to her.

"You don't look fine," Vickie insisted. "Let me at least come in and make you a cup of tea before I go."

"No. I want to be alone. If you don't go—"

Vickie's heavily made-up face bore a mix of astonishment and indignation. "Don't take a header, honey. I was just trying to be a good neighbor." With that he gave his red wig a haughty toss, turned on his spiked heel, and stormed down the hall toward the exit.

This time Sarah watched him actually leave the building. Then she quickly slammed her door and bolted it. She slid right down to the floor, bringing her knees up to her chest. Did she have the strength to even tear away the wrapping?

What perverted gift had he sent her this time? Another heart-shaped locket? No, the package was too big. More chocolates? A second wreath? No. Romeo wouldn't settle for repetition. He would have something new for her. Yet another demented token of his affections. But what? Everything she could conjure was too gruesome for words.

Finally, unable to stand the agony or the suspense another minute, she tore away the paper, revealing a rectangular corrugated mailer. Hands trembling, she cautiously lifted the flap at one end.

A red velvet box slid out. Heart-shaped. Tied with a white satin ribbon. Under the ribbon was a folded sheet of white paper. Another excerpt from Melanie's diary? Another *love letter* from her sister's killer?

Sarah's stomach churned. She slipped the paper out and unfolded it. Postponing opening the box and seeing what depraved gift he'd chosen for her this time.

She steeled herself as she began to read—

Dearest Sarah,
    You struggle with your longing, your emptiness—just as I do. We're parts of a whole, Sarah. We both know too well the fragile line between pain and ecstasy. The others (even Melanie) were incapable of filling that terrible void inside me. As for Emma—well, I knew even as I held her heart in the palm of my hand, still pulsing, that it would fail to satisfy. Don't weep for Emma. I gave her my heart for a time. As a token of my absolute devotion, I give you hers.

                                    Soon, my love,
                                    Romeo

In a blind savage frenzy, Sarah jerked off the lid.

There, nestled on a bed of bloodstained white velvet, in a half-frozen state—a human heart.

A strangling sound erupted from Sarah's lips. Bile spewed from her mouth. When there was nothing left inside of her, she clutched her cramping stomach and continued to have dry heaves. Too spent to move, she sat in her vomit, her head pressed against her knees, her mind catapulting back in time—

> *"There, there."*
> > *"I hate him. I hate him, Mommy!"*
> > *"There, there."*
> > *"He's a terrible man. He does disgusting things!"*
> > *"There, there."*
> > *She clutches the sleeve of a pale yellow robe— the birthday present she never saw her mother wear before. "Don't ever leave me, Mommy. You're all I have. You're the only one who loves me."*
> > *"There, there. There, there, baby."*

She heard a pounding noise behind her head. Dazed at first. Then she pulled herself out of her reverie. Vickie again? Ready to strike, now that she'd read his latest missive?

The cop outside. *Got to get up. Get to a window. Shout to him.*

"Sarah? Damn it, Sarah. Are you in there? It's me, John. Open the door." Allegro's shout was followed by another series of fierce bangs.

"John?" What was he doing here?

Something smelled awful. Oh, God—it was her own vomit. She began to cry.

"Sarah? Please, baby. It's okay. Open the damn door."

"No, no, it's not okay."

"Sarah, you've got to let me in."

A vision of a woman with a black eye and a swollen jaw flashed in her mind. She squeezed her eyes shut.

"Do it right now, Sarah."

He sounded so stern, she flinched. Pulling herself to her feet, she dutifully reached for the lock.

In his eagerness to get in, Allegro pushed at the door the instant he heard the lock turn, knocking Sarah back as it swung open.

"Jesus," he gasped the instant he laid eyes on her.

She waved him away wildly. "No, no. Don't come near me. I've had—an accident. I'm so ashamed. Don't be mad at me. Please." It wasn't her voice coming out of her. It was the voice of a frightened little girl. A fissure in time had materialized, and she'd slipped right through it to the past.

"You were sick, Sarah," Allegro soothed. "There's nothing to be ashamed of. I'm not mad. Let me help you get cleaned up, Sarah."

"I'm smelly and disgusting!" she screamed, dropping to her knees and putting her hands over her face. "Everyone knows that."

Allegro knelt in front of her. "Sarah, you just got sick to your stomach and threw up. As soon as you get out of that robe and take a nice hot shower, you'll smell as sweet as ever."

His words were like a balm, cajoling her from the terrors of the past, easing her back to the uncertainties of the present. Slowly, she lifted her head. "I don't think . . . I can manage, John."

"I'll help you, Sarah. If you'll let me." He rose, trying to lift her to her feet.

She shook her head.

"Please, Sarah."

"Not yet. First—first—I have to tell you."

"Tell me what?"

Her eyes fixed on the floor a short distance from where he stood. Allegro turned to see what she was staring at. "Jesus . . . Christ."

Sarah lunged for him, grabbing at his trouser leg so abruptly, he lost his balance and fell to his knees. A crumpled paper—Romeo's letter—dropped from her hand. Allegro picked it up, but he couldn't tear his eyes from the red velvet box. From what was inside it.

"It's . . . Emma's," she gasped, a long low moan rising up from her throat. Oh, God. She started to heave again.

∎   ∎   ∎

Allegro lifted Sarah in his arms, carrying her into the bathroom. Her mind was a thing apart. Fear, anguish, revulsion vied for center stage, the emotions, like miniature live-action figures, arguing shrewishly over who deserved top billing. *You can all have your time in the spotlight. Don't be greedy.*

He dropped the lid on the toilet seat and eased her down onto it. "I'll fill the tub for you." He mentally vetoed a shower because he didn't think she could handle standing. "While you're bathing, I'll go clean up inside, okay?"

She sat there like a limp dishrag.

"You got anything in the house for stomach upset?" he asked.

She cringed. Vickie had offered to bring her over something for her stomach. Vickie. She had to tell John about Vickie. Later. When she could think straight. If she would ever be able to think straight again.

Allegro slid the medicine door open, rummaging. He found a roll of antacid tablets and peeled a couple out. "Here. Chew these."

"Can't," she mumbled. The thought of chewing anything made her stomach muscles convulse.

Tossing the chalky tablets into his own mouth instead, Allegro leaned over to run the water in the tub. He spotted a plastic bottle of bubble bath in the shower caddy and half-emptied it.

"How's that?" he asked.

She gave him a blank stare.

"Okay, listen," he said, matter-of-factly. "I'm going to get you out of that robe and help you into the tub. Will you let me do that, Sarah?"

He watched her closely. Was that a faint nod of consent? He wasn't sure. The thing he didn't want to do now was panic her. Or force her into further retreat. As it was, she was practically catatonic.

"I'm just going to untie the sash first," he told her.

Careful not to touch anything but the tie, he slowly undid it. "Easy does it."

The robe fell open. She was naked underneath. He wasn't prepared for that. His hands darted out to draw the robe closed, but then he saw that she seemed oblivious to her exposure.

He helped her to her feet. "Okay, steady now. The water's going to feel real good, Sarah." She offered no resistance as he slipped the robe off her. He tried to keep his eyes off her body, but he wasn't wholly successful.

"Can you step into the tub, Sarah?"

Her vacant eyes fixed on his. "I used to have nightmares of being gobbled up."

He lifted her in his arms. She was light. Just short of skinny. When he lowered her into the warm bubbly water, she made a sound somewhere between a purr and a growl.

"Water too hot?"

She didn't answer, but he knew it wasn't. Easing her into the tub, his arms had gotten wet up to his elbows. His jacket and shirt-sleeves were soaked. And the fronts of both had Sarah's vomit on them. Watching her closely to make sure she didn't sink all the way down into the water and end up drowning herself, he got out of his jacket and shirt. His pants had suffered only mild damage. Grabbing a face cloth from the towel rack by the sink, he dipped it into the tub water and scrubbed at the vomit on his trousers.

There was still the mess in the foyer and living room to clean up. And the box, the letter. The heart. Needed to deal with that, too.

"How does it feel?" he asked solicitously.

She said nothing. But some o˙ her color was coming back.

He stroked her cheek. "You're going to be fine, Sarah."

She placed her soapy hand over his, holding it captive against her face. "Don't . . . leave me, John."

"I won't, Sarah."

She closed her eyes, still clutching his hand. "I was dreaming about my mother before—before Vickie knocked—" She stopped abruptly, her eyes flying open. "Perry couldn't have delivered that note, the— the—" She couldn't get herself to speak of Emma's heart. "Unless he escaped from the hospital. He didn't, did he? That isn't why you came here tonight? Why did you come here, John?"

A fresh rush of paranoia assailed her. She yanked his hand away from her face. "Why are you here?" she cried.

"I'll tell you later. Right now, you just soak in this nice warm water and try to put everything out of your mind. You don't have to be afraid, Sarah. I'll stay with you. You'll be safe."

Allegro scooped up some of the soapy water in the palm of his hand and let it trickle down over her shoulders.

"*He* did this."

Allegro drew back and stared at her. "Who did what?"

"My father used to bathe us when we were little. Me and Melanie. He'd put us both in the big tub and wash us and splash us." Another flash from the past that she'd buried. She felt like a grave robber, only it was her own grave she was pillaging.

"But this one time I splashed him back, and he'd forgotten to take off his watch. It was a very expensive gold watch. Not waterproof. And I ruined it. He was so angry. He yanked me out of the tub. I remember standing there on the cold tile floor, soaked and shivering. He didn't even hand me a towel. It was like I wasn't even there. After that, it was only Melanie in the tub with Daddy."

"*With* Daddy?" Allegro echoed.

"What?" *A slip of the tongue? No. It was true. Her father had taken baths with her sister. Melanie'd once told her. "It's a secret, Sarah. You can't tell, or Daddy will be so mad he'll send you right off to reform school."* She'd been too young to know what a reform school was, but she could tell by the way Melanie said it that it was a bad, dark, scary place. She never breathed a word.

Allegro saw her getting wild-eyed again. "Forget it. It's okay, Sarah. I must have misunderstood."

"Misunderstood?" Dizziness swept over her. Why was she sitting naked in her bathtub having a conversation with a bare-chested man? "What happened to your clothes? Why'd you take off your clothes?"

"You threw up all over them."

She flushed, her wet hand going up to her mouth. "Oh, God, how could I forget? You ready to call the men in white coats to cart me off?"

He smiled. "No. Do you want to be carted off?"

Tentatively, she smiled back. "No. I'll settle for a little privacy, though."

"You sure you're going to be okay?"

"Yeah. The worst is over, right?"

Allegro nodded, but he couldn't look her in the eye. She was in no condition yet for the truth.

He got to his feet. "You've got a nightgown hanging here on your door hook. You want me to bring you in a clean robe?"

" 'Fraid I'm robed out," Sarah said, sounding more like her old self. "The nightgown will be fine. If you rummage through my bureau drawers, I'm sure you can come up with a T-shirt for yourself."

"Thanks." He got to his feet.

"John?"

"Yeah?"

"You won't leave?" She could hear the desperation in her voice, but this time it didn't matter. It didn't matter if he knew how scared she was. How much safer she'd feel if he was with her. As if he didn't know anyway.

Allegro smiled reassuringly. "No, Sarah. I won't leave. I'll be right here when you get out."

He was halfway out the door when she called to him

once more. "John—there's a new bottle of Scotch on top of the fridge."

He hesitated, then nodded.

As Allegro closed the door behind him, Sarah couldn't stop herself from wondering: Had he been drunk the night he was supposed to have beaten up his wife?

The stink of her vomit still lingered faintly in the living room, although Sarah saw that Allegro had done a good job cleaning up the mess. And thrown open the windows to air the place out.

He was sitting on her couch, his elbows on his knees, his head in his hands. The bottle of Scotch was on the coffee table. For a minute she thought he might already be feeling the effects of the booze.

"Where . . . is it?" she asked, looking furtively and in vain for Romeo's latest and most horrifying special delivery—the wrapping, the mailer, his letter, the red velvet box with Emma's heart. *How wonderful if she'd imagined it all. Rather be crazy than sane just now.*

Allegro snapped to when he heard her voice, twisting his head around to see her. She looked like a waif in that shapeless, calf-length pink cotton gown.

"I sent everything off with Pollock to the lab. Forensics."

"Pollock?"

"The cop posted outside."

Some bodyguard. "How could—Romeo—get past him?"

Allegro scowled. "Pollock says he heard something down your alley about an hour ago and went to check. Turned out to be some stupid cat. Knocked over a trash can cover. He spent a few minutes checking around back there just to make sure things were in order. Giving the bastard more than enough time to slip the lock on the outside door with a credit card, duck in, make his *delivery*, and get out."

Sarah vividly pictured the cat rubbing up against her kitchen window in the darkness. That obscene heart dangling from the white choker around its neck. The image transformed itself into something hideous. Its neck was slashed, blood oozing from the open gash. Onto the golden heart. Dripping down inside it. Coating the photos of the two sisters a bloodred.

Allegro saw her go pale. He reached for the bottle of Scotch. "Come sit down and have a drink."

She was surprised to see him snap the seal on the cap. So he hadn't had anything to drink. Yet.

She shook her head, but she did come around to join him on the sofa. When she got a full view of him, a harsh laugh broke from her lips.

"What is it?"

"The shirt." Across the front of it in bold black letters read, *Trust in Allah, but tie up your camel.*

"Yeah," he said, patting the lettering on his chest. "I guess that pretty much covers it."

She sat down next to him. "One of my clients gave that to me. Hector Sanchez. He's an artist who was blinded in a motorcycle accident."

"Isn't that the guy who—?"

Sarah gave him a guarded look. "Who what?"

"Who found that package from Romeo waiting for you outside his studio. The box of chocolates. And those notes."

Sarah's eyes darkened with suspicion. "John . . . I never told you . . . how I got them. Where. I never told anyone. I just said Romeo'd sent them to me."

"Sarah, don't look at me like that. Mike told me. He spoke to Sanchez."

The breeze from the open windows sent chills through her. The night fog seeped into the room.

"Mike spoke to Hector Sanchez?" There was no concealing the suspicion in her tone.

"That's right."

He's lying. She'd tripped him up. She'd never mentioned Hector to Wagner either.

She edged away from him.

"Sarah, what's the matter with you?"

"How could Mike have spoken to him? How did he even know Hector existed? I never mentioned him to either of you."

"Sanchez phoned Mike. Well, he phoned Homicide asking for the person in charge of the Romeo case. Mike took the call. He told Mike about the package from Romeo."

That rang true. Knowing Hector, it wasn't hard to believe he might have called in to Homicide and told Wagner about the package. Or put two and two together from the way she'd acted and figured it came from Romeo. "Sanchez was real worried about you. Mike assured him we were on the job. I'll tell you, Sarah, I think your artist's got a crush on you." Allegro paused before adding, "I don't blame him."

Her brow furrowed. "Why did you come here at this hour, John?" A professional call? Or a personal one?

He didn't look happy with her question. So much for her pathetic stab at romantic fantasy.

"It isn't Perry, Sarah. He's not Romeo. Someone turned up and provided him with an airtight alibi for the night of your sister's murder."

Given Romeo's latest delivery, Sarah more than suspected it. Still, it was the last thing she wanted to hear.

"Why'd he try to kill himself?"

"I'm not saying he's not fucked up. Just that he's not Romeo."

"So that's it," she said starkly. "Back to square one."

He gave her thigh a brief touch. "I know in the scheme of things this isn't much comfort for you, Sarah, but when Perry came to a little while ago, he insisted he made it all up about having sex with your sister. I thought you'd want to know that—that Melanie didn't—sleep with him."

"Well, that's his story now. Maybe he was so tormented by guilt, he wants to deny it ever happened."

"Dennison says that Perry shows all the signs of—"

"Dennison? You talked to Bill Dennison?"

"He was over at the hospital when Mike and I got there. To check on Perry. Dennison *is* his shrink. Although Perry refused to see him."

"Was he still there when you left?"

Allegro regarded her quizzically. "Dennison? No. He decided to give Perry a day or two to settle down. Prescribed some antidepressants for him. We didn't say anything to Dennison about Perry's alibi. For now, we're keeping that under wraps."

Sarah was only half listening. "What time did he leave the hospital?"

"Close to ten-thirty. I saw him heading for the elevator as we were going into Perry's room."

Sarah's throat went dry. "Then he could have done it. Bill could have delivered that—that *parcel* here."

"A lot of people could have delivered it, Sarah. Just about anyone but Robert Perry. The field is wide open again, I'm afraid. Do you know exactly when that package showed up at your door?"

"It wasn't there when I got home around eight."

"Eight? You left the hospital with Mike at six-thirty."

"We went for a bite to eat before he dropped me off." Sarah rushed right on, not wanting Allegro to question her about what she and Wagner had talked about. "Anyway, I was in bed by ten-thirty. Woke up from a bad dream at eleven-fifteen. Then my next-door neighbor knocked on my door. She—I mean, he—was on his way out, or so he said, and he saw the parcel."

Allegro grinned. "Vickie Voltaire? Some looker, according to Mike."

Sarah scowled.

"Hey, don't worry. He's not my type," Allegro teased, trying to coax a smile out of her. He didn't succeed.

"Vickie could have left it for me, John." She told him

about their earlier encounter at her door. How Vickie'd pretended to leave, how he'd tried so hard to convince her to let him come in and take care of her. Even her theory of how he could have entered the buildings of the victims in drag.

"We'll definitely have a talk with your neighbor."

"You think it's far-fetched, right?"

He stared at her, hard. "I think you're smart. I like that in a woman."

There was an awkward silence. Sarah never knew how to handle moments like this.

"Then again, if it wasn't Vickie who left the box, I still vote for Bill." Sarah wondered if Allegro remembered her confessing that she and her ex-brother-in-law had had a brief fling. "He had keys to the building and to my apartment. I gave them to him about eight months ago. And asked for them back a month later," she added quickly.

"And he refused?"

"No. He gave me back the apartment key, but said he'd lost the other one. He wouldn't have even needed to waste time slipping the lock."

Allegro scowled. "First thing tomorrow morning, we have the locks changed."

"It was a mistake, John. The thing with me and Bill."

"Although," Allegro continued as if not hearing what she'd said, "I suppose if he has a copy of the key to your apartment, he might have risked putting that package inside instead of leaving it at your door. That is, assuming it was Dennison."

"Not yet. He's enjoying his game too much."

"Some game," Allegro said.

"Yeah. He starts playing by screwing with my head first," she said bleakly, "and then he's going to work his way down."

Allegro eyed the bottle of Scotch. Maybe one shot—

"What time did you say Bill left the hospital?" Sarah asked.

"Around ten-thirty," Allegro said.

"That gives him forty-five minutes before Vickie knocked my door and told me the parcel was out there. He could have even kept the—the heart—in a freezer somewhere in the hospital." *And Melanie's heart? Was her heart still there?*

Allegro saw the color bleed from Sarah's face again. He stood. "You've been through enough tonight. What do you say I tuck you into bed, and we'll hash all this out in the morning?"

She grabbed his arm. "It makes sense, John. And remember the other night after that attempted break-in here. I called Bill, and he wasn't home."

"We questioned Dennison. He says he was out walking his dog."

"Did anyone see him?"

"Look, Dennison's right up there on our list of suspects. We'll check out where he went after he left the hospital."

"What about his alibi for last night? When Emma—"

"Believe me, we'll question him about that, too. But based on next to nothing, we can't go barging in on him at this hour and give him the third degree."

He glanced at his watch. "It's after one. You need some sleep. What I will do is post someone outside Dennison's house and make sure he stays put until we get over there and question him thoroughly. Will that make you feel better?"

She gave him a bleak look. "He's out there, John. Romeo's out there waiting to rip my heart out—"

He put his arms around her. "I'm getting damn fond of that heart of yours, Sarah. You think I'm going to let anything happen to it?"

"I don't know if you can stop it from happening. I don't know that anyone can."

"I've got three men outside now, a cruiser swinging by every thirty minutes, and I'm going to camp out right here on your sofa. I promise I won't even blink too long, okay? I'm a night owl anyway. And you already know from the last time someone tried to break in here that I've got twenty-twenty hearing," he added with a lame attempt at humor. He got serious again real fast. "That fucking maniac isn't getting within a mile of you, Sarah. You have my word on that."

She reminded him that Vickie was only a few yards away. Or would be when he got home.

"Yeah," he said, "but I'm right here."

Allegro's gaze shifted from Sarah to the unopened bottle of Scotch on the table. "Do you mind if we deep-six the booze? It doesn't mix with guard duty."

She looked over at the Scotch. Was his drinking problem so bad that he couldn't trust himself to stay away from it?

"Be my guest," she said quietly.

"It's not as bad as you think it is, Sarah."

"How do you know what I'm thinking?"

"I just figure, why make a fight hard when I can make it easy. Booze is a temptation. I won't deny it. But there are some temptations I've been finding even more enticing lately. And those I've got to fight the hard way."

Was he talking about her? Was she really a temptation? Or was this more about pity than longing? She was certainly feeling pretty damn pitiful at the moment. But when she looked him in the eye, Sarah saw only tenderness there. Would she ever know the truth of his feelings? She wasn't sure. She only knew the truth of hers. At least she was beginning to think she did.

She started to say something, then faltered.

"What is it?" he pressed.

A flush threaded through her cheeks. "I was going to say something dumb and coy about my sofa being lumpy." She felt so foolish and inadequate. And if she kept on with this nonsense, Allegro would soon discover just how foolish and inadequate she truly was.

The corners of his mouth turned up. "You know—it does look kind of lumpy. Of course, all the better to stay awake."

To her dismay, Sarah blurted, "I don't want you to spend the night out here on the couch. I want you to spend it in my bed with me. If you don't want to, I'll understand. I look like hell, I've acted like a raving lunatic tonight. I practically accused you of being Romeo. I'm totally screwed up, John. In more ways even than you know." She talked fast because otherwise she knew she'd lose her nerve.

He slipped his hand behind her neck and drew her face close to his. Until their lips were barely touching. When he spoke, she could feel his words against her mouth. "We're both fucked up, Sarah. I won't hold it against you if you don't hold it against me."

I'm desperately searching for the balance
between darkness and light. I see it in
you, too. Our desires are tangled in a
nightmare that we share.

_____

M.R. diary

22

Sarah lay on her back on the right-hand side of the bed, hands crossed over her chest, not moving a muscle. Like she'd been laid out in a coffin. A disquieting pose, to say the least. Yet she couldn't budge. Embarrassment held her captive. She'd invited Allegro into her bed, and now that he was lying beside her, she found that she'd dragged all her old fears right under the covers with her. Making for very cramped quarters. To add to her discomfort, she was stark naked. In a fleeting moment of abandon when they'd first entered her bedroom, she'd flung off her nightgown. She'd regretted it almost instantly.

"Sarah?"

Should she pretend to be asleep? Spare herself further humiliation?

"I'm sorry, John." She'd wanted so desperately to have sex with him—still did—but she couldn't let herself go.

He rolled onto his side so that he was facing her, propping his head on his hand, elbow dug into the mattress. "Would you rather I went back into the other room?"

She turned her head to him. Though the room was

quite dark, the headlights of a passing car on the street illuminated his face for an instant. Not an easy face. Not peaceful. Grooves of melancholy, turmoil, and bitterness bit deep into his features. But it was a face that snagged her heart. She could feel it beating now with a clumsy longing.

She waited until the car went by and their faces were bathed in blackness again to ask, "What do you see in me, anyway?"

"All the things you can't."

She placed her hand on his bare chest. He'd taken off the T-shirt, but he was still wearing his trousers. "The bad as well as the good?"

"Depends on how you define bad."

"I don't define it. I just try to keep my distance from it."

"Can you do that?"

"Yes. It's an art, really."

"Bullshit."

She withdrew her hand. "You're right. It's a defense. Ask Feldman. He'll tell you. Or maybe he has already."

"Forget about Feldman."

"I can't. He's right here in bed with us. Shadow of my shadow."

"I love you, Sarah."

She gave an awkward laugh at his entirely unexpected confession. "When did that happen?" Even as she asked the question, her mind was busy denying the veracity of his declaration. How often did a guy use that tired phrase just to get laid?

Allegro rolled over onto his back. "The exact moment?" He smiled faintly. "When you threw up all over me."

"Now you're making fun. Or else you're very peculiar. Either way, a disappointing answer." As if any answer wouldn't be.

"Things aren't only one way or another, Sarah."

"What way are they then?"

He didn't respond for a long while. She thought at first he was trying to work his way out of the hole he'd dug himself. Then, when another minute or two passed, she knew he wouldn't answer her at all.

That was when he spoke. "One time I was home alone with my kid. He died seven years ago. I never told you I had a kid, did I?"

She shook her head. He hadn't told her. Wagner had.

"Danny was home sick. He'd been sick for a couple of weeks. The doc said it was bronchitis. That he should be getting better. Only he wasn't getting better. Grace was all worked up. Begged me to take the day off because she was worried about Danny. She always worried."

"So you stayed home with him?"

He nodded. "I told her to get out for a while. Sent her off shopping for something or other. 'Cause she was driving both me and the kid nuts. I was in the kitchen making him some soup for lunch when I heard him call for me. I went running into his room, and he was hanging over the edge his bed, puking up his guts. I rushed to him and held his head. And all I could think the whole time, his vomit splattering all over me, was that I loved him so much. So much it hurt."

Sarah could hear the hurt in his voice. She could feel it. His. Hers. Pain was another link between them.

"Grace walked in later. Danny was fast asleep, and I was just sitting there beside him on the bed, stroking his forehead. I was crying. I didn't even know it. She said to me, 'I never saw you cry over anyone before, John.' And she was right."

Slowly, he turned to Sarah. She could feel his eyes on her even in the dark. "Tonight, when you got sick and I had to take care of you, it felt so much like that time with Danny, I got all teary-eyed. And I thought to myself—I love this woman. So much it hurts."

Sarah lay very still, but her mind was anything but. *Had he known his son was going to die? Was that part of why he was crying? Did his eyes well up tonight because he knows I'm going to die, too?*

As she slept, Sarah's cheek rested against a spot just below Allegro's right shoulder, her breath warming his damp skin. His arm was starting to go numb, but he made no attempt to move it.

Her lips parted. He wondered if she talked in her sleep. But only a whimper escaped. When a car whizzed by, fleetingly illuminating her face, he saw a single tear running down the ridge at the side of her nose. Before it got to her upper lip, he captured it with the tip of his tongue. The taste was salty and sweet at the same time. Arousing.

Sarah threw an arm across her face as she slept. A low, fretful noise rumbled in her ears. The noise was making her whole head vibrate. It woke her up. She lay very still, trying to decipher the sound. Picture where it was coming from.

> *She sees brown eyes. Wide with panic. They're her eyes. She's trying to cry out. But the sound is muffled. Because there's a large hand pressing down over her mouth.*

The memory sharpened. Sarah saw herself, naked, pinned down on a bed. Just a girl. Only a child.

> *"I knew I couldn't count on you. No matter what you try, you're a disappointment."*
> *She whimpers. It hurts.*
> *"You're just like your mother. Two of a kind. Blubbering, pathetic, frigid." He spits out each word. "Just go upstairs to bed. I don't even want to look at you."*

She stumbles off the sleep sofa, crying out as her shin smashes against the metal bar that frames the mattress.

Her father yanks her by her hair and stares her down. He isn't done with her yet.

"This never happened. If you ever say it did, you'll be sorry for the rest of your life. Because then everyone will know how you came in here and tried to make me do bad things to you. Everyone else will know what a terrible little girl you are."

A loud moan involuntarily escaped Sarah's lips.

Allegro switched on the lamp on her cluttered bedside table. She winced, bringing her hands up to block the glare and shield herself from his all-too-perceptive stare.

"Shut it off. Please, John."

Instead, he grabbed her wrists, forcing her hands from her face. A surge of panic raged through her like an avalanche.

"Tell me, Sarah. Get it out."

She kept her eyes shut. "I lied. To myself. To Bernie. To . . . everyone."

"What did you lie about?"

"It wasn't . . . just Melanie. He . . . my father . . . molested me, too. I . . . let him. What's worse . . . I . . . wanted him to. I wanted him to . . . want me. Love me like he loved . . . Melanie. But he didn't. He was disgusted with me because I cried when it hurt."

She buried her face in her hands. "I thought if I told Momma . . . about letting him do it . . . to me . . . she would have hated me, too. And then there wouldn't be anyone left to love me."

Allegro held her tight. "It's okay, baby. I understand. I love you, Sarah."

She wasn't listening. She was still caught up in her terrible guilt. "But I was jealous. I wasn't even . . . thinking of Melanie, of my mother. What she was . . . suffering. I was a spiteful, ugly girl."

"No. Never," he said. "You were just a sad, confused child."

"What I did was monstrous. Letting him. God, it's so sick."

"Is that why you took those pills?" He grasped her wrists, his fingers brushing the scars. "And did this?"

Sarah let her head fall back onto her pillow. The cover slipped down to her waist, leaving her breasts fully exposed. Allegro lifted it back up over her.

She managed a shallow smile of gratitude as she clutched the blanket tightly around her. "I . . . suppose. Although I was blind to it at the time. Blocked it out completely. Feldman thought I was suffering from depression over my mother's death. He didn't know the half of it. But then, until tonight, neither did I. And I didn't want to, despite all of Feldman's efforts to get me to open up— explore my feelings. I was a lousy patient."

"Maybe he was a lousy shrink," Allegro offered.

Sarah shook her head. "Whatever else he might be, he's not that."

They looked at each other, then Sarah's gaze fell on her scarred wrists.

"I sliced them a couple of months after I started college. Over a senior I was crazy about who dumped me. Turned out, he hit on every decent-looking freshman around. I made it easy for him. I threw myself at him. And held on for dear life until I caught him going at it with my roommate."

Allegro was silent.

She laughed dryly. "Yeah, pretty obvious, huh? Déjà vu all over again."

"Are you going to keep trying to kill yourself until you succeed, Sarah?" His voice was like a caress.

"And disappoint Romeo by beating him to the punch?"

"Don't talk like that."

"How should I talk, John?"

He took hold of her wrists again, tenderly this time.

She watched as he pressed the scarred tissue of each one in turn lightly to his lips. The gesture triggered a pulsating charge of desire and desperation deep inside her.

When he released her wrists, she slid her fingers over his lips. "Don't let me die, John," she whispered, then leaned toward him, exchanging her fingers for her mouth. His mouth opened against hers, but he didn't touch her body. Not even after she let the cover drop to her waist, exposing her breasts again.

She reached over to turn the light off, but Allegro shook his head. "I want to see you," he said hoarsely.

She stiffened. But she offered no protest as he rose from the bed and pulled the sheet all the way off her. She lay still, shutting her eyes to his scrutiny.

"Open your eyes."

"This is hard for me, John."

"Do you want me?"

"Yes . . . but I'm so scared."

"You can stop me at any point. If you tell me to stop, I will. I promise you. Do you believe me?"

"I'm not sure."

"Take the chance, Sarah. You've faced your demons."

"Not all of them. There's still Romeo."

"If you let Romeo deny you what you want, Sarah, he's won."

"You say all the right things, John."

"Because this is right. What we're feeling. What we both need." He was on his knees at the side of the bed, his fingers curled around the edge of the mattress.

All Sarah's muscles tightened reflexively—preparing for a sexual assault.

But there was no assault. Allegro didn't even move to touch her. She lay in the light, utterly exposed, surprised to see her nipples hard as pebbles. She experienced a rush not only of arousal but of optimism.

She was giving herself permission to want to make love. Not out of jealousy or revenge or even desperation. Maybe, in a crazy way, she'd earned this. She'd paid for her crimes with so much suffering, surely she deserved a chance to finally know what it was like to feel passionate abandon.

"Yes." The word slipped from her lips. She watched him clumsily wriggle out of his pants and briefs and climb into bed. Before she lost her nerve, her hands moved jerkily around his neck, pulling him closer. Her body tensed as his erect penis rubbed against her thigh.

He caressed her so tenderly. Fingers cruising lightly across her rib cage. Tip of his tongue lightly circling a nipple. A hand lovingly tracing the tops of her thighs. Soft lips gliding down over her quivering stomach.

His foreplay was gentle and sensitive, and she wanted to let go, but even as she urged herself to relax, her arms crossed over her chest, her hands clenched into fists, her nails dug painfully into her palms.

"I don't think I can do this—"

"Yes, you can, Sarah. Trust me. Let me love you."

She tried. She lay very still as he slid down the bed, gently urging her legs apart. Then his head was between them, and she gave a sharp little cry as she felt the tip of his tongue make contact with her clitoris. Instinctively, she clamped her legs closed in a protective effort, but she only succeeded in holding him captive there.

Her head thrashed back and forth on the pillow as he persisted in his single-minded task. Not just the tip of his tongue now, but the whole of it. Long, lush, thorough strokes. She writhed uncontrollably—her hips beginning to move against him, her body divorcing itself from whatever resistance still clung to her mind.

He withdrew his tongue and began to nip at her labia —lightly, sensually.

The sensation caused her mind to explode into a flashback of the terrible dream she'd had right after Melanie's murder.

The faceless man lowering his head to her breast. Drawing in her nipple between his hot, moist lips. Flicking it to erection. And then it happens. Caught unaware. The sear-

ing, excruciating pain of it. He's bitten her nipple off. And he won't stop there. He is munching away at the tissue of her breast, gnawing right through the bone. Closer, closer to her heart—

"No!" she screamed at the top of her voice, kicking and clawing at the demon head devouring her, eating her alive. *Not my heart. Not my heart!*

Jerking his head up, Allegro got a knee smack in his jaw. He let out a sharp cry and tried to grab at her flailing legs to pin them down, but she was uncontrollable.

Sarah was fighting for her life—arms and legs striking out ferociously, slamming Allegro in the chest, the stomach, his shins, too close to his groin for comfort. He cursed hotly, struggling in vain to hold her down, to quiet her frenzied shouting.

The explosive splintering of her front door brought them both up short. Allegro leaped from the bed, snatching his trousers up off the floor as Mike Wagner, followed by Rodriguez and Corky, burst into the bedroom brandishing their guns.

A stunned silence from the intruders. A gasp from Sarah, who grabbed for the sheet to cover herself. Allegro pulled on his trousers. He zipped his fly, the sound luridly loud.

Wagner quickly shifted his gaze from Sarah to Allegro, who was now pulling the T-shirt he'd borrowed from Sarah over his head. There was no hiding the confusion and consternation etched on Wagner's features. He took a nervous step back as Allegro turned and started toward him. Sarah, wrapped in the sheet now, looked anxious, too. Like Allegro might deck his partner for—if nothing else—lousy timing. But he strode right past Wagner, leaving the bedroom without a word to him. Or to her. Seconds later, what was left of the front door slammed shut.

Rodriguez and Corky shared a look.

Wagner's features evened out, although he avoided making eye contact with Sarah. Instead he looked back at the two detectives. "Okay, boys. Do what you can with the door, then get back out and take up your watch," he snapped officiously—slipping his gun back into his shoulder holster.

As the detectives turned to leave, he had one more order for them. "And neither of you saw anything here tonight."

"Right," they both mumbled, as eager to get out as Wagner was to be rid of them.

Again, her front door slammed shut.

Wagner remained standing in the center of the bedroom. After a moment, he asked, "Are you okay?"

Sarah, hot with embarrassment, nodded shakily, praying he wouldn't ask any questions about the scene they'd just charged in on. At the moment, she wasn't even sure what had happened herself.

"I was worried about you. I got word from Pollock about the latest—delivery."

"Do they . . . know yet? If it's really—Emma's—?"

"So far it looks like a . . . match."

Sarah winced but said nothing.

"Anyway, I drove over here to check that everything was quiet. That you were okay. Then we heard screams, and—"

"It isn't what you think."

"Look, it's none of my business, but—"

"That's right," she said stiffly.

"Did he—hurt you, Sarah?"

She looked away. "No. No, he didn't hurt me. I think . . . I hurt him."

"I don't understand."

She met Wagner's intense, worried gaze. "I panicked, Mike. For a moment I even thought—" She stopped abruptly.

"Thought what?" he persisted.

"Nothing. It's crazy." She glanced over at her nightgown, lying in a heap on the floor.

Wagner got it for her. He turned his back as she slipped it on.

"I've got a great idea." Sarah said. "Have a cup of tea with me."

"I'll put the water on."

"Mike?"

"Yes?"

"Why didn't you ever mention to me that you spoke to Hector Sanchez the other day?"

He gave her a puzzled look. "Who?"

"Hector Sanchez. My client. He phoned you on Thursday, didn't he?"

"What makes you say that?"

"He didn't phone you?"

"No. Sanchez? I never heard his name before. He told you he talked to me?"

A cold wave rocked her. What the hell was going on? "I must have misunderstood."

"Maybe it was John he talked to," Wagner suggested.

"Yes. Maybe it was."

"Tell me more about John's wife."

Wagner looked over the rim of his teacup at Sarah. They were seated at her kitchen table. It was almost two in the morning.

Slowly, he set the cup down in its saucer. "What do you want to know?"

Sarah had her hands folded in her lap. She clenched them together. Her cup of tea remained untouched.

"John told me she jumped out of a seventh-story window."

Wagner nodded.

"So it wasn't a cry for help. Or a way of getting attention. She had to know she wouldn't survive that kind of fall."

"I guess I never thought of it that way."

"Why did she kill herself? Was it because of their son's death?"

Wagner ran his finger up and down the teaspoon beside his cup. "I suppose in part."

"And the other part?"

"Sarah, why are you doing this? Why are you asking me these questions? Are you in love with John?"

"You said he beat her."

"Once. It happened once. And who really knows the true story? Maybe he wasn't the one. Maybe she did it to herself. You didn't believe it was him."

"But you did."

His face was miserable. "Look, John's drinking was way out of hand. Maybe they got into a fight and he didn't realize what he was doing. As far as I know, it never happened again."

"He's still drinking."

"Not as much as before. Never on the job anymore. Look, I couldn't pick a better partner than John. He's never once let me down. Sure, he's had his problems, but I'm certainly not one to cast stones."

"And you think I shouldn't be either."

"I think you should get some sleep."

Sarah nodded, but she knew there wasn't a chance in hell she'd sleep that night. And she wasn't too optimistic about any of the nights to come.

Allegro phoned her late Sunday morning. She had her answering machine on so she could screen her calls. The press was hounding her even more, now that Emma Margolis's death had become the hot news item of the moment.

"Sarah, I know you're there. Please pick up."

She stood by the phone, hands clamped together.

"We need to talk, Sarah. My head's spinning. And my jaw's not too great either. I'm sorry about last night, Sarah. I should have known better. I shouldn't have rushed you."

There was a long pause. Sarah's breath caught. Was he going to hang up? Did she want him to?

"Sarah, the other reason I called is—I had a long talk with Dennison over breakfast. He says he went straight home from the hospital last night and was back at his place by ten forty-five. The thing is—a neighbor who was out jogging saw him drive up closer to eleven-thirty. So he's lying, which means your theory definitely could hold water. He could have made it over to your place first. And there's something else even more damning."

Again, he paused.

"Sarah, are you listening to me?"

Her hand was clammy as she lifted the receiver to her ear. "Yes."

"I'm sorry, Sarah. You've got to believe how sorry I am."

"What's the something else?" Her voice was curt.

Allegro sighed. "Seems Perry's been real agitated since he came out of the coma. When the doc on duty said he'd have his shrink come in, Perry was adamant about not wanting to continue treatment with Dennison. Wanted someone else. Anyone else."

"Did Perry say why?"

"Not at first. The doc says Perry got even more worked up when he asked. Kept repeating it was too dangerous. Went on about how it might not be safe for his wife. How she could be next."

"I don't understand," Sarah said.

"He finally got Perry calmed down enough to talk. Perry seems convinced that Dennison's Romeo. And Perry's terrified that if Dennison finds out he blew his cover, the shrink might kill his wife."

Sarah's grip on the phone tightened. "What makes Perry so sure it's Bill Dennison?"

"That afternoon when Perry and Emma left the tea shop, Perry did follow her. And he says that as he was turning the corner onto her street, he saw Dennison and Emma walking into her apartment together. He says they looked real chummy. That Dennison had his arm around her shoulder."

Sarah sank down onto a nearby kitchen chair.

"Are you still there, Sarah? Are you all right?"

"What will you do now?"

"I'm taking a photo of Dennison back to Emma's neighborhood. Show it to that old woman across the street. And other neighbors. See if anyone can confirm Perry's story. And we'll lean hard on Dennison. Go over the accounts of his whereabouts on the nights of each of the murders until something breaks. You had a gut feeling about him almost from the start. I should have paid more attention to it. Sarah . . . about last night—"

"Anything more from forensics?"

"What? Yeah. The heart's a match. They're going over —the rest. We'll have more later today."

"Did Emma have family? I know there's her ex-husband, but she didn't mention parents. Siblings." *Did Emma have a sister?*

"Her mother's been notified. She's a widow. Lives in Michigan. She wants to have Emma buried there. As soon as the autopsy's finished. There's also a younger brother. He's flying out here on Tuesday to make the arrangements."

There was an awkward silence.

"Have you found the other woman yet?" Sarah asked. "The one whose heart—"

"No. Not yet."

Sarah's eyes welled up. Who would discover Romeo's mystery victim? A husband? A boyfriend? Someone who'd really loved her? Cherished her?

"Can we talk, Sarah?"

She swiped at the tears with the back of her hand. "We are talking."

"I mean face to face."

"I need a day to—recuperate, John. Call me tomorrow at the office."

"Are you sure you're ready to go back to work?"

"I've got to stay busy. Or I'll go nuts."

"Okay, I'll call you in the morning. Say around ten."

"Okay."

"Sarah?"

"Yes?"

"I never meant to hurt you. Or scare you."

"I know," she said before she hung up. And she be-lieved it. But would she have, if he hadn't told her about Dennison? If it didn't look like things were pointing to her ex-brother-in-law as the killer? Stilling the hysterical but distressing notion that Allegro could conceivably be Romeo.

There was still his odd claim that Wagner had spoken to Hector Sanchez. Could it have happened and with everything else going down, Wagner simply hadn't remembered? Easy enough way to find out. Call Hector. Ask him if he phoned Wagner.

She rang Sanchez up, but he was out. She left a message. Five minutes later, her phone rang. Thinking it was Sanchez, she picked up.

It wasn't Hector Sanchez.

Music oozed out of the receiver. *Rhapsody in Blue.*

At 9:20 on Monday morning, Wagner and Allegro were in the Homicide squad room with the ten detectives now assigned to the Romeo task force. Allegro was standing at the chalkboard, firing out orders. He'd just come back from Emma Margolis's neighborhood and hit the jackpot. Not one but two people in Emma's building—both of whom had been away for the weekend—corroborated Robert Perry's claim that Emma had entered her building late Friday afternoon with a man who matched Dr. William Dennison's photo.

Frank Jacobs, an electrician who lived in apartment 3B, was going out on an emergency call on Friday when he saw Emma and Dennison entering the lobby together. Dora Cheswick, resident of apartment 5A directly across the hall from Emma's place, was leaving her apartment—on her way to spend the weekend visiting her sick mother in Burlingame—when she saw Emma and Dennison entering Emma's apartment. Both eyewitnesses had chosen Dennison's photo without hesitation out of a dozen Allegro showed them. Both agreed to come in to see if they could pick him out in a lineup.

With a new prime suspect on the hook, there was an air of revitalized optimism in the squad room. Allegro was breaking the men up into teams, each pair assigned one of the Romeo murder victims, Rodriguez and Johnson taking over Emma Margolis, he and Wagner staying in charge of the Melanie Rosen file. Every piece of information would be gone over ad infinitum, all witnesses requestioned, photos of Dennison circulated around to everyone who knew any of the victims. Pollock would be checking out all recent missing persons files, trying to track down the still-unidentified owner of the decomposed heart that Romeo'd swapped for Emma's.

"Okay, boys, you all know what to do," Allegro concluded.

Wagner watched the team file out. "What do you say, John? We ready to bring him in now?"

Allegro shrugged into his rumpled sport jacket. "Why don't I get him while you connect with some of our old pals from Vice? Like that ex-hooker who runs that club in SoMa. Show Dennison's photo around. See if anybody recognizes him. Let's get as much as we can on the bastard."

"Right." Wagner stuck a butt in his mouth as he got to his feet.

"Oh, and what about that S&M joint out in Richmond? The one Sarah told us Emma and Diane Corbett went to."

"Still trying to track it down," Wagner said, lighting up.

"Corky, time to make the rounds of the sex clubs again." Corky waved and left.

They were heading out of the squad room when the phone rang.

"I'll get it," Wagner said.

Allegro nodded and hung around to see if it was anything important. Maybe even Sarah jumping the gun and calling him instead of waiting for him to phone her.

"Homicide. Detective Wagner here."

There was a faint pause on the other end of the line. "Oh, hello Detective. I don't know if you remember me."

The woman's voice was vaguely familiar.

"It's Lorraine Austin. Karen's mother? We talked the other day? You came into my jewelry store. On Kearny Street. Well, not really my jewelry store. I don't own it. I wish I did."

"Yes, of course I remember you," Wagner said. "How are you, Mrs. Austin?"

"Oh, fine thank you. As fine as can be expected, that is."

"Yes, I understand." Wagner rolled his eyes in Allegro's direction.

"I hope I'm not disturbing you, Detective Wagner, but this morning an old high school friend of Karen's stopped in the shop. With her fiancé. To pick out an engagement ring. I had no idea she'd even moved to San Francisco. Karen never said a thing to me. But it turns out Ericka spoke to Karen on the phone only days before—before Karen died."

Wagner waited as he heard the woman sniff back tears.

"The thing is, Detective, you'd asked me if I knew anything about a psychiatrist Karen might have seen for therapy or dated, and I'm afraid I wasn't very helpful. I didn't really think Ericka would know very much about Karen's personal or social life either. After all, they'd only spoken on the phone that one time."

There was another pause.

"A daughter doesn't tell her mother everything," she

said quietly. It was a statement she'd made to him during that first interview.

"Did Karen say something to Ericka about Dr. Dennison?" Wagner asked as Allegro waited at the door to the squad room, his attention sharply focused on the side of the phone conversation he was able to hear.

"Well, no."

Wagner glanced at Allegro and gave his head a slight shake.

"But Karen did mention that she was dating someone new, someone she really was very attracted to."

"Oh?"

"Karen said she was dating a cop. A police officer."

Wagner's eyes shot to Allegro.

"What is it?" Allegro mouthed.

Wagner's gaze remained fixed on his partner. "Is that all, Mrs. Austin? Is that all she told her friend?"

"She didn't give Ericka his name. But she did say he was unlike any man she'd ever dated before."

"Any other details?" Wagner asked.

"No. I'm sorry. That's all she could tell me."

Allegro's brows knitted together.

"Well, thanks, Mrs. Austin," Wagner said. "We'll certainly follow up on it," he said, hanging up.

"Karen Austin's mom?" Allegro asked.

Wagner nodded.

"What was that all about?"

Wagner rummaged through some papers on his desk. "Nothing. Just a sad, lonely mother in mourning grasping at straws."

"What did you tell her you'd follow up on?" Allegro persisted.

Wagner shrugged. "Nothing really. She thinks her daughter may have been dating someone at her company. She didn't even know his name."

"You okay?"

"I'm okay. Sometimes talking to the victims' families —it gets to you, you know?"

"You've got this funny look on your face, Mike. Like something's percolating behind it. What gives?"

"What are you getting all paranoid about? I told you—"

"If it's about the other night, you guys bursting in on me and Sarah—"

"Look, that's none of my business, John." He paused. "But to be honest—"

"Yeah, go ahead. Be honest, Mike."

Wagner shrugged. "She's been through hell. Maybe this isn't the best—the smartest time—she's pretty vulnerable right now, and—"

"And what?" Allegro's tone was growing increasingly belligerent, Wagner's increasingly circumspect.

"Nothing. I'm going to mind my own business. How's that?"

"Fine. That's fine." Allegro was at the door. "You coming?"

"In a few minutes. I want to jot down a couple of notes in Karen's file about the mom's call. Keep everything up to date."

"Right," Allegro said. His eyes fell on the phone. Should he call Sarah now? She was probably at work already. Had she made her decision? He desperately wanted to see her. Everything had gone utterly—not to mention embarrassingly—wrong the other night. He wanted to make it right tonight. Maybe he'd call from a phone booth downstairs. More privacy.

"See ya," Allegro said, shuffling out the door.

As soon as Allegro was out of sight, Wagner went over to a bank of filing cabinets along the far wall. He pulled open a drawer of closed files, searched through them until he found the one he wanted. He pulled the slender file out, opened it, and withdrew the top sheet of paper. It was the autopsy report on Grace Allegro. As he folded it and slipped it into his jacket pocket, he returned to his desk, flipped through the phone book, found the number he was looking for, and dialed.

"Lawry's Jewelry Store."

"Mrs. Austin?"

"Yes?"

"It's Detective Wagner. Sorry to bother you."

"Oh, it's no bother, Detective. We haven't any customers. One of those quiet days."

"I forgot to get your daughter's friend's full name and address. A phone number if you—"

"Oh, of course, Detective. She and her fiancé put a deposit down on a beautiful one-point-four-carat diamond ring. Naturally, I took all the pertinent information. I should have it right here in my file cards. Yes, here it is under F. Ericka Forster. Soon to be Dawkins. Ericka did tell me she was taking her husband's name. They often don't these days. I thought it was nice. I guess I'm old-fashioned. I think Karen would have done the same. At least I like to think so."

"I think it's a nice custom myself. Not that I'm married, but if I did get married—well, anyway, if I could get in touch with your daughter's friend—"

She gave him Ericka's address and phone number.

"I wish I could do more, Detective Wagner. I haven't heard anything in the news about that man in the hospital being officially charged yet. That's why I wanted to tell you about the policeman. You never know."

"Thanks, Mrs. Austin. Always smart to check everything out." Wagner's eyes drifted to Allegro's empty chair. "You're right. You never know."

"Not that anything can bring my baby back. I just pray you have your man. That no other lovely, vibrant young woman will fall prey to that monster. No mother wants to survive her child, Detective Wagner."

Wagner was surprised to find his eyes welling up. "Yes, Mrs. Austin. I'm sure that's true."

While the public may view him as barbaric, inhuman, savagely warped, Romeo believes (with utter conviction) that he's a misunderstood romantic.

Dr. Melanie Rosen
Cutting Edge

23

A squad car delivered Sarah to the rear delivery entrance of her office building at nine-thirty Monday morning. Slipping inside unnoticed, Sarah hurried over to the service elevator just as it was opening. A janitor pushing a cleaning cart got out. She entered the empty elevator and pressed the button for the seventh floor.

On three, the elevator stopped and the doors slid open. A tall man with a baseball cap pulled low stepped in. Sarah let out a gasp of alarm as her eyes shot to the man's shadowed face. She made a desperate effort to sidestep him and escape before the doors slid closed, but he easily blocked her path.

The elevator started to rise, then jerked to an abrupt halt. Bill Dennison had pressed the emergency stop button.

"Don't be scared, Sarah. I'm not going to hurt you. I have to talk to you."

She willed herself to face him squarely. "How did you—?"

"I drove over to your place yesterday after a very disturbing grilling by your pal, Detective Allegro. But the area was swarming with SFPD and reporters. I thought maybe I could slip around the back, but the bastards had it cordoned off."

"So you called me instead? A little *musical* interlude?"

"Don't be idiotic. When I tried again this morning, I spotted you sneaking out, and I followed. Once I figured where you were going, I sped ahead. Watched you come in through the rear of the building. Raced up a few flights of stairs to beat out the elevator. I'm still pretty fast."

She could smell a sickly mix of Dennison's musky aftershave, his sweat, the ammonia from the janitor's cart. The scents made her queasy. "Why did you do it, Bill?"

"I told you. I have to talk to you."

"That's not what I mean."

He rolled his eyes. "I am not Romeo, Sarah. I am not some demented sadist."

Sarah flinched.

Dennison's eyes flared. "Jesus. She told you."

Sarah shook her head lamely, not knowing what he was talking about.

He drew closer. "I never did anything to your sister that she didn't want done. That she didn't beg for. Did she tell you that, too? How she couldn't even come unless I . . . hurt her first? Melanie was the one that was fucked up, Sarah. Not me. But I never held it against her. It never made me love her any the less."

Sarah's pulse was pounding in her ears. *Have to keep cool. He won't kill me here. He can't. It's got to be the same way as he did the others. It's a ritual he can't vary. A compulsion to do the same deed in the same way over and over again. Wasn't that what Melanie'd said?*

Dennison was only inches away. His normally handsome face looked haggard. "You told the cops, didn't you? About me and Melanie. About me and you."

"No. I didn't, Bill—"

His eyes narrowed into menacing slits. He grabbed hold of her. "The cops don't buy that it's Perry, do they? Even though it's being given big play on the news that Romeo's been caught. It's a ruse. They suspect *me*. That's

why Allegro showed up at my doorstep yesterday morning, hounding me with more questions. It's because of
what you told them—"

"Bill, I swear—"

"And because I treated two of the victims and happen
to have once been married to a third. It does look bad,
doesn't it? But that's purely circumstantial. Sarah, you of
all people know how much I loved Melanie. And she loved
me, too. It was this obsession she had with your friggin'
father. Like he was some kind of a god. Nothing I ever did
or said or thought could hold a candle to him. That's why
I started screwing around. That's why I left her. That's
what drew me to you, Sarah. At least you didn't have this
crazed father fixation. You didn't hold every man up to
him as an ideal."

As he spoke, his fingers dug deeper into Sarah's flesh.
He might not kill her here in this claustrophobic, almost
airless cage, but he could hurt her with impunity.

His mouth twisted into an ugly smirk. "Ironic, isn't
it, that Dr. Simon Rosen, this man who was so perfect, so
brilliant—the only person in the universe as far as Melanie was concerned who ever really understood her—
would end up not even knowing who she was half the
time. I thought finally she'd be able to let him go. I really
believed we had a shot at a second chance."

"If you're innocent, Bill, then go to the cops, talk to
them—"

He snickered. "Oh, that's brilliant advice, Sarah. And
to think I once really thought I was falling in love with
you."

A rush of anger overcame Sarah's terror. And her
good sense. "What about Emma? Did you love her, too?"

He shook her hard. "What do you know about me
and Emma?"

"That you were with her the night she was murdered," she blurted. At least she didn't tell him Perry'd
provided that information. Like Perry, Sarah didn't put it
past the murdering bastard to strike out at Perry's wife in

revenge. Or had he taken care of her already? Was Cindy Perry the owner of the unidentified heart?

Dennison's jaw went slack. He swayed, releasing her to grab on to the wall of the elevator to hold himself up. "Emma and I had a drink."

"Champagne?" Sarah taunted.

He shot her a dark look. "Brandy. We had brandy." His face twisted. "Okay, I was attracted to her. She was attracted to me, too. That's why I terminated the therapy. But these past few weeks I haven't been having an easy time of it. I know it was dumb, but I felt this need to—to connect with someone. I craved a little tenderness. Understanding. Affection."

As Dennison spoke, Sarah surreptitiously inched her way to the right, keeping her eyes on his. *A few more feet and she could get to that big red alarm button on the bottom right of the console. If she could only get her legs to move. If they'd carry her that far—*

She thrust out her hand, but before it got to the alarm button, Dennison grabbed her wrist and shoved her across the elevator. She slammed against the wall.

He was staring at her as if he'd never seen her before. "Oh, crap. Are you hurt? I wasn't trying to hurt you. It's just that I'm panicked, Sarah. I'm completely innocent, but if my name is linked in any way as a possible suspect in these slayings, my reputation will be destroyed. I'll lose my practice. I'll be ruined. Maybe I'm not the world's greatest psychiatrist, Sarah, but I do help a lot of people." He leaned toward her, pinning her against the wall. "I swear I was only at Emma's place for an hour. We didn't even have sex. She said she didn't think she could handle it. And I understood. I swear I did. Besides, she said—" He stopped abruptly.

"What did Emma say, Bill?"

Dennison's watery blue eyes widened. "Oh my God. She said she was expecting a friend to drop over later."

"A friend?"

"I thought she was trying to get rid of me. But she

had to be telling me the truth. She was expecting him. Romeo. And he kept the date."

Like he kept all the others.

Sarah seized the opportunity. "You have to tell the police, Bill. Come up with me to my office. We'll phone Allegro."

He shuffled back from her. For a moment, she thought she'd won his cooperation. But then his mouth snaked into a sneer. "You don't believe me. That cop won't believe me either. But then again, I've got something on your pal Allegro, so maybe we can strike a deal."

"What could you possibly have on John?"

"Oh, so it's *John,* is it? I had the feeling there was something going on between you two. Psychiatrists are very perceptive people, even those of us who haven't conquered Mount Everest like the eminent Dr. Simon Rosen. When Allegro was grilling me yesterday, he kept referring to you as Sarah. Not Miss Rosen. And something about the way he said 'Sarah—' "

"Whatever might be going on between us is none of your business, Bill."

"Did he tell you he was seeing her?"

"Seeing who?"

"Melanie?"

"They worked together. She was consulting—"

"No. I mean for therapy. He and his wife. The one who killed herself."

"What are you talking about?"

"Melanie discussed the case with me. She saw Allegro and his wife for treatment. Melanie was the one who had the wife committed. And you know what—the records on the case aren't on her computer. They're gone. As if they never existed. Not in her closed files either. Now, how do you suppose those files vanished into thin air, Sarah?"

"I don't believe you."

"They were hot for each other. Melanie and John. He was fucking her, all right. Just your sister's type. Rough, crude, uncivilized. You can bet he had no trouble making her come—"

Something snapped inside Sarah's head. Without warning, her resolve to play it cool, try to humor him, appease him, was replaced with a cold fury. "You liar! You filthy pervert! You coward!" she screamed, pummeling his chest with her fists. She was no match for Dennison. After momentarily being surprised by her assault, he easily caught hold of her wrists and wrenched her arms behind her back.

He was sweating profusely. "You are crazy, Sarah. You need help. You really do."

"Hey! Anyone in there?" The voice seemed to be coming from above them. "Are you stuck?"

Before Sarah could respond, Dennison clamped one hand over her mouth, his other snaking tight around her waist. He dragged her over to the panel, pressed the *start* button, then *B* for basement. The elevator jerked back into motion.

Sarah's heart and mind were racing. When they got to the basement, could she break loose from him and make a run for the exit? Scream at the top of her lungs, hoping someone was in earshot and would come running?

The elevator came to a stop, the doors sliding open onto a dank, shadowy space bathed in sickly yellow light. Empty and stone silent. "Don't do anything stupid," he warned. "It won't be worth it."

Sarah saw the doors start to slide closed again. Saw her only chance. She shoved Dennison hard, catching him off guard, propelling him out of the elevator into the basement. He lost his balance, stumbling to the ground.

"Sarah—Sarah, please—"

The doors slid shut.

An exceedingly perturbed Andrew Buchanon, his bony face harried, his shoulders stooped, scurried over to Wag-

ner as soon as the detective entered the reception area of
the rehab department.

"Where is she?" Wagner asked brusquely.

"She was completely hysterical when she came in.
Fortunately, one of our other counselors seems to have
managed to calm her somewhat. She did tell him she
wasn't physically assaulted. I do think, though, that she
may need to be hospitalized for a psychiatric evaluation.
She's extremely distraught. Not that I don't sympathize,
but it's most difficult with clients coming in and—"

"Shut up," Wagner said sharply.

Buchanon's thin lips instantly froze.

Wagner pointed a finger at him. Like it was a gun.
"Where is she?"

"In Mr. Grossman's office. Look, Detective, we're all
quite distressed here. If there's anything any of us can
do—"

"I already told you what the hell you can do."

Bernie'd rolled his wheelchair right beside Sarah. He had
his arm around her shoulder. Both looked up when the
door opened.

Wagner strode over to Sarah. "Did he hurt you? Do
you need to see a doctor?"

She was pale, but her eyes were clear. "No."

"What happened?"

"Dennison, that fuck, cornered her in the service elevator, that's what happened," Bernie erupted. "Why
wasn't there a cop with her?"

Wagner ignored him, his gaze fixed on Sarah. "John's
waiting for him at his apartment. And we've got men on
their way to his office in case he heads there instead.
Meanwhile, I have to take a statement from you, Sarah.
But I don't want to do it here."

"There's no way you're gonna bring her down to
some grim interrogation room," Bernie protested.

"My place is on Laguna," Wagner told Sarah. "Less

than a ten-minute drive. I'll make you a cup of tea, and we can talk there." He glanced at Bernie. "If you'd like to come along, that's okay with me."

"I'll be fine, Bernie. Don't worry."

"Will you stay at my place tonight?" Bernie asked.

"Under the circumstances," Wagner stepped in, "I think it would be wise for us to put Sarah up in a hotel under police protection. I assure you, we'll take good care of her."

Sarah thought about Allegro, about how he'd sworn he'd protect her, too.

Sarah looked up at the roiling clouds ready to explode with rain as Wagner helped her out of his car in front of a narrow apartment building on Laguna.

"Funny," she said. "The weather was perfect for weeks on end. Since Melanie's murder, it seems like it's been raining every day."

"I do a great rendition of that song about the sun coming out tomorrow," the detective teased gently.

She smiled. "You're a sweet guy, Wagner."

"Yeah, yeah. That's what they all say."

He guided her inside the pale ochre apartment complex, up one flight to his apartment.

"This is nice." Sarah stepped directly into his living room with its off-white walls, nubby gray tweed carpet. The natural pine shutters on the windows were folded back, allowing a glimpse of Lafayette Park.

She felt like even more of a slob as she contrasted her chaotic mess with Wagner's tidy, stylish digs. Even the oversize glass ashtray on the coffee table was spotless, though the faint smell of cigarette smoke lingered in the air. The spare furnishings—a futon sofa, a low black-lacquered coffee table, a pair of wicker barrel chairs with print cushions—had an Asian flavor and Sarah guessed he'd purchased most of the stuff in nearby Japantown. No paintings, only a large rectangular silver-framed mirror over a fireplace that looked as if it had never been used.

"Have you lived here long?" She deliberately opted for small talk. Not ready to dwell on her harrowing encounter with Dennison. Not wanting to reflect on those distressing innuendoes he'd dropped about John.

"About six months. Haven't really had a chance to fix it up yet. Just bought a few of the basics. Lacks the woman's touch, huh?"

"It's very clean."

Wagner grinned. "That's because I'm hardly ever here. Look, I'll make the tea and you just relax for a few minutes. When you're ready, we'll go over what happened between you and Dennison." He'd already radioed his partner from the car. No surprise that Allegro hadn't found the psychiatrist at home or at his office. An all-points bulletin was in the works.

He headed toward the kitchen to put on the kettle.

"You live alone?" she called out.

"Yeah. I was living with this woman out in Berkeley for a few months, but she decided she couldn't handle being part of a cop's life."

"I'm sorry." She folded her arms across her chest. Felt her hammering heart. Dropped her arms.

"Don't be," he called back. "It isn't like we were made for each other."

When he returned a few minutes later, he was carrying two steaming mugs.

Sarah was sitting in one of the barrel chairs. After setting the mugs on the lacquered table, Wagner took a seat next to her, pulling a small tape recorder out of his pocket.

"Why don't we just get it over with?" he cajoled gently.

She began haltingly. It was especially difficult recounting what Dennison had told her about his sex life with her sister. But what was the point of hiding it from Wagner? He'd already read Melanie's diary excerpts.

"He swears he's innocent," she said. "That he only stayed with Emma for an hour. That she was expecting someone else. Romeo, according to Bill."

"Right," Wagner said sarcastically.

"It's possible. I don't know. The thing he seemed most worried about was his precious reputation. That doesn't exactly fit my idea of Romeo."

"What does?"

"I don't think Romeo really cares about anything but his obsession. His seductions. Nothing else matters."

"Romeo's also a great actor. Now, did you cover everything?"

Everything except that bombshell Dennison had dropped about John, his wife, and Melanie. She sat silent, twisting her hands in her lap.

Wagner leaned forward. "What is it, Sarah?"

"Nothing. It's only . . . what if you're wrong this time, too? What if it isn't Bill?"

"We've got a link already between him and three of the victims. He treated two of them. He was married to— your sister. We've got eyewitnesses placing him at Emma's apartment the night of her murder. For chrissake, Sarah, he practically did you in that elevator."

Sarah blanched.

"I'm sorry. I can be such an insensitive jerk—" He looked stricken.

"No," she said. "You're not either, Mike. You're a nice, decent, sensitive guy. And you're right. Bill probably is—"

"No, wait. You're right, Sarah. We've got to keep our options open until we have Dennison dead to rights. Matter of fact, we're also checking on that neighbor of yours. That drag queen. John told me about your suspicions about that character."

She met Wagner's eyes. "Did you know John and his wife saw Melanie for therapy?"

"What? Where'd that come from? We were talking about the case against Dennison and that drag queen."

She hesitated. "There is—a connection. With Bill Dennison, anyway."

"I don't get it. What connection?"

"Just answer my question, Mike. Did you know?"

"Oh, well—" he hedged.

"You did know." Sarah felt a tightening in her chest.

He sighed. "She told me. But what does this have to do with—?"

"Melanie told you?"

"No, of course not. John's wife. Grace."

"You knew Grace?"

"Not well. The first time we actually talked was a day or two after she dropped the assault charge. She called. Asked if I'd meet her for coffee."

"Why did she want to see you?"

"I don't know. I guess because I was his partner."

"What does that mean?"

"She was upset because John had moved out. That he wanted a divorce."

"And?" Sarah felt like she was pulling the words from his mouth.

"And she thought maybe I could talk to him. Actually I suggested they go into couples' therapy. Grace told me she was already seeing a shrink and that John wanted nothing to do with it. Some guy. I don't remember the name. Not Dennison," he said.

"John told me they were separated at the time she killed herself. He didn't say anything about wanting a divorce. Did he move back home?"

Wagner shook his head. "About a month later she almost OD'd on pills. John never said a word to me about it."

"Grace told you."

"She called me a couple of weeks afterward. I guess she saw me as her link to John. That's when she told me they went to see your sister. I think Grace was kind of delusional by then."

"What do you mean?"

"Oh, she was talking all kinds of crazy stuff. You know—"

"No. I don't know," Sarah said, her urgency increasing with Wagner's escalating evasiveness.

"I don't really remember much of what she said, Sarah."

"Did she say she thought John was attracted to my sister?"

Wagner shrugged. Then, eyeing the tape recorder, he reached over and switched it off. "Grace was nuts, Sarah."

"He was attracted to Melanie," Sarah insisted. "And Melanie was attracted to him. John told me so himself."

"Okay, then, why are you asking me these questions?"

"Because I don't know if the attraction began before Grace killed herself. Or how far the attraction went."

"What are you saying, Sarah?"

"It's not what I'm saying. It's what Bill—"

"What? He told you there was something going on between John and your sister? Come on, Dennison's wigged out."

"That doesn't mean he was lying." She couldn't shake the feeling that she was still seeing everything through a gauze curtain.

"Sarah, listen to me. You'll feel a hell of a lot better when we catch Dennison and the evidence starts rolling in. There are a dozen men working on this. I've got a couple making the rounds of the sex clubs in town right now. Tonight I'm hitting them myself. Somebody's going to recognize Dennison, and all the pieces are going to fall into place. You'll see."

Why was he working so hard to convince her?

Wagner took a long drag of his cigarette, rose, and took off his sport jacket. A paper slipped out of his pocket and floated to the floor near Sarah's feet. She picked it up and was about to pass it on to Wagner when she caught the name Allegro on the top of what she saw now was a form of some sort. She gave it a closer look.

An autopsy report. On Grace Allegro.

She eyes shot to Wagner. "What is this?"

"Nothing." He snatched it from her hand. "Hey, our tea's cold. I'll make up some more," he said, putting out his cigarette in the spotless ashtray.

She followed Wagner into his galley kitchen. He turned the burner back on.

"Why did you pull that report, Mike?"

He stared at the stainless-steel teapot. "A watched kettle never boils. My mother used to say that."

"Damn it, Mike. If you know something, you've got to tell me."

He turned reluctantly to face her. "Are you really in love with John, Sarah?"

"Oh God, you do know something."

Before he could respond, his pager went off, startling them both.

"I've got to call in," he said brusquely, heading over to the wall phone at the end of the counter.

His back was to her, and the kettle began whistling, drowning out his words. By the time she'd shifted the kettle to a cool burner and shut the other one off, he'd hung up. He remained in that position so she couldn't see his face. She could, however, see his shoulders slump.

"What is it?"

"Dennison's off the hook." There was a tightness in Wagner's voice. Like he was holding back a lot of frustration. And anger.

"What? How?"

"That was Rodriguez on the phone. Calling from Mercy Hospital."

"Who's at Mercy Hospital?" Had Dennison tried to kill himself, too? He had certainly seemed desperate enough. Or worse—had Romeo killed again? Was she somehow to blame for yet another act of violence?

"Not who. What."

"I don't understand."

Wagner sat down at the kitchen table. "Rodriguez

questioned a colleague of Dennison's. Shares his suite of offices."

Sarah took the chair across from him. "Carl Thorpe."

"Yeah. Thorpe went to bat for Dennison's good character, even mentioning that Dennison volunteered to be tested as a possible bone marrow donor for Thorpe's son, who was diagnosed with cancer a year back."

"Bill was tested at Mercy Hospital?" Not much of a deduction on Sarah's part.

"It gave Rodriguez the opportunity to check out Dennison's blood workup. At first he thought he hit the jackpot. Dennison and Romeo are the same blood group and type. 'A' positive. Enough, coupled with the other evidence, to book Dennison, get some more blood, and do a full DNA workup."

"But there was a problem?"

"Rodriguez's snitch pointed out some other number on Dennison's chart. His HLA. Rodriguez says it's a test required for histocompatibility or something like that. Whatever, he phoned it in to the medical examiner, and it seems Romeo's HLA and Dennison's aren't a match."

"So that automatically eliminates Bill as a suspect?"

"Pretty much. The ME will do some further checking, but—"

"But it doesn't look hopeful." Sarah finished grimly.

"You can still press assault charges."

Sarah didn't even respond to his suggestion.

The kitchen was eerily silent except for the faint hiss still emanating from the kettle. Wagner lit another cigarette, took a drag, exhaled.

"There's still that neighbor of yours. Vickie, right? What we need is to get our hands on a photo of him as a *him*."

"I can do that," she said.

"What?"

"He's got one. I saw it." *Yes, focus on Vickie. She had suspicions galore about the drag queen. If somebody at a club remembered him—possibly with one of the victims—*

She caught Wagner's troubled expression. "What?"

"Nothing."

"You don't think it's Vickie. Then . . . who?"

Wagner nervously smoothed back his hair. "I didn't say it wasn't Vickie."

Sarah slapped her palms down on the table. "Damn it, Mike! Stop dancing around this. We're not going to make it go away. Why'd you pull Grace Allegro's autopsy report? Why'd you skirt the whole business of John and Melanie having had an affair? We both have these dumb thoughts about—about him. We're telling ourselves it's nuts, but—"

The phone rang. "Jesus," Wagner cursed under his breath. "What next?"

He picked up. After a second, he said, "Hold on," and held the receiver out to Sarah, a muscle jumping at the side of his jaw. "It's him."

She read it all in Wagner's face. Her hand was like ice as she took the receiver, her eyes never wavering from his.

"John?"

"Bernie told me Mike brought you over there. Are you all right?"

"Yes."

"Do you want to press charges against Dennison for assault? I'm afraid that's all we've got. Otherwise he's in the clear. One of our men—"

"Mike already spoke to Rodriguez," she said in a flat, expressionless voice.

"Another perfect suspect bites the dust. The whole team's about to pull their hair out, we're all so damn frustrated. Rodriguez wants to call in a psychic. I keep thinking of that cunning bastard out there, laughing at us, running us around in fucking circles."

Sarah's eyes strayed from Wagner's intense face to the window. The hard rain had finally come. Once again she was drowning in a sea of loss and confusion.

"Look, I've had it for today," John was saying. "Why don't I swing by Mike's and—?"

"No," Sarah snapped, unable to conceal the frantic note in her voice.

"I thought we could go out for dinner tonight. Please, Sarah. I know what you're going through. It's breaking me up inside."

She could feel the tears coming. She couldn't hold them back. *Can you feel my adoration and devotion? . . . Initiating you to the exquisite pleasures only I can give you? I know what you're suffering. What you need . . . because only I can understand. . . .*

She looked imploringly at Wagner. He took the phone from her.

"John. She's pretty shook up. Dennison may not be our boy, but he scared the bejesus out of her, cornering her the way he did."

"Let me talk to her again, Mike."

Wagner looked at her inquiringly. Sarah shook her head.

"Give her a little time, John."

"Put her on, damn it!"

Wagner gave her shoulder a sympathetic squeeze, then clasped his hand over the mouthpiece. "You gotta talk to him, Sarah."

Reluctantly, she took the receiver back, forcing out the words, "I'm here."

"Sarah, I know how scared you must be. What I'm going to do is pick you up and get you settled in a hotel under another name. Corky will be there with you. I'll be there the whole time, too. Outside your door, if that makes you feel better. You can bolt it, chain it, do anything you want that will make you feel safe. I'm not going to let him get to you. I told you that before, and you believed me. You still do, don't you?"

"Yes. I believe you," she said, with excruciating effort. Her arm dropped to her side, the receiver slipping from her fingers. Wagner caught it before it hit the floor.

"John. Listen, Sarah doesn't look too good. I think

she ought to see someone. Maybe get something for her nerves."

"Feldman," Sarah said hoarsely as she leaned against the wall.

"She wants to see Dr. Feldman. I can zip her right over to the Institute. Why don't I give you a call from there after we see what he says?"

There was a pause on Allegro's end. "Okay, but call me as soon as you know anything. And Mike—"

"Yeah?"

"Tell her—"

"Yeah?"

"Never mind. I'll tell her myself when I see her."

Wagner hung up the phone. "Should I call Feldman first and make sure he's available?" he asked Sarah, but she wasn't listening.

Her face was flushed, her lips twitching. She'd thought she was in love with John. Now she was thinking John might be Romeo. So why didn't her escalating suspicions—hers and Wagner's—alter her feelings for him?

Was this how it was with Melanie? With Emma? The others? Had Romeo—John—mesmerized them all? As he had her? Had they fallen in love with him, too? Even after they realized the truth? Was the redemption he'd offered the others what she, too, craved? For her crimes. She'd even confessed them to him. Oh God, he had wooed her—

"Sarah."

"Tell me what made you suspect him," she asked hollowly.

"I don't suspect him."

"What was it?" she persisted. "The drinking? Was he having an affair with my sister while his wife was seeing her for therapy? Did you know about that, too? Did Grace find out and tell you?"

"Sarah, please. There is no way that the man I've worked side by side with for close to a year, a man I really care about, is some raving nutcase killer in his spare time."

"Do you think I *want* to believe it? Even the vaguest possibility makes me sick."

"You don't think I feel sick?"

"Why'd you pull out his wife's autopsy report?"

He didn't answer. Worse—he looked away.

"You suspected something, Mike. That's it, isn't it?" She was having trouble catching her breath. "You think he killed Grace."

"The coroner ruled it a suicide."

The tiny kitchen seemed to be swallowing all the air. Sarah strode back to the living room, pacing back and forth. Wagner hurried after her.

She paced for a minute or two, then dropped into one of the chairs. "When did Grace—die?"

Wagner sat down on the futon sofa across from her. "Seven months ago."

"And—Diane Corbett?"

"Sarah, you're making a big leap here."

"Stop it, Mike. It's the same leap you're making, and we both know it." Desperation was etched into every word. *Please. Not John. Anyone but John.*

Wagner sighed heavily. "The murders started a few weeks after Grace died. But so what? All right, Grace did say John got a little rough with her when he was drunk, but hey, manhandling your wife when you've tied one on is a long way from—from what Romeo does to his victims."

"Did you suspect murder right off?" Her tone was eerily calm.

"No, of course not. I still don't. When John came in that morning and I told him I'd got the call about Grace, he looked devastated."

She regarded him with a stark gaze. "And hung over?"

"He always looked hung over."

"You had a feeling back then. I can see it in your face, Mike."

"What are we doing? Sarah, let's just stop now. Please."

"Tell me." *No more shadows. No more secrets. No matter how terrible.*

Wagner turned pale. "I don't know. You could make a case, I guess. He lived only five minutes away from her place. She didn't leave a note. She had an airplane ticket in her pocket. He came in late that morning."

"If she was leaving, why would he need to—get rid of her?"

Wagner raised his eyes to the ceiling. "She called me a couple of nights before it happened. Said she was going to try to talk John into giving it one more shot. See if, once she got back from Hawaii, rested, tanned—you know—got herself together—maybe he'd want to give it another go."

Spots danced in front of Sarah's eyes. "You think he pushed her out of that window."

"We're both just getting carried away here. And I'm going to prove it. Give me a couple of days—"

"I want to know everything, Mike. Damn it, I need to know. What else?"

He sighed, resigned. "Okay, something came in today. I got this call. It—threw me. Not that it's anything but wildly circumstantial, Sarah."

"Go on."

"Karen Austin, Romeo's third victim, was dating a cop. She told a friend. I only found out today. I haven't told John . . . yet."

His eyes fell on her. He looked forlorn, pained. "And there was you, Sarah. The way John came on to you."

"Like he came on to Melanie?"

He looked away. "I don't know for sure that they were having an affair, Sarah. I swear. But when she started consulting with us, I could feel there was something between them. Hell, I was attracted to her, too. She could turn it on—" He put his hands up to his face. "Jesus, I didn't mean it that way."

She drew Wagner's hands back down, held on to them.

He gave her a brief, grateful smile. "Then Saturday night. Hearing your screams. Bursting into your room and finding him—"

"Don't," she pleaded. "I told myself I was overreacting. He didn't really hurt me. I panicked. I was having these flashbacks from my childhood. Terrible memories. I was getting everything mixed up. Feeling unhinged."

Wagner smoothed back her spiky hair from her damp forehead. "It's going to be over soon, Sarah. I promise you."

She clutched his arm, her eyes flashing with a spark of hope. "Wait. What about that night when Romeo tried to break into my apartment? John was right there with me. He couldn't be two places at the same time."

Wagner seemed to brighten, too. "No, that's true enough."

She struggled to piece together all the events of that rainy night—going out to dinner, coming back to her apartment, her going off to the kitchen while John carried his wet jacket into her bathroom—

She gasped.

"What?"

"He could have done it then."

"What are you talking about?"

"I never heard anyone trying to jimmy that window in my bathroom. Only John heard it. What's to say he didn't pry the window open earlier? He went into the bathroom when we first came back. It could have been a setup, an alibi for him as well as an excuse to leave the apartment, supposedly to hunt down Romeo. It was while he was out there that another letter got slipped under my door. God, it would have been so easy."

"Wait a minute," Wagner said. "What about Vickie? That drag queen? He could have done it every bit as easily. Jimmied the window. Slipped the letter under your door. I bet you, we could put a whole case together against him,

Sarah. We find one link and I'm telling you, we'll have the whole damn chain. We'll be kicking ourselves for our off-the-wall suspicions about John."

Sarah was as eager as Wagner, if not more so, to point the finger at any other suspect. And she had been the one to bring up Vickie in the first place. The phone rang again. Absently, Wagner reached for it.

"What are you still doing there?"

Wagner's eyes shot to Sarah. He mouthed, "John."

Sarah blanched.

"She got sick, John," Wagner said. "She's lying down. I was about to call Feldman. See if he could come over here. What do you think? Do shrinks make house calls?"

"I called him already," Allegro said. "I thought she'd be there. Let me talk to her, Mike."

Wagner held the phone out to her. She shook her head wildly.

"She's asleep, John. I don't think it's a good idea to wake her."

"Look, I've got a lead I've got to follow up on, but leave word for me what's happening there. Feldman told me he might want to admit her to the hospital for a couple of days' observation. If not, check her into the Royale on Bush. Register her under the name Wilson. Susan Wilson. Same if she's checked into the hospital. I'll have Corky there in twenty minutes."

"What's the lead?"

"Probably just another dead end. I'll let you know if it's anything. When she wakes up, Mike, tell her I'm thinking about her. Okay?"

"Yeah. Sure. I'll tell her, John."

An hour later, Sarah was in Stanley Feldman's office. He'd canceled two appointments in order to see her.

It felt eerie, almost surrealistic to Sarah at first. Like his office was this tranquil, untouched cocoon, totally separate from the world that was spinning out of control beyond its four walls. As usual, Feldman sat in his traditional place behind his desk, his hands folded one over the other on his forest-green blotter, note pad to his right, his bland expression awaiting whatever interpretation she chose to place on it—calm, concern, disinterest, disgust, tenderness, irritation, lust. But had he crossed the boundaries? Or was it her mind that had crossed them?

She almost opted to stretch out on that black leather chaise. The fresh, white doily was in place. And she felt so drained, it was tempting to lie down. But in the end, she took a chair across from his desk.

She tried to hold her hands together in Feldman's composed manner, but ended up twisting and wringing them. "I don't know why I came."

Feldman nodded.

"I used to be able to tuck my mind away, but it won't stay where I put it anymore. I know you think it's better this way, but it's tearing me apart." She laughed harshly. "Great symbolism."

Sarah saw the psychiatrist wince, but the look he gave her was sympathetic.

"So you feel your psychic pain gnaws at you from the inside. And Romeo is planning the assault from the outside. Each a powerful, destructive force in its own way. Each must be revealed and defused if you are to feel safe."

She hesitated. "There are some things I'm not ready to talk about. But I do know I'll have to in time. If there is time."

"You are afraid time is running out."

"Romeo seduced my mind, and now—" Her voice faltered as she added, "I think he may have already begun the seduction of my body. He said I was saving myself for him, that only he could make me burn inside. And it's true."

"What exactly is true?"

It took great effort to get the words out. "That I'm in love with a man who may be planning my murder," she said huskily.

"John Allegro?"

"You think so, too."

He shook his head. "I only know that he has feelings for you. It was obvious when he came to talk to me the other day. And just a short while ago, when he called me—"

Sarah's eyes stung with tears. "I've shared a lot with John. But if he is Romeo, then he's understood more about me from the first than I understand about myself even now."

"What does he understand?"

She wrung her hands. "That I must be like Melanie. Like the others. That deep down, some part of me must be asking to be abused and debased, tortured. Because I still love him. Even knowing that he's my torturer, my killer. I have this awful, helpless feeling—that my fate was sealed a long time ago. And Romeo knows, better than I, that there is no escape ultimately. You always pay for your sins."

"Talk to me about the other Sarah."

She gave him a confused look. "What other Sarah?"

"The one who's fallen in love."

"With a killer. A madman."

"Wait. We'll leave that supposition for a moment. For that's all it is, yes?"

"Yes. Even now we're—they're—investigating someone else. My neighbor." A spark of hope came back into her voice.

Feldman bridged his fingers together, his manner impressively calm. "So talk to me about this feeling of being in love."

"I didn't think I could. I didn't think I was capable of loving someone. Oh, I love my friend Bernie. But I mean—" She struggled with how to put it.

"Sex?"

She felt herself blush. "Yes."

The color in her face faded fast. "But I screwed that up, too. That's me. I've always screwed up better than I've screwed."

"In this instance, perhaps it was wise, Sarah. If you believe John Allegro is Romeo."

"You think that's why I'm in love with him? Because I think he's Romeo, not because I don't?"

"Is that what you think?"

"I could have bet a million bucks you were going to toss that back in my face, Feldman."

"What you think is what's important, Sarah."

"I'm still holding on to the hope that it's Vickie, the transvestite who lives next door to me. I suppose that's terrible, too. Despicably un-PC. But better Vickie than John. Better anyone than John."

"So you've answered your own question."

"Which one? I've got a load of 'em."

Feldman did his usual silent shtick. Gave her time to sort it out for herself.

It didn't take her very long. "Oh. Whether I'm in love with John Allegro because he is or isn't Romeo."

He smiled faintly. Her reward.

Oh Sarah. I can still hear the two of you outside the den that night. Your confusion and tears. His rage and lies. I'm sobbing under the covers, the sheets still warm from his body, his semen still warm inside me. Hating him. Loving him. Sarah, Sarah—forgive me, Sarah.

M.R. diary

24

"I wish you'd change your mind about this, Sarah," Wagner said as they drove away from Feldman's office at the Institute and headed toward the Mission District. It had stopped raining. The sun was even burning through the ever present fog.

"I won't."

"Then let me—"

"You know my plan's smarter."

"And more hairy for you," Wagner argued.

"Not if you play your part."

"I know we've both got our hopes up here, Sarah, but we also have to face that it's a long shot. Even if anyone at those clubs recognizes your neighbor from that photo that you said yourself is at least ten years old—"

"It would be a start. Something to follow up on," she persisted. She looked over at him for some hint of optimism. Instead, Wagner's face was disturbingly impassive.

"You can't shake your suspicions about John, can you? Are you humoring me, Mike? Do you think Vickie's even a long shot?"

"Of course I do. Would I agree to this risky plan of yours if I didn't?"

"But." She knew there was a *but*.

Wagner shrugged. "You read me too well, Sarah. I'm going to have to show his photo around, too." He didn't have to mention John by name.

Sarah said savagely, "You're not going to come up with anything."

"I'm not going to come up with anything."

Sarah glanced at him. Did he believe it?

Neither of them spoke for several minutes, the only sound coming from the hum of the Firebird's engine.

They stopped at a red light on Market. A kid was hawking papers on the street. Romeo's name shrieked from the headlines. Wagner glanced over at her, then fixed his gaze on the stoplight. "There were bruises on her face —Grace's. It was in the autopsy report."

Sarah was thrown by his remark. "What of it? She fell seven stories, didn't she?"

"Landed on the back of her head."

"What are you saying?"

"Nothing."

"You don't think it's nothing. Why was her death ruled a suicide?"

"A combination of your sister's psychiatric evaluation and the psychiatrist's where Grace had been committed. Both reports indicated that she had strong suicidal tendencies and had, in fact, made several unsuccessful suicide attempts. The medical examiner explained that the bruises on her face could have been the result of injuries sustained during her fall. There was a lamppost near where she landed. It was possible her face grazed some part of it before she hit the pavement."

"But you don't think so. You think she got John to go over there that morning, pleaded for him to give her a second chance. That he got mad. Beat her up again. Then maybe she threatened to press charges against him, and he panicked or got pissed and threw her out the window. Is that it?" she shouted.

"Shit, Sarah. Don't kill the messenger."

"Even if that happened—and I'm not saying it did—why would that set John off on an appallingly sadistic killing rampage? His wife wasn't raped, mutilated. Her heart wasn't ripped out. It doesn't fit Romeo's pattern."

"I don't know. Maybe it was the trigger. Melanie said there's usually a triggering event." The light turned green, and Wagner drove across Market. "And a high that comes afterward with having gotten away with murder. There's a sense of empowerment. Melanie talked about that, too. How one terrible deed can trip open the lock to macabre sexual fantasies the killer may have been successfully containing until that point. And that once the line is crossed—when fantasy becomes reality—there is no going back."

"What did John say when she was telling all this to the two of you?"

"He agreed with her. He believed that Romeo couldn't stop even if he wanted to. That the only way to end it was for someone else to stop him."

Sarah's desolate gaze fixed on Wagner's profile as he drove through the crowded, noisy Mission streets. "And are you going to be that someone?"

"Yes, of course I remember you, Mike." Vickie smiled fetchingly as he switched his gaze from Wagner's police ID to his face. "Don't tell me you're looking for our darling Sarah again."

"No. This time I'm looking for you."

Vickie's arched eyebrow dropped a notch. "Oh? And why is that?"

"I'd like to ask you a few questions. Mind coming down to headquarters with me?"

"It's a lot cozier here."

"I'd like to have you look through some mug shots."

"I can't imagine why. I haven't seen anyone. Who would I identify?"

"We know Romeo's been hanging around here. Possibly posing as a vagrant in the street, a delivery guy, some scuz hanging out in the porno store. You may not realize you've seen him, but you start looking at those mug shots, and one of them might jump out at you."

Vickie's big crimson lips pouted. "I'm not crazy about police stations, Mikey."

"Believe me, I'll treat you like a queen."

Vickie giggled. "With a line like that, how can I resist?" He spun around on his three-inch heels. "I'll just grab my purse and dab a drop of powder on my nose."

A couple of minutes later, he was back, keys in hand.

"Here, let me," Wagner said gallantly, slipping the key ring off Vickie's finger as he pulled the door closed.

"And I thought chivalry was dead," Vickie cooed.

Blocking the door with his body, Wagner slipped the key in the lock, turned it once to the right to throw the bolt, then emitting a raspy smoker's cough, threw it back to the left.

As they headed down the hallway Vickie slipped an arm through Wagner's and gave him a playful smile. Wagner smiled back.

As soon as Sarah saw the "odd couple" heading for Wagner's car, she slipped out of the doorway of the porno bookstore and hurried into her building.

As Wagner'd promised, the door to Vickie's apartment opened freely with the turn of the knob. Wasting no time, Sarah shut the door behind her and crossed the studio to the oversize closet down the little corridor.

The hatbox was right where it had been the last time. She snatched it off the shelf without hesitation.

There it was—right on the top of the pile of papers. The faded five-by-seven glossy of Vic and Momma at the beach.

Her gaze fixed on the young man in the photo. The casual yet possessive way his arm was flung around his mother's shoulders, the intimate smile on his face as he looked down at her. And his beautiful red-headed mother with that cruel line to her mouth. Had she abused him? Tormented him? Made him feel powerless and inadequate? Produced the kind of rage and hatred of women in him that Romeo had to feel in order to carry out his heinous crimes?

Hurriedly, she dropped the photo into her tote bag. She was desperate to leave the confining space. The smell of stale air and cheap perfume pervaded the closet.

Then she thought of what Wagner had said earlier. Even if *Vic* did hang out at those sex clubs, it wouldn't prove anything. Something more substantial was needed to convince Wagner he was on the wrong track about Allegro. And as much as she hated to admit it, she could do with a little more convincing herself.

Melanie's diary. Her yearbook. The photo album. Any one of those would do the trick for sure. *And her sister's heart. No, she couldn't bear to find that.*

Wagner would keep Vickie occupied for at least an hour. Not all the time in the world, but the apartment was small. She'd start in the closet, systematically work her way through the rest of the studio apartment.

Vickie *tsked* as she started to step into the passenger side of Wagner's car. "Shit, I've got a run." He glanced down past his short, tight black miniskirt to the tear in the black pantyhose running down his muscular right thigh. "Give me a sec, honey, while I run back and change."

Wagner, already behind the wheel, popped out of the car as Vickie shut the passenger door.

"Hey, what's the big deal? We're going down to the police station, not dancing."

"I don't care where we're going. I'm not going anywhere with a run like this."

Wagner scooted around the car and cut Vickie off as he started down the street toward his apartment building. "I'm tight for time, sweetheart. Give a guy a break. What's a little run between friends?"

Vickie tapped Wagner's chest with his long, shiny red fingernail. "You pull the car up to the building and double-park, and I'll be back out before you can say Rita Hayworth."

"Yeah, sure. I know how you girls are. First you have to change your pantyhose. Then you decide the skirt isn't really right. And maybe you really should wear a different blouse, change the earrings—"

"You're taking more time with this little speech, Mikey, than it's gonna take me to make the change."

Wagner gripped Vickie's arm. "Come on. Why don't we take care of business and you can spend the whole afternoon playing dress-up when you get home?"

Vickie's coyness vanished in a flash. "Why the bum's rush? How come you're so damn eager to get me downtown? Look here, I'm either doing you a favor by going along with you of my own free will to that detestable police station or that's a warrant in your pocket, darlin'."

Reluctantly, Wagner stepped aside. Sarah'd had more than enough time to slip into Vickie's place, get the photo, and escape into her own apartment to pack a few things. The unmarked cruiser with Corky behind the wheel was already out front, waiting to take her, not to the Hotel Royale on Bush, as Allegro had ordered, but to a motor inn on Lombard per his orders. And since Corky was a buddy of his, Wagner got no back talk when he told him not to divulge Sarah's whereabouts to *anyone*.

Wagner was about to get into his car when he remembered Vickie's unlocked door. Vickie already had his key in the outside door to the building when Wagner caught up with him.

Vickie ran the tip of his tongue across his top lip, throwing Wagner a droll smile as they headed down the hall to his apartment. "You planning to help me change, honey?"

But Vickie's teasing smile winked out when he found that his door was unlocked.

"Shit." Wagner shrugged sheepishly. "I must have turned it the wrong way."

"Or else some bastard broke in. Why don't you go first?"

Sarah was still in Vickie's dressing room, rummaging around in a carton of fashion magazines she'd found behind a rack of flouncy party dresses, when she heard a door slam, followed by voices.

Wagner and Vickie. What the hell?

Her eyes shot to the open dressing-room door. She sprang to her feet, shutting it, careful not to slam it in her panic.

"I'll just be a minute, honey." Vickie calling out.

"I'm timing you." Wagner's voice.

Sarah's heart was hammering as she heard Vickie say, "Damn. I just remembered, this was my last pair of black pantyhose. I'll jump into leggings instead. I've got this gorgeous new pair in chocolate brown leather that's to die for."

The leggings in question were dangling a foot away from Sarah's face. In a flash, Sarah darted for the carton, swept the magazines in, and shoved them under a rack of clothes, diving in after them.

The door to the dressing room opened as she disappeared behind a rainbow of drag queen costumes.

A couple of seconds later, she heard Vickie gasp in alarm, then exclaim, "What the fuck—?"

"Problem?" Sarah heard the note of anxiety in Wagner's voice. Nothing compared to the heart-stopping trepidation rolling through her.

"I'll say there's a problem. Would you just look at this?"

Sarah began sweating profusely. Had she shoved the damn hatbox onto the wrong shelf? Forgotten the lid?

Wagner's footsteps came toward the closet.

"I'm looking. I don't see anything," Wagner insisted.

"The leggings, for chrissake. That fucking saleswoman told me they were a size sixteen, and I took her word for it because I was in this mad rush and didn't have time to try them on. I didn't even check the ticket. But it's right here in black and white. Size twelve. Size fucking *twelve*. Now how do you suppose I'm going to get these long lithe legs of mine into those itty-bitty things? I swear, she did that on purpose. Knowing it was a final sale. Well, that's the last time I shop in that crap-hole of a boutique."

Wagner snatched a royal blue velour jumpsuit off the rack. "I like this number better anyway. The color brings out your sexy eyes."

"You really think so? Or are you bullshitting me, too?"

"Do I look like I'm bullshitting you?"

"You've got damn sexy eyes yourself, baby," Vickie crooned. "We could have ourselves a grand ol' time right here instead of wasting it down at some grimy, stinky police station."

So much for Vickie being straight, Sarah thought. Unless he—Romeo?—swung both ways.

"How 'bout a rain check?" Wagner was saying. "I really do need you to go through those mug shots, Vickie."

"Okay, okay. But you could at least help me slip out of these old things. Here, baby, start with these buttons."

Sarah felt decidedly uncomfortable. Wagner, however, was handling the awkward situation like a pro. She'd spare him, and herself, at least some of the embarrassment by never mentioning that she was still in the closet while he was helping Vickie with his costume change.

"Why here of all places?" Wagner asked, hanging back by the archway of Melanie Rosen's living room at a little past seven that Monday evening, eleven days after Melanie's murder.

"I'm not sure," Sarah admitted. She stared at the faint

indentations in the Moroccan rug where one of her sister's two caramel silk love seats had rested. A bloodstained piece of the expensive rug had been hacked off and removed. As well as the Shaker pine coffee table. All of these evidentiary items had been carted away by the police to be dissected and analyzed for clues, like the victim herself.

The dusky light that filtered in through the nickel-size spaces between the closed teakwood Venetian blinds cast a moribund gloom over the room.

"It's mine now," Sarah said. "My father deeded it to Melanie, and she left it to me in her will."

Wagner gave her an incredulous look. "So you've decided to take up residence so soon?"

"Temporarily. I'm not making any plans for the future."

"What the hell was wrong with the motor inn? You didn't like the view?"

"I need to be here, Mike. I can't explain it. Call it my way of making peace with Melanie. Peace with myself. Besides, who'd think of looking for me here? Not even Corky knows where I am. After he stationed himself outside my motel room, I called a cab, snuck out the patio slider, and got picked up at the diner across from the motel. I rang your pager as soon as I got here."

She walked over to her tote bag and pulled out the heisted photo of Vic and his mother. It was all she'd come up with at her neighbor's place. Not a single clue connecting him to the murders.

Wagner grimaced. "We went through a lot of trouble to get that photo. I hope it pays off."

"What are you going to tell John when he finds out Susan Wilson isn't registered at the Hotel Royale?" she asked as Wagner stuck the photo in an envelope she knew already contained John Allegro's picture.

"I haven't figured that out yet," he admitted. "Don't worry. I'll come up with something." He tapped out a cigarette and started to light up, pausing to ask if she minded.

"No. But those things will kill you."

"I'm going to quit once—" He stopped. They could both finish the end of that sentence.

"Did you locate that club in Richmond?"

He nodded. "I'll hit a couple in town first, then head out there."

"Will you call me first thing in the morning if—if you find anything?"

"I'll come by tonight when I'm done."

She shook her head. "No. It'll be late, Mike. I'm going to turn in early."

"Sarah, this is nuts. You can't stay here all alone."

"I'll keep the lights off, the shades drawn. I won't answer the phone if it rings. Really, I'll be fine, Mike."

"I'll worry about you anyway."

"Now you sound like my friend Bernie."

Wagner smiled.

Sarah smiled, too.

By nine that evening, Sarah was also beginning to question what on earth had possessed her to come back to Scott Street—a house crammed full of painful memories and appalling atrocities. Had she really thought her return would somehow scare the demons off? Show them that they couldn't terrorize her any longer? That she was stronger and more powerful than they ever imagined? If so, it wasn't working.

She paced through the silent house, downstairs through the office quarters and upstairs through the apartment that she had once shared with her father and sister. A streetlamp in front of the house cast a sickly greenish aura over the rooms, making it just possible for her to find her way around.

Walking among ghosts. *Are you here, Melanie? Dad? Romeo?*

For so long, she'd tried to remove herself physically and emotionally from the abuse she'd both witnessed and experienced as a child. Melanie's murder and Romeo's insidious assault on her mind had brought it back. Now she churned inside with so many turbulent emotions— fear, anger, frustration, grief, lust, love. That evening in Tiburon with John, she'd even had a glimpse of happiness.

When she got to the master bedroom, once her father's, then Melanie's, she went over to the bureau near the door and pulled out one of Melanie's nightgowns—a lovely rose print in soft cotton knit with gentle smocking on the bodice. She held it up to her nose. It still bore the faint scent of Melanie's perfume. Sarah used to hate the smell of perfume, especially that one. Now she found it oddly soothing. Like when she was little and had worn her dead mother's favorite bathrobe—not yet ready to let go.

In the mirror above the bureau she caught sight of Melanie's brass bed—stripped to its antiseptic box spring. Slowly, she crossed the room. A devastating wave of sadness swept over her. Falling to her knees, she pressed her face to the edge of the bed. She knelt there for a long time.

At first the faint strains of the melody melded with her raspy breaths. Wailing musical notes. But as Sarah's breathing stilled, the melody remained. More distinct now. No question as to what she was hearing. *Rhapsody in Blue.*

Terror coursed her veins. Where was the music coming from?

Downstairs. From one of the rooms downstairs.

He was here. Romeo was here. Sneaking in through a window? No. No, a key. Melanie must have given him a key. Yes. He was her sister's lover. Her father-substitute. The only other man who could give her what she craved. . . .

Sarah clamped her hands over her ears. Didn't help. The music, her anguish, her fear reverberated inside her head. No escape.

No, no, no. This is what he wants. To corner you. Make you cower. Submit.

She sprang to her feet, flew out of Melanie's bedroom. On the upstairs hall credenza—a silver candlestick. Snatching it up, she clutched it to her breast. Hesitated. *No. Don't think. Act. Your only hope.*

Creeping soundlessly down the stairs. Not even risking a breath. Her only hope—to catch him off guard.

The music remained faint even as she reached the foot of the stairs. At first, she thought it was coming from Melanie's waiting room. So dark in there. Impossible to see anything. Anyone.

And then she remembered. The speakers on the wall. But the source of the music was a small stereo system in Melanie's private office.

That's where he was. Where he was waiting for her. Her killer. Her seducer. Her lover?

Gripping the candlestick with both hands, Sarah stealthily slid open the doors of Melanie's consulting room. Just wide enough for her to slip through. The room was hazily illumined by moonlight. It appeared empty. Music filtered softly through the air.

Sarah's eyes fell on the closed door leading to her sister's private office. *Yes. In there. Waiting. Yearning. Beckoning with a siren call. Romeo . . .*

On automatic pilot crossing the room. Holding the candlestick up with one hand as she reached for the doorknob. Allowing only one thought in her head. *Get him first.*

Not until she was cautiously turning the knob did she become aware that the music had ceased. When? Was she still hearing it when she entered the consulting room? The doors were open wide enough for the sound to travel from the waiting room. She'd stopped paying attention.

Maybe he'd shut it off. Better to hear her approach.

Her hand froze on the knob. What was she doing? What was she thinking? She remembered. *Get him first.*

Yes. That was the plan. What other choice did she have? Too late to call for help if he was already here.

She burst into the office, wildly swinging the candlestick back and forth in front of her. *Come on, you bastard, you fuck, you heartbreaker. . . .*

No one jumped out at her. This room, like the others, appeared empty.

Hiding. Preparing to spring out at her. *Like monsters do.*

She flicked on the lamp on Melanie's desk. Still clutching the candlestick. No one leaped out.

Had he come and gone? Was this yet another of his perverse *romantic games*?

She made her way over to the stereo. No CD of *Rhapsody in Blue.* No cassette tape. Where was it? Had she really heard—anything?

A sudden loud blast of music made her yelp in alarm. Until she realized it was a rock song and not a rhapsody. Coming from a car outside whizzing past the office window.

She sank down on the edge of Melanie's desk, cradling the candlestick in her lap. *You're really losing it, Sarah. Letting that overactive imagination of yours get totally out of hand.*

The next morning Sarah woke up confused and disoriented to find herself in her old bedroom on Scott Street—the one Melanie'd turned into guest quarters. And like every morning since her sister's murder, she woke wishing that this was all a terrible nightmare.

Instead her waking hours had become more horrific than all her terrifying nighttime dreams put together.

Her eyes fell on the phone beside her bed. Bernie. Yes. He could always be counted on to give her spirits a lift. Almost always. Besides, he'd be worried about her.

He picked up on the first ring.

"It's me. Sarah. And I'm fine," she said, beating him to the punch.

"I hope you know you're going to pay for my ulcer treatment."

"You don't have ulcers."

"I will."

"Oh, Bernie, what a mess."

"You heard the news, huh?"

"What news?" she asked, her anxiety returning in a rush.

"Another . . . body without a heart turned up last night. Some poor hooker. Left in a hotel dumpster near the Hall of Justice. Cops haven't given a statement yet, but since whores aren't Romeo's bag, they're saying on the news we could have a copycat killer on the loose now, too."

"No. It's him," she whispered bleakly. "He needed another heart."

"What's that supposed to mean?"

"Nothing. Forget it."

"Where are you anyway, Sarah?"

"It's a secret."

"Since when do we have secrets?"

Her eyes welled up. "Since forever, I'm afraid."

"Sarah, are you crying?"

"Not yet."

"You need a shoulder to do it on?"

"It would be nice." But it wasn't Bernie's shoulder she was thinking of, it was John's. Why did everything in her patchwork of a life have to be screwed up? Why couldn't there be one inch of fabric without a wrinkle in it? One smooth, clean, simple little stretch?

"Say the word, sweetie, and I'll hop into my spacemobile and deliver that shoulder to you pronto."

"I love your shoulder. I love you. But I'm tired of crying. I only called to tell you not to worry."

"Fat chance."

"Well, I'll speak to you soon, Bernie." She started to hang up.

"Oh, wait. I almost forgot," Bernie said. "Hector Sanchez called the office a half-dozen times yesterday, wanting to talk to you."

"Shit. I wanted to talk to him, too. I'll give him a call. Thanks, Bernie."

"Sarah, stay in touch, you hear?"

"I will. I promise."

As soon as she hung up, she dialed information and got Hector Sanchez's phone number.

It rang four times before he picked up.

"It's Sarah Rosen, Hector. Did I wake you?"

"No. I was painting. I think this one might be almost decent. You have to come by and tell me whether I'm right. When you're up to it, of course."

"Is that why you were trying to reach me?"

"No. It was about that last time you were over here. You know, when that package showed up on my doorstep."

How could she forget.

"Yes. What about it?"

"Well, it isn't about the package actually, but about the degenerate who delivered it."

"What about him?" Sarah was finding it hard to breathe.

"He must have dropped it off right before I came back with Arkin."

"What makes you say that?"

" 'Cause of the smell. It's a thing with blind people. Their other senses get heightened, you know what I mean. That creep's smell was still in my hallway. He might even have still been hiding there. I'm telling ya, Sarah. The smell was real strong."

Sarah exhaled slowly, recalling John's inimitable smell —a blend of peppermint breath freshener and booze.

      ∎   ∎   ∎

Wagner called later that morning. "Did I wake you?"

"No. Did you—find anything?" she asked.

"Nothing conclusive."

"I heard about the hooker." She hesitated. "They found her right near . . . the Hall of Justice."

"The missing heart."

"Why a prostitute? That doesn't fit the profile, does it?"

Wagner said grimly, "I think you were right about him cracking. He's losing it."

"Yeah. I guess I *was* right."

"I know what you're going through, Sarah. Believe me—"

"Mike, I've got another plan—"

"Sarah."

"I've got to know for sure it's not John. Otherwise, I swear I'm going to go crazy. And whatever you tell yourself, you need to know, too."

She could hear him drawing in on his cigarette as he thought it over. "Okay, I'll listen. That doesn't mean I'll go along with it."

"I think you will, Mike. I think you have to. We both have to."

As soon as Sarah hung up with Wagner, she phoned Allegro. They talked for about twenty minutes. Set a date for that evening. He'd come over to Melanie's at seven.

Shortly after five P.M., Sarah called Bernie, only to get his answering machine. She left a message at the beep.

"Oh, Bernie, I wish you were there—"

A click followed by a raspy breath at Bernie's end made her stop short. "Bernie?"

There was no response.

A vein pulsed in Sarah's temple. "Bernie? Is that you?"

And then she heard—faint at first, slowly growing louder—what had become Romeo's *special* voice. *His* Rhapsody in Blue. Not a chance it was a delusion this time.

"No, no, no!" she screamed into the mouthpiece. "Dear God, no!"

Bernie returned her call twenty agonizing minutes later. He'd been out. Having coffee with Tony. A rapprochement. She didn't tell him about the music. Or about how terrified she'd been that something had happened to him. She knew now it had been just another of Romeo's warped pranks. Hopefully, it would be his last.

Each kill fuels more intense, challenging and violent fantasies and fosters more desperation, decompensation. If he's not stopped he'll ultimately self-destruct. But no one can predict when or what it will take.

Dr. Melanie Rosen
Cutting Edge

25

Romeo feels a rush. He strips down. Showers. Scrubbing his skin nearly raw. His heart's beating a hundred miles a minute. Zinging with excitement. Everything's moving faster now. But that's okay. The rhythm feels right. Feels good.

Only a little while longer. He stretches out on his bed. Everything's going to go perfectly. He can feel it like an extra heartbeat.

Emma was a great dry run. A perfect dress rehearsal. But Sarah will be opening night on Broadway. The pounding pulse at his temples sounds like applause. A standing ovation from a packed house.

Look. In the front row. All of his women. Clapping wildly. Except for Melanie.

Where's Melanie? He searches the crowd frantically for her. She's got to be there somewhere. She wouldn't miss this brilliant performance for the world.

Ah, there she is. In a special box seat. Applauding loudest of all. Appreciating his skill, his artistry, his orchestration, to the fullest. As he knew she would. Yes, Melanie was special. She gave him more than the others. Not only her heart but her intimate and revealing diary, which has become his bible. He especially loves the parts where she wrote about him. And the parts about Sarah, of course. He can never read them without getting a huge hard-on. Sometimes he whacks off, deliberately letting his come splatter on the page he's reading. It re-creates the delectable image of the last time he came in Melanie, came all over her. And heightens, to an almost unbearable pitch, the vision of what it will be like with Sarah.

He takes up his remote, switches on his TV. The five o'clock news has just begun. There she is. Lead story. Just like on every news show since early that afternoon.

Sarah's already speaking, her exquisite face filling the screen—

". . . Romeo has deluded himself into believing that I'm vulnerable to his charm. That, like his other victims, I will ultimately find him irresistible. That I need him as much as he needs me. But he's wrong. I'm not fooled by any of his tactics. What's more, I'm beginning to see the cracks, just like I said I would. He's trying to hold it all together, but he can't. He's spiraling out of control. He knows it. And I know it, too."

Sarah's face is replaced by that of the newscaster, an attractive brunette with prominent cheekbones and a too-wide mouth. "That was an excerpt from Sarah Rosen's taped interview done earlier today with commentator Tom Lindsay at an undisclosed location. Miss Rosen, sister of slain psychiatrist, Dr. Melanie Rosen—"

Romeo turns off the television. Closes his eyes. Pictures Sarah. Plays her earnest little spiel over in his head. Her vain attempt at self-deception makes him even more turned on. *I'm not fooled either, baby.*

Sarah will absolve him of all his sins. Sarah will be his forgiveness. All the fury, despair, and acts of violence will explode in their union. In her surrender lies her deliverance. And his.

There is a roaring in his head again. But now it isn't applause. It's a jumble of sounds—an engine, sobs, music.

She materializes as she always does. And always in the

same place. Behind the wheel of her brand-new, shiny two-seater baby blue sports car. He's beside her. They've pulled over onto a desolate cutoff on a country road. A tape is playing. He wants to hear it now, even though she doesn't. Gershwin's *Rhapsody in Blue.* Her favorite, he reminds her. But her sobs are drowning out the music.

"You're breaking my heart."

Not her voice this time. His. He's saying those words. Shouting them in her ghost-white face, his eyes filled with rage and the pain of betrayal, his voice full of anguish and accusation. YOU'RE BREAKING MY HEART. YOU BITCH. YOU GODDAMN FUCKING BITCH.

He's so busy screaming into her face, he doesn't even see the knife plunging in and out of her chest at first, doesn't comprehend that it's his hand wielding the weapon. Until her blood's spurting out of her like a geyser, all over his face, almost blinding him. But he doesn't stop. He keeps driving the knife in and out, in and out, in and out. In rhythm to the closing bars of the Gershwin concerto.

Ha! And to think she'd accused him of having a tin ear.

I want to give myself so completely to him that it will finally release me from the chains that have bound me to you all these many years.

_____

M.R. diary

26

Sarah studies herself in her sister's full-length mirror. She's wearing one of Melanie's outfits. A silky suede tank dress. Midthigh. The color of grape soda. Because it hangs slightly on her thinner frame, she has belted it at the waist with a black suede sash.

She doesn't look like herself. Not like Melanie either. Somebody new. Unique. Provocative. Exotic.

"Are you ready? It's almost seven."

She spins around, her face flushed. She hadn't heard him come into the bedroom. "Yes."

He steps farther inside. "Remarkable."

She fidgets nervously with the sash.

"Sarah, you can still change your mind," Wagner says. "When the doorbell rings, I can go down there and tell him—"

"What? That I chickened out at the last minute? No, Mike. I have to go through with it."

"I'll be within a stone's throw of you the whole time, Sarah."

"I should check on the roast."

He stops her as she turns away from the mirror. "Remember. Get him to remove his gun. And, Sarah—be careful."

"You talk like a man who believes John's guilty. I thought you were the one who said it can't possibly be him. That the only reason you were going along with this was to put my mind at rest? To convince me of his innocence?"

"And if nothing happens, will you be convinced?"

She stares deep into his eyes. "Something is going to happen."

The downstairs doorbell rings. Her breath jams in her throat. Can she really do this? For a moment she has the sensation that the floor's slipping away.

Wagner draws her closer, brushes her lips with his. "For luck," he murmurs, then hurries off to hide in the kitchen.

She meets Allegro at the top of the stairs. She sees he's clean-shaven. Jacket's freshly pressed. Even his hair's trimmed. He's holding a fragrant bouquet of flowers.

He does a double-take when he sees her. Whatever he was preparing himself for, it wasn't this.

"You like?" she asks coyly. *No. Tone's all wrong. Too girlish.*

"You sure you're ready for this?" he asks, brushing off her question.

"Ready for what?"

"I wasn't sure you ever wanted to be alone with me again."

"Come sit in the living room. Dinner will be ready in a little while. I'll pour us drinks."

"I've been kind of thinking of going on the wagon."

"I'll pour you a club soda."

"Like I said. It's still only a thought."

She leads the way, her eyes darting toward the kitchen door.

"That is some dress, Sarah."

She turns back to him. "You look nice, too."

He puts the flowers down, wraps her in his arms. "This is good, baby." He kisses her deeply, leaving her breathless, dizzy.

When she pulls away, she says, "Your gun hurts my ribs."

He slips off his jacket, undoes the buckle of his shoulder holster, and shrugs that off, setting it on the coffee table. "Better?"

Her throat's dry as sandpaper. She glances at the gun. It's still easily within his reach. *This isn't going to work. I'll never carry it off.*

"What's wrong, Sarah? I thought this was what you wanted."

She sighs. "I—I thought so, too."

"Don't be afraid, Sarah." His tongue darts out and sweeps across her lids, along the curve of her neck, circling her ear.

She shuts her eyes again, searching desperately inside herself for the courage. It has to come from her. If she's learned nothing else through this whole ordeal, she's learned this. *See what I've learned, Feldman? And you, Melanie? Aren't you proud of me?*

The candles flicker. A faint breeze. *Has Mike cracked the kitchen door open? Is he watching?*

She pulls away. "I can't. I can't do this. Please go, John. Please. Go now. Don't ask any questions. Please."

He tries to reach out for her, but she backs away.

He lifts his hands as if in surrender. "Okay. If that's what you want."

"Yes. I'm sorry."

He sighs heavily and is going for his gun holster when the kitchen door flies open.

"Leave it there, John." Wagner's standing at the doorway, service pistol in hand. Silencer fitted to the end of the barrel. His eyes shift to Sarah. He smiles.

"It's okay, Sarah," Wagner says.

"No—"

Wagner puts a finger to his still-smiling lips. "Everything's going to be fine now."

Her heart's pounding. *Fine? Nothing's fine. This wasn't the plan.*

"What are you doing, Mike? Let him leave. I can't do it." She rushes toward him. Allegro tries to stop her, but Wagner gets to her first. Wraps his free arm around her waist, his gun still aimed at Allegro.

Screwed up. Lost. No way out.

Sarah pleads, "Please, Mike. This isn't the way we were—"

"It's no use, Sarah," Allegro says. "Mike's doped it all out."

Wagner smiles slyly. "Pretty paltry double-cross. Sarah pretends to get cold feet, sends you off, John. Then you wait out of sight, catch me in the act, bring me down."

"Face it, Mike. It's over," Allegro says.

"No, not over yet. This is the grand finale. Romeo's going to strike one last glorious time. And Michael Wagner's going to be the cop to bring him down."

Wagner eyes her now. "Didn't I promise you, Sarah? *Soon.* Remember? You should be honored. You're the one I chose from all the others, Sarah. I've saved the best for last."

Sarah can only stare at him. He's talking crazy, but he looks utterly normal, completely sane. Hard for her, even now, to fully believe he's the sexual psychopath who slaughtered her sister, Emma, those five other hapless women.

He presses his lips to her hair. "Mmm. You're wearing Melanie's perfume. It smells better on you." He breathes in deeply. "I know how you've longed all your life for the one person who could free you, Sarah. Not your father, like you thought. Me. Romeo. I'm the only one, baby." His hand glides up her rib cage, cups her breast.

She struggles to break free.

Wagner laughs softly. "Yes, fight me, baby. That's what gets my heart racing."

Allegro makes a move for his gun holster.

Wagner grins at him, releasing the safety on his pistol. "I don't think you want to do that, John." He snatches up his partner's weapon, empties the shells into his pocket, tosses it across the room. Then he focuses back on her, the smile gone. "You did spoil the surprise part of the party, Sarah. You don't know how much I wanted to see the look of astonishment on your lovely face when I revealed my true identity to you. It really was one of the highlights with Melanie."

Her sister's name on his lips disgusts Sarah. "But not with me. You fucked up big-time, Mike. Hector smelled your stinking cigarette smoke in his hall—on that package you left for me. You told a stupid lie about his calling Homicide. The rest was easy," she gloats.

"Easy as your sister. After I saw her at that sex club, I waited a week to call her. She was hot. Had to see me right away. We walked hand in hand in the rain. Had drinks in a bar on Lombard. Then she went to the ladies' room. Left the door cracked open. Stayed there a long time. I finally went in to see what was keeping her. She was standing by the sink. Naked. She wanted it so bad. But I made her wait. I made her wait a long time. Until she was desperate. As desperate as she was for your daddy." He smiles crookedly.

Sarah knows he's deliberately baiting her. All part of the sick game he'd started right after he'd killed Melanie and set his sights on her. She can't—won't—let him see it's working. "Did you wait until all of your victims were desperate, Mike?"

"All of them. Even Grace." He shifts his gaze from her to Allegro. "Grace loved it, Johnny. The rougher, the better. Oh man, she could take a beating. And give great head. Grace ever give you great head, Johnny?"

Allegro leaps for him, but stops abruptly when he sees Wagner press the barrel of the gun against Sarah's temple.

"Grace could feel it, Johnny. She was the one that got me going," he says. "The trigger, like Melanie said, that set Romeo off. It all fell into place for me the morning I showed up to drive her to the airport. She begged for one last fuck before we took off. Only she freaked when I went to tie her up. Bondage was the only thing that didn't turn Gracey on, John. She started screaming. I got pissed. The window was open. It was so easy. Anticlimactic, you know? Had to make the best of it, though. Whacked off right after I sent her flying. I came just seconds after she went splat." He gives a small, indifferent laugh.

Sarah sees Allegro's eyes fill with tears. *Oh John, I'm so sorry.* But she feels a shred of comfort—even courage—as she sees him swiftly pull himself together.

"Grace wasn't your first, though, was she, Mike?" Allegro says cryptically.

Wagner gives him a curious look. "Oh, and who am I leaving out, Johnny?"

Allegro's lips curl. "You left out the one who really got you going. Your momma. She was the first, wasn't she, Mike? Numero uno? I read the whole file on her murder. The Ledi cops faxed it up this morning after I decided to go digging into your past. Nineteen stab wounds. All in the chest. Two poor schnooks who happened to be in the wrong place at the wrong time took the rap."

"Shut up." Beads of sweat erupt across his brow. This gets to him. Momma's off-limits—*You're breaking my heart, baby. . . .*

"And I talked to your stepdad up there in Ledi today, too. Guess what? Thursday wasn't his birthday. His birthday's in May. And he hasn't seen you in months. We did have a nice chat, though. He told me all about how you used to like to crawl into bed with your momma. Before she got married again, of course. She confessed it all to your stepdad, Mike. Every juicy little detail."

"Shut the fuck up about my momma!"

Wagner's whole face is altering. A cruel slant to the mouth now. A merciless glint in the eyes. The very timbre of his voice has changed. Cold, savage—insane. He's holding her so tight, she can almost feel his heartbeat against her skin.

Over by the love seat. He pulls out a pair of handcuffs from his jacket pocket, orders her to cuff Allegro. She refuses. He rams the barrel of the silencer into her mouth. She can't swallow. She's going to choke.

Allegro sticks out his hands. "It's okay, Sarah."

As she reluctantly goes to put the cuffs on him, Allegro makes his move. With lightning speed, he shoves Sarah to the floor and flies at Wagner, smashing his fist into his partner's jaw.

Sarah hears Wagner growl in pain. Followed almost immediately by a second sound, like the popping of a champagne cork. But Sarah knows it isn't a cork, it's a bullet spiraling through the chamber of a silencer. And then she hears a thump. A body dropping.

Time suspended as she lies there on the carpet, face down, paralyzed with fear. *Don't let it be John. Oh God, don't let it be John.*

An arm circles her waist, gently lifting her. "It's okay, Sarah. It's okay, now."

Her heart shrivels up. Romeo. She feels herself breaking apart, shattering. Her newfound fragments of courage are running for cover. Grief is filling all the empty spaces inside of her.

His moist, hot lips on her bare back above the scooped-neck dress. His free hand tugging off the sash around her waist.

She gasps in horror at the sight of Allegro sprawled on the carpet. Blood oozing from his temple. His face a grimace of agony.

"Don't worry, baby. I just grazed Johnny," Wagner says, kicking the table out of the way. "Wouldn't want John to miss the whole show. Makes me hot just thinking about it." He pinches her nipple cruelly through her dress. When she whimpers, he presses the cold steel barrel of his gun to her lips. "Shhh. I know you're excited, but no noise yet, baby."

Allegro's shirt is drenched in sweat. He grits his teeth. "Mike, I'll kill you. I swear."

Wagner looks amused. "Cuff him like a good girl, Sarah."

The room spins. Wagner grabs her hard by the scruff of the neck. The pain makes her dizziness pass.

"Do it, Sarah, or I'll shoot him where it's really gonna hurt." Now he's aiming at Allegro's groin. "And just to show Johnny what a nice guy I am, we'll let him keep his hands over his crotch. When he gets real hot watching us, he can whack off. I owe him one for Grace."

"You're pathetic," Allegro mutters. "Tell me, Mike— is that what you did? Whack off every time your momma and stepdaddy went at it?"

"I could blow both you and Sarah away in the blink of an eye, John."

"And spoil your dream date with Sarah? Everything you've been longing for. You're wigged out, but you're not dumb."

"This is more than a date, John. You wouldn't understand that. This is a sacred night. But you're right. I won't let you ruin it. For me. For Sarah." He gives her a nudge in Allegro's direction.

Her hands are trembling, but she clicks the cuffs over John's wrists.

"Now take the set out of his pocket and cuff his ankles," Wagner orders.

At the armoire. Aching with pain and trembling all over. Throat so dry, it hurts to swallow.

"Choose the music," he commands, trailing the barrel of the silencer lightly down her spine. "Something you like to dance to."

"I can't dance."

"That was years ago, Sarah. Get over it."

"How—?"

"Melanie wrote about your dance classes. How Daddy was so disgusted with his little girl with two left feet. Oh, Melanie didn't miss much, baby. She wrote down every delicious, sordid detail of her life and plenty of yours, for good measure. About the sleeping pills. Carving up your wrists. I know everything, Sarah." He licks the side of her face. Not like a puppy dog trying to please its master. Like a wild animal tasting its prey. "Okay, I'll pick the CD, baby. You need a little time to heat up."

Reggae music blaring.

"Mmm. Melanie loved this sound. The way her body swayed to the beat. Close your eyes, Sarah. Feel it."

He slips his hands down the top of her dress, inside her bra, cupping her bare breasts, finding the nipples. His fingers are teasing, playful.

Shame washes over her. Such a familiar feeling. She's as helpless now as she was when she was a child. Against her will, another man is violating her body. Her rage roars in, expunges her shame. *This is not my doing. This is not my fault.*

Sarah's eyes connect with Allegro's. She sees his anguish, frustration, rage, and helplessness.

"If only you knew how long I've been waiting for this one perfect moment," Wagner whispers in her ear. "Long before Melanie. Long before reading all about you and your naughty deeds in her diary. You're the one, Sarah. You've tried to run from your true nature most of your life, just like I have. Tonight, we're both going to end the lies."

"Yours maybe, not mine."

"I knew you'd be tougher than the others. That's how I knew you were special. You have to go through the pain to find true fulfillment, my love. And that can only come from complete submission."

Allegro laughs sourly.

Wagner shoots him a look. "Let's see if she's wet, huh, Johnny?" Without warning, he yanks off her dress. Slips his hand down her panties. "Not creaming yet." He sounds more amused than annoyed. "I knew you'd be the toughest to break, Sarah. My greatest challenge. I dreamed of this, baby. It's perfect. You fight it the hardest, and you need it the most. I'm going to open your heart to the truth," he says.

Sarah's eyes fix on Allegro's. For support, strength, courage. Then she defiantly meets Wagner's gaze. "You think you know the true me, Mike, but you don't. I'll never see you as my savior. Only what you really are. My torturer. My murderer."

"That's right, baby. Fight it hard. In the end, your surrender will be so, so sweet."

"I hate you. Despise you!"

He pulls off her panties so that she's fully exposed. Makes a lewd slurping sound. Completely deranged.

Over the arm of the love seat, face down.

He snaps his black leather belt in the air and lands a light, stinging blow on her buttocks.

"A teaser," he tells her, then increases the intensity. The thrashing raises raw, red welts on her battered flesh. He's now using his free hand to press down on the back of her head, shoving her face into the cushion to muffle her screams. "Are your juices flowing yet, baby?"

Allegro's bullet wound is excruciating. Can't focus. Seeing double. But still battling. "Why don't you uncuff me, you fuck? Let a real man show you what to do."

Wagner laughs. The belt lashes out again.

She's gasping for breath. Suffocating, like in her dream.

Naked, on her back, splayed out on the cushions of the love seat. Wagner wipes the sweat and tears from her cheeks. "Romeo knows what a bad little girl you are. Sneaking peeks at Daddy's door, watching him play hide the pecker with your big sister. Is that what you fantasize about most, Sarah? Getting it off with Daddy. Wanna play Daddy games with Romeo, princess? Act out all your fantasies about doing it with Daddy?"

"Like you did with your mother?"

She sees something flash across his face. A memory that brings back his own sense of helplessness? But it only lasts for a moment, before his features are cold and hard again. "Momma never hurt me. No woman's ever hurt me. You all think you're such hot shits. But you're nothing. She was nothing. She had her cherished boy, and she tossed him away like so much garbage. Picked that stupid, drunken shithead. You know what it was like watching that fuck's prick go up inside my mother? Yeah, Sarah. You do know. You know all about watching. I don't have to tell you."

In the kitchen, swooning from pain, fear, revulsion. He holds her up, his arm clamped brutally around her rib cage. She can't breathe.

I can tune it out. But once I tune out—repress it—he's won. I will not let him win.

He bangs her into a chair draped with a light green surgical gown. Clear latex surgeon's gloves laid on top of it. Bile rises in her throat.

Several objects lie neatly displayed on the kitchen table. The white silk scarf, the bottle of Perrier-Jouët, and a shiny black snakeskin-bound book. Melanie's diary. Thick with the pages of her sister's torment, shame, and frustration.

Sarah's eyes fix on one particular item. Set apart from the others. A red velvet box. Shaped like a heart. Tears roll silently down her cheeks. She looks away, only to see him lifting a carving knife from the counter, ceremoniously placing it across the lid of the cr mson box.

"You've won her heart at last, baby. Her forgiveness as well as mine."

Back in the living room. Wagner's dressed for *surgery*. He sets the uncorked champagne bottle and the heart-shaped box on the coffee table. Places the carving knife on the cushion of the love seat. Puts the gun down at his feet.

John lies slumped on the floor about ten feet away. His shirt is stained with blood, and his face has a sickly pallor of death. But to Sarah's amazement and joy, she sees his eyelids flicker open and flit to Wagner's gun before he closes them again.

Wagner misses the silent interchange. He's too busy admiring Sarah's naked body. "Such sweet firm titties, tight little ass—"

Her wrists pinned behind her back with the silk scarf, she can only glare at him. "What about Vickie's tight little ass? I was there, Mike. Hiding in the closet. I could hear you panting—"

"Naughty, naughty, Sarah. You do know what happens to sneaky little girls. They get exactly what they deserve. Romeo's got to give you what's coming to you. What you really, really want. Down on your knees, baby."

"Never. Eat shit."

He slaps her hard across the face. "Poor baby. You want the pain. I understand." He raises his hand to strike her again.

"No, please. Don't. Don't hit me again. Please." She steps away from him as she's pleading. A few feet. A couple more.

He makes a game of it. Matching her step for step. Moving his hips to the reggae beat. Grinning. "See, we're dancing now, baby."

She makes it almost to the center of the room before Wagner grows bored. "That's enough, Sarah. Get down on your knees."

Manufacturing a sigh of surrender, she obeys, looking up imploringly at him. "Okay, okay. You win. Is this what you want? For me to be contrite? To be obedient? To give in and do everything you say?" As she prattles on to Wagner, Allegro arduously snakes his way across the carpet.

Wagner rests his hand on her head. As if he's giving her his blessing. "Doesn't it feel better? Letting go? Letting me take charge?"

"Yes."

"Yes, Romeo," he says.

"Yes, Romeo," she repeats dutifully. *Oh, John, hurry. Please. Please.*

Wagner smiles but suddenly twists it into a grimace. He blinks twice, his arm jumping off her waist, lurching for her neck. "What—?"

He gives her a dazed look, then looks dumbfounded at his shoulder. Together, they stare at the red splotch spreading down the sleeve of his pale green surgical smock.

"Fuck," he growls, grabbing her savagely, shoving her in front of him. He spins around to face Allegro, who's propped up against the love seat, the silencer-fitted gun clutched in his cuffed hands.

"Another shot, Johnny?" Wagner taunts, using Sarah as a shield as he drags her closer to Allegro.

All the color is gone from Allegro's face. "Sarah, I'm sorry. . . ." His eyes flicker closed, his hands drop to his lap, the gun slips off his thigh to the carpet.

Wagner laughs maniacally. Blood trickles down his arm, but he seems oblivious to his wound. Making quick work of binding her ankles, he carelessly shoves her onto the love seat, then kneels over Allegro and tests for a pulse.

"Tough old dog. What do you say, my sweet? Should I put him out of his misery?"

"No. No, please. I'll do—anything. Just let him live. Please. I'm begging you."

He yanks her off the cushions, back onto her knees. "That's right, Sarah. You'll do anything for me. But it's got nothing to do with that lump of shit lying there. It's not him. You need to atone."

"What about you, Mike? You murdered all those women. Even your own mother."

He circles her neck with both hands. His thumbs press in. "You should talk," he hisses.

"Stop," she pleads. "Stop. I can't . . . breathe."

Wagner tightens his grip. She's strangling to death. Just like her mother.

Oh my God . . .

"There, there. Tell mommy why you're crying."

"I hate him. He's a terrible man. He hates me. He hates you, too. All he loves is Melanie."

"That's not true, Sarah."

"I'm not the bad one. It's Melanie. She's the bad one. She's the one that makes him do those dirty things, not me. I wouldn't let him. But Melanie does. She loves it. I know. I saw them. I saw them."

Wagner's slapping her, dragging her back from the abyss of memory. She stares into his face. He's smiling. But then his features blur. Sarah's no longer seeing him. She's seeing her mother. Hanging from a noose in the attic.

Daddy'd warned her she'd be sorry if she told. . . .

On her knees, wedged between his legs—the supplicant, at her master's feet. The lights are dimmed. The rhapsody plays.

He's smiling tenderly. "See, Sarah. We are soul mates. Because we both killed our mothers."

"How . . . did you know?"

"Melanie wrote all about it."

"But she couldn't. She didn't—"

"She heard you crying. Heard your momma trying to comfort you. Heard you ratting on her and your daddy. You not only broke your momma's heart, Sarah. You broke Melanie's, too. You killed them both."

"Yes. It's true." The wailing, rhythmic strains of Gershwin's concerto drown out Sarah's raspy breaths.

He strokes her cheek, her throat, her breasts. Her body is boneless. "Oh, Sarah, I treated you the best right from the start. Showered you with love letters, gifts, the best parts of Melanie's diary. To bring you closer to the truth. What really hurt was your childish infatuation with John. It almost killed me seeing you in bed with him. You can understand that, can't you?"

She nods. Ironically, painfully, she understands not only Mike Wagner's rage but his guilt, his hurt, his feeling of futility. She understands, too, his terrible sense of abandonment. She's come finally to the unalterable truth not only about him but about herself. The sins of the fathers. And the mothers. Borne by the children.

He circles his almost fully erect penis with one hand while the other caresses her breasts. The look on his face is primal. Plagued. The final bars of the rhapsody fill the room. "I don't really want this to end," he says mournfully.

She smiles timorously. "Let's have one last toast."

He stares into her eyes as he reaches for the champagne bottle. He's forgotten the glasses. Frantically, he rushes back to the kitchen for them. Everything has to be perfect. When he returns he fills the two fluted goblets. "What shall we toast to?"

"To . . . forgiveness."

He hesitates.

"It's time," she coaxes gently. "Time for us both to let

go of the hurt, the envy, the malice, the sickness. Time to forgive them all. Time to forgive ourselves."

He brings the rim of a goblet to her mouth, runs it provocatively across her lips. "Say it first, Sarah. Say, 'I want you more than life itself, Romeo.'"

She looks up into her killer's face. Her breathing has evened out. Her voice is calm, accepting. Even tender. She says, "I want you more than life itself, Romeo."

His lids flutter shut; his features are almost angelic. "Perfect. So perfect." Then he opens his eyes and tips the goblet up so she can drink. "To forgiveness, my perfect love." He takes a long swallow from his glass, then lowers it and smiles bittersweetly at her. "It's time, baby. Redemption. Absolution." His gaze shifts from her to the cushion beside him.

His lips part, but no sound emerges. For a moment it's like a strip of film jamming in a projector. Everything comes to a dead stop. Everything but the pounding Gershwin climax.

"Sarah, Sarah—you've ruined everything, you dumb slut." His voice is thick with the intense frustration and fury at the destruction of his precious ritual. He screams uncontrollably into her face: "The knife, cunt. *Where is the fucking knife?*"

She spits a mouthful of champagne right into his blazing eyes. Blinded, his hands reflexively reach up to shield his face.

Pulse pounding in her ears, sweat pouring off her naked body, she slices through the last of the silk at her wrists.

The glinting steel blade flies past his stinging eyes. He emits a guttural, soul-searing shriek, his features painted with the wretchedness of the damned.

Sarah plunges the knife deep into the monster's chest.

It's over in a heartbeat. Romeo's last.

Epilogue

Sarah settles herself into the now familiar chair behind the anchor desk at the *Cutting Edge* set. She's come to tape her segment. Just before the director cues her, John gives her a reassuring nod, whispers, "This is the last time, Sarah," then steps away from the camera.

The red light flashes on. Sarah has written notes on a piece of paper, but it remains folded on the desk as she begins.

"I've shed so many tears these past weeks. For my sister Melanie, for Emma, for all the other women whose lives were desecrated and ended by that madman. I feel close to them all. I am one of them. All of us suffered terrible betrayals. All of us were trapped in guilt and shame. These are feelings I still struggle against each and every day. But I'm the lucky one. I have the chance to fight for the joy and happiness we all deserved.

Melanie . . . and you, Momma . . . I wish I could take your hands in mine and we could walk together from the shadows into the sunshine. But, I make you one vow: I'll carry you with me here in my heart."

About the Author

ELISE TITLE was a psychotherapist for fifteen years and for several years worked with inmates in high-security prisons. This is her first novel of psychological suspense. She lives in New England.